THE GREENLING

THE GREENLING

a novel
by david booram

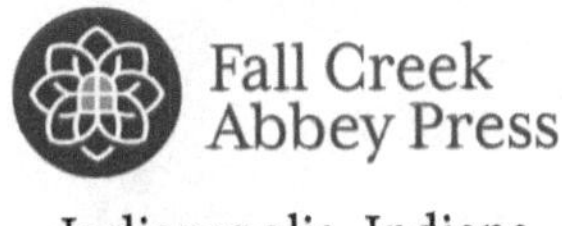

Fall Creek
Abbey Press

Indianapolis, Indiana

For Edwin Herman Theising,
my grandpa and first eco-hero, who
lived off the land because of necessity,
farmed organically because of conscience,
and loved God's big green book because of joy.

and

For Michael Anthony Russo,
a friend who loves at all times –
in life, death, and everything in between –
who courageously entered the darkness with me.

CONTENTS

*"The obsession with power has completely transformed
the life of man and dangerously stunted
his concern for beauty."*

Rabbi Abraham Joshua Heschel, *The Insecurity of Freedom*

*"We find it difficult to conceive
of evil and beauty together.
The fear of the beautiful
that ran through the elder ages
almost eludes our grasp."*

J.R.R. Tolkien, *On Fairy Stories*

Family Ties

THE GREENLINGS
(Ireland)

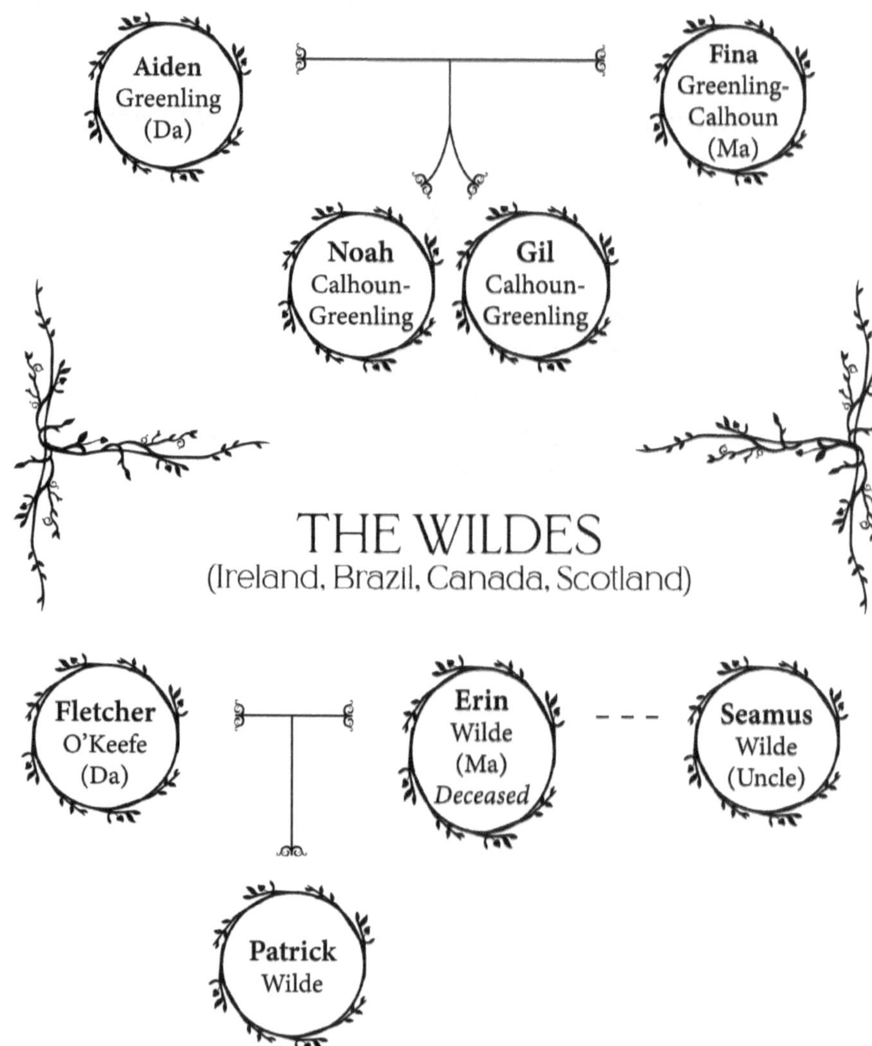

THE SENNHEISERS
(Germany)

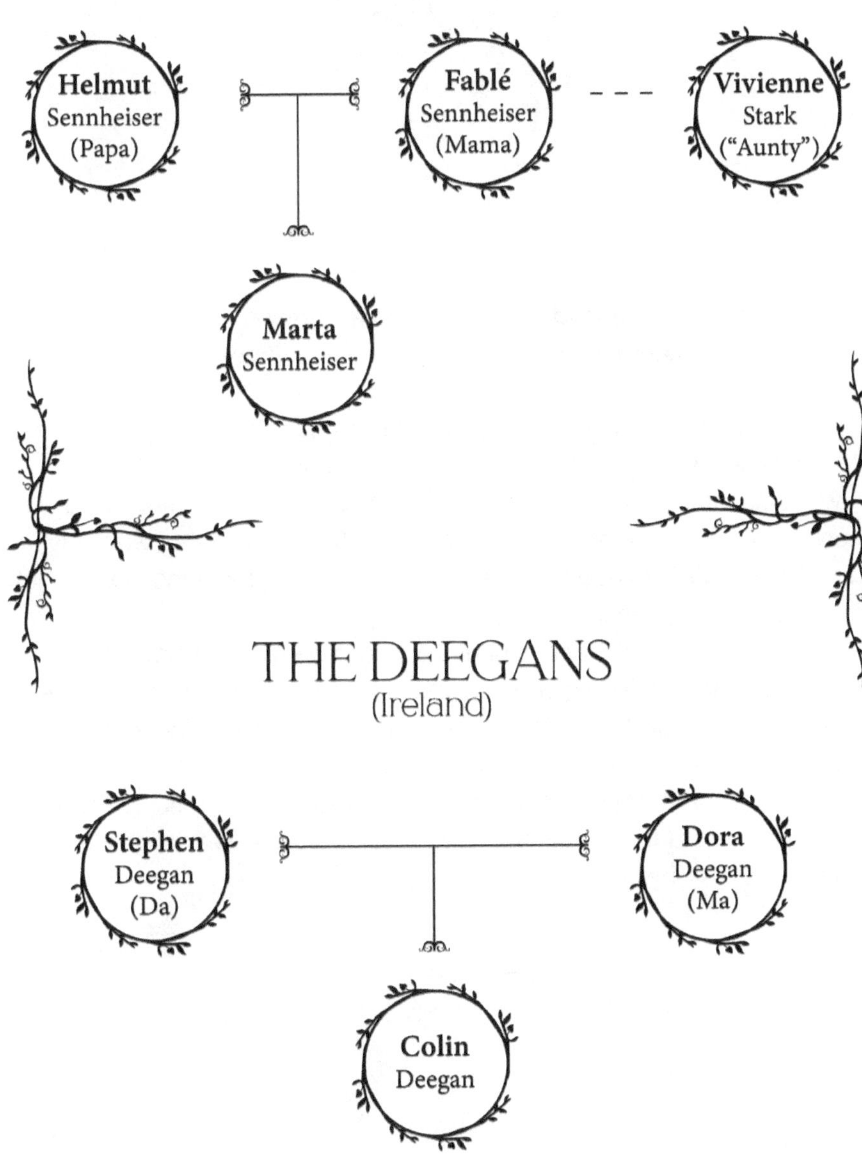

ᑭART ᐅNE

Episode 14: Extinction is Forever
HOLO-POD Hosted by Noah Calhoun-Greenling

"The recent release of multiple robotic lions in Tanzania's Tarangire National Park was designed to incorporate both native and feline-bots into several new prides. Africa's need to attract more tourists, or should I say—their money—has sparked the trial in an effort to attract more safari wannabes. The aim, I'm told, is to assure the safety of wealthy visitors who want to get up close to the big cats.

"But, it seems the experiment has ended in complete failure—possibly bringing about devastating consequences to the social order of the larger cat's family systems. Now, without their living counterparts, the replica lions appear stuck in an endless loop—circling or pacing back and forth with nothing to react to. There are growing concerns that this artificial intrusion will cause even further stress to an increasingly scarce lion population throughout the African continent."

Spring 2060

Kilkenny, Ireland (95° F / 35° C)

"You're such a weirdo!" Her words don't come off as mean, just bitingly honest. Behind the sarcasm lies a deep bond of friendship, a commitment that's becoming more and more costly as they get older.

"You think I don't know that? Whenever I look in the mirror, I see *Noah the Strangeling* tattooed on my forehead."

Dark gray clouds drift across a dirty-looking sky above the run-down courtyard at Loreto Secondary School in Kilkenny. The two girls find a spot to be alone, sitting shoulder to shoulder under one of the giant oak trees, trying not to be overheard. But it's hard to have a private conversation surrounded by three dozen other high-school seniors who eat their lunches at splintered, gray picnic tables, gossip, watch HOLO-VIDs, or play the latest time-wasting games.

"It happened again, just last night," Noah whispers, her words softly lilting, to her friend, Shea—brushing a strand of her golden-red hair away from her emerald-green eyes. "It's kind of beautiful and kind of, well, strange. I woke up in the middle of the night, and the moon was pouring through the window. I was half awake, and all of a sudden, a shadow swooped up and got darker and darker. Like something... or maybe *someone*... was moving closer to the window."

"Sheesh. Weren't you scared?" Shea interjects, her coal-black eyes narrowing as she listens.

"Absolutely. My heart was pounding. And my mind was racing, trying to keep up—so I crawled to the window and looked out. The moon was so bright that, at first, I could only see its black silhouette. Then my eyes got used to the light, and I saw its two huge yellow eyes."

"You're kind of creeping me out, Noah. What was it?"

The wind picks up, and the trees around the bricked patio sway, announcing a storm's approach. Students grab papers that rustle and put their books and gadgets in their backpacks—ready to make a quick dash inside.

"Not more than two meters away in the wych elm was this enormous snowy owl, just looking into the window, staring at *me*. Its eyes were this mixture of gold and red. They looked like fire... like someone was looking through them at me."

There's a rustling of clothing and quiet footsteps, but Noah and Shea are so immersed in their conversation they don't hear Colin and his gang creep behind them.

"What's all this about Greezling? Still livin' in yer wee little fairyland? Ya' know, while ya' gurlies live in yer fantasy land, some of us have to live in the *real* world." Colin's mates bob their heads up and down, sarcastic grins mocking the two girls.

"Shut up, Colin! You're such an effin' grease bag," Noah fires back.

The tall, muscular boy doesn't bother to respond. Instead, he points to his black Amazon skull cap. "Ya' know, me da lost his job because of this kind of shite. He's talking about taking yer ma to court, ya' know."

Colin actually drools, a saliva trail escaping the corner of his mouth as he spits out the words. "Yer such a dweeb."

"Ain't she just that," Gannon, the shorter boy, gloats. "Everyone here knows yer stuck somewhere between second and third grade. We'd probably feel sorry for ya' if ya' weren't so full of yerself."

Other students nearby turn their heads to see what the ruckus is all about. Some join the circle and surround the two girls.

"Noah, I used to really like you, ya' know," the girl, Keelin, adds. "You were fun, different, quirky in a cool sort of way. Now, ya' just come off as a strange little misfit. You're either trying *way too hard*, or you're completely bonkers. Even though ya' do all these *big things* that get ya' on the HOLO-NET, no one wants to be a mate to ya' anymore. Ya' know why? Because they know they'd be snubbed, just like Shea here is."

Noah jumps to her feet to face the bullies. Shea tugs on Noah's sleeve, trying to get her to back away. But Noah looks each of them in the eye while she waits. Anger rages in her now. She squares her shoulders and channels a warning.

"You all should be ashamed of yourselves. Me the misfit? *You* don't fit anymore. *You're* the problem, and a time's coming when you'll just be spit out like a piece of rank cod. Yeah, Keelin, I *used* to be fun. But that was before my eyes were opened. And different? You're damn right I'm different!"

Noah pauses to look around at the others who have joined the circle. *Why can't they all leave me alone? I probably should just shut up,* she tells herself—instead, she takes a deep breath and then spits out her final words. "Your petty little lives are totally redundant—one hundred percent—you're completely irrelevant to everything that *really* matters."

The two boys and the girl look at each other for a couple of beats and then break out laughing. They turn around and walk away, mocking Noah's diatribe, eager to report the latest lunacy to the others sitting around their tables. As they leave, a swarm of tiny midges descends around Colin. He slaps the exposed skin of his cheeks and arms as the ravenous little insects take quick, sharp bites.

On the courtyard's perimeter, sitting on a bench underneath an ancient wych elm, is the science department's new student teacher, Patrick Wilde. He watches from the tree's shadow and feels a vibration mushrooming from the earth through his lower midsection and into his chest. As Noah turns toward the building and walks through the doors, the sensation drains back down and out through his feet. He waits for a moment, puzzled. *What on earth was that?*

Noah's brother, Gil, darts through the squeaky back door, slams his brown canvas book bag on the kitchen table, and starts rummaging through the fridge. The vertical glass door on the unit's right side glows violet-blue, revealing neat rows of micro-greens and mushrooms.

His hands start to shake—his forehead slick with sweat. He needs sugar.

Revise that. He needs something to eat, but he craves a sugar fix.

As usual, his ma just has a few leftovers, a container of cricket flour, and some weird-looking leaves and seeds from her foraging. He picks a bowl up and sniffs—"meh"—then sticks out his tongue. "Why can't we just be like everybody else?"

Ma's bare feet coming down the stairs hardly make a sound. She stands in the doorway for a moment, the afternoon sunlight revealing streaks of gray in her shoulder-length auburn hair. There's a faint trace of smokiness that still lives in the mossy green walls. Herbs and vegetables hang down in baskets from the kitchen's wood beams. Dented copper pots and iron skillets are grouped above a well-seasoned hearth.

Still wearing her work apron from the shop, she watches her son rummage in frustration. "He needs his da," Fina tells herself. What am I saying? I need him. "Ever since Aiden left, Gil and Noah just keep drifting farther and farther apart."

The boy's lanky frame stiffens, sensing his ma's presence. He closes his eyes and takes a deep breath, trying to calm down. When he's amped up like this, he usually regrets what comes out of his mouth, especially at home.

"Hi, Gil. How was school today? I bet you're looking forward to your weekend."

"Hey, Ma. It was alright. Can't say that for Noah, though." His gray eyes point outside where his sister sits in the old tree swing, her face brooding at something in the distance.

"What do you mean?" Fina asks softly.

The volume and pitch of his voice rise. "I guess what I mean is it's *not* alright! She did it again. Got into a big to-do with some of my mates about all her imaginary friends. Why can't she just keep all her psycho stuff to herself? It's killing me. You know why? When the kids are done slagging her off, they start in on me. You know what I wish? I wish somebody would *really* put her in her place! Maybe that would finally shut her up."

Fina just listens, the sad look in her eyes expressing grief and remorse. The chronic ache in her heart over the distance widening between her two children seems to become more acute with each impasse they fail to navigate.

She looks out the window and sees the fissured, gray bark of the ancient wych elm in the backyard. The tree's solid presence quiets her mind, but her heart feels troubled. *Gil's right. Noah is going through something. And she doesn't care how it affects the rest of us.*

"Son, I know it's hard on you. It's hard on Noah, too—"

Gil interrupts her—fists clenched, jaw tightened. "I don't give a damn about Noah right now, Ma. Can't you see how stupid she makes *me* look? Do you ever ask *her* to consider how impossible she makes *my* life?"

Ma cautiously puts her hand on his arm. "Gil, I'm sorry. I see your point. Of course... I do talk to her about her relationship with you. And I try to get the two of you to talk to each other about what's been building up between you. But it seems like both of you are too stubborn or too hurt to really listen." She pauses; a breathy exhale whispers through narrowed lips before she continues. "Just because I'm the parent here doesn't mean I can fix everything. This is something you and Noah will have to fix. Or if you don't, it will just break down until it's beyond repair."

Gil looks down at his hands and shakes his head. Quickly pulling his arm back from his ma's hand, he stands abruptly, then storms toward the hallway, turning around with narrow, angry eyes.

"No, this is on her, Ma. I'm done. She knows where to find me."

Fina lets him go, brushing a strand of hair from her face, her mouth tightly pursed. Her gaze wanders to the shelf, where there is a cube holding a HOLO-VID taken on holiday at Connemara two years ago—Noah and Gil have their arms over each other's shoulders, heads thrown back as they laugh at some silly joke shared between them.

They were inseparable then, she recalls—wiping away a tear from the corner of her eye. *But they've always been so different, too. How did I describe them to the headmaster last spring? Noah—the compassionate intuitive. Gil—the pragmatic realist.* She shakes her head and lets out a loud, long sigh through her nose.

Has there ever been a pair of twins less alike than these two?

Spring 2048

Poppelsdorf Palace, Bonn, Germany (93° F / 34° C)

Helmut Sennheiser hums along as he listens to Wagner's Ride of the Valkyrie. The pilot-bot in his black Mercedes-Benz S-Class continually reads his mood through its guidance screen and adapts the car's speed and aggressiveness accordingly. The soaring music matches the pride he feels at becoming the youngest minister of the German government's Bundesministerium für Wirtschaft und Klimaschutz. He fully realizes that the recent right-wing political victories are what ensured his appointment to one of the sixteen Federal Ministries. That it would be the Ministry of Economic Affairs and Climate Action was far beyond what his populist party could hope for.

Yet here I am, he tells himself, *overseeing Germany's economic policy—ready to reverse the left's reckless advances.*

He feels especially good about today's kill. His predecessor's carbon emission goals would have toppled the country's economic prowess not only in Europe but also worldwide.

He pats the breast pocket of his suit coat and feels the rectangular outline of his real power. A smirk widens his thick, black mustache. *It's incredible... these reversals aren't won by debate or compromise... they come from a tiny little book.* He's amused, really—with how he quietly secured the needed votes. He relives his off-the-record conversations with several opposition members—how they squirmed at the book's contents—how quickly they flipped their support. He shakes his head at how simple it was.

Not one of those spineless bastards wanted the list of lust, greed, or narcissism to come to light. The coup de grâce was the HOLO-VID of presidium vice-chair Emil Erker and his cronies lounging in a room full of naked porn stars. A few seconds of those images spinning life-sized around them and, they quickly saw the light and switched their support for the Russian Natural Gas Initiative—no debate needed!

His face still wears a crooked grin as the car enters through the gate of his residence in Poppelsdorf Palace exactly on cue for the climax of *The Valkyrie*. He looks around, satisfied that despite the region's once-in-a-millenium flooding, the additional pumps installed around the home's perimeter have made the property an island of safety. As he pulls underneath the tasteful carriage porch of their executive residence in the Bonn suburb, he's surprised to see his wife, Fablé.

She's wearing a smart, form-fitted charcoal suit—her raven hair severely pulled back. She's frowning at him as he exits the car. His eyes move to her side, both hands tightly holding their nine-year-old daughter, Marta, by the arm.

"What's the problem here, *meine liebe* and *liebling*? You both look as if someone's been shot," he says jokingly.

"You tell him, Marta. Go on," her mother insists, tightening her grip on the young girl's upper arm, her school uniform wrinkling under her fist.

"Papa, I'm so sorry," Marta says, fighting through tears, her long dark curls quivering as she tries not to cry.

"Sorry for what?"

The girl looks down at her papa's feet. "I knew you'd say no. So... so I joined a club at school and had one of the older students write your name."

Helmut looks at his wife, his brow forming a question mark. She shakes her head, her dark purple lips twisted in disgust, and shoves a handwritten note toward him.

Mr. and Mrs. Sennheiser,

I'm informing you that Marta received a three-hour detention today. She and four other nine and ten-year-old students in the Pollinator's Club were caught hanging posters on school property. As you should know, we have strict policies prohibiting students from protesting at school.

I am informing you quietly because of your political position, which, as

Helmut's eyes narrow, moving back and forth between his wife and daughter. They soon turn as dull and lifeless as coal and come to rest on the little girl. A deep furrow settles on his broad forehead. *What the hell's the matter with her?* He wonders, his frustration building. *She's clueless about the stakes there.*

"How long have you been a part of this, Marta?" he demands.

The girl reaches up to rub her tiny fingers over the animated charm on her necklace. Glancing up through silver-blue eyes, she shudders, then quickly turns her face away.

When she finally finds her voice, she mumbles, "Um... just a couple months. My friends... they asked me to go with them to it. And you know how much I love butterflies."

Helmut frowns with displeasure—blind to the tears trailing down her thin cheeks. "Marta, I'm disappointed in you. Not only did you go behind my back, but you did something that goes against everything I stand for. What did these damn signs say, anyway?"

Marta sees her shame mirrored in her papa's eyes but quietly answers. "The signs I made said, *'Don't b-e-e a hater, save a pollinator'* and *'B-e-e on their side, stop insecticides.'"* She tilts her head up and looks at him imploringly, "Is that so bad, Papa?"

Helmut and his wife exchange a black look that communicates their agreement. They both know they can't have a young tree hugger sprouting in their own family. What would his political allies think? They'd mock him out of the party's center. They are merciless if one's own house isn't in order.

Marta sees the cold, distant look on her papa's face, glaring at her in a way she's never seen before. "I'm so sorry, Papa. Please... please forgive—"

He cuts her words short. Helmut reaches down and firmly takes Marta's arm. Fablé lets go of her daughter and watches as he marches the small girl around the side of the house. The sun disappears behind thick, dark clouds as they enter the backyard. He releases her from his grip and orders the yard-bot to uncoil a garden hose to begin watering. Soon, a spot of soft earth develops by a big holly bush and quickly fills with muddy, umber-colored water.

"Sit down here, Marta. Now!" he says sternly, pointing at the filthy brown spot. "Let's see how much you love this nature shit after you've wallowed in it. Now sit!"

Marta looks down and starts to whimper, her dark curls damp from the windy spray. "No, Papa! Please! I didn't mean it... I was being so naughty... I won't do it again... I promise."

His face grimaces, struggling to block out the childlike petition. He doesn't give himself time to think or feel but takes her by both shoulders and shoves her until she falls on all fours. As he pushes her, the necklace breaks and slips into the cold mud. The dirty water splashes up on her face and straightens her long, dark curls, now clinging to her small, slender cheeks.

He notices the splats of the dirty water on his trouser legs. "Damn it, see what you caused now." His voice then turns icy and low. "Remember, I told you to sit. Don't crawl or stand up. Just stay there until I tell you to get up." He turns and leaves her in the cold, brown sludge as if he were throwing out the trash and marches toward the back door.

Marta's hands sink into the thick muck as he leaves, her tiny fingers searching for the life-like butterfly medallion that Papa gave her on her last birthday.

❧❦❧❦❧❦

Later that evening, the low-pitched doorbell chimes—it's Aunt Vivienne, here to babysit. Papa is in his tux, and Mama is wearing her flowing black and white floral dress, ready to attend another exclusive fundraiser. Marta watches from the winding stairway as her mama and aunt greet each other, kissing on the cheek and then hugging as if they are gently dancing.

Marta knows Vivienne is not a real Aunty. She's been told that the Sennheiser and Stark families have a strong bond going back to their great-grandfathers in the mid-1900s. Something about electricity and energy—she doesn't really know what all that means.

"Please, Viv, see if you can talk some sense into her," Fablé implores as they walk arm-in-arm into the sitting room. "You and your mother have such a unified front, both in the party and with the media. I envy you and hope to have the same with Marta. I just can't understand what got into her to pull a stunt like this."

Vivienne slips off her red leather blazer, throws it on the sofa—her exotic fragrance drifts in the air—then places her hand on Fablé's shoulder, trying to reassure her. "I went through a stage like this when I was little, too. It will be okay. She's still naive about how the world works. She'll come around. Besides," she says with a conspiratorial wink, "she looks up to me, and if there's one thing I've learned, it's how to get what I want. You remember how we were when we were teenagers. Now you and Helmut go on. You need to focus on tonight and what might come of it."

Fablé steps back and briefly considers this self-confident, sensual woman. She offers a demure, knowing smile toward Vivienne and then strides toward the front door, never stopping to look back.

Looking up the stairway, Vivienne sees her niece spying on the two women, ducking behind the railing to be unseen.

"Okay, Marta. Your little spying expedition is over. Let's go upstairs. Time for your bath. Or should I say your *next* bath? No matter what your papa tells you, a mud bath is not the best way to care for smooth skin like yours and mine." Vivienne winks. A question mark purrs in her throat, making Marta feel that they share some special secret.

Looking like a street urchin with dirty cheeks and soiled clothes, Marta tilts her head toward her aunt and takes her outstretched hand. They head up the dark red carpet on the curved staircase and walk into an enormous dressing room that splits into his-and-her hallways, each ending in its own extravagant bathing spa. Vivienne smiles. Even though Fablé is furious with her daughter, she's ordered a steaming bath for her to soak in.

Marta stretches her hands up in the air, and Vivienne helps the girl out of her clothes and then steadies her as she gets into the large French bathtub. The storm is becoming more violent, rain peppering the ceiling-high windows. After she soaks in the sudsy water for a few minutes, Marta looks at her aunt and asks sincerely, "Why does Papa always get so upset with me? I really *do* try to please him, you know. But then I always seem to do the wrong thing, something that gets me in trouble. I don't think he even still loves me."

The girl's lips quiver—tears well up in her silver-blue eyes framed by her dripping dark curls.

Vivienne studies her niece's feline features as she considers how to answer. "My little munchkin. You never have to worry about your papa or your mama not loving you. They will always love you. It's just that they are under a lot of pressure now. They are fighting a good fight—for you and our people."

Marta scoops up some bubbles and stares at them. She then smashes them between her tiny hands, shooting suds in all directions. "I know, Aunty. When they don't think I'm around, they're always talking about how bad things are. I hear them say they're going to fix things—the way they're supposed to be. But sometimes... sometimes I feel like they're trying to fix *me*."

Vivienne takes her time to answer, slowly shaking her head as she ponders her niece. *Marta's so bright and so sensitive—a very dangerous but valuable combination.*

"My dear little Marta, it might seem that way, but that's not it at all.

You're not the problem. Hear me? You're still young. It's alright for you to mess up and make mistakes. That's how you learn." Vivienne caresses the girl's wet cheek and then continues, her voice soft and gentle. "Listen, munchkin, it's important to let the adults decide what's best for the future. So, you need to listen and learn from them. But for now, though, it's also okay to play with your dolls and stuffed animals... to love the butterflies and be worried about their future. They're beautiful, aren't they? But soon, you'll see, and I'll help show you, that things aren't as wonderful as they seem. Then you'll have to grow up and decide which side you'll be on. What you'll fight for."

Marta looks down at her toes poking up out of the water and then scoops up a handful of sparkling suds. She looks at the water and the bubbles, then turns to her aunt. "It's like the water's real, but the bubbles are just pretend. And you know how much I like to pretend." She blows on the bubbles she's holding, and they both watch them drift and pop. "But I think I'm ready. I want you to teach me what's real and what's make-believe. Isn't that what you try to do?" She looks straight into her aunt's eyes, not blinking or looking away. "I've seen you on the HOLO-NET telling people about real science. I want to know what real science is."

Vivienne looks down at the young girl, a smile slowly forming on her wide mouth. "Did I just see you grow up right before my eyes? You look bigger. And smarter, too. Of course, I'll teach you. I'll teach you everything I know about everything. Then your mama and papa will love you even more than they ever have."

Marta's pale blue eyes wander back and forth as if calculating a new math problem. Her aunty watches her niece's troubled face—then scoops her up in a soft white bath towel and rubs her dry as they watch the dirty water disappear, leaving only a small, brown ring around the shiny platinum drain.

Spring 2051

A diverse band of women—some sporting suits and heels, others draped in bohemian hippie garb, along with young mothers and their elderly grandmothers—women from all walks of life—flutter excitedly into the teal and yellow herbalist shop, Down to Earth. Most have given up wearing makeup when walking outside. It's just too much effort to constantly be bothered with blotting the perspiration away before it all runs down to the neck. Barney, the small brown-and-white terrier who's considered by many to be the mayor of the Marble City, sniffs the air and wags his tail approvingly as they pass by.

Instead of the usual mismatched collage of community event flyers taped to the window, the only signage is the large green-and-brown poster with the words SUPPORT AMAZON LIMITATION ACT #235 printed in bold, block letters.

In the past, socially concerned and politically engaged women like these would have advocated for better schools for their children, gender wage equity, or reproductive rights. It's not as if these are not still frontline issues for them. But recently, Kilkenny's women have rallied around another troubling front.

The perimeter of the small space is crammed with dried herbs, salves, and oils—scents of lavender, sage, and other mysterious fragrances invisibly swirl through the air. Fina watches the eclectic group of two dozen women enter her shop and grab a glass filled with an effervescent, dark, amber-colored drink. She nods at her husband's Greenling kinfolk, Grace Ellyn and Haven Bay. They return the gesture and gaze back through their clan's characteristic green eyes. Noah studies the pair, feeling like she's looking at a distant reflection of herself. *Will I look like that in twenty years?* Shea, standing next to her now, reads her friend's mind and looks back and forth between Noah and the two older women, flashing an exaggerated smirk at her.

The growing band greets one another with hugs and broad smiles. Some even dance a little jig while others crowd around the open floor space in celebration. Fina, dressed in a flowing muslin dress, her rich red hair plaited in Celtic braids, moves from her place beside her daughter Noah to the center of the floor. There, she begins to slowly turn around and speak in a clear, lilting brogue. Noah reaches out to hold her friend Shea's hand.

"My dear Sisters, what can I say? We did it! And oh, my. What a long, uphill fight it's been. After almost four years of having almost everything you could think of thrown at us, we somehow prevailed. And our little David took on Goliath and landed a well-placed stone."

Women sandwiched into the tiny shop breathlessly whisper, "Yes. Yes. Yes." Noah watches, smiling proudly, caught up in the circle's spirit and determination.

"It's been said by many wiser than me that local problems need local solutions. Well, in the case of our children's and our land's future, our *global* problems need *local* solutions. As you all know by now, our county council has approved the recommendation to enact Amazon Limitation Act number 235 by a vote of eight to one."

Several cheers ring out. Fina smiles and motions with her hands that she's not finished yet.

"And we know how compulsive the drive to want and to consume has become. If truth be told, none of us are immune to it either, are we? So we can't self-righteously act like this bill is for someone else. We need ordinances like this to help keep *us* accountable. So first and foremost, this legislation is for us here in this room."

The group claps their hands, a few whistle, nodding in agreement, while a few shout, "Áiméan, Fina!"

"So, Friends, raise your glasses to celebrate all we've accomplished. Not just for us but for our children's children's children and all the other creatures who deserve to live as they always have. Starting next week, we're going on a diet—a shopper's diet!" Fina chuckles and then continues. "One Amazon delivery a month should be more than enough for any of us, right?

And if I'm right, some of us may go through a wee bit of withdrawal!"

The rag-tag group snickers at the jab; glasses, filled with the malty Smithwick's ale, clink. "Sláinte," they shout, spilling their drinks on one another as they hug, teetering between laughing and crying at what they've accomplished.

Noah and Shea weave their way to the center, still holding hands. When Fina catches sight of them, she beams at the two and pulls them in. As they hug, Noah feels something furry wriggling between their legs. *Barney!*

His tail is wagging, thumping against their three legs excitedly. Noah giggles and quickly smiles down at him. He cocks his head, looking every bit the mayor of Kilkenny, and locks his gaze on her. The next moment, he quickly closes and opens his left eye.

What's that? Noah rapidly blinks in puzzlement.

Barney sits down and throws his scruffy head back. As his furry cheeks draw up into a toothy smile, he squeezes his little eye shut and then opens it again.

He winked at me. Barney winked!

Stephen Deegan comes home long after his shift is over to the rundown bungalow he calls home. The heat is unbearable—the tenth record day in a row. He swerves on unsteady legs after stopping off at Ryan's Bar, stumbling through the yard's brown, knee-high grass. His wife's eyes betray the disgust and fear she holds for the man. She rudely shushes her son, Colin, a quick nod thrown toward the other side of the house. He gets the message and hustles away to the backyard, careful to avoid the empties from several cases of Macardle's ale.

Deegan looks up at the slovenly-dressed woman. Wet, dark sweat rings stain her gaudy blouse's armpits.

"What's it now?" he barks.

Dora says nothing, she just opens the HOLO-EM so they both can see.

He groans as he sits down on the broken cement steps. Sweat drips from his ruddy forehead into damp eyebrows before stinging its way around his blood-red lids. He squints through unfocused eyes, trying to read the words hovering in the air between them, then gives up.

"Just tell me what it says, woman," he snaps, running his hand over his thin, greasy hair. "I left me damn readers in the truck."

His wife takes a quick drag on her hand-rolled cigarette and lets out an exasperated puff. "It says you've gotten the sack. You've lost your bloody job, Deegan," she yawps with a deep, raspy voice. "I don't know why they've waited this long. But now you've lost it to that Fina Calhoun and all her goddamned lady bountifuls. It says you, along with twelve of your mates, are finished with your delivery positions. Service *no longer needed*. You hear me? Whatcha gonna do about that?"

Colin has snuck up to the corner of the house, listening. *Noah's ma? What's she gone and screwed up now?* He shakes his head, trying not to breathe, but the hot, dry air triggers his cough. His ma's eye catches a glimpse of him. She shakes her head slightly and then turns back to her husband, ready to fend off what's to come.

Deegan slowly stands, grabbing his wife for balance—his weight almost pulls her off the stoop—then unsteadily weaves through the broken-down screen door. "Don't worry about it, woman. It's nothin' for ya' to be about. I'll take care of 'em. Now, where's me dinner?"

⚘❦⚘❦⚘❦

Two days later, a dark gray panel van pulls down the alley next to Down to Earth. It's after two o'clock in the morning, and the street is empty except for a trio of mangy cats stalking the giant rats that have become common. Barney, sleeping in the recessed storefront across the street from Fina's shop, stirs from his doggy dreams when he hears the engine's sound. The driver turns off the ignition and lights a cigarette. The cabin is already thick with smoke and smells of spilled whiskey. Someone hacks uncontrollably in the back, earning black scowls from the others. The passenger in the front seat is rapidly tapping his foot.

After five minutes, the driver nods, and the three men, dressed in dark clothes and balaclavas, quietly exit the van. They carry hurling sticks and a bag filled with cans of spray paint.

Looking down the street, they see no one and quickly move about, painting an Amazon logo with the "A" connected by a frowning arrow arching to the "Z" on the wood and brick shop front. Another writes GREEZLING HOOR in all caps, along with other nasty slurs.

"Bee-utiful." The leader steps back as he admires their work. Glancing both ways and seeing no one, he nods to the other two. He looks up through the balaclava's opening at the security HOLO-CAM and raises the middle finger of his right hand toward it. For a second, the gesture reveals the man's shoulder, showing a faded tattoo of a hideous sea monster and the phrase "Drinking Squid."

They quickly disappear into the building's shadows and begin bashing the three big windows and walls. Jars of herbs and salves, bins filled with crickets and buffalo worms, all neatly stacked on high rows of shelves, crash to the floor from the violent impact. Barney sits up and—fully awake now—bares his teeth and growls at the three intruders.

They step through the broken glass and ravage the snug little shop. As they do, cases alive with giant grasshoppers, kept as micro-livestock, tumble and break open. Despite their savagery, or because of it, sweet and musky scents soon fill the air. After two or three minutes, they stop. Breathing hard, they look around and see the floor covered in glass, plants, dried insects, and oils. Each one unzips his fly and pisses away on the scattered, broken debris. Done, the leader nods, and they head out through the window and jog slowly away down the dark alley. Barney sees their retreat as a signal to give chase. His barking and snapping hurry their pace toward the van. As the leader opens the door, he spins and winds up his hurling stick for a full swing at the little noisemaker. The blow lands squarely on the small terrier's frame, bowling him over onto his side, where he lies lifeless in the alley's muck.

Marta's dark curls bounce into her face as she runs down the staircase, running her hands along the Christmas garland her mama hung yesterday.

"I love Christmas so much," she squeals, racing to find Papa.

Like in most families, the holiday seems to officially begin on the day the Christmas tree is brought home—her mama just told her that today's the big day to find their tree. Marta races through the back door and finds her papa in the small outbuilding, putting some tools in the truck's storage bin. When he sees her, he extends a hand toward her and quickly slips the other into his bulging coat pocket.

Seeing a questioning look on her rosy cheeks, Papa laughs—places his large hands on her shoulders, and steers his bundled daughter into the front seat.

"Come on, little munchkin! Let's go Christmas tree shopping!" She waves rapidly to Mama with her small, mittened hands as he tells the truck's pilot-bot to start the engine and back them out of the long, curved driveway.

Helmut turns the pilot-bot off to drive manually and steers the massive Hummer H7 past the Rhine River's recently built and controversial levee system. The fifteen-meter-high floodwall blocks their view for several miles until they pass the city's limits. There, Papa turns onto a series of smaller highways, then one-lane roads, and eventually turns into a narrow, unplowed gap—tires biting into the smooth, untainted snowfall. A wonderland of sparkling white snow dots the branches of the massive red pines, mid-sized blue spruce, and Norwegian firs across the landscape.

After a few miles, he pulls off into a small turnaround where they park. Marta notices a big, yellow sign on a large pine trunk.

NO TRESPASSING
PRIVATE PROPERTY - KEEP OUT!
NO HUNTING, LOGGING, OR TREE REMOVAL
VIOLATORS WILL BE PROSECUTED

After reading the words out loud, she flashes a surprised look at her papa, who just shrugs as he grins back boyishly. "Here we are, Marta, dear. Are you ready to find our Christmas trees for us?" She nods—her unease about the sign now gone—her silver-blue eyes sparkling with wonder.

As they step out of the truck, Papa pulls his black balaclava down over his face. Marta's tall, red boots sink into the snow until its deep, white powder pours in over the top. She shivers, feeling the sudden chill creep down the lining. He puts his arm around her and gives her a pair of rough leather gloves—smaller but the same as his. They head into the woods, the snow crunching under their feet, her papa carrying a well-used tree saw. Their breath sends puffs of little clouds into the air. Her short legs march through the deep snow with great effort. After walking for several minutes, her eyes squint, and she points to a perfectly formed, six-meter-tall blue spruce.

"That one, Papa," she squeals. "I want that one."

"A good choice, my little munchkin." They walk toward it, and he bends a knee deep into the snow. "Here, Marta. Help me with the saw."

Together, they place the jagged metal blade against the rough pine bark. For a moment, it's as if the tree shudders, exhaling a few small puffs of snow onto them. Marta squeals, then puts her hands back on the handle, and Papa puts his on top of hers. They find a steady rhythm moving back and forth, the blade cutting into the evergreen's skin-like bark, then deeper into its fleshy heartwood. She smells the release of the crisp pine scent just before she notices the sap seeping from the gash they've created. The blade keeps biting further into the pulpy tissue, almost severing it from its oozing base. They put down the saw and stand. Papa then steers her back and gives the trunk a quick, sharp kick. At last, the tree, heavy with snow on its branches, pivots, and thuds to the ground on its side.

Marta bounces up, clapping her leather gloves together. "We did it, Papa. We did it! Yay."

Helmut's smile widens. His eyes reflect the pride and pleasure he feels for her. "Yes, we did. I couldn't have done it without you." As he studies her rosy face, he sees the innocent delight in her young eyes. *Was I ever that childlike?* He wonders, then quickly shakes off the feeling and reaches for the pine's broad branches.

"Now, Marta, you grab that side, and I'll take this one," he says. "Let's drag it to the truck."

After loading it in the truck bed, they head back into the field of pines and find two more trees, just like the first one.

Marta looks up, thoughtfulness written on a quizzical brow. "Papa. What do we need three trees for? We've always only had one before."

Helmut watches his daughter for a moment, concealing how badly he wants her admiration. "Because, Marta, this is a big year for your papa. Our party has promoted me, and we'll be hosting a lot of important people at our house this month. I want to show them how special we are."

Marta looks confused and shakes her head, showing she doesn't understand. She *does* take in the hopeful look on Papa's face as he speaks and stares into the pale blue sky. She looks up in the same direction and smiles. *How cool will it be to be the only kid at school with three huge Christmas trees?*

BRRAAAP... BRRAAAP... BRRAAAP... BRRAAAP. Her thoughts are interrupted by the piercing noise of a four-wheeler that rattles like the tin cans she strings out behind her bicycle.

A skinny man in a green snowsuit shuts off the ATV's sputtering engine and takes his helmet off. His hair is pure white—a short, scruffy beard covers his chin and cheeks. He stares at them for a few beats before getting off the four-wheeler and walking with a slight limp in their direction.

His steel gray eyes narrow as he sizes Helmut up. "*Scheisse*, man! What's the matter with you? Can't you read?" Thrusting a thumb at the sign on the tree next to him. Helmut's eyes go flat and never leave the man. Marta steps behind her papa. Her wool-covered head leans out to watch.

The old man stares back, then surveys the scene and spots the three pines strapped to the truck bed. Not waiting for an answer, he wades through the snow toward it.

"What in God's name have you done, you theivin' son-of-a-bitch? It's been fifty years since we replanted this forest, and you... you just come along, acting like it's nothin' to no one... and cut it down." He looks at Marta, his hawklike eyes and nose aiming straight at her. "What for? Hmm? For you, little princess? For some cheery little Christmas picture?" He lets out a loud, exasperated sigh—the younger man's silence elevating the moment's tension. "Come on, the damage is done—help me get these unloaded. They can rest here where they belong."

The man reaches for the truck gate and begins to open it. Helmut makes sure his balaclava is in place, then unzips his coat and reaches into the interior pocket. He pulls out a small, black Walther PPK .22 and points it toward the other man's back.

"You can stop it right there, old man. We aren't unloading anything."

The old man struggles and spins around, unsteady on his bad leg. If he's startled by the gun pointed at him, he doesn't show it.

"Hey, put that damn thing away! Are you crazy? This is my land! And these," he says, pointing at the three spruces, "sure as hell ain't yours. These are *my* trees! You hear? I told you what we're going to do."

He squints at Helmut as if sizing him up. "I can see it in your eyes. You haven't ever shot anyone before. And you're not gonna start today."

Helmut's face hardens as his eyes narrow. He raises the barrel of the gun over the man's head and pulls the trigger.

POP!!! The wood's silence is abruptly broken for a split second. Marta shrieks as her small frame jerks. A few mourning doves, protectively nestled in the three felled pines, shoot off over their heads, their wings whistling alarm. Birds hidden in the surrounding woods explode into the air. It's as if someone abruptly struck a metal drum and then stopped. A deadly silence quickly rushes back around them.

The man, still ducking, now rants at Helmut, "What the fuck are you doin', man? This isn't a game you're playing."

Helmut's voice is slow and threatening. "Finally, you speak truth, old man. Now get your greeny-weenie ass on that ride of yours and get the hell out of here. *Mach Schnell!* Before I change my mind."

The old man backs his way carefully to the ATV. He doesn't bother putting his helmet on. He wants to keep his eyes fixed on Helmut. The engine fires up and vibrates with its chaotic rhythm, announcing that the confrontation is over. The snowdust from the ATV's tires drifts behind the man until he's out of sight.

Papa pulls his balaclava off, looks at Marta, and flashes a cocky grin. "Let's go, *meine* munchkin. I think we've got what we came for." He slips the gun back into his coat while putting his other arm around his rosy-cheeked daughter. Marta's eyes look down at the trampled snow, confused by what just happened—unable to look at her papa.

Spring 2054

Kilkenny, Ireland (95° F / 35° C)

Noah switches off the auto-glide to pedal and steer the bike herself. The gentle wind conceals the fact that it's too hot for this early in the morning. Her long red hair clings to her neck and face from the sweat as she rides. Even so, she enjoys biking the three miles to Jenkinstown Wood.

Being only thirteen, she feels proud that her ma trusts her to refill the diminishing herbs for the shop. Today, she hopes to spot some weasel's snout in a small clearing her ma says used to be rich with it. Finding the rapidly disappearing herbs and medicinal plants is now nearly impossible.

Leaning her bike against a cracked, half-barren maple tree, she adjusts her knapsack on her shoulders and walks toward the wood's opening. As she walks along the dusty path, she passes a large oak and notices its heavy, bent limbs and deep, curved peels of tree bark. She feels her heart physically respond, its beat slow and heavy as if trying to push sludge through her chest.

Gently placing her soft, small hand on the tree's pale, fissured bark, she whispers, *Are you alright?*

The gray giant's distress slowly fans out in an arc of silence. For a moment, an unearthly lifelessness envelopes Noah. Suddenly, she's overtaken—her hands and arms begin to tremble uncontrollably—the ground itself seems to vibrate with a subterranean rage.

After several minutes, unable to move, she finally breaks contact. *What in the world was that?* Her legs are shaky, her body still wobbly as she begins walking again, her boots kicking up little dust clouds.

She travels for a few kilometers, surveying the sparse undergrowth. *Whenever I come here now, it feels like a desert—not the way it used to be—it feels like death... it's almost impossible to find a spot of green with flowers anymore.*

POP! POP! POP! Noah flinches, then ducks. Gunfire—something she's never encountered in these woods before.

She freezes and drops to a crouch. Her heart pounds and quickly fuels a collision of mixed emotions. She feels... afraid... uncertain... peeved... torn. *I better just back away and go home,* she tells herself. *No, that's the coward's way out;* her protectiveness for the woods pushes back. *Whatever it is... it's totally wrong,* she finally reckons. As she cautiously creeps in the direction of the shots, she sees the back of a tall, wiry boy with an ugly, fluorescent green skull cap.

"Hey!" Noah yells, wanting to be sure he knows she's there in case he might turn and shoot in her direction. "What in the world are you thinking? Don't you know people walk here?" Her voice sounds shrill—her anger edged with fear.

The boy whips around to face her, a matte-gray pistol dangling from his long, lean arm, still too heavy for him. *It's Colin. That makes sense,* she thinks to herself.

"Well, if it isn't the little Greezling herbie 'erself. Why ya' sneaking up on me ya' mutter? I might 'ave know'd ya'd pop up and spoil the day. Want some of this?" He steps toward her and makes a suggestive gesture with his hips, doing his best to shock her.

She just shakes her head and sneers. "You're so gross, Colin." Unafraid, she inches toward him, smelling the sharp, sulfurous afterburn of gunfire. "You just surprised me. I usually don't see anyone else in these woods. And besides, you shouldn't be out here shooting things up. You're not old enough to have a gun like that by yourself."

He stands there, glaring intimidation. Noah holds his gaze and then looks behind him. Several empty beer cans are scattered among a patch of honey cap mushrooms. Both the cans and the tiny fungi look like someone has run them through a dull meat grinder.

Looking back at him, she screams, "Colin, you're such a monster! Those little mushrooms are defenseless. I hardly see any of them anymore." She walks toward them and stoops to the ground, her lips quivering, ready to weep.

The boy turns and watches her hovering like a mother hen over the carnage he's created. Something about the scene loosens a memory of his da shouting at him when he was six. *What the fuck are ya' doin' boy? Real men don't play with gurlie shit like that.* And then his pissing all over the flowers he'd picked for Ma.

He pushes the thought away and sneaks up beside her, undoes his fly to urinate on the few mushrooms still standing.

"Here, let me water the little buggers for ya'!"

He laughs at her as she grabs a stick lying beside her and stands up—her face an angry red—her eyes weighing her chances.

"Why don't ya' try it? I'm up for it when ya' are," he taunts.

The birds go quiet—the leaves become still. Noah realizes how alone she is now. She feels vulnerable yet foolishly unafraid. Her muscles tense. She straightens her shoulders. Her breathing becomes slow and heavy. The adrenaline's been building ever since she discovered it was Colin. She barely notices that she still has a choice here. Her fingers trace up and down the rough bark of the stick. *Either walk away,* which her jacked-up state tells her *not* to do, or *whack the little prick in the balls.*

Instead, she hurls a feral howl at him. "Get out of here, you bloody hooligan! I'll report you if you don't. What do you think your da would say if he found you'd taken it? I've heard how he deals with you when you cross the line."

He looks at her blandly as he zips his pants up, making a theatrical production of it. They silently square off for an uncomfortable few more moments. Colin makes a gross snort, then abruptly turns and heads toward the road.

Left alone, Noah's breathing becomes erratic, her chest heaving, as if she's just run a sprint. After her mind settles, a quiet hush emerges from the forest, surrounding her like a soft cocoon, blanketing her in its calm. Then she hears, almost as if words were spoken directly into her brain, *"We were ready just in case."*

Noah's brow furrows—stumped by the words' origin—even more bewildered by the phrase's meaning. *Ready to do what?*

Spring 2057

Dallas, Texas, USA (125° F / 52° C)

The aristocratic, silver-haired woman signals her husband's HOLO as the car door opens for her. Fine, dusty sand blows through the open rear door, peppering the backseat's screened fabric that absorbs most of the troubling particles. She quickly slides in and unwraps her designer sand scarf as the pilot-bot closes the door. The air purification system quickly evacuates the floating motes and replaces them with fresh 02 from the oxygen concentrator.

She huffs through her skinny nose. Lips tightly turned down in a frown—miffed because he's not home—irritated with herself for assuming he would be.

"Charles, I knew you'd let us down! Simon and I are heading over to the zoo now. We're tired of waiting. I don't know how anything can be more important than your grandson, but obviously it is. Join us there if you can... or if you want to."

Helen abruptly ends the message, turns to the freckled little boy twisting his shirt in his tiny hands, and says, "Let's go, cowboy!"

After giving the limousine's pilot-bot their destination, her countenance softens. Her rigid shoulders relax as she feels some generosity toward her husband returning.

"You know, Simon, your Grandpa Cha-cha is the one who rebuilt the Dallas Zoo. After the zoo-pandemic, he bought the whole complex and brought it back to life." The boy's large eyes go wide—a small, lifelike ani-bot of a tiger paces on his lap—hanging on to his mo-ma's words. "Before that, the smell was horrible. You couldn't know when the animals would come out to be seen. Plus, there were thick bars and glass cages between you and them. But now, that's all changed. Thanks to Cha-cha, you can walk right up to them and be with any animal you'd like. You can even climb up on the bigger ones."

Not wanting to burst the boy's sense of wonder, she leaves out the fact that the zoos are now populated, not with real animals, but with a limitless supply of convincing robotic renditions. In the experimental sections, robotic replicas of extinct species—giant pandas, African mountain gorillas, and black rhinoceroses—wander lifelike, surrounded by stunning holographic scenery.

ᎧᏇᎧᏇᎧᏇ

Charles Cartright, better known as 'The Chief,' listens to his wife Helen's HOLO-EM and chews his large bottom lip. *That poor kid... he hasn't a clue how messed up his mama is. Shit... if Lily's neighbor hadn't found her, we'd be planning her funeral instead of checking her back into BrightStar.*

He looks at his HOLO-WATCH. A face like John Wayne's glares back as if reading his mind. *"Ten minutes 'til your next meetin', pardner,"* the old cowboy announces—time enough to send a message back to his wife.

"Helen. Listen. No excuse... but... I can't make it today. I know—you told me so. And I promised." He pauses, a long exhale escaping his big chest. "I did run out to BrightStar. My father-daughter session was this mornin', remember? That was a goddamned shitshow. She looked awful—eyes like a caged animal's. And then... you know... every word I said just set her off... it just made things worse."

His voice falters for a short minute. "I'm telling you—we're losin' her, Helen... Fuck, she's probably gone already." He wipes the growing pool from his eyes. "I'm okay. Just doin' my best to keep it together. Don't bother waitin' up. I've got a helluva day. Love ya', darlin.'" He quickly disconnects the HOLO, never thinking to ask Helen how she's doing.

He strides down the hall, enters a large, glass-walled conference room, and takes his place at the head of a thirty-foot, black walnut table. He's flanked by a contingent of twenty nouveau-yuccie PR-heads. They and their predecessors have operated as the greenwashing agents for the Trans-Natural Economic Coalition for decades.

It's not that the job's gotten harder, he reminds himself. *It's always just more of the same shit. But it's relentless. A new generation's idealism is just like some of the young colts me and my daddy used to whip into shape. First, you have to break 'em, then you gotta rein 'em in, and then, you saddle 'em up and take 'em wherever the hell you want 'em to go.*

"Damn it! You're failin' here, people. Have you all seen the latest pollin' numbers? They're fuckin' atrocious." The Chief's tone drips with insult. "Can't y'all figure something out to get some buy-in for this vision? *My* vision? I think my seven-year-old grandson could do better than this. Why's everyone still upset with all these useless animals dyin' off? Most people didn't even know they existed in the first place."

He glares around the table. Each one puts their head down, avoiding the slim chance of eye contact. "Change the damned narrative! We... don't... need... extinct... animals anymore. You read me? This is my fuckin' eco-legacy here! I want every boy, girl, man, and woman to believe that a planet populated with robotic animals is a better future. A better world than any that's evolved before."

The old man looks every bit his age with a full head of pure-white hair paired with a sizable paunch. But there's an unquenchable fire in that gut. His glare, reminiscent of a hungry lion, surveys each one around the table before he launches in again.

"And *you*, y'all can't even seem to find the vision, let alone sell it! You've had three months to come up with a strategy that actually works. And what have you given me? Play-Doh in Happy Meals! I want people out there to be so in love with the idea that they're trippin' over each other to invest in this brave new world. Y'all understand? There will be consequences if you can't deliver. And they will be unpleasant, right B.B.?"

The mountain of a man, standing off to the side, nods ever so slightly, flashing a gold cap on his top incisor. His giant afro looks like an ebony halo, though the scars on his face and arms make it obvious he's far from being a saint. As if on cue, B.B. plucks the gold, optical-zoom prosthetic eye from his left orbital socket—flings it in the air like a piece of candy, and catches it in his mouth. After swishing it around to clean it, he unceremoniously spits it into his hand and squeezes it back in place with a wet *PLOP!* Those around the table shudder and squirm. A few visibly gag.

If the money doesn't light a fire under their overpaid yuccie asses, maybe the fear of God will, the Chief reckons as he turns and walks past B.B., never slowing to look back.

Summer 2057

Dublin, Ireland (95° F / 35° C)

After boarding the bullet train, Noah, her ma, and Shea settle into their compartment and enjoy the flowing montage—small villages, woodlands, hillsides, and broad fields of gold and russet—that streams by the window, accompanied by the peaceful whir of the train's wheels.

Despite the pleasantness of their travel, Noah bites her lower lip and shakes her head in frustration. *I'm so fed up with it all... what's it going to take? Diesel engines still pull all our trains. People say, "We're for cleaner transportation," but nothing ever changes, really.*

Sensing her friend's sulky mood, Shea pulls out a travel game of *Othello*. Soon, they are immersed in the board's complex strategy, while their trip to Dublin continues on unremarkably. When they arrive at Heuston Station, they find an orange-and-green kiosk where they rent three solar-powered scooters—the girls, now sixteen, are finally old enough to pilot their own. With their backpacks containing a change of clothes, they pick their way through the city streets' overflowing gutters and park their rides four blocks from their destination: the Leinster House. From there, they walk the remainder of the way on foot over the elevated walkway system—without it, the flood zone would be inaccessible.

The impressive three-story building used to be the ducal mansion and now houses the Oireachtas, the Irish government's center of power.

Ma and the two girls walk past several uniformed *gardaí* who observantly watch them pass by. They then head inside an unpretentious front door and pass through the security checkpoint. After their bags are returned, they find a public toilet where they change out of their jeans and into clothes more suitable for the presentation. As Noah looks at herself in the mirror, she straightens her tangled, copper waves, rubs on a small amount of honey and beeswax lip gloss, and mouths to herself, *"Here we go."* She still hasn't gotten over the shock that the project she has given herself to this last year has actually brought her here.

Her ma interrupts her daughter's musings and catches her eye in the mirror, a look of motherly pride passing between them. "Come on, girls. We best head over now to the Dáil."

They stuff the rest of their belongings in their bags and head out the door toward the entrance to the large hall. As they're walking, Shea reaches out and stops Noah. "Here, give me that," she insists, snatching the bag from her friend's shoulder. "You've got this, Noah. You always do."

Noah replies with a nervous smile. "Thank you."

The room is already packed and alive with the buzz of countless separate conversations. A slender, mocha-skinned young man is waiting there. When he sees them, he steps forward and introduces himself.

"Hello. My name's Duncan. And you—you must be Noah."

Noah takes his hand, thanks him, and then introduces her ma and Shea.

They follow his lead, slowly walking down the aisle as he continues to speak. "I'm one of the parliamentary assistants here at the Dáil, and I'll be taking care of you this morning. We're really delighted you're here, and I'm personally thrilled about all this."

Noah meets his gaze, puzzled, feeling as if Duncan is a little starstruck at meeting her. Now that's a new one!

"Is there anything you need before I take you to your seats?" He asks.

The three shake their heads while thanking him. He then spins around and takes them to the front row of the visitor's gallery. The expansive room is semi-circular. In front are two single rows facing one another—the lawmakers sit there. Its plush furnishings tastefully blend the rich ochre walls with deep cherry wood and tan leather. Noah glances over at her ma and Shea. I wonder if I look as out of place here as they do.

Although she won't have to speak—her presence is primarily symbolic—Noah anxiously swallows and takes long, slow breaths while she awaits the anticipated announcement.

After the gathering of politicians settles down and gets to the day's business, she pans the assembly, her green eyes weighing those around her. So these are the ones who'll determine our future. You'd think, with things in such a crisis, they'd have more to show for it.

"And finally," her broodiness is interrupted by the short, balding chairman, "in keeping with our tradition of selecting the proposal for our annual student holiday competition, we are pleased to announce this year's winner. We are honored to have 16-year-old Noah Calhoun-Greenling with us today."

A few of those seated nearby smile as they look her way. Feeling conspicuous under their gaze, she forces herself to keep her eyes trained on the speaker.

"She is a passionate young woman who has championed the environmental needs and problems of not only her hometown, Kilkenny, but now the rest of Ireland. Each one of us encounters the impact of this predicament merely by coming to work at the Dáil, as it is surrounded by the sea's encroachment on our capital.

"As you all know, our people have had a rich and lengthy love affair with the Emerald Isle. Being a small island means we are especially vulnerable to the changes in the rising tide. Unlike many larger nations, we remain unified that climate action and sustainable practices must be a high priority—no matter the costs.

"Although our previous awards have gone to more uplifting holidays, we applaud Noah for recognizing the sobriety of the moment. Therefore, we declare that October 22nd will now be known as Earther's Lament Day—a day when Noah will summon the country's youth to a wake for the planet—a time to remember and mourn our non-human kin."

Sporadic applause eventually takes root and politely ripples through the room at the speaker's words.

"We thank you, Ms. Calhoun-Greenling," the man says, inviting her to stand. When Noah takes to her feet, all heads turn in her direction. A mild blush colors her neck and cheeks. Feeling conspicuous and uncertain about what to do next, she looks at her ma and Shea, who both nod reassuringly. She stands up, shoulders thrown back, feeling her confidence return, and then raises two fists and begins to knock her knuckles together—a gesture inherited from the Greenling clan for when words are insufficient—the motion making absolutely no noise.

After Noah, her ma, and Shea suffer the obligatory photo-op with the talkative speaker, they head back to the washroom to change into their street clothes. On their way toward the door, they run into Duncan, the young man who had greeted them earlier as they entered the hall.

"Off so soon? I wish I could join you. It gets a bit dull around here after a large event like today." He pauses a moment and then continues, "I wanted to catch you before you left to let you know that if I can do anything to support you, give me a shout. Frankly, most of these student holidays have been pretty weak. You remember, don't you? *'Ireland Loves Ice Cream'* and my personal favorite, *'Hurling for Her.'* But what you've come up with is bold; it's original, and frankly, I'm surprised they took the risk. Anyway, I'll send my contact info so you have it. I'd really like to see your idea get some traction and succeed."

Noah feels her ring vibrate and watches the HOLO-EM with his name bloom. She nods and smiles gratefully. "Thank you, Duncan. We'll see. We're off to meet with some of the folks at ECO-UNESCO. They were super helpful in getting my holiday proposal in good shape. Now they want to talk about promotion."

"That sounds wonderful," he says, gently touching her arm. "And Noah, congratulations. Who knows, Earther's Lament might open doors that you've never dreamed of."

She looks at the young man, who, for a moment, seems younger than she is. Or does she somehow seem older? *Strange times. Strange times, indeed,* she thinks to herself, then scurries outside into a howling gale.

They arrive at their destination with soggy, mud-splattered pant legs. The brick, three-story building is plain, with a Rolling Donut kiosk on the first floor. Before heading upstairs to their meeting, they pop in and order two dozen jam-and-cream fingers. Each eats one on the way up, laughing at how they look, sporting various smudges of raspberry jam and custard on their faces.

There's a simple sign at the top of the third floor with the name ECO-UNESCO stenciled on what looks like a burlap sack. Opening the door, they see several casually dressed men and women in a conference room. Everything looks used, vintage, or upcycled. The rust-colored rug is stained, and the ceiling looks as if it might fall in if they slam the door too hard.

An energetic woman in her mid-thirties steps out of the room and approaches them with a broad smile.

"Hello, you must be Noah. My name is Poll," the woman says as she reaches out to shake Noah's hand. "I'm the director here, but we're an egalitarian lot. We are *so* looking forward to putting our heads together and getting behind this beautiful concept you've come up with."

"Hi. It's good to meet you. Thanks for taking the time—" Noah starts to say but is interrupted by the woman.

"Take the time? Are you kidding? We think this could be the biggest thing since Greta Thunberg was honored with the George Cross in 2033." The woman's enthusiasm is genuine and radiant. "So, who have you brought along with you?"

Noah turns to her left. "Well, this is my ma, Fina Greenling-Calhoun." The two women shake hands as they warmly appraise each other.

"And this is my best friend, Shea." Noah puts her arm around Shea. "I couldn't do any of this without her by my side. And these are donuts from the shop on the street," Noah says, offering the bakery bag as if she's presenting a precious jewel.

Poll takes the greasy white sack daintily between two fingers and says, "Come on back. Everyone's anxious to meet you and get started." They follow her into the conference room, again struck by how unpretentious the furnishings are.

Maybe it's that pompous hall we were just in—or maybe it looks like someplace I'd see back home. But this feels real—like things matter here.

The five women and three men who make up the staff greet their three guests and introduce themselves. They're just about to sit down when the door swings open with a whoosh and slams hurriedly. The sound of high heels echoes as a tall, well-toned woman approaches. She gracefully leans down to take off the blue spikes and puts them in her bag, now standing barefoot in the conference room doorway.

"Hi, you must be Noah. So nice to meet you," she says, looking at the young redhead with piercing, coppery eyes. "I'm Journi Preston."

"Hello, I know who you are! I've been watching *Environmental Watch* since I was a little girl." Noah's cheeks reveal a slight flush at meeting one of her heroes. "It's great to meet you, too!"

Journi smiles, then turns to the group. "Sorry I'm late, everyone, but my lunch with the director of the EPA and her staff went... well... you know how Bobby is. She just kept going on and on. I eventually had to interrupt her and break out of there."

"Well, we're glad you made it. So, let's get started," Poll says.

For the next two hours, she adeptly guides the meeting, drawing out ideas from the group that will soon become the roadmap for the Earther's Lament Day national campaign. Shea and Noah's ma sit next to the wall, here to provide moral support rather than to contribute directly.

A central focus of their strategy is to pool resources to develop a HOLO-POD that targets Irish youth. ECO-UNESCO has strong support in most schools, and the schools' teachers have always come on board. But they decide to turn things upside down. They want the youth, not the schools, to drive things. With some luck, they hope to take advantage of Noah's youthful passion and take the message viral. Then, down the road, who knows? With Journi's HOLO-CAST reach, maybe in a year, they can expand the concept into a worldwide movement that will host Earther's Lament Day events in their nation's communities.

As the meeting is wrapping up, Journi's HOLO ring vibrates. She steps out to accept the connection, then quickly leans back in through the room's doorway and says, "This is going to be big, friends. I hope you're ready!

Gotta run."

She tiptoes to the door, mocking a teenager's sneakiness at coming home in the middle of the night, and disappears. The group chuckles.

People gradually say their goodbyes and make their way to the door. But Noah's eyes seem distant—focused somewhere beyond the room she's sitting in. Lost in her thoughts, her gaze flickers between excitement and apprehension. *How did I get here... and where on God's green earth is it going?*

Spring 2058

Poppelsdorf, Bonn, Germany (98° F / 37° C)

Vivienne, in her low-cut purple cocktail dress, leans back on the cream-colored loveseat. Across from her, in two deep burgundy leather wingbacks, sit her handsome hosts, Helmut and Fablé Sennheiser, equally dressed for the occasion. What's become Germany's near-relentless rain beats on the high clerestory windows around the room's perimeter.

"Here's to next week," Helmut says, lifting his fluted glass toward Vivienne.

"To next week," the two women echo. The delicious bubbles from the Dom Perignon Rose' Luminous Label Champagne bring the trio a smile of shared pleasure. Helmut closes his eyes and takes a deep breath in. The two women's perfumes mingle to form an exotic blend. One complex, deep, and powerful, a pungent blend of feral pheromones. The other, flushed with nectar-laden pistils and stamens, alluring in the purity of innocence.

Vivienne looks at the couple across from her before setting her half-empty glass on the live-edge bubinga table. The table is so glossy that she can see her face in its reflection.

"*Danke schön.* I really didn't relish celebrating alone tonight," she lifts her glass and tilts it toward the couple, then takes another long sip.

"We certainly can't have you celebrating by yourself, dear." Fablé winks, the champagne's effect causing her dark eyes to shimmer.

Vivienne smiles with dark, wet lips and lets her eyes linger on the other woman for a moment. "The AFD's global gathering will attract our biggest allies—the Swiss People's Party, the Brothers of Italy, the Hungarian Fidesz Party, and the rest.

"You both know—getting here has been quite a struggle. And now that I'm here, I feel... I want to propose something. I'm not getting any younger. My image..." Viv pauses, thoughtfully sampling another mouthful of champagne. "Rather, my physical appeal as the movement's pin-up girl isn't what it—"

Both Helmut and Fablé try to interrupt, but she waves them off.

"Thank you, both of you. But I've made up my mind. It's time we found a new voice, a new face." She pauses, takes a deep breath, and then continues, slowly and carefully enunciating each word. "So, if you'd allow me... I'd like to take Marta under my wing. I'd like to mentor her to become the next generation's rising star for the party. She's bright, we have a good rapport with one another, and if I'm not mistaken, she'll have your good looks and great figure, Fablé."

The couple glances at each other through glassy eyes, stifling a tipsy giggle, their thoughts, for a moment, almost telepathic. *Our daughter, the next Vivienne Stark! What could that do for our future aspirations?*

The conversation continues and briefly touches upon a few practical issues.

"Well, I think that settles it! Agreed?" Helmut announces as if he's just sold his old Mercedes to a good friend.

"Agreed," the two women say, tittering as they clink their empty glasses.

"I'm off to the cellar for another bottle. I'll get the good stuff this time," he says with a seductive wink. He considers their entangled affair as he walks down the dim stairs. He's been with both women, and his wife knows it. Hell, Viv knows that Fablé knows.

As he's gone, neither of the women notices Marta seated on the upstairs landing above them. Her silver-blue eyes record every move, every expression her aunt makes. She brushes a strand of her long black hair from her pale face and smiles a wicked little grin she's been practicing in the mirror. Turning to go back to bed before she's discovered, she looks back. Through the stairs' railing, she catches a glimpse of her mother as she drops to her knees in front of Aunt Vivienne to give her a long, passionate kiss on the mouth.

Fall 2058

Kilkenny, Ireland (88° F / 31° C)

Birds chitter in her ma's haphazardly planted backyard, where Noah retreats to search for extinct or near-extinct species on her HOLO. Her denim overall shorts are embroidered with the names and images of vanishing creatures. She surveys account after account of the past two centuries' toll on the biosphere. On one HOLO-VID, she recognizes Journi Preston's voice narrating a stream of disturbing images.

"The blue-throated macaw, the brown spider monkey, the humpback whale, the American burying beetle, the Siamese crocodile—all at risk of disappearing forever. And these are just a small sample of the bloody wounds from a hemorrhaging planet. Add to it the other vulnerable life forms, and the estimate swells to over sixty percent at certain future risk—a future that now hurtles toward the present faster than ever."

Leaning against the ancient wych elm, she feels as if the tree is also weeping at what it has heard—the countless beautiful creations now shattered beyond hope.

Gil comes out from tinkering in the garage. He sees her weeping under the tree and sits down beside her. On her HOLO-VID, a pair of red pandas lie dead from hypothermia. She's already told him about the killer freeze that caused their death—two of only two hundred thought to exist still.

"Hey, sis. Why are you doing this to yourself? I watch you come out here and get engrossed in this stuff. It's just making you miserable. Even Ma's concerned," he says softly.

"Concerned?" she shoots back, wiping her nose on the back of her wrist. "That's what I'm trying to do. Be *concerned*. Actually, I'm outraged! Carbon neutral? Sustainable? Renewable?" She ticks off the words, almost yelling now, her sarcasm mocking the beloved environmental slogans. "I'll tell you what. I'm sick of all their political bullshit! Can't you see what we've lost, what we're losing—while nothing ever really changes?"

Gil sits quietly for a moment, then answers, "I know. I really do, but it's just... it's just so damned big, Noah. *Too big.* Can't you just be... I don't know... hopeful or something? There are really smart people working on this. Some of us are still optimistic—things are starting to change—with all the advancements in tech and energy and—" She wags her head and tries to interrupt him, but he presses on.

"—you just sit out here all alone, obsessed with the problem, not really looking for solutions. You're still just a kid, remember?" His eyes glare at her, his exasperation spilling out. "I don't know why it's so damned hard for you to just act your age... you're only sixteen... now for the love of God, just lighten up... will you?"

Noah clenches her fists. *Who does he think he is telling me where to get off? I don't remember asking for advice.* Her green eyes stare through him for a moment. Then her head turns and peers at the HOLO, putting her finger on the image of the dead pandas, slowly tracing their small furry forms.

"That's why I can't be optimistic," she mumbles, her voice now deflated. She presses her hand into the floating scene as if she could resuscitate the lifeless pair. "There's nothing hopeful about any of this for them."

༄ ༀ ༄ ༀ ༄ ༀ

Colin and his da are home alone watching Manchester United play Arsenal on the HOLO. The only time he's ever felt a scrap of connection with the old man is when it involves a Smithwicks and football. Tonight, Manchester is winning two to one. Beating Arsenal is the one thing left that still seems to make Stephen smile. Colin is bragging about how he and his mates hassled Noah and her little eco-hippie fest when the game is interrupted.

"What the shit?" Stephen hollers.

"Good evening. I'm Patricia O'Neal with a special report. We'll return to the game shortly. Today, two hundred Earther's Lament Day gatherings took place around Ireland."

The HOLO shifts to three different secondary school grounds, filled with students hosting the solemn services. As the newscaster continues, a headshot of Noah, her copper mane surrounding her lightly freckled face, comes into focus.

"Ahh... can you believe this, Da? Speak of the goddamned devil. I was just tellin' ya," Colin moans as the reporter continues.

"The student-led observance was the brainchild of Kilkenny student Noah Calhoun-Greenling, whose holiday proposal was adopted by the Dáil last year. The day-long event was co-sponsored by ECO-UNESCO and the Environmental Watch of CHN Washington. The two hundred schools that participated today represent one-fourth of the secondary schools in Ireland."

The report continues and provides an overview of the day's activities, showing several HOLO-VIDs of students dancing, reading descriptions of extinct animals, and even one of several boys and girls lying in an open grave.

Colin shakes his head and takes a long drink of beer from his bottle. "Man, this is so embarrassing to watch, ain't it, Da?"

"The event was applauded by the Swedish climate activist Greta Thunberg. Young Noah has been compared to Ms. Thunberg; some even view her as the heir of the well-known activist. However, others, such as well-known climate contrarian Vivienne Stark, who has often debated Ms. Thunberg, call the event a publicity hoax. Ms. Stark was unavailable for comment, but we were able to get a reaction from her protégé, Marta Sennheiser."

After displaying images of the two older women, the HOLO-VID switches to Marta Sennheiser, who wears short-shorts and an airy apricot blouse dotted with butterflies, her hair's dark ringlets surrounding silver-blue eyes.

Stephen and Colin look at each other, father and son smirking as they raise their eyebrows at the young woman's attractive image.

"I really can't believe the lengths some of my peers will go with their alarmism. Maybe it's to make up for the attention they didn't get growing up, or, I don't know, perhaps they have some twisted vendetta against humanity. Noah's stunt isn't harmless. It's dangerous—and at its core, it's blatantly anti-

human. Promoters of this degrowth movement, like her, have already ruined the lives of millions of people who are just struggling to give their children a better life."

While she speaks, scenes appear showing union strike lines, people begging on the streets for food, and vacant factory buildings that have recently closed.

"Fuck, yeah. The little fox *nailed* it. That's what happened to me," Stephen shouts, his words slurred and exaggerated.

The newscaster continues, then cuts to a rebuttal from ECO-UNESCO's executive director, Poll Quinne. When she finishes speaking, the HOLO shifts back to the newscaster with smaller images of students gathering on various school grounds.

"Whatever either side of this debate might have to say, the facts of today's Earther's Lament Day seem to speak for themselves. An estimated 20,000 students in Ireland's secondary schools seem deeply concerned by what they see happening to our planet. And so, they chose to remember and mourn the non-human dead and dying with whom they feel a deep sense of kinship."

"Bwah..." Stephen waves dismissively at the HOLO, mocking the game's untimely interruption. "Go fetch me another cold 'un, will ya, lad?"

As Colin gets up to go into the kitchen, the image of the newscaster fades. Then the HOLO-CAST abruptly shifts to a commercial in which a polar bear is vacationing at Old Head Beach—wearing sunglasses, sipping a cocktail, and praising the SPF 250 sunscreen, *Polar Pal.*

It's been a week since the Earther's event at Noah's school. Walking through the halls, she notices how other students glance toward her. She tries to act normal, whatever that means. But it's unnerving to feel watched. And on top of that, she's not sure how well it *actually* went. Of course, a few of her friends went out of their way to say something encouraging. But she wonders—*is it possible for anything to make a dent in these teenage brains?*

Her literature teacher, Mrs. Kearns, intercepts her at the door. "Noah, Mr. Hawkins would like to talk with you. Get along to his office and then come right back."

"Oh, okay, ma'am. Is everything alright?" Noah responds, concern in her voice.

"I haven't the faintest idea, dear. Now go on with you."

Noah moves quickly through the empty hallway; her footsteps on the worn, gray marble floor loudly echo against rows of outdated lockers. She attempts to tame her thick, frizzy hair the best she can while making sure none of her lunch is still stuck between her teeth. She enters the outer room of the headmaster's office, runs a hand over the well-worn oak benches, and then takes a seat. *I've only been here a few times—but dang—whenever I'm here, I start to feel little—like somebody else is in control.*

The door opens and jars her out of her thoughts.

"Come inside, Noah. It's good to see you. I hope I'm not interrupting your day too much," the balding man says with a smile and a quick wink.

"Not at all, sir. I was just settling in for Mrs. Kearns' lesson on Seamus Heaney's poem, *Death of a Naturalist.*"

"Oh, a wonderful choice. The grief of innocence lost. Good for her." Noah nods, waiting for him to tell her why he wants to see her.

"Sit down... sit down," he says, pointing at the chair opposite his. "I'll keep this short so you can go back to class. But I want to personally congratulate you, young lady. Last week's event was quite a triumph. You were spectacular! How you managed to create an experience that weaved the facts of the climate crisis with the pathos of eco-genocide was brilliant. Just brilliant! Well done."

Noah sits up a little straighter—a faint flush on her neck reveals her pleasure and discomfort with his praise.

"As you know, we took a survey after the day. One of the questions we asked was whether or not they had subscribed to the *Extinction is Forever* HOLO-POD. Guess what? You scored a whopping ninety percent! Isn't that grand? Anyway, I thought you'd want to know.

"I know ECO-UNESCO wants to fire up other students nationwide for next year's Earther's event. And I believe, if our school is any indication, you have a tiger by the tail! Is it okay to say that? Oh, my... idioms of speech are such slippery slopes."

Noah barely hides her snicker at the man's feigned embarrassment. He looks back at her over his half-moon readers, a mischievous twinkle in his middle-aged eyes. As he wraps up their meeting, he stands and suddenly begins to feel a low vibration on the floor around him. It patters beneath his feet, then gently moves up his legs, and finally blossoms in his chest.

Noah—her squinted eyes revealing her own bewilderment—watches him as he looks down and studies the grain in the worn oak floor. For a moment, it seems to come to life and swirl within the planks until it quickly settles back into its solid form again. *Strange*, he thinks to himself. *I haven't felt that since I hiked in that old-growth woods at Fhaltaigh Millennium Forest years ago.*

Still unable to find any explanation for these experiences she keeps having, Noah hesitates briefly and then interrupts the moment—thanking him for his support. As she walks to the door, she turns around and looks at him with a playful smile. "You felt it too, didn't you? Kinda weird, isn't it? It's real, you know—all of it."

The headmaster's eyes widen, as if he's just caught sight of an ancient dryad—always glimpsed, never seen. *Who knows? Maybe the old tales are truer than I thought.*

Noah spins around and exits the office, slowly making her way down the hall toward her classroom. While walking, she looks out a window and notices a giant beech tree. The instant her eyes rest on its stately form, her mind fills with an inaudible impression: *"We stand with you too, dear friend. Thank you."*

She stops in the middle of the hallway for a moment, tempted to look around to see who spoke. But she knows—no one will be there.

℘ART ℘TWO

Episode 57: Extinction is Forever
HOLO-POD Hosted by Noah Calhoun-Greenling

"I bet you didn't know that there are over ten thousand virus species that can infect us humans. Because of changes in the climate and shared land use, the infection rate from wild mammals to humans is skyrocketing. You know why? It's simple—we're now sharing land with species that were previously geographically isolated from us.

"This 'zoonotic spillover' is directly caused by the link between global environmental change and the increased emergence of unknown diseases. Haven't you wondered why people seem to get sicker and sicker with diagnoses we've never heard of before?

"One mega-study looked at over three thousand species of mammals and then envisioned scenarios regarding the viral impact of climate change and land use in 2070. Guess what? The model predicts that these species will migrate to new regions with cooler and higher elevations, more biodiversity, and areas of high human population density.

"What's it all mean? This epochal migration will result in the largest cross-species transmission of viruses in human history—an estimated four thousand times greater than what it is today."

Winter 2059

Dallas, Texas, USA (15° F / -9° C)

The view of the Dallas skyline looks like a scene from Mars—stunning. Everything's dazzling from the view through the wall of windows on the seventy-first floor of the Bank of America Plaza. But the accelerated creep of the Chihuahuan Desert has created a perpetual haze around the city that quickly morphs into massive, sometimes deadly, dust storms. Every inch of the town is now etched beyond repair.

The Chief lounges in his private lair, surrounded by the big game trophies he, his dad, and his granddaddy have shot. He's sitting as he watches a Community HOLO Network environmental report, his back toward the door, in a tall office chair covered with the skin of a Siberian tiger he killed.

As the unquestioned supreme leader of the Trans-Natural Economic Coalition, or T-NEC, he's remained unwavering in his commitment to knowing their opponents—even if, like today, watching the opposition on CHN sends his blood pressure skyrocketing. For over half a century, he's relentlessly ensured that T-NEC dominates and dictates the policies and future of every significant economic sector—energy, mining, agriculture, manufacturing, technology, and finance.

Merton, his long black hair slicked back, is dressed in a dark blue suit and white shirt cinched at the neck with a turquoise bolo. He walks through the low-lit outer office and stops for a moment at the door, his hand over the surgically implanted echo-bot behind his ear that connects to his HOLO ring.

"Hey, Ma. Sorry to interrupt. But I gotta go now. I'll talk with you tomorrow, okay? Love you." He lets out a deep breath, then goes in without knocking—careful to close the arched wrought-iron door behind him.

He sees the back of his boss's head—the mane of flowing white hair looks like the images he's seen of Aspen, Colorado before the winter bake. *How ironic the old man chose a nickname linked to the Indians. Just yesterday, he was still raging about the money the Natives keep costing him.*

Standing behind the man, Merton watches, getting a kick out of the Chief's expletive-filled harrumphing. The HOLO-VID zooms in on a trim, middle-aged Dr. Seamus Wilde in a tweed sports coat and open neck, looking every bit the part of a well-trusted academic.

"With record temperatures around the globe, we urge everyone living between thirty degrees latitude north and south to monitor their energy consumption carefully, especially megacities like Los Angeles, Beijing, New Delhi, Tokyo, and Seoul. Our predictions show that if individuals adjust their energy consumption by fifty percent, it will reduce our impact on this trend by fifteen percent."

While he speaks—his Irish accent lilting through the dire report—vivid scenes materialize in the room's surrounding space—dense smog smothers empty playgrounds, amphibious vehicles boat through major thoroughfares, and devastating wildfires rip through densely populated middle-class neighborhoods.

"We also demand an immediate forty percent cap on the production of petroleum, concrete, and other non-essential chemicals in the US. We hope that if the US takes the lead with these bold actions, the rest of the world will follow. If our global leaders can find the political and personal will to implement these measures, we just may buy another year before a total cascading meltdown of all ecosystems.

"But we are hurling through uncharted global territory. All big strategies have failed. The only option left is to face the crisis as an army general would—drafting an ever-evolving battle plan, year after year after year, with no end in sight. The fact is, the impact of the human species on the planet is now officially catastrophically irreversible."

The HOLO-VID returns to Journi Preston, the program's anchor, seated behind her news desk. Even when seated, her height—nearly six feet tall—conveys an unshakable strength and confidence. Her dark, almond skin and prominent, copper-colored eyes, when paired with the faint trace of a South African accent, endow her with an aura of global authority.

"Thank you, Dr. Wilde. Personally, I find myself quite sobered by your frank assessment today. We greatly value your perspective and this important call to action." She turns toward the camera, the studio lights shimmering on the tight curls of her caramel-brown afro, and offers a warm, open smile. *"And that's this week's report Environmental Watch on CHN. I'm Journi Preston. We'll be back next week to inform and inspire you to help reset our planet's future. Have a safe weekend."*

The Chief spins the high-back chair around, only half seeing Merton, and then launches into one of his frequent, profane rants.

"Damn that Preston. And Wilde, too. I thought the news was supposed to be *objective*. That's just a fuckin' infomercial for all those prairie fairies." He pauses, his face scrunched like a paper wad. "She's got balls—I'll give her that. Can you believe it? She's requested an interview with me after lunch today. And I'll do it. I seem to be the only son-of-a-bitch able to uncoil the noose she tries to put around our necks. It makes you wonder if somebody leaked our agenda for next month's board meeting. If I find out there's a mole, so help me God... damned liberal degrowth twats!"

The man stops and coughs forcefully. When he's finished, he gulps down the last half of a glass of water and bangs the glass down. He picks up where he left off, his voice raspy but strong.

"I'll tell you, Merton, we should all be saluted as heroes. Can you imagine the jobs we'll create if we bump global production across all sectors for Q two and three? Or... the money we'll make? How does she think it's any of her fuckin' business!? Her show's just the kind of drip, drip, drip we *don't* need right now. Those liberal eco-nuts could make our path through Washington a goddamned slog."

The Chief takes a ragged breath, his face flushed, and finally looks up to acknowledge the other man's presence. "What is it, Merton? Whaddya want?"

"Sorry to interrupt, sir. Just wanted to update you on a few things," Merton says, sitting in the chair across from the big man. "You asked me to be on the lookout for any emerging neo-energy threats we might need to consider targeting. I've identified six new and viable concepts being fast-tracked through some of the startups' research and development. A few of their models show definite potential, both economically as well as their projected scalability. One is in India, another in South Korea, two in the US, another in Germany, and one in Finland. With the recent evolution of quantum computing, their approaches are spawning some truly novel solutions."

"Damn it, Merton, I can't have this green stuff pollutin' the air right now. I have our bi-annual petroleum summit next month. There'll be hell to pay if there's a whiff of legitimacy given to these fuckin' energy squatters. Some of the corporate weaklings are already getting twitchy about the market and the damn *optics*." He rolls his eyes while making air quotes for the final phrase.

"Yes, sir. How would you like me to handle it?"

"Like before, damn it! It's always worked before. You know the playbook. Act interested, act passionate about the potential, act like a learner. And then buy the damn things up so we can merge them into some division and write white papers that never see the light of day."

Merton studies the Chief for a moment. He notices the deep bags under his eyes. The sagging jowl betrays his age and fatigue. But underneath the shrinking exterior, he sees what has always ignited his admiration and allegiance—the ruthless drive to win and a willingness to do whatever it takes—not only to control a single sector but to dominate the entire global market.

"I'll take care of it, sir. Any parameters?"

"Merton, just get it done! Now get out of here and get to work."

As the door closes, the Chief turns and looks out the bank of windows over the Dallas skyline. He lets out a soft groan, his eyes unfocused as his mind fills with the memory of his daughter raging at him in the rehab center. After a few minutes, he shakes his head and turns his attention back to his desk. He scans the list of corporate heads to bully into compliance and initiates a few HOLOs while he eats the rest of his lunch.

Feeling like he might be coming down with something, he kicks his shoes off and lies on the sofa for a short power nap. When he finally sits up, exhaustion takes over, and he slumps back down, almost passing out. The room spins, his heart pounds, and pools of sweat burst from his pores. His collar tightens around his beefy neck. His chest seems to have a boa constrictor wrapping him in its deathly embrace.

Before he passes out, he shouts at the HOLO for his assistant, Marie, and cries out in a pathetic whimper, "Help. I'm dyin'. Call someone... quick. Oh, fuck. I'm... I'm..."

☙☙☙

Journi Preston listens to some relaxing nature sounds on her HOLO as she waits for her interview with the despotic czar of the Trans-Natural Economic Coalition himself. She takes a deep breath and lets it out slowly. *I'm not sure I can stomach this today.* Inwardly, she's churning. *Breathe, Journi. Keep breathing.* Her jaw softens as she prepares to occupy the same room with the man. *Doesn't matter how many time I've done this—choosing my professional self over my personal feelings—it's always the same damn struggle.*

Suddenly, the doors from the outer office explode open, admitting four EMTs followed by a gurney-bot, and move quickly toward the Chief's door.

Journi finds a corner of the room that allows her to be inconspicuous, her journalistic curiosity piqued by the unfolding event. She hears mumbling from what sounds like the Chief's weak voice responding to the medical team's questions. There's the loud rattle of equipment and decisive instructions between the two men and two women. She conceals her HOLO-CAM to record brief glimpses of the evolving scene—the EMTs trying to save the man's life in the adjacent room.

Without warning, another woman marches into the waiting room. Her non-descript appearance is remarkable only in its ordinariness. Both her face and clothing are plain, pale, cool, and forgettable. She stands calmly in front of Journi, her eyes incongruent, one wide-eyed and one narrowed, seeming to transmit some secret of her own.

"You shouldn't be in here, Ms. Preston," Marie curtly announces.

Journi pushes back, miffed at the woman's tone. "I'm sorry. What do you mean? I have an appointment with the Chief at 2:30, remember?"

"Oh. Of course. That's right." Her expression briefly reveals her mental lapse but then quickly recovers. "As you can see, things are a bit chaotic right now. I'm sure you understand. I can HOLO your office and make arrangements to reschedule when he's back in the office."

"Of course. Let me gather up my things and get out of your way," Journi responds, then makes her way toward the door, glancing over her shoulder to catch Marie smiling.

Toronto, Ontario, Canada (-27° F / -33° C)

"They just rushed him off to the hospital! He was crying like a baby."

Seamus doesn't respond but quickly disconnects the encrypted HOLO. *I get it. But damn... stick with the plan, woman.*

The longcase clock counts the seconds in the professor's quiet office at the University of Toronto. Seen through the large door's old glass panes, the back of his partially grayed hair and ponytail are the only evidence that he's in his study. His hands are shaky. Staring at the flooded courtyard below, he lets out a long, low breath, trying to still his jumpiness. He sips the fifteen-year Redbreast Irish whiskey he poured after he learned the plan was in motion. After a few swallows, he turns the glass around, beginning to feel the calming effect of alcohol.

He recalls how Marie became one of a handful of environmental protection protégés at the school. *Underneath all those good manners, she had a wicked little tongue.* Later, his sister Erin recruited her to join the initial phase of their covert, long-range plan. Marie's been a one-woman sleeper cell in the Chief's office for almost ten years now. Not knowing the details, he's always suspected she has a personal score to settle with the man.

His heart begins to pick up speed again, so he pours another drink. *My god... what were we thinking? This will never work. It's just too desperate... too late!*

He pauses, losing himself in his thoughts again. Finally, he shrugs his shoulders and lifts his glass, as if toasting his late sister. *It's all moot now, Erin. Phase one of Operation Hail Mary has begun.*

Opening his HOLO, he writes what he hopes is a cryptic post on the subreddit, *r/thetitanic.*

> Hey, Bigfoot, we cracked the hull! Things may get a bit choppy, so keep your life vest on.

He disconnects the HOLO and flops back in his chair, hands running through his disheveled hair. Suddenly, a flood of grief and sadness surges from the depths of his soul. Even as he closes his eyes, he can't stem the tears that follow.

Oh, Erin... how can I do this without you?

Dallas, Texas, USA (29° F / -2° C)

Merton speeds his deep purple Mercedes-Benz SL AMG 71 into the Baylor University Medical Center entrance, wrapping up his HOLO connection.

"Sorry, Ma, I gotta go. I'll talk with you tomorrow." He nearly hits an elderly man and woman walking to their car in the handicap parking bay. "Love you, too."

After he jams his car into the space beside the couple's dust-covered, blue Toyota Corolla, the older woman shouts at him while he sprints to the hospital entrance. Looking back over his shoulder, he sees the woman taking a nail file out of her purse, ready to scratch the car's passenger side door. Before he can yell at her, her husband quickly stops her. Both then turn to face Merton and flip him off with their crooked, bony fingers.

After getting directions from the hospital's roving info-bot, Merton hurries to the intensive care unit and finds Room 1034. He's surprised to see a quarantine sign on the Chief's door. *Maybe it's a ruse to keep the press out,* he thinks to himself. *Pretty brilliant, actually.* He puts on the required yellow gown and facemask, walks in, and sees the old man hooked up to two IV drip lines and a control panel of flashing monitors.

B.B sits in the corner, wearing a black military-grade vest made from spider silk. He thumbs through a HOLO-MAG, his eyes constantly surveying the surroundings. The Chief is being attended to by a Filipino nurse, who nervously finishes her tasks and leaves.

The person lying in the bed is a shell of the man Merton saw just that morning. All the arrogance and aggression seem to have escaped like hot air from a deflated balloon.

"Chief, it's me, Merton. What happened?"

The Chief quietly murmurs—slits for eyes. "It feels like every damn inch of me's been scraped raw from the inside out. The itchin', the pain. It's drivin' me crazy! Can't they do somethin' to make it stop?"

He reaches out with a meaty hand and grabs Merton's with a vice-like grip that shocks the younger man. He knocks a picture of his daughter, Lily, to the floor—pieces of glass scattering everywhere. His eyes widen at the smashing noise, then lock onto his hatchet man.

"Damn it, Merton, what are you doin' here? You need to take care of business. Let these people do their job. Now get out of here and do yours!"

The old man's eyes roll back in his head, and he drifts back into a drug-induced stupor. Merton shakes his head. His eyes burn with tears of shock. He releases the Chief's now limp hand from his own.

Merton disregards his mentor's bullying and sits by the bed. He recalls his dad's friendship with the Chief. *If you can call it that*, he snickers, *Pop was weak.* Ever since his dad died, Charles Cartright has fulfilled Merton's need for a combative father figure to batter him into shape. *Part of me wishes he'd just go ahead and croak... but not quite yet.* He feels a competing mixture of unquestioned devotion and growing discontent toward the old man, the latter fueled by a worm of greed and envy.

I can't believe that it's still not time. When will all the fucking pieces be in place... with the board... with all the damned self-interest factions? He lets out a long, frustrated breath, the day's events starting to unravel the tail-end of his self-control.

Twenty years, and I still feel like I'm on probation... the Harvard hatchet man, still trying to win his approval. He chews his bottom lip, feeling a twinge of remorse for his ingratitude. The unfamiliar emotion is suddenly interrupted by the Chief's incoherent mumbling and labored breathing. He quickly sublimates his uncomfortable guilt with a more familiar one—domination.

As he turns to leave, Merton looks over his shoulder and takes one final look at the big man lying there—looking as vulnerable as any other sick piece of flesh in this hospital, wrapped up like an expired piece of meat.

B.B.'s unsmiling eyes meet Merton's for a long moment, and then both nod, acknowledging a shared allegiance. He pushes the door open, sheds the mask and gown, and hurls them into the metal bin.

❧ ☙ ❧ ☙ ❧ ☙

On her way toward the bank of glass-tube elevators, Journi Preston notices Merton. He's yelling at someone on his HOLO, then abruptly disconnects, shaking his head. His clothes look dusty and rumpled—not sporting his usual put-together self. *The man makes my skin crawl. And I have very thick skin!*

He's staring out one of the twenty-foot windows, watching a mini dust devil in the parking lot—hands crammed into his jacket pockets—his frame anxiously rocking forward and back. She hates to approach him, but the journalist in her overrides her personal feelings. She quietly walks up beside him. He doesn't even turn to see who it is.

"Hey, Merton. How is he?"

He stares down at his feet and shakes his head in exasperation, jamming his hands further into his pockets. "Oh, of course. It has to be you. That piece you ran about him a few weeks ago was bad enough—the way you spun his accomplishments to look like betrayals of the human race. Now you have the nerve to show up here riding that self-righteous high horse of yours. Tell me. Why? What do you think you'll find here? A man fighting for his life? A medical team working overtime to figure out what's wrong with him?"

The tirade accelerates—his face flushed—eyes still red. "Just leave it alone! Leave *him* alone," he shouts.

"Woah, buddy. Calm down. I'm sorry, friend, but you know as well as I do. This is news. *He's* news. He doesn't get a free pass like the rest of us get when we're rushed to the hospital."

Merton glares at her now, but she's on a roll and presses on, her voice escalating.

"He's been the kingmaker of every multinational CEO on the planet. Nothing happens with fossil fuel, coal, natural gas, electricity, chemicals, agriculture, battery manufacturing, or the entire nuclear universe without his blessing. If he's taking Gas X, we have a right to know what's happening."

She knows she's crossed the professional line, but what the hell, it's been said.

He smirks at her as she finishes her rant. *You know, even though she's a liberal twat with a PhD, I'd still do her if she'd keep her mouth shut.*

"Well, well, well—that's more like it, JP. Good to see the self-promoting little bitch is back. You know, playing the selfless, high-minded journalist doesn't fool anyone. Admit it. Deep down, you're as much of a shark as I am," he says, his eyes slowly descending over her body and then back up again. "See you around, Preston." After a few beats, he quickly turns toward the revolving doors and out into the red, dusty heat.

She watches him as he jogs to his car, and then she turns back toward the elevators. The adrenaline begins to flow freely through her body's core. He's right—her appetites are on the carnivorous side. And if she didn't know better, this heightened sense feels almost as good as being aroused. As a journalist, a hot story like this is something she lives for.

Journi steps onto the third floor and begins to follow a blue illuminated line her HOLO casts to guide her. She stops when she overhears a quiet but lively disagreement taking place behind the nurse's station. Pretending to interact with her HOLO, she increases the volume and listens in with her audio implant.

"This is so wrong! The family thinks he had a heart attack. We all did, until the lab results came back," whispers the petite Filipino to her fellow nurse. "Don't you think the family has a right to know?"

"What are you talking about, Bernie? Know what?" the other nurse asks.

"I'm not supposed to say anything... a few minutes ago, three cardiologists and the hospital's CEO were huddled together outside Mr. Cartright's room. One of the white-coats said that based on the patient's ECG and troponin levels it *couldn't* have been a heart attack... it looked more like some kind of poison." She takes a deep breath and looks around before she continues.

"The director seemed panicked and warned them... he's worried about reporters... Then he said something that made the hairs on the back of my neck crawl... that if they're right about the kind of poison it is... *'we've got a much bigger crisis on our hands.'"*

The other nurse looks at Bernie, confused, and shakes her head. "It's not your problem. Just keep your head down. Who knows, maybe they know something you don't?"

As Journi pretends to disconnect her HOLO, she looks down the hall and sees a giant hulk of a man outside what she presumes is the Chief's room. *Security detail,* she tells herself. Having already gotten much more than she'd hoped for, she blurts out loud, as if to no one.

"Wrong floor. Why do hospitals have to be so confusing?" She then slips into the elevator, her satisfied grin reflected on the mirrored walls.

Spring 2059

Dallas, Texas, USA (112° F / 44° C)

Seamus Wilde slips on his tan corduroy pants and pats his midsection. Congratulating himself, he studies his figure sideways in the hotel mirror, his salt-and-pepper hair pulled back in a ponytail. *Not bad for an aging academic!*

Before putting on his favorite sports coat—the one with the cocoa-colored "professor patches"—he checks to make sure the pockets are empty. He's noticed himself becoming a bit more forgetful lately. *The last thing I need is for some operational detail to tumble out at the lunch today.*

His HOLO interrupts, chirping like a song sparrow. After the birdsong begins to repeat more loudly, he accepts the connection from Brett, the young assistant assigned to him for the week.

"Dr. Wilde, the limousine is ready to take you to the Convention Center. Would you like for me to ride with you?"

"Thank you, Brett. Would you cancel the ride for me? I've decided to stretch my legs and walk there. Can you meet me inside the conference room doors?"

"Of course, sir. See you then."

Seamus quickly glances at himself in the mirror and then leaves. As he waits for the elevator to take him to the lobby, the woman known to her boss in Dallas as Marie slips up next to him. Inside the elevator—doors closed— she hands him a box of Cuban cigars and then quickly exits on the thirteenth floor.

After descending to the ground floor, the doors open, facing out toward the gold-toned lobby of the Omni Dallas Hotel. As Seamus steps out, he gives the small box a toss in the air and turns toward the skywalk.

Merging with the crowd, he is soon carried up a spiraling escalator to a wide platform that crosses over Ceremonial Drive, where he begins walking toward the convention hall.

"Seamus, wait up," someone with an east-coast accent calls out from behind him on the skywalk. He turns around and sees Dr. Fortuna jogging on short legs, trying to catch up. The man's scalp shines with perspiration underneath his thinning, white hair. He's out of breath, the movement of his chest betraying his neglected physical fitness.

"Hi, Arthur," Seamus says. "I was hoping we'd bump into each other. How's Sylvia and the kids?" The Director of the Global Infectious Disease Institute provides a brief update on the homefront and then abruptly changes the subject.

"Seamus, I need to make this quick. There's been a recent incident here in Dallas. My team's been brought in to take an initial look. It's too early to say, but we may be looking at a new parvovirus strain."

Seamus nods slowly and meets the man's words with a concerned frown.

"We have a high-profile patient who presented with the classic symptoms of a heart attack. But when the cardiac team at Baylor Med Center ran their diagnostics, they were confused by the results. More than confused, they're completely stymied. I won't get into the details here, but it's concerning. The cardiac team's trying to keep it under wraps for now. They've classified it as a simple cardiac episode. That, hopefully, will buy us some time to see what we're up against."

"Thanks for the heads up, Arthur. Anyone I know?"

"Sorry, Seamus, I can't release that information to you right now. I wanted to brief you on the incident in light of your sister's inter-species mutation research. This virus could be one of those bugs that quickly learns how to jump species, from canines to humans. Pretty scary if that's the case, given the number of families that have a little Rover or Spot at home. The best estimate is that there are half a billion dog owners worldwide. You get the picture."

"Thanks for letting me know, Art. I'll keep it to myself. And let me know if there's anything I can do to help."

"Thanks, Seamus. I'll let you go. I hear you're presenting this morning. Sorry, I'll have to miss it. I have to meet with my team in an hour to see what progress they've made in finding out what we're dealing with. We'll talk soon."

Seamus offers his goodbye and continues walking. Arthur tilts his head as he watches his friend walk down the sky bridge. He studies the man's shoulders, his stride. Wondering—though not exactly sure *what* he's wondering or *why*—just wondering, like a familiar sixth sense that stirs in him during a crisis.

Seamus takes several deep breaths as he walks away, trying to act normal. *My God, that was a little too close,* he thinks to himself. He picks up his pace toward the escalator, feeling troubled that the toxin has been detected so quickly, but also relieved to have a friend open a backdoor to keep him updated.

He walks into the conference hall and strides up to the stage to find the moderator who will introduce him, attaches his HOLO to the auditorium's transmission system, and gets ready to rattle the minds of those gathering to hear his Annual Planetary Risk Assessment speech.

After his presentation, Seamus greets several prominent luminaries in global environmental affairs. Most, like him, look either like aging academics or young eco-nerds. They enthusiastically express appreciation for his words and his strong call to action.

Also scattered among the dispersing crowd are several corporate executives, easy to spot in their custom-tailored, dark-blue suits and uniform haircuts. Over the years, Seamus has worked with many of the environmental watchdog organizations to identify and blacklist the most egregious violators. *If you added up all the destruction they've inflicted on the planet, it would make what the rest of us have done look like a light feather-dusting.* His disgust is written on his face as he weaves through their circles, barely refraining from spitting on their shoes for their shameless greenwashing.

As he moves to leave, he spots Brett in the crowd and flags him down. "Brett, I have one more thing. Would you stop by McFinn's Florist on Garland Road and pick up the twelve small terrarium gift boxes they have on order? One of my colleagues asked if I could have someone pick them up for him. They are under his name, Charles Cartright. And while you're at it, stick one of these cigars in each of the boxes. Here's the list of where to have them delivered."

Brett scans the list and smirks, nodding as he takes the box from Seamus. *He gets the irony of the gift,* Seamus notes. The list he's given the young man contains many of those smug bastards he just passed in the convention hall, including the former vice president, Tommy Thompson.

"I'll take care of it right away, sir. Anything else?"

"No, I think I'll head out and walk around the block before the next session begins. Thanks, Brett."

The young man quickly moves outside and steps into a dust-covered taxi-bot. Seamus follows him out, moving more slowly. As soon as he exits the door, he regrets the decision to take a walk in the scorching, late-morning heat, but decides he needs to stretch his legs. He covers his mouth with his sand scarf and moves quickly toward the glass-enclosed sidewalk. After a few blocks, he turns to walk back, the sun at its zenith, removing the last of the skyscraper's shadows and now bearing directly down on the sand-etched canopy.

Pausing for a moment, he wonders at the fury he's unleashing. *Oh, Erin. Why aren't you here to be part of all this?* Knowing he won't hear a response—and feeling the extreme heat radiating from the glass's silica overhead—he quickly returns inside.

Sitting behind the Chief's burled red oak desk and looking out over the dusty Dallas skyline, Merton smirks, feeling something he's only felt once or twice before. *God-like. Messianic.*

He loosens his turquoise-studded bolo and unbuttons his collar. His chest swells with satisfaction. His head leans back with growing pride. *He never talks about it—hell, he acts like he's immortal. But the old devil needs a fucking succession plan, especially now.* He lets out a long, frustrated sigh. *So, how do I make sure that I'm the one tapped?*

He steeples his fingers as the chair gently rocks. Weirdly, the image of a children's Bible his mother used to read to him pops into his mind—the one with colored cartoon figures. He can see the pages now. He can even smell the cheap ink they were printed with.

There was one where Christ was tempted by the devil—standing over a pathetic, powerless Jesus. The scene then morphs in his mind—rather than imagining Jesus, Merton envisions himself. *Now, I'm the chosen one—the all-powerful one. But instead of kneeling—fuck that—I'm in control. I'm the one tempting the devil.*

He opens his HOLO, ready for his daily check-in with his mom, but is interrupted by an insistent chirp from his echo-bot. He spins the chair around and makes a circle-like gesture to receive the incoming call. In front of him floats an image of Griffin "Smack" Daniels—balding, unshaven, a former Navy SEAL, and CO of Upstream, T-NEC's preferred private military contractor. He's seated in mottled shade on the hood of a camouflaged Humvee, streams of sweat swimming on his large forehead. Behind him lies a barren wasteland filled with dead scrub and rippled, rum-colored sand.

"Hey, Smack. You look like shit. Where the hell are you, buddy?"

"You know I'd have to kill you if I told you," he shoots back at Merton. "You're not my only client, you know. But I can tell you that the snake meat and camel milk are starting to grow on me."

"Well, don't get too comfortable out there." Merton snickers. "Thanks for returning my HOLO—I've got a job for you and your crew if you're interested. You got the bandwidth? Or should I look someplace else?"

"It depends. What's the focus of this so-called 'job'?"

"We've got six R&D start-ups in four countries that... how should I put it? Need to be acquired, discredited, failed, or just plain disappeared. In short, they need to be made irrelevant. The Chief's authorized any means necessary, so I'll leave operational details up to you. Just make sure it's not linked back to us."

"What's your budget and time frame?"

"Just get it done. You do that, and we'll pay you $250,000 per cancellation. Multiply that by six... you can do the math. *And* we need it done by the end of September. That's a hard deadline. You good with that?"

"I'd have to see some details about the targets, but it's feasible if they're all near major cities."

"Alright, I'll send an encrypted HOLO-EM, and you can let me know if you boys are in."

"Roger that. Good doing business with you, Merton. I gotta run and blow up some stuff, or I won't be home to kiss my wife and kids before bedtime."

The HOLO dematerializes. A framed picture on the desk of the Chief's troubled daughter and grandson smile back at him. Merton stares at it for a moment, then shakes his head, half-whistling while he exhales. *What a waste. Who the hell needs family? Mom and me. That's it. Anything more— that's dead weight.*

He quickly spins back toward the window, the sky a dull red, the sun glaring through shifting spires of swirling sand. *Now that's a more fitting backdrop,* he tells himself—grinning as he imagines the cartoon devil bowing down to lick his dusty Texas boots.

Arlington, Virginia, USA (97° F / 36° C)

Journi Preston kicks her shoes off and sits in her simple office at the CHN complex in Crystal City. Instead of awards or photographs with the rich and powerful, the walls are covered with large images of history's worst ecological disasters—Chernobyl, the Dust Bowl, the Deepwater Horizon oil spill, the Great Smog of London.

Looking out her window at the snarl of commuters fighting through dense, blue smog, she steeples her fingers, considering her options.

She asks her HOLO to reach out to Noah. After a few chirps that sound like a yellow warbler's spring song, the girl accepts the request. She appears to be outside, lying in the grass, surrounded by a grove of trees. A tiny twig still clings to her tangled red hair.

"Hi, Noah. Hope I'm not interrupting anything. How's your day going so far?" Journi casually greets her young friend, sounding as if they've known each other far longer than they have.

"Oh... hi, Ms. Preston. I'm fine. Good, actually. We got out of school because the air quality was so bad. I mean, that's bad, but going home early is good."

"Listen, call me Journi. Alright? I'm calling because I have a proposal for you. How would you like to come to Washington?" She pauses, letting the question sink in. "I'd like to do a feature interview with you. I think it's time to breathe some life into the environmental youth movement. So, what do you think?"

Noah sits up cross-legged and closes her eyes for a moment, looking away from the HOLO. "Ms. Preston—"

The woman interrupts, "Noah, call me Journi. Remember?"

"Journi, then... that sounds amazing!"

"The station will take care of your transportation. We have a small solar plane that can pick you up. It doesn't need to be a long trip. Maybe three days, so you won't miss much school."

"Wow! Are you kidding me?"

Journi chuckles at the young woman's lack of pretense while shaking her head. "Of course not."

"Okay. Let me talk to my ma and da."

"Of course. And Noah, I really look forward to what this might mean, not just for you but for all of us. Take good care."

"You, too. And... thanks! You've been such a huge support," Noah replies, ending the connection.

Three weeks later, Noah finds herself outside Washington D.C., peering through an office window and trying to identify the U.S. Capitol and National Mall through the haze over the Potomac River. Despite the poor visibility, her green eyes are wide with wonder. *I can't believe I'm really here. Just a few days ago, Shea and I were lying in my yard, blowing dandelions into the sky.*

"Quite a sight, isn't it?" Journi interrupts. She sticks her head into the room, indicating that Noah's few quiet moments alone are finished. "We better get in there. But first, we need to stop by makeup."

"Makeup?" Noah asks with a playful grimace. "I thought that was just in the movies."

"Come on. I know you're a natural beauty, and freshening you up won't take much." Journi winks as she nudges Noah to the door. "Oh, how I wish I still had your skin. But your hair... hmm... it may need a little more attention than it's used to."

Noah inspects herself in the HOLO-360 mirror, noticing her eyes are bloodshot and still half-open after the late night flight. Her hair looks like it always does, a wild and living thing with a mind of its own.

After Margaret works her magic in the makeup room, putting Noah's hair in a half-up style, they head to the HOLO-CAM studio and find their seats. The lights are bright but bearable.

Just before they get started, Margaret rushes in. "Here, let me put this on." She pulls out a brilliant Tree of Life hair clip and begins working it into Noah's hair. "I felt like something was missing, so I asked the 3D Manu-Print for some ideas and voilà! What do you think?"

Noah examines herself in the HOLO-360 mirror and quickly flashes the stylist an appreciative smile. "I love it! Thank you so much, Margaret. It's perfect."

After the woman exits, Journi turns in her seat. "Ready? Now, Noah, I want you to relax. Just be yourself. I know everyone says something like that, but I mean it. We'll be recording, so there's no pressure to get it perfect.

I *hate* perfect. Let's aim for something real, something unfiltered. How's that sound?"

Noah takes in this powerful, well-put-together woman seated next to her, suddenly recalling why she likes her. And more than that... why she trusts her. *She cares about what I care about—about what really matters.*

Noah nods in agreement, her reddish-gold hair floating around her face, and says, "Let's do it!"

The interview begins with the kind of background questions she'd expected: where she's from, what her family is like, her interests, and so on. Then, Journi smoothly shifts to the main focus of the segment.

"Noah, your nation's political leaders have awarded you quite an honor. What would you like people to know about Earther's Lament Day?"

"Well, last year on October 22nd, students in my home country, Ireland, stopped to lament what we've done to our planet. This year, we'd like to see it spread beyond our nation. We chose to hold it on the exact opposite date as Earth Day, which is April 22nd. Earth Day is a day to show support and to celebrate the gift of our home. It's a wonderful tradition. But it's not enough. It seems to me that all the bleak statistics and inspiring calls to action haven't made any real difference."

Journi leans in and interrupts, "Why do you think that is?"

"I think it's because we've forgotten how beautiful... how alive and interconnected... how mysterious our planet really is." Noah takes a long breath and then continues in her lilting Irish accent. "In our country, we set aside time after someone's died to pay our respects. We hold a wake to honor the dead. We gather together to remember... we share stories... we shed tears. It's quite moving. Quite clarifying, too. So my hope for Earther's Lament Day is that it will create time and space for that. Space to not only grieve, but also lament."

Journi pauses briefly, then asks, "Noah, what's the difference between grief and lament? They sound like the same thing to me."

"Well, for me, grief is what I feel when I experience the loss of something. Personally, I've felt devastated by the countless creatures, many I've never even heard of, that are now extinct. It's as if entire families, or neighborhoods, or even cities were here one day and then gone the next. Forever! That's what's happening every single day in both the human and non-human realms. So, grief is my feeling the tragic sadness of it all.

"But lament... lament is what I *do* with my sadness. You see, it's not enough to just feel sad. I have to engage with it. Lament helps me do that. I cry. I rage. I share stories, my questions, confusions... without trying to put a happy face on it."

"So what's your hope for Earther's Lament Day?" Journi asks.

"My hope..." Noah quietly repeats as she looks off into the distance. "I hope that by grieving together and holding vigil in this way, students worldwide will get in touch with their personal connection to the plants and creatures we've lost. That through crying out together, naming our losses— just as if someone from their own family was killed—they'll be changed. Their hearts will be changed. Their values will be confronted and turned upside down. I hope that our sense of connection to all living things grows."

Journi waits a few seconds for the words to sink in. "That's quite a vision, Noah. I'm sure there's far more to your own story than we've touched on today. Perhaps we can have you back sometime to learn more about you. But for now, please know that I, for one, will not only be watching but also personally participating with students here in Washington. *Environmental Watch* and this station will devote the entire day's programming on October 22nd to helping you, our viewers, participate in an Earther's Lament event where you live."

Journi turns and looks directly into the HOLO-CAM. "CHN will have a list of sponsored sites in the US and abroad where you can join others. We also have prepared a Leader's Guide for students who would like to host an Earther's Lament Day at their school, college, or university."

Shifting her eyes toward her guest, Journi offers a sincere smile as she finishes the segment. "Noah, thank you for helping us feel the anguish of these mounting ecological losses, along with the invitation to recover a sense of personal connection with all of life. This is Journi Preston for *Environmental Watch*. Thank you for joining us."

"And that's it," the video producer announces.

"Whew," Noah exhales. "I can't believe how fast the time went. And how exhausted I feel."

"Welcome to my world," Journi answers. "I have to take a power nap after some of the interviews I give. But you... you make me feel inspired. I'm not sure how the idea of lament can inspire me, but somehow, it does. I'll try not to overthink it."

Noah takes a long, deep breath, a smile of contentment stretching across her face. *I feel lighter... more grateful. Grateful for Journi, for a chance to experience something beyond Kilkenny. For a sense that my life has purpose and meaning.*

Journi interrupts her musing and brings her back to Earth. "Want to grab some lunch?"

"That sounds great," Noah replies. "Any good sushi restaurants nearby? Anything from the seas of Ireland is battered and deep-fried."

"I know just the place," Journi says, arching both eyebrows.

৩৮ ৪৫ ৩৮ ৪৫ ৩৮ ৪৫

Noah and Journi playfully fight over the last bite of the spicy grasshopper roll at the small restaurant, Takeshi Sushi. Journi gives up as if defeated in battle and drops her chopsticks.

"Okay, Noah. I think this morning's interview was excellent, especially for a rookie. We'll have to see how it plays, but I'm pretty sure it will be a hit. Especially with your peers."

"Well, either way, Ms. Preston—I mean, Journi... it's been an amazing experience for me," Noah responds gratefully. "Everything, really—"

"Here's the deal, Noah," Journi interrupts. "I hope we're just getting started. This morning was a bit of a trial run, and I'd say you passed with flying colors. I've already approached the station and some private foundations. They'd like to get behind you and fund a larger media presence. I think it could give Earther's Lament Day a huge lift, not just in Ireland, but worldwide."

Noah's face registers her surprise. "I'm not sure I understand. What do you mean?"

"Well, I'd like you to have a five-minute weekly segment on my show. We can talk about its focus later, but I'd love to have you, along with your voice and perspective, as part of our program. Also, these foundations would like to fund the production of your own HOLO-POD. I know ECO-UNESCO is helping with the Irish initiative, but this would be global. And if you need it, I'll help you access CHN's network of environmental experts and activists. So, what do you think? It's a once-in-a-lifetime chance to make a difference on environmentalism's biggest media platform."

Noah's mouth goes wide, a look of amazement written on her face. *What in the world's happening here?* The words of Duncan, the handsome young parliamentary assistant at the Dáil, pop into her mind. *This just might open doors you've never even considered.*

Journi leans forward and pops the question. "So? Are you in?"

Noah takes her time to answer. She picks up a slice of ginger with her chopsticks, holds it between her and Journi like she's giving a treat to a tail-wagging puppy, winks, and says, "You bet I'm in. When do we start?"

Journi grabs the ginger dangling between them and pops it into her mouth, puckering her lips as she swallows.

"We need to celebrate!" Journi announces while motioning for the waiter-bot. The intelligent service cart quickly responds and rolls up next to the table, ready for instructions. "Bring us your coconut ice cream, a banana sushi roll, and two spoons... please."

The two women giggle as the food carrier's feminine, Japanese voice acknowledges their order, reverses directions, and scurries off toward the kitchen, skillfully avoiding other oncoming carts and patrons.

Bern, Switzerland (89° F / 31.5° C)

Marta sits up straight next to Aunt Vivienne at the Kursaal Bern Convention Center in the city's downtown district. The recent flooding from the Aare River, made worse from glacial melting into the Aare Gorge, caused quite a traffic slowdown. Late, along with everyone else, they barely had time to compose themselves after the sudden drenching.

Viv looks sideways at her 'niece' and studies what she sees. Despite Marta being only seventeen, the final touches of the teenager's makeover have transformed her into an alluring young protégé of the older woman. The detailed kinetic tattoo—a wine-colored butterfly emerging from its cocoon that floats, spiraling up and around her arm until it disappears under her loose-fitting sleeve—was the brainchild of her amazing body engineer's brilliant design.

After the emcee introduces her, Vivienne walks up the stage's steps, sporting her leopard heels, skin-tight jeans, and gaping neckline beneath a brown fur jacket. Her burnt-orange lipstick is flawless, framing her oversized mouth and perfect teeth. The crowd, mostly made up of middle-aged men, love her. And she can see it in their eyes. Their not-so-veiled desire ensures they will eat up whatever she chooses to feed them.

"Thank you for inviting me to share a few thoughts with you today. I am thrilled to be here and very excited to be part of this historic gathering. But before I continue, I'd like to introduce you to a remarkable young woman: my godchild, Marta Sennheiser."

Marta stands from her front-row seat and walks in a practiced way onto the stage beside her aunt. She waves as people shout, "We love you, Vivienne," and then someone up front yells, "We love you too, Marta!"

"Thank you," Vivienne responds, then continues. "Marta represents what we're fighting for: our children and their futures. Marta is to be tomorrow's face of our movement. So stay tuned; you will be seeing a lot more of her in the days ahead."

The crowd applauds, interspersed with a few enthusiastic wolf whistles. Vivienne flashes a seductive smile, seeming to ride the wave of attention projected toward her with genuine delight.

As the crowd's emotions subside, her demeanor becomes somber. "As you know, I have been speaking, writing, and debating with others about the times we live in—the crucial nature of the choices before us. Choices for the kind of world we live in. The kind of people we will become. The kind of future we will pass on to our children.

"We are often characterized—mischaracterized, really—as unintelligent, unfeeling, barbaric, and anachronistic. Nothing is further from the truth. If only our detractors would take the time to listen without bias, they would find that we have our own positive ambitions, ideas, and qualities.

"Are we, as we are often accused, Anti-Nature? No! We are not Anti-Nature! But we are also Pro-Science. We're committed to sensible environmental policies. And we're also Pro-Innovation. But most importantly, we are Pro-Human!"

She pauses while the applause rises, then falls.

"I'm often quoted as saying, 'I don't want you to panic. I want you to think.' But I'm afraid that's almost impossible now. The far left is doing shameful things today." A chorus of 'boos' swells around the convention hall. "They are taking things away that belong to us. Taking our freedoms away. Taking our futures away. At the same time, they promote policies and laws that are blatantly totalitarian.

"Now my message is this: 'I want you to panic so that you will think!' I'm sounding the alarm! Without fear and panic, we will follow sheep-like into economic annihilation. Who will be left to care whether or not there are polar bears or giant redwoods if humanity is thrown back to the primal wilderness we've worked so hard to emerge from?"

As she continues, she commends the attendees for their many sacrifices and vigilant efforts to improve the world by promoting positive, pro-libertarian ideas.

"I want you to know, in case no one else tells you, each of you plays an essential role in the national and international movement's battle for limited government, for personal liberty. We must unmask this Trojan horse offered by climate alarmists for what it is—the real threat to our planet.

"You," she says, pointing at the crowd, "along with other sober-minded academics, writers, financiers, and entrepreneurs—You along with the local and national elected officials who fight the good fight—You fight for HUMANITY! And I thank you for your service! Every single one of you."

Having played her part, Vivienne finishes, taking a deep bow that's met with roaring affirmation. The already-standing crowd breaks into applause and then chants her name. "Viv-i-enne! Viv-i-enne! Viv-i-enne!"

As the gathering's headliner, she's accomplished what she came to do, whipping their emotions into a throbbing frenzy. Now, in the days that follow, when they discuss difficult choices and make concessions on substantial funding or tactical disagreements, they will have been unconsciously softened and seduced by her allure. They will embrace the proposed compromises and agree to what's asked of them. For, deep in their souls, on some level, they feel as if they are doing it for her—secretly fantasizing that she would reward them with a private moment together.

Men are so predictable, so easy to manipulate, she thinks, as she and Marta shake several meaty paws on their way toward the hall's exit doors.

As Marta watches, she wonders if Viv's life is always this exciting—how hers will unfold in the years to come. Flashing her wicked little grin, she follows her aunt to the door, aware of every eye that watches her backside.

❧ ❦ ❧ ❦ ❧ ❦

As Marta enters the large foyer, a HOLO-NET reporter with Royal-Net approaches and asks her to comment on the explosive rise of Noah Calhoun-Greenling's Earther's Lament events.

She flips her dark hair out of her eyes, smiles at the middle-aged man, and acts as if she's trying to decide whether to say something or keep it to herself.

"Well, it seems like a desperate stunt to me. I hope it's untrue, but I wonder if the alarmist left is simply using poor Noah, or exploiting her unfortunate vulnerabilities.

"I've recently been told, and I apologize if it's too personal or meant to be confidential, but... um... I think the public should know—I've learned that Noah *actually thinks she can talk with trees.* Who knows what she'll come up with next? Little green men? Now, I don't want to judge her, and I can imagine how much stress she's under. But I've spoken to a few of her classmates, who confirm the story. They've even hinted that she's said things about herself as being 'called' or 'chosen.'

"Most people... you know... think *that* kind of behavior is unnatural—maybe even a sign of some sort of mental illness. Seeing things. Hearing things that aren't there. Are these hallucinations? Schizophrenia? Maybe bipolar? I don't know. But I do wish her well, and I hope and pray that if she needs help, she won't be too proud to ask for it. Thank you."

She looks at her aunt, who gives her a knowing wink and steers her toward the elevator doors.

Kilkenny, Ireland (94° F / 34.5° C)

Noah's been buried since she came back home—between catching up with school and sleeping, she's had little time for anything else. The trip to Washington felt like a massive whirlwind—unsettling and exhilarating.

She heads up to her room after school for a HOLO meeting Journi has set up. Looking in the mirror, she frowns as she examines her hair—*it looks like* it's *been through a whirlwind!* Same with her room—dirty clothes scattered in every direction.

Her HOLO ring chimes with an incoming connection that blossoms before her.

"Hi. Noah? Miles Davis here."

Noah frowns skeptically. *Where's your trumpet, Miles?*

The young HOLO-POD producer smirks when he sees Noah's reaction. "Go ahead—ask me."

"Huh? Oh well, are you... or were your parents just really into be-bop?"

He laughs good-naturedly. "Neither. It's a nickname I got in college for driving twenty *miles*"—air quotes accentuate his namesake—"for the best pizza around. I can almost smell Lovely Rita's fennel sausage sitting here."

Noah laughs along, glad her last name isn't Ark.

"Well, let's get down to business. Ready to dream up a show?" Miles asks, signaling their cue to begin. "I've already talked with Journi for her perspective. But she's made it clear that this is your baby all the way."

For the next ninety minutes, he asks questions about her values and how she imagines the show. She tries to impress on him that her focus isn't primarily on what the human species fears or needs but on everything that's being *lost*.

"Miles, my biggest concern is the shrinking numbers of incredible life forms who also call this planet home."

He nods, affirming the angle she's taken. "Got it. Loud and clear, Noah. You do know the pro-human, growth-at-all-costs camp will hate it and counter everything you say, don't you?" Noah frowns and slowly bows her head in response. They continue fine-tuning the concept and eventually settle on an approach they think will maximize the program's viewership and impact.

Noah sighs, flopping back on her bed, and lies there, looking up at the ceiling fan slowly rotating. Miles watches, smiling softly toward her—a mild vibration rises in his midsection—as the silence expands and grows.

The fan blades above gently stir her frizzy red hair for several moments. Miles continues to quietly observe this young woman three thousand miles away until—the buzz still pulsing in his chest—he detects the slightest hint of a smile on her freckled face.

What about... she wonders, unsure what Miles will think of it.

"What?" Miles asks tentatively.

She rolls over on one elbow and looks at his face in her HOLO. "Miles, listen. I know you're the pro here, but... I was just staring up at the ceiling, and... well, I felt something. It's hard to explain, but I think I know what to call the program. Want to hear it?"

He nods, the vibration escalating.

"Extinction is Forever!" She makes her voice sound like a jacked-up HOLO DJ, while her hands widen in an exaggerated shimmy. Noah's neck quickly turns a soft pink—too late, she remembers that they've just met—feeling embarrassed by her charade. She becomes quiet, anxiously trying to read his response. "So, what do you think? Is it stupid or what?"

Not missing a beat, he practically sings. "Noah, I love it! No need to think twice about it!" A wide grin conveys his reassurance.

"Really? You really like it?"

After a few warm exchanges of appreciation, Noah takes the lead to end the conversation. Miles feels the buzz taper down to nothing. A relaxed emptiness, like the silent wake made by a passing ship, having suddenly opened, now gently closes within him.

❧❧❧

After Noah finishes with Miles, she immediately initiates a HOLO with Shea. Her friend's face materializes, wearing a serious, concerned expression.

"Hey, Shea. What are you up to? I just finished meeting with Miles—the producer of this new HOLO-POD Journi's setting up for me."

Shea stares back, not saying a word.

"What's going on? Is everything okay?"

Her friend swallows hard and shakes her head. "You haven't seen it, have you?"

"Seen what? Spit it out, will you? You're starting to worry me."

"There's a new HOLO-VID of Marta out, and she... um... she says some pretty awful stuff about you and—"

"What do you mean?" Noah interupts—her brow and mouth frown in aggravation.

"You know how she is, how she comes across as all... concerned." Shea's voice is taut. "In the latest snippet, she calls you crazy... um... I mean, she makes it sound like you're bipolar or schizophrenic. It's just—"

"That little—" Noah's nostrils flare as she breaks in again. "I can't believe—well, I guess I can. So what? Even if I'm *on the spectrum*"—she adds air quotes, dripping with sarcasm—"so are seventy-five million other people. And I'd sure as hell rather be one of them than Marta and her bloody corporate crooks."

Finished ranting, Noah abruptly says goodbye to Shea and disconnects. She stares out the window at the gnarled limbs of the big wych elm and lets out a long, heavy sigh. Her expression shifts back and forth, as if she can't decide whether to scream or cry.

Why does this still wind me up? You'd think I'd be over it with all the name-calling... all the bullying at school. She notices her fists are clenched, her breathing ragged. *JUST LEAVE ME ALONE.*

As she takes a deep breath, trying to calm herself, a large blue-and-white bird flies onto the exact branch where she'd once seen a snowy owl. There was electricity then, but it was darker and older. But now, she feels a different energy reaching out toward her. It's younger. It's concerned and supportive.

"Hello there. Whatcha doin', little buddy?" Her tone shifts, becoming soft and gentle. She bites her lip and shakes her head as she hears herself. *What's wrong with me? Other than Shea and a couple others, I feel more connected... more understood by a bird than the people I know.*

At that moment, the energy between them spikes—*What the... I've never felt that before*—then slowly fades. As it dissipates, Noah studies the jay who cocks its head and briefly gazes back at her before flying away into the nearby woods.

৯঵ ৳৹৯঵ ৳৹৯঵ ৳৹

Over the next few weeks, Journi keeps watch from afar, observing Noah and Miles's progress as they produce the first several episodes and agree on a launch date. *Now it's time to figure out how to gain a global following,* she tells herself.

She looks out the large office window, the D.C. skyline curtained by the past week's record deluge. Nearer to CHN studios, she can glimpse a flooded Ronald Reagan National Airport—transformed now into a large, semi-permanent lake—the most recent casualty of the Potomac River's ten-foot surge.

"I told you so," she almost shouts, wishing the do-nothing politicians across the river would hear. Reeling her frustration in, she kicks off her pumps and props her feet up on the desk—ready to brood over the challenges and possibilities ahead.

Okay. The marketing team's on board. Check! They're already sounding the drum beat. Check! But how are we going to get at the youth culture? That's got to be Noah's primary audience. What about sports? Nah—feels like a miss. Media? Hmmm—which ones? Scientists? No, too... cerebral.

Journi chews her bottom lip, feeling stuck. She calls for some music on her HOLO and closes her eyes—discarding her unproductive, churning thoughts. The tambin flute of West Africa's Fulani people soon grounds her—rich with its breathy, earthy tones. Abruptly, a polyrhythmic djembe announces the song's end. The final sounding sparks an idea. *That's it!*

She swings her bare feet to the floor and stands up—eyes suddenly wide open. *Music. Musicians. Of course! The microphones they have are the farthest-reaching on the planet.*

Journi's name pops up on Noah's HOLO ring between classes. She steps outside into the courtyard and opens the connection—Journi's image blossoms in front of her.

"Noah, are you sitting down? Guess what? We got 'em—well, we got four out of five. E-nuff, Begging for Mercy, Lisa-Lisa, and Stand Up have all agreed to shift their band's promo weight and get behind Earther's Lament Day."

Noah drops her hands to her sides. *No way! That's so lethal,* she tells herself, heart galloping, temporarily speechless.

"I'm still serving Brendon Baxter guilt sandwiches daily, but I think we're in great shape with or without him."

When Noah finally finds her words, tears run down her face. "Journi, are you serious? Stop—really? You're joking." In answer, Journi just tilts her head and smiles. "Oh my god! You did it. You really did it, didn't you?"

"No, dear, *you* did it. I showed the bands our uncut interview and then gave them the backstory. They loved the pitch. It was like asking a dog if it wanted a treat. They practically begged me to let them do something. Each of them, in their own way, told me they had a feeling they were given a platform for something bigger than fame and fortune. Noah, they've been looking for something like this, something big and global they could lend a hand with."

Still stunned, Noah struggles to find her words—the sound of her voice subdued. "Thank you, Journi. Thank you for believing in this. For believing how important this is." She pauses, her green eyes glistening. "For believing in me."

Journi looks back at Noah with an expression of playful pride. "Ahh... slow down. Don't get all gushy on me. I'm not doing this just for you, you know. Well, I sort of am."

Noah takes the bait. "Who says I'm getting gushy? Can't a girl just say thank you?"

"Well, if that's it, you're welcome!" Journi's soft eyes and warm smile linger for a moment, saying more than words—conveying her growing admiration and hopes for Noah.

Three of the bands are already on the road. Lisa-Lisa conducts her final run-through before she launches her new concert tour—Ex is Forever—in two days. Each group adjusts their setlist, with Earther's Lament Day becoming the climax of their shows. Over the next month, word spreads as the buzz goes viral—*Extinction is Forever's* follower count skyrockets, placing it in the top-ten HOLO-PODs with over five hundred thousand listeners. After three months, Noah's HOLO program has amassed over two million subscribers, the majority under twenty-five.

James Johnson III lazes outside his Frank Lloyd Wright-style mansion, the Olympic-sized swimming pool reflecting hazy moonlight and the burnt-plastic smell of wildfire smoke lingering in the atmosphere. After unbuttoning his shirt, he glances up and spies Astrid's silhouetted figure from their bedroom window. *Mmm... be there soon,* he promises, more to himself than to her.

Settling in for a few quiet moments after a long day, he eagerly anticipates his first sip of the Last Drop 2010 Buffalo Trace Bourbon. But first, he raises his glass to propose a toast to himself—*to the sweet life.* The smooth, honey-colored liquid carries its warmth slowly down his throat. A proud smirk curls his lips as he calculates the value of a single mouthful. *Seven hundred dollars... and worth every penny.*

He unwraps the cigar that the Chief gave him. He found it in some weird little terrarium, which he left behind at the hotel, but pocketed the cigar. Usually, the old man expects gifts from *him,* not the other way around. *Is the crusty bastard getting sentimental? Nah! Never!*

Sniffing the long, dark figurado cigar stirs his senses and brings him fully to the present moment. He smiles as a memory of his first smoke floats into his consciousness, activated by the tobacco's rich, old-leather scent. *God, I wish Grandpa Spitz was here. He'd have loved this!*

After he cuts off the end with the cigar guillotine, he lights it ceremoniously with a double-torch flame. Satisfied it's lit on all sides, he then takes in a long, delicious draw. He leisurely lets the rich, warm tobacco roll around in his mouth before exhaling a giant cloud into the atmosphere above him. Soon, even the moon is veiled by the dense smoke.

He replays his conversation with Merton earlier in the day. These lab-meat factories have sought to infringe on the agribusiness for decades now. Up to this point, he's managed to contain it within the small margins of their protein monopoly. But with this latest breakthrough, any household that can afford a low-priced kitchen gadget will be able to produce their own protein as easily as telling a kitchen-bot to bake bread in the morning.

Merton seemed to understand the scope of the problem and assured him that stopping it before it became a threat was a top priority of T-NEC. *I'll leave it to them to figure out*, he silently concedes. *At least for now.*

❧❧❧❧❧❧

Two hours later, Astrid Johnson rides the elevator down from her third-floor bedroom. Her pair of Shih-Tzus—Missy and Beau—follow along, decked out with matching pink bows, curious about their late-night mission. She knows her husband often works late into the night, given the transnational scope of his agribusiness, Fendide. Still, after dinner, he told her he just wanted to relax for a few minutes by the pool. She's surprised, and slightly miffed, that he's not come to bed yet. *I knew I shouldn't have bothered putting this damned thing on for him.*

As she steps onto the veranda and sees her husband on his lounge chair, she considers how tired he must be. Her mood softens, and she notices he's fallen asleep with a cigar in his hand. *Lucky he didn't burn himself,* she chides, taking in the whiskey bottle and half-empty glass.

"James," she says quietly, coming around to face him. "It's time to turn off the lights and come to bed." Looking at his face, she sees the sweat on his forehead. His jowls are red with broken blood vessels. He begins to moan as if in a deep stupor. She reaches down to feel his head. He's burning up. Fumbling around on the table next to him, she triggers an EMERGENCY-HOLO, then sits beside him and waits for the EMTs while she tries to manage her growing panic.

After the paramedics rush James to the hospital, Astrid follows in her white Alfa Romero 45 Stradale. The two forgotten pups wander the pool area, looking for something to eat. Simultaneously, the pair find the half-smoked cigar and begin fighting over it—their pink bows soon trampled from the tussle.

The following morning, Astrid sends a HOLO-EM to her maid, Juanita. In the chaos of her husband's health crisis, she has completely forgotten about her two dogs. Juanita's more than willing to come in early to pick Missy and Beau up and take them to their doggy daycare.

James is stable but not improving. So the two pups spend the rest of the week at the kennel, delighted to play with the a hundred-and-twenty other dogs that pass through Fur Baby Spa and Dog Hotel. After a few days, they become lethargic, and both develop fevers. The on-call vet quickly quarantines them from the others, but not before it's too late.

Midland, Michigan USA (92° F / 33° C)

Barry Thompson, the grandson of former Vice President Tommy Thompson, has been looking forward to his poker game all week. As the U.S. congressional representative of Michigan's Second District, he takes pride in being a politician 'out among the people!' Tonight, that means playing poker with the executives of Foster Compounds, the nation's largest manufacturer of both toxic and non-toxic chemicals. Of course, Barry rarely finds himself in the company of anyone who doesn't max out their annual PAC contributions—unless it's the waitstaff at one of the many five-star restaurants he seems to live in.

The back room of Chip Connors' resort cabin is loud and lively as the men deal several rounds of Texas Hold'em. They try to avoid talking about business, but every once in a while, they nudge Barry to tell them about what's happening on the Hill. The truth is, it's the only reason they put up with the young braggart. He sits on the House Committee on Energy and Commerce, and though most of the committee's work is public record, some of the most crucial reports are marked classified. Whenever Barry manages to garner attention for passing along something labeled "eyes only," he feels his personal and political stock rise. The bull market inside him becomes an irresistible drug.

Sitting back in the brushed leather chair, he lights up the cigar his grandfather gave him at lunch last week. Flying nano-bots soar over him like small eagles. The tiny smoke-eaters quickly absorb the thick cloud. Grandpa T.T. had invited Barry to the Capitol Hill Club to celebrate his new role within the New Freedom Caucus. He's felt the old man's approval growing over the last few years, something his father seemed too stingy to offer. After taking another deep draw on his cigar, he starts dropping hints about the most likely inquiries under consideration against several municipalities. Most have to do with unsafe drinking water or dangerous levels of heavy metals and ammonia released into the atmosphere by chemical or manufacturing plants.

As he continues to outline the specific nature of the cases, the long ash on his half-smoked corona miraculously stays attached. The men try to stay focused on his words, but after several rounds of scotch, they are mesmerized by the end of Barry's cigar. Over the years, the four have developed the habit of turning everything into a betting game. A frustrated glance passes between them—ready to interrupt him to wager how long the gray crisp will hang on.

After one last drag on the cigar, Barry's eyes suddenly roll up into his head. At first, the men think he's lost his train of thought. Then, profuse sweat breaks out all over his body. It's as if his skin has sprung a thousand leaks. He looks around the room with dark, vacant eyes, seeing straight through the others.

"Oh, God. I think I'm sick—my head's going to explode!" Cigar ashes scatter, then float in the air—the tiny eagles swirl and dive in their manic, reckless pursuit. "Stop that noise, will you? HOLO someone! I think I'm dying," he pleads, and then collapses onto the green felt table, spilling cards, poker chips, and glasses onto the tiger-striped oak floor.

Summer 2059

"*OK. OK, todos. Muchísimas gracias. Gracias* for coming out tonight!" Lisa-Lisa shouts to over nine thousand fans. Her short, black-and-gold hair is pasted with sweat around her pale, round face, and her show at the Auditorio Nacional is nearing its climax.

"You all know that this tour, this concert, isn't about me. And... it isn't about you, either. It's about *them*." She points behind her to an enormous HOLO that replaces the stage's backdrop. "ALL OF THEM!" Hundreds of swarming, swirling creatures spring to life, visually pulsating to the drummer's heartbeat rhythm.

The crowd spontaneously starts to chant, "THEM. THEM. THEM. THEM." Following their cue, Lisa-Lisa's arms sweep the air back and forth as if she's conducting an immense and powerful orchestra. She lets the chant grow and then eventually motions for quiet.

"Everything that lives... everything that breathes on this tiny blue planet—the human, the *non-human*—all have a sacred right to live, a sacred duty to protect and preserve.

"So... I beg you. Please. Sign up. Stand up. And make sure you show up at your school or city on October 22nd for Earther's Lament Day. I've met Noah, the girl who's behind it all. Let me tell you, she's the real deal. She's just like you and me, with a heart that bleeds blue and green for our Mother Earth.

"Together, we can be the change. But before that, *we* need to *be changed*. We need to be forced to face, to experience what we've lost— what we're losing every day. Only if we let ourselves feel our solidarity, not abstractly, but with love and grief, can we have any hope to slow down what we're doing to our home."

Lisa-Lisa pauses, her words echoing, until all that can be heard is a deep, collective sigh.

"That's right. Breathe. Breathe for yourself, and remember those who can't breathe." The lights drop suddenly, the arena black as night. Gradually, HOLO images of plants, trees, insects, fish, reptiles, birds, and mammals appear and float above the audience's heads. They seem to move, fly, swim—just out of reach.

Lisa-Lisa then begins to sing, with no instrument other than her voice carrying the song's sad refrain.

"A world... we've stripped... of wonder..."

As she sings, these virtual creatures of planet Earth begin to struggle—one by one. *"Can't breathe!"* they seem to cry. Their emaciated ribs and vacant eyes stare down at the swaying concert-goers.

"Only... shadows... fill... the spaces..."

Some in the audience try to reach up. Too late, the creature's sad figures wither like collapsed balloons. Their demise accelerates in unison, fading into nothingness until the cave-like space goes black as night. Like death. Extinction. Forever.

"Now... now... now... they're all... gone... gone... gone..."

Her voice lowers an octave, and the song's final three words echo like a death knell. The crowd is crushed into a gaping wound of soundlessness. The absence of noise is only interrupted by a clearing of a throat or shuffle of a foot.

She waits—one beat, two beats, three. Then Lisa-Lisa lights a blood-red candle and speaks softly to the hushed audience.

"Out of respect. As our way of honoring the loss, I want to ask that we all depart in silence tonight."

She then turns and exits the stage, holding the candle to light her way. The house lights come up slowly to a pale, soft level as the crowd consents and leaves without saying a word.

Toronto, Ontario, Canada (91° F / 33° C)

Seamus's HOLO announces a connection from Dr. Arthur Fortuna, the Global Infectious Disease Center's director. Other than a few written communiques concerning the toxin incident, Seamus hasn't spoken directly with the man since they bumped into each other in Dallas at the Planetary Risk Conference. *It's about time, old friend. I wondered when I'd hear from you.*

Seamus smiles as the man's head materializes before him. "Hello, Arthur. It's good to see you."

"Hi, Seamus. Thanks for seeing me. Am I catching you at a bad time?"

The man's question amuses Seamus. *Why do some people ask if it's a bad time and others ask if it's a good time? I guess when your world is haunted by lethal pandemics, it's always a bad time.*

"No, Art. I always have time for you. What's up?" Seamus asks, sensing that the director isn't in the mood for small talk.

"I'll get right to the point. We've been working on that novel parvovirus I mentioned a few months ago. It's been pretty tricky to determine much about it so far—we have such a small sample to work with. The patient I mentioned survived, though he still has some significant respiratory issues. He's on oxygen and will probably stay on it the rest of his life."

Seamus's face appears neutral, incongruent with the gravity of the conversation. "I'm sorry to hear that. So, are there any more cases, or is this just an isolated one-off?"

"We're investigating a handful of other events that seem like they may be related, but we're not one hundred percent positive yet. Should know more in a week or two. A few other cases are popping up around Minneapolis, too. We've traced most of those back to a dog kennel there. This bug could be a real bitch if it infects the canine pet population and then jumps to humans."

Seamus begins to perspire as Arthur tells him more. He never meant for the operation to get out of hand like this. *What's there to say? In a war, there will always be collateral damage. With the population at nine billion, maybe some pruning of the human species is in order,* he rationalizes to himself—not sure if he completely believes it.

"Arthur, I don't know what to say. This is beyond alarming. What do you need? How can I help?"

"Well, for one thing, we need to develop a vaccination for the dogs. If they *are* the carriers, then there's a ticking bomb in a third of the households worldwide. The risk is even higher in advanced countries, where half of all homes have at least one of these little fur balls living under their roofs."

The older man's eyelids sag, as do his shoulders. Getting this off his chest seems to have taken something out of him.

"Let me see if we can generate some ideas for handling the virus in the canine population," Seamus offers. "If we could even just develop a kind of reverse mutation that would mitigate the interspecies jump, that would help protect human life, even if the dogs still succumbed."

"Thanks, Seamus. Any help you can offer is greatly appreciated. There's one last thing—there's a strong possibility that the virus doesn't occur naturally but was engineered. There's evidence of gene snipping and biological glue that is beyond the pace of all known pathogenic mutations. It could've been the Russians or Chinese or one of the jihadist states. Hell, with our frightening AI capabilities, it could be some nut job working out of a high-school chemistry lab!"

The man's sardonic grin is short-lived. "Just wanted you to know that there could be a bigger problem than just the virus. Did I just say that? *A bigger problem* than something that could kill a third of the planet?"

"Art, I'll look into it. I appreciate you letting me know and for your trust in sharing this with me. When you get a chance, can you forward everything your team has been working on so far?"

"Of course, Seamus. And I appreciate *you*. I've been needing to share this weight with someone outside the Center. Sometimes, it feels like I'm trying to shield Earth from a planet-killing asteroid with nothing more than a broken umbrella. I've got good people around me, but none of them seem like peers. Take good care, friend."

The HOLO switches off, leaving Seamus feeling more alone than he's felt since Erin died. He stands slowly on unsteady legs and then heads toward his university laboratory. He and Erin used it to further their covert research in the Amazon while she taught alongside him in Toronto. *Who knows? Maybe lightning will strike twice in there. Yeah, right.*

After he disconnects, Dr. Fortuna looks at the generic-looking man standing next to him known as Wilson. He doubts it's the man's real name. It seems the National Security Agency amuses itself by perpetually playing spy games of one kind or another.

"That was perfect, Director. This lead you provided is the best intel we've received so far," Wilson, or whatever his name is, says.

"Sure. Do you need anything else from me? In case you haven't noticed, I've got a global pandemic I'm trying to prevent."

"No, that's all. Thanks for working with us on this. I know it's not easy to investigate a friend. But believe it or not, our friends and colleagues are usually the least suspected sleeper agents. I'll leave you to saving the world, Doctor. Let me know if anything else of interest presents itself."

Arthur Fortuna nods and then looks down at the report on top of a stack of papers on the cluttered desk. He rubs his eyes, trying to recall how they got here. To recalibrate, he forces himself to remember the events that led him here.

Two months ago, the Center's research lead contacted him with a theory. It suggested that the original virus cultured from the Chief originated in the Amazon. He was then told that the secondary wave of infections shared the same biogeographical and genetic signature.

He was aware of only a handful of legitimate research facilities in that region. So he immediately sent a team to locate the source. They searched diligently for three weeks. Nada. It was as if the virus had appeared out of thin air—or from some small lab functioning off the grid.

The Amazon is a veritable cornucopia of unknown biocompounds. Arthur is well aware of black market bosses and alternative-treatment entrepreneurs conducting questionable or illicit research in the jungle. It's possible that the virus could be traced to one of these.

But there was only one site in the region that he knew of personally that could create this bug. So, he presented the idea to the NSA director. After that, the investigation became a runaway train that has now jumped the track, heading straight for his friend, Seamus Wilde.

What have I done? he asks himself, teetering on regret, his resolve weakening. *Too late now. I just hope it was the right thing to do, old friend. And this ruse will save lives—even if it destroys yours.*

Dallas, Texas, USA (118° F / 48° C)

The lively chatter from the boardroom inside the Bank of America Plaza's penthouse abruptly halts as a big, white-haired man is wheeled in, guided by B.B., an even bigger mountain of a man. The Chief is an imposing figure, enveloped in pervasive whiteness that cloaks him from top to bottom, skin to teeth. He wears a white linen suit, white shirt, and tie, completed with pure white socks and loafers that make him look like a mashup of Pope John Paul II and Mark Twain.

The younger man who pilots the wheelchair is a living shadow—sporting a large, circular, black afro, coal-black skin announcing his pure African descent, and a black leather jacket stretching its seams in every direction. No one knows what the initials stand for, but everyone's settled on the nickname 'Big Bastard'. B.B. looks around the room, expressionless, scanning for anyone who might pose a threat to his boss.

Scowling at figures in the room, the Chief speaks to his companion as if those around the table are merely a collection of useful tools.

"It's alright, B.B. I've known most of these hustlers since we were in prep school. I still don't trust them, but they know better than to try to get rid of me. They need me. That's the best insurance for stayin' alive. Good old corporate greed."

B.B. steps back and relaxes slightly but keeps his mirrored sunglasses on, sweeping the room with his hidden glare.

"Okay, you sons-of-bitches. I called y'all together to let you know we've got a problem. Not on our end, mind you. We've got our fists wrapped around the balls of every politician and every government on the planet. On top of that, we've created a culture of addicts—thinking they can have it all, they just keep buying up your products at a rate that doesn't seem to have any limits. But we do, in fact, have a problem. Don't we, B.B.? Or should I say a *future* problem?"

The Chief slowly takes off his glasses. *This is what my Lily deals with—users just don't seem to have a choice. Or do they?* He starts polishing the lenses with a white handkerchief he's removed from his suit coat pocket.

"B.B., get me a drink, but be sure to add a little something extra to it for me." The men and women around the table exchange worried glances.

"As I was saying," the Chief continues, "we've got a growing problem. This commie, liberal, environmental movement is swelling into something we've yet to see. Can y'all believe the amount of press that little Irish bitch is getting? At the latest count, she's captured a hundred million followers.

"Now we all know these dumb kids will follow anything that looks like the next big revolution. We've seen it before. But we also know these dumb little fucks will become dumb *big* fucks in ten years. And then they'll have something they don't have now. *Money!*

"Hell, they may even start to think they've got a choice—about what to buy or even worse, what *not* to buy. Shit, who knows? They might even start believing *they* can reset the whole god-damned global economy for something better." He pauses to take another sip of his drink, then slams it down with enough force that the ice and liquid explode from the glass, landing in a spreading pool on the table. "Damn it! They don't get to decide who lives and who goes extinct! We do. Or, more precisely, *I do!*"

The man picks up the dripping glass, closes his eyes, and takes a long, slow drink from the bent straw. When he finishes, he looks slowly around the room with the ferocity of a lion who hasn't eaten in a while.

"Listen. We're not here to brainstorm or any of that candy-assed stuff. Y'all have people who do that for you. What I'm here to tell you is that you need to crush this thing before it gets completely out of hand. Don't bother coordinating. Just do it. I want speed! I want intensity, you hear? Now get out of here! You all have a job to do. Actually, two jobs! Yours and mine."

B.B. walks over to the man, leans down, and whispers in his ear.

The Chief smiles a wicked, old-man grin. "Well, hot damn! One of those rock bands that's helping fuel this crap is playing right here in

Dallas tonight. I bet one of your corporate goons could find a way to bring the house down on this Begging for Mercy show. Now, wouldn't that be something to see? Let's see which one of you sons-of-bitches can make those choirboys beg?"

He pushes his big body up straight in the wheelchair, surveying the room one last time, then signals for B.B., who pushes him through the door, trailing behind like a well-trained rhino.

Two men in navy-blue coveralls and bandannas pulled over their faces jump out of a beat-up, white-panel truck parked outside the rear service entrance to the American Airlines Center in downtown Dallas. A gritty haze hangs in the air and quickly begins covering the truck's window with a fine layer of sand. The venue's staff is in fast motion as they gear up for the arrival of the fifteen thousand people ready to hear Begging for Mercy. Kicking up dust clouds and carrying a large duffle bag filled with tools, the two men blend in easily, not raising so much as a glance from the security guard playing a HOLO game by one of the triple-sized garage doors.

They quickly head downstairs into the belly of the arena, where there is a tight, twisting network of wires and pipes. Finding the line that snakes underneath the stage, they shut off the valve and head in that direction. Underneath the stage, one of the men punches several small holes along the main gas line to the stage. The other takes out a small timing device and readies an auto-ignition switch. When finished, they open the valve of an acetylene tank, pointing the torch head toward the ignition switch.

Finished, they walk quickly back to turn on the stage's gas line and then move quickly up the stairs. The security guard is still there, chatting with an attractive young woman who briefly turns and looks at them. Seeing nothing remarkable other than two grown men in navy-colored onesies, she refocuses her attention on the guard's dark-blue eyes and wide Texas smile.

The men hop into their truck and pull several blocks away. The driver turns their ride around on Payne Street, now facing it directly toward the American Airline Center—a haze of sunlit dust softens their view. Thirty minutes pass, and then they watch as a rushing swell of the arena's staff and work-crews frantically pour out from every exit.

BWOOM! BWOOM! BWOOM! A brilliant flash of hot light torpedoes from the mammoth arched windows. Shrapnel-shaped pieces of glass explode in every direction. Black smoke aimlessly roils through twisted steel frames. Instantly, hundreds of car alarms are triggered, masking a deafening silence that hovers over the surreal scene.

Soon, fire trucks scream past toward the smoking behemoth.

The man in the passenger seat sends a HOLO-EM.

> Smoke's on the water, boss. I think tonight's concert is officially a no-go.

Fall 2059

Kilkenny, Ireland (87° F / 30.5° C)

The two girls are upstairs in Noah's bedroom, wrapping up the final preparations for the second Earther's Lament Day at school. Shea—wearing *Don't Wake Me* PJs—has her knees tucked under her petite body on Noah's bed, watching through her dark, hopeful eyes as Noah hurries about the room, double-checking everything.

"Just two days away. Can you believe it?" Shea says as she rises and heads to the adjoining bathroom.

"Uh-huh," Noah agrees, not bothering to look back at her friend. "Ready or not, eh?" Noah flips through a thick stack of photos of animals, insects, plants, and trees—a sudden waft of the myrrh-scented rice paper drifts through the room—and then puts the images in her rucksack. *I can't believe Journi found the money to send packets to anyone who wanted to host an event.*

"I wonder how many kids will actually show up," Shea speculates, her words garbled as she finishes brushing her teeth. "This kind of reminds me of *Día de Muertos* from World Culture last year. Kids really got into that, remember? This feels like that... except way more relevant."

Shea turns out the bathroom light and then crosses the room, where she flops back on the bed. Noah nods imperceptibly, silently studying her best friend. *You're amazing, Shea... always there for me. And here you are again, trying to cheer me up, putting your reputation on the line.*

Noah has also been wondering about the turnout, trying to keep her expectations low. She sits on the edge of the bed and, after a few moments, answers. "Didn't someone say, 'A prophet is not welcome in their own hometown?' Or, in this case, their *own high school*. I don't know, Shea. I'd be happy with thirty or forty showing up. It's not going to be like last year—that was a mandatory assembly. And this is the *whole day*."

"Oh, come on, Noah." Shea sits up, reaching for Noah's hand. "Have you

forgotten how many people around *the world* watch your HOLO-POD?"
She pulls Noah down beside her, putting an arm around her, and leans her
head on her friend's shoulder. "We need to stay positive, think positive. Can
you believe I'm saying that? Usually, it's you telling me to have a little faith."
Shea sits up and playfully pokes Noah in the ribs. "Listen, girl. I. Have.
Faith. In. You."

Noah giggles, then sinks into her friend and feels Shea's steadiness. She
realizes just how edgy she's been for the last few weeks—her nerves, the
main thing energizing her actions. But now, that anxious feeling seems to
drain out of her body. *Strange*, she thinks. *I feel relaxed. Relieved. At peace.*

"Thanks, Shea. I can't imagine doing this without you. Thanks for
hanging in there with me," she says, kissing her friend on the cheek.

After a few moments, Noah straightens up. "When all this is done, how
'bout us going to get matching tattoos?" Shea turns toward her.

"Umm... okay. Sure. What did you have in mind?"

"I don't know. Some near-extinct creature for sure." They look at each
other and nod, as if sealing a silent agreement.

At the same time, Noah's HOLO ring chimes. She opens it to view
her ma's message, her face floating before them, darkness concealing the
landscape behind her.

"Hello, dear. We're all finished up at the field behind the school. Donnel
O'Malley has been so kind and generous to let you use it. He even brought
out some lights so we could see as we worked in the dark. My friends from
the shop came and carried wood to the fire stations. Your da, Uncle Liam,
Uncle Ronan, and some of the other Greenling men came and dug the most
enormous hole this town has seen in an age or two. So, I think you're all
set. I'll be home soon. And Noah..." Her ma's voice catches. "I'm so proud of
you. We all are."

Her ma's image fades, and the two girls lie back on the bed, just like they
used to do when they were little.

The silence absorbs their worried exhaustion and covers their spinning
minds like a warm blanket until they both fall asleep side by side.

When Ma gets home, she quietly heads upstairs. Her shirt and jeans are smudged with powder-dry soil. *It's been a hot, long day, but worth it,* she thinks to herself. Turning off the light in the stairway, she walks by Gil's door. She hears the buzz and thumps of a HOLO-GAME and considers knocking, but instead chooses to leave him alone.

Then, she stops in front of Noah's room. The light is still on, so she lightly raps on the door. No answer. She carefully turns the old brass knob and pushes the door with her shoulder. It sticks slightly but doesn't squeak. As she looks in, she sees the two girls sleeping beside each other. She walks over and gazes at them. *More than friends,* she considers. *Sisters? Or something else?*

As she watches them lie there together, she remembers *her* best mate, Shannon, and is suddenly swept into the past—its joys as well as its sorrows. *Where are you, Shana-banana?* Long ago, she lost track of her friend. But seeing Shea's arm draped over Noah stirs a longing for her best friend that she's not felt for a very long while.

Leaning over, she kisses both girls on the tops of their heads, walks to the door, and turns off the light.

Standing in the open field under the clear morning sky before sunrise, the two girls are dazed by the chorus of stars encircling a scythe-shaped moon above them. Shea reaches for Noah's hand and gives it a firm squeeze. Something about the scene brings a hush, an active silence they choose not to break.

Together, they arrange the tables with the stacks of scented photo cards and complete their final preparations. Thanks to the school's Optical AI Club wizardry, the visual and audio HOLO transmitter is turned on and ready to beam.

A few close friends and other student volunteers soon arrive in a small, hushed procession. Quiet greetings are exchanged.

"James, David. Go light the fires." Noah directs the boys toward the field's perimeter. One by one, the small group watches as the twelve fires encompass them. The flames quickly climb onto the larger logs and begin to illuminate the gold and green field. Others carry guitars, drums, violins, flutes, and tin whistles, spreading them out on blankets before each fire. *This is happening,* Noah tells herself—her determined eyes alive with reflected fire. In front of each fire is a large, upright carving—one for each family of planetary life: fish, birds, reptiles, trees, and so on.

Soon, they notice tiny pinpricks of light approaching from all directions—first two, then five, then twenty, then too many to count. Students step into the circle of light, holding candles. Their glowing flames are quickly absorbed by the larger fires.

The volunteers steer the growing group to the tables, where they instruct them to pin a card with an image of an extinct or near-extinct animal or plant over their hearts. Next, they tell them to connect their HOLOs to the *Extinction is Forever* network. As they do, the animal, plant, or tree in their photo comes to life above their heads. The scene quickly fills with running, slithering, flying, swimming, and swaying creatures.

"It's beautiful," Noah whispers. "If only it were real."

After the students check in, they're directed to form a large circle in the middle of the field, facing in. The center is bathed in light from three tall torches on long poles. The participants' young faces are dimly illuminated by the warm, golden flames burning before them.

Seated amid the flaming sticks are several of the Greenling clan—Noah's immediate and distant relatives. The small band sits shoulder to shoulder, facing out, and straddles colorful drums of various shapes and sizes. As the circle of students is completed, a slow rhythm emerges from the drum circle.

The various HOLO images of the students' creatures fade, and then disappear. A soft, collective sigh ripples around the larger circle. A HOLO of a tiny wych elm seedling is then illuminated as it hovers overhead in the circle's center, seeming to glow from some magical source from within. The drumming builds in speed, complexity, and volume as the tiny seedling descends to the earth. There, it begins to grow, morphing into a young sapling, spreading limbs that extend overhead. Unseen winds ripple through countless twisting leaves. The tree gradually ceases its upward, outward expansion—an enormous replica of the ancient species.

Mournful female voices slowly emerge as four flying figures come into view—from the north and south, east and west. One appears to be a young child, another an adolescent girl like the students gathered around the circle. Another is a haggard, gaunt adult. Finally, there is an elderly woman in her last decade. Noah—just beyond the tips of tree's branches—furrows her shadowed brow, bewildered at their sudden and unscripted appearance. *Who are you? And why are you here?*

The students—not needing to be told that these are banshees—think it's all part of the day's event.

Noah knows better, though. "*Bean sídhe*," she whispers. Their appearance seems to meld both vegetal and human features. Moss-like hair surrounds faces with deep-set emerald orbs that have witnessed too much suffering. Skin resembling tree bark covers hollow cheeks stained with sap-like tears. Shreds of long grasses and feathery roots flow around their bodies like burial gowns.

They silently land on the tree's large branches, then nod in unison toward Noah, as if waiting for her to begin. Her initial shock is soon replaced by bewilderment. *What are they here for? To participate? To scare us away? Or maybe... something else?*

Noah shakes her head and pushes the questions aside, realizing that everyone's waiting for her. She then turns her attention back to the students gathered around her. Her lilting words, carried by the HOLO transmission system, surround the listeners with the rhythmic sound of her voice.

"Good morning, friends of the earth! Your brothers and sisters, the fish, the insects, the reptiles and amphibians, the birds and the animals, the flowers and the trees are moved by your presence. We live in a beautiful world, don't we? In fact, it's the beauty of the world that draws us together.

What we love... what we care about... has the power to change us. And what we're unwilling to tolerate has the power to change the world."

The circle of boys and girls nod their heads. Their defiant eyes dance with the reflected light from the fires and the golden glow of the giant tree.

"But today," Noah continues, "isn't about trying to change anything. Today, we gather to lament the loss of the unimaginable beauty that has disappeared. Forever. But listen... our lament isn't about giving up or letting go of hope. Our lament is an act of resistance."

Those in the circle listen—their faces somber.

"Today, you will be guided through a variety of stations. Some of Earth's earliest protesters recounted and lamented the crucifixion of their resistance leader, Jesus, by walking what they called the Stations of the Cross. In the same spirit, I'd like us to think of this field as a place to lament our planet's Stations of Extinction. And just as those ancients demonstrated their solidarity and shared grief by tracing on their foreheads a cross made from black ashes, we will make our own sign—a sign of tears."

Noah and her volunteers then walk around the circle with small jars filled with ashes from an evergreen yew mixed with wild flax oil. They use their thumbs to draw tear-like marks on the students' cheeks. As they do so, the lifelike HOLO image of each person's plant or animal reemerges above them.

Noah, her eyes expressing both fierceness and grief, slowly casts her gaze on each student as she turns around in the center. She spots some whose ash is already streaking from tears. She smiles faintly, and then breaks the silence.

"One last thing. You will hear a gong struck at the top of each hour to announce the time. Whenever you notice that your companion creature is fighting for its life, come and join the others at the perimeter fire that matches the number of gongs that were struck. It will be easy to find. The fires are placed around us in a circle like a giant clock. Then, when you come, we will take time together to remember each one lost and the miracle that was each one's life."

The sun has gradually risen, and a faint mist hovers over the ground.

The sky, however, resists dawn's optimism and remains a dull blue-gray. The circle of students takes their cue and slowly disassembles, drifting in all directions to the various Stations of Extinction.

Standing alone in the center now, Noah looks up at the wych elm and spies the four banshees. They are now rocking forward and back, in unison, as if in the pains of childbirth. She finds herself bobbing her own head in time with their steady movements. *What on Earth are you doing here? Do you approve of all this? Are you here to support us... to show us how to lament?* At that exact moment—they seem to read her mind—the four beings stop rocking and fix their deep-set eyes on her. Like a dirge inside her mind, she hears their voices harmonizing.

"No, dear child. We are here to witness the beginning of an ending. We are here... because of you... because of what's to come."

As soon as their words cease, they launch into the sky and begin their keening, circling high above the perimeter's twelve fires. Noah looks on in wonder as they spiral round and round in some magical, ancient dance. *I can see what's ending, but what's coming?*

As the day progresses, knots of students shift from place to place—some to locations where they dance, others to areas with musical instruments, others to tables with snacks and hot tea, and still others to the many fires around the perimeter. Some even go down into a deep, open pit to lie down on the dark soil to experience extinction's finality. Their movement from above looks like a colony of ants, moving in random, swirling patterns that teem with life and purpose.

While they move about, the wych elm in the middle of the field—by the magic of the HOLO—begins to slowly drop its large, tooth-edged leaves and scatter them on the ground, eventually baring every branch and twig.

Just before noon—the sun shrouded by murky, unnatural clouds—Noah's ears pick up fragments of heckling from the opposite side of the circle.

When she turns around, she quickly spots the unruly, disrespectful gang. *Why am I not surprised they'd show up today?*

The ringleader, Colin, has rallied his favorite hooligans. They rudely break the solemn mood with their loud mockery, imitating pig snorts, monkey cries, braying donkeys, and honking geese.

Boiling inside, Noah clenches her fists and jaw, then stomps toward the mob.

"Hey, ya' buncha wankers!" Colin shouts. "Maybe ya' want to say a little prayer or dance a little dance for us, too. How about a little love for us humans?"

"That's right," Keelin yells, mocking the dancing by shaking her hips back and forth. "If you have your way, you'll ruin the lot of us with all this green shite." With equally dramatic taunts and gestures, the others hurl noisy insults toward the somber event.

Noah is livid. Completely unafraid. She just stands there for a moment, glaring at them, ready to rush into the middle of the pack, kicking and punching.

Then, she notices Gil standing at the back of the small group, neither participating nor opposing them. Noah lets out a long, frustrated breath. *Of course, my good ol' brother would be here with them.* The twins catch each other's eyes, but Gil quickly looks away, turning to face another direction.

The small group starts gyrating in a contrived, erratic dance while continuing to mock the event with their fake wailing and boo-hooing.

Losing control—exasperated at their vulgar insults—Noah screams, "GO TO HELL! All of you. You all should be ashamed. Especially you, Gil. NOW GET OUT OF HERE!"

She turns and tramps away, the united chorus's howls—"Ahh... ooooooh... ahh... ooooooh!"—fading behind her as she returns to the circle.

After several steps, Noah becomes aware that she's being followed; something—or someone—is trailing above her. She looks up and sees the adolescent banshee hovering a few meters overhead. The creature's deep-set green eyes stare at her as if silently pleading, waiting to be released. Noah pauses, and then conveys assent with a half-flick of the wrist. *Go! Have at it.*

The flying wraith seems to explode with motion and screams away toward the hecklers.

Before she can turn, she hears Colin cry, "What the fuck's that?" Noah spins around, seeing the terror in their wide eyes and gaping mouths. Unsure of what's happening, they turn and run, bumping into each other, trying to get away from whatever is now overhead. Colin shoves Gil hard, then pushes the others out of his way. Just as he's almost broken free, the banshee suddenly descends like a falcon diving for its prey. He wails as he falls to the ground, and then shivers as the unnatural being passes through him as if he were a dim HOLO image.

Noah smirks and shakes her head at the chaotic scene. *Show's over!* she tells herself, then returns to the circle, moving toward an intricate wooden statue carved from a large log—this one of a giant stag beetle. Seated before the likeness of the jumbo-sized insect is her uncle Liam and his Irish uilleann bagpipe. He's playing a slow piece that gives Noah the feeling of a bumbling beetle. The image makes her smile.

"*Thank you,*" she mouths to her uncle as their eyes meet. He winks back, his grizzled cheek almost touching an eyebrow.

Other musical instruments lay on a blanket in front of the large beetle for anyone wanting to join in. A boy Noah's never met picks up a guitar and begins to strum along. A girl picks up a violin and, after tuning it, gently strokes the strings.

Around the statue, Greenling women—dressed in earthy greens and browns with flowing ribbons—begin to dance in a small ring. At times, their steps are filled with joy and humor, imitating whatever creature group they seek to honor. Eventually, they subtly shift to movements that express overwhelming loss and grief. A few students overcome their shyness and join the circle, dancing their own joys and sorrows.

GONG... GONG... GONG... GONG...

Shea holds a cloth-wrapped mallet and stands next to a wooden cart holding a large Chinese gong. When the students hear the call, they look up at their animal or plant to see if it's still holding on, or if it has finally succumbed. Those with struggling creatures traipse toward the fire at the five o'clock position around the perimeter.

Noah steps up next to Shea and waits. A group of around thirty eventually joins them and stands shoulder-to-shoulder around the fire. After a few minutes, Noah steps forward and invites them to introduce their companion for the day, urging them also to read a few words about them.

Janice, stunningly beautiful with wide, blue eyes that sparkle like diamonds, steps toward the fire. She slowly turns to face the others, her countenance mirroring a beautiful sadness. With her delicate fingers, she unfastens the photo card pinned over her heart and begins to read.

"I've been blessed by the company of the giant ibis today. The giant ibis is a wading bird found in northern Cambodia. It's the largest member of its species." Noah is struck by the contrast between Janice's irresistible allure, her naturally feminine style, and the utter ordinariness of the bird she affectionately describes.

Holding the bird's card, Janice's hand trembles as she continues. "The giant ibis is a lowland bird... mainly living in marshes, swamps, or lakes. Its diet includes eels, small amphibians, and reptiles, along with locusts and cicadas. The species traditionally has not been—" She stops and gulps for air, then continues, "—has not been fearful of humans unless harassed or hunted.

"However, today, it's listed as critically endangered. The primary reasons are the drainage of wetlands, the epidemic of clear-cutting forests, and finally, extreme droughts. The combination of these factors has pushed this docile bird over the edge and stolen its hope for a future on our planet. The current giant ibis population hovers around two hundred birds worldwide. And these numbers are, at best, optimistic."

Janice reaches up and wipes a tear with her hand, smearing the ashes across her cheek. She quietly moves back to the circle's perimeter, and another student steps forward to introduce their companion. One by one, the tearful readings continue until each one has finished.

After a few moments, Noah walks to the center, struggling not to break down, and softly says, "Thank you for sharing about the life and struggles of these plants and animals, our brothers and sisters. Like us, they were born, they grew, they learned, and they played. They found homes and food, found mates, and raised young. We were no more the center of their lives than they were of ours. Yet, we are better for their having lived among us. Just as we are poorer now for having caused their disappearance."

She pans the group with mournful eyes, her mouth pursed in regret. "When you're ready, step forward and release your photos into the flames. As the fire consumes their images, so together, we witness our planet's grave losses."

The students step forward. Some kiss the image, while others simply float the pictures into the searing blaze. As they do, a fragrance is released from the burning of the myrrh embedded in the cards. The smell is astringent and bitter. Like incense, it lingers and surrounds the somber band around the fire. Soon, it dissipates and then disappears into the atmosphere.

Attracted by the smell, the four wailing banshees descend and drift in circles around the fire. Their mournful keening crawls like a spider across the students' flesh. The sound is a chorus of primal lament and anguish.

When the cards eventually shrivel into nothingness, the students pick up buckets filled with water and douse the flames. They stand and watch the fire smolder for a few minutes, soon sputtering into empty silence.

The banshees crisscross above Noah as she walks to the open pit the Green-lings have dug. It gapes like a battle-scarred crater. Grave markers etched with the names of extinct species surround it. The sight of them hits her like a punch to the stomach.

Other students begin trailing toward the giant hole as well. Some have already seen the sign pointing down a wooden ramp and have descended to the bottom. They lie down on the soft, dark soil with closed eyes and seem to be asleep. Stains of mud and blots of wet earth soak into their clothing. No one rushes through this station. Some remain there for long stretches, unmoving and silent. Eventually, most are overcome with weeping, tears streaming down their faces, mingling with what's left of the ash markings from the morning. After the last group of students climb out of the pit, they gather around the open grave and take up shovels to begin the bleak task of filling the grave from the surrounding mounds of earth.

❧ ☙ ❧ ☙ ❧ ☙

As the sun sets, the group appears subdued, weary. More than that, they are all physically and emotionally exhausted.

Noah stands underneath what remains of the bare wych elm. The tree towers, a naked, giant sentinel—still glorious with outstretched limbs—reaching like a skeleton toward the heavens and the horizons. She picks up an Irish tin whistle and begins to play the ancient folk song, *Foggy Dew*. The entire group of students turns toward the sound of the stirring rebel's anthem and drifts to the center, forming a large, tight-knit circle around her. The only light remaining is the dull, pale, sickly sunset and the three torches within which Noah stands while she plays—the notes fierce and troubled but also delicate and pure.

After the last note echoes and then fades away, she invites the gathering to conclude their day by reading together the *Liturgy of Extinction* projected on the HOLO in front of them.

"It's dark now. What do you hear?" Noah asks.

"We hear the wind, the waves, and the rain," the group responds.

"It's dark now. What do you hear?" She asks again.

"We hear our buses and planes, our cars and our trains."

"It's darker, ever darker now. Who are you missing?" The refrain comes with broken words and gentle sobs as the weary mourners list a litany of lost creatures—monkeys and macaws, beetles and butterflies, toads and tree frogs, ivies and ibises. Noah's voice rings out like a death knell. The four banshees drift down beside her, quietly keening.

"*It's late!* So very late. What are you missing?"

With the last dredges of emotion and grief, the group responds, "We have no plants beneath our feet, no trees overhead!"

With what feels like her last breath, Noah cries out in a voice that lacerates the darkness. Even the banshees recoil, taken aback by the piercing climax.

"It's late! So very, very late. What have you lost?"

Quiet weeping merges with the whispered final phrases.

"We have lost our home. We have lost our brothers and sisters. We have lost the very gift of Life itself. The replaceable destroying the irreplaceable."

Noah stands still, the silence expanding for several moments. After the quiet pall has settled over the group, she takes out her flute and begins to play again. She has no words to dismiss them. Soon, she stops, slowly looks around the circle, and knocks the knuckles of her closed fists together three times. Each looks at her through sad, tired eyes. Together, they return the gesture.

Silence. Wind is the only sound heard. The assembly seems glued to the ground, almost too stunned to move. Then, a few turn and drift away into the dark until one by one, they disappear, leaving the empty field.

Noah is finally alone. The banshees, too, have departed into the night sky. Shea stands off in the distance, respecting her friend's need for solitude.

Noah lets herself sink into the dark brown earth beneath her. She begins to cry tears she's held in all day—the weeping she denied herself as she guided others into their grieving hearts. Now, she welcomes the flood. The sobs rise from her depths, impossible to resist.

"*It is finished,*" she murmurs—searching the sky for something. The moon? The stars? But... nothing. Not even a tiny vibration from the buttons of moss or tufts of grass underneath her. Nature seems to have abandoned her—offering no support, no acknowledgment that she even exists. The smothering charcoal blankness above is the only thing peering back at her small, collapsed figure.

The young woman sits outside alone in the dark. Cradling her long-stemmed wine glass, she slowly sips the first swallow of Trimbach Gewürztraminer she just poured. The humid night air barely plays with her dark curls, offering only the slightest coolness to the perspiration on her neck and exposed arms and shoulders. The view from the rooftop patio of her father's penthouse on the Kurfürstendamm is breathtaking. Even so, she scowls, not really seeing the angel-like halos cradling the structures that surround her.

Though Marta and Noah have never met, she follows her as carefully as if she were an obsessed stalker. Vivienne has repeatedly warned her that Noah may become the most dangerous force of her time. Though known to exaggerate wildly in public, in private, her aunt is shrewdly understated in her assessments and predictions. At nine o'clock, Marta instructs her HOLO to find CHN news and tops off her drink. A life-sized image of Journi Preston blooms in the darkness.

"Good evening. And welcome to this special edition of Environmental Watch on CHN. Thanks for being with us. One year ago today, young Irish environmental activist Noah Calhoun-Greenling launched a daylong event she calls Earther's Lament Day. She, along with students from her school and twenty thousand other secondary students from more than two hundred Irish schools participated in a ritual of planetary grief.

"The focus was directed toward our planet's extinct and near-extinct flora and fauna. She claims these disappearances can be directly traced to human causes. She has repeatedly called out corporate and industry executives to take responsibility for what she calls 'policies of planetary betrayal.' If left unchecked, she warns, and I quote: 'these excesses will result in the unstoppable and total collapse of the biosphere's diversity.'"

As Journi speaks, images of last year's event are displayed, followed by footage of the corporations and CEOs Noah has named as most responsible for blocking meaningful climate remediation.

"One year later, it seems that students worldwide, along with large

numbers of younger and older adults, agree. Today's Earther's Lament Day appears to have exceeded last year's participation a hundredfold. Conservative estimates suggest that as many as two million people participated in today's events. Every continent, including all developed and developing countries, hosted some form of the daylong ritual."

Several more HOLO-VIDs appear from diverse schools and locations—one from Kenya and another from Brazil. There are images from Japan, the Philippines, and Hong Kong, where police attempted to interrupt the gatherings.

Interspersed with the images are interviews with students from around the world who share why the event mattered to them and how they were affected. A blonde-headed boy in Stuttgart sums up what others seem to convey.

"A lot's been said about my generation's pandemic of anxiety. It's true... I'm terrified of the future. But now, I see that I'm not only afraid, I'm buried under something... it feels like an invisible mountain of grief and guilt is on top of me." Traces of tears on his dirty face underscore how deeply the day has touched him.

"I've probably cried more today... than my whole life. Something inside seems like it's shifted. I feel like I can go home and... I can sleep. I mean, really rest for the first time in a very long time."

As the program wraps up, Journi returns to the foreground and closes the day's coverage.

"All in all, the day appears to have been an enormous success by any measure. Ms. Calhoun-Greenling indicates she is committed to expanding the event every year. When asked what she hopes the event will accomplish, she said, 'I hope it will engage my fellow students holistically—speaking to their hearts, emotions, their conscience, and sense of justice. I hope it will inspire their minds and the need for clear thinking about the problems we've inherited from our parents.'"

"This all sounds very promising for those who care about these issues. Well done, Ms. Greenling. Well done. I want to thank you all for joining us. And on behalf of Environmental Watch and CHN, I wish you a very good

night.”

Marta frowns, her tightened lips exhaling frustration as the HOLO image evaporates into the night's thickening mist. She reaches for the half-empty bottle. The last few drops dribble into her empty glass. Her shadowed eyes land on the tattooed butterfly on her wrist. It struggles to emerge from its cocoon, then breaks loose, spiraling up her arm and out of sight. Bemused by the ink's magic, she wonders, not for the first time. *Where does it go when it disappears inside me?*

PART THREE

Episode 17: Extinction is Forever
HOLO-POD Hosted by Noah Calhoun-Greenling

"In 2033, CRISPR-based gene drives were formally and globally implemented. The goal was simple: to modify the population of mosquitoes and eventually cause their total extinction. As predicted, the consequences have been significant. Truthfully, for many species, it's proving to be downright catastrophic.

"Take, for instance, the purple martin. Before the selective elimination of the little pest, ornithologists estimate that its diet consisted of over two thousand mosquitoes a day. The bird still has to eat, so what does it do? It switched its diet to other insects, and the competition for food became even more extreme, affecting all other species. So now, the insect population is totally overwhelmed, not only collapsing the birds' food source but also stressing the pollinators who keep the plants reproducing. And yes, mosquitoes are—or rather, were—an essential pollinator.

"What really frosts me is that it's all about not being bothered by a pesky little bite. Of course, the little buggers carry diseases, but there are readily available cures for all of them. To me, it's about as stupid as not liking the soggy bother of a rain shower and then someone deciding to blow up all the clouds. See how that turns out!"

Winter 2060

Palo Alto, California, USA (50° F / 10° C)

Brian Sterling walks up to the nondescript building in Palo Alto, carrying a small alligator-skin satchel. He's dressed casually yet carries himself in a way that exudes the apparent ease of the wealthy. When he gets to the door, he removes his custom-made Vuarnet Glacier Round Sunglasses. He looks up at the sign above him, pausing to read the name NEO-VULCAN in red-and-black magneto script. Shining from his hand, the mineral lenses from the sunglasses reflect the brilliant blue light onto his tanned face.

After entering, he notices the attractive brunette receptionist smiling at him. Her full, red-orange lips surround her perfect teeth, which match her perfect figure. She takes longer than expected to speak, seeming lost in her appraisal of him. *Apparently, my little antic at the door paid off,* he tells himself.

Eventually, she breaks the spell to welcome him. "Good morning, Mr. Sterling. I trust that your trip was... uneventful." She pauses coyly. "That is, unless you *prefer* some adventure."

He feels thrown off for a moment, his pulse's tachometer registering the change in RPM. He's expecting a dull financial negotiation with the startup's young CEO, Philip Bucannon. *But who knows?* He now wonders to himself.

"Well, let's see, if I wasn't up for a little adventure, would I be considering getting into bed with a group called *Neo-Vulcan*?" he responds playfully.

"Touché," she replies in turn. "Mr. Bucannon is on his way to his office from the research facility. Let me take you there. Can I get you anything while you wait?" He's still a bit distracted, not knowing exactly how to read her. *Or does he?*

"No, I'm good. By the way, what's your name? I didn't catch it."

"Oh, sorry, I don't think I told you. I'm Carly. But most people call me

Van." She answers as they head down the hallway.

"Well, thanks for being so helpful, Van. And, please. Call me Brian. Though, everyone who knows me calls me Skip."

"That's a fun name. Like skipping stones, right?"

"Well, it started there. I could skip a stone farther than all my friends. But it really stuck after I bought my first yacht. A beautiful vintage Oceanco Black Pearl. Some friends and I took it to Barbados, and they all started calling me Skipper. 'Aye aye, skipper' this and 'aye aye, skipper' that. It stuck, and then it just got shortened to Skip. How about you? How'd you get pegged with the nickname Van?"

She turns toward him in the narrow hallway and angles her body closer toward him in a way that no one would confuse with being professional.

"Don't tell anyone here... it was because of my boyfriend's van in high school. I was young and naive. Actually, I was pretty stupid. I didn't really care back then what people said about me. Anyway, I spent more time in the back of that van than around my dinner table. Not as glamorous as yours." She finishes with a wink, then slides around into an open doorway.

"Here you go, Skip. Philip—also known as *Mr. Vulcan himself*—will be here shortly." She leans on the door frame and bites her bottom lip, studying him as he walks to one of the steel benches. "Make yourself at home. And let me know if... I can get you anything." She waits a beat as her offer lingers, then slowly turns and walks away.

Left alone, Sterling wonders. *Did that just happen? Or was it some kind of pre-negotiation ploy to soften me up? Regardless, it's an entertaining way to get started!*

Philip Bucannon bounds into his office, looking more unkempt than expected.

"Sorry to keep you waiting," the nerdy-looking business executive says, reaching over to shake Sterling's hand. "The team just made a breakthrough and wanted to bring me up to speed before moving to the next phase."

He quickly moves to a seat next to Sterling and loosens his tie. "Listen, I appreciate you coming all the way out here. I know we're a small operation, but—"

"Glad to do it," Sterling gently interrupts. "Your prospectus really got my investors' attention."

Taking a deep breath, Phillip presses forward. "That's great. So, where do we begin? Need anything? Did Van make you comfortable?" Sterling nods his head. "You have the financials, key data points, and our projections. Sorry, I can't give you more details on our proprietary research. But I guess you appreciate that side of the business."

Sterling likes the man. And for him, that always makes the job easier. If you're going to steal a target's pet project from under their nose, it helps to have a soft spot for them.

The two men efficiently cover the expected ground. Sterling skillfully minimizes the potential risks to Neo-Vulcan while exaggerating the strategic and personal benefits to Phillip should he decide to cash out. Since both of their teams of lawyers have reviewed the agreement, there's no need to get too far into the weeds.

"So, do we have a deal, Philip? Or should I call you 'Mr. Vulcan' like everyone else?"

Philip laughs. "Philip's fine. Yep! We have a deal!"

The CEO walks to a tall, industrial liquor cabinet and pulls out a bottle of Balvenie Twenty-Five Rare Marriage scotch. He triggers his internal echo-bot and shouts, "Van, get in here. Time to celebrate!"

As he serves three generous pours of the amber liquid, Sterling says in all genuineness, "I *knew* I liked you."

Van soon dances in, makes a little twirl, and picks up the remaining glass, clinking it with Sterling's and then the CEO's.

"Meet my wife," Philip says. "Mrs. Vulcan herself." She snuggles up next to her husband while still eyeing their new partner like an amused kitten.

After the second round of drinks, Sterling excuses himself and tells the couple he has to get back to report in. They say their goodbyes—Van still sending pheromones his way, making him mildly envious of Mr. Vulcan.

Back in the rented Cadillac Escalade, he darkens the windows and initiates a HOLO. In a few seconds, a man's head floats in front of him.

"Hey, Smack. Bird's in the nest. Just wrapped things up here."

Smack smiles. "Atta boy, Skip! Feels like old times. I owe you one. By the way, let's get a crew together and go sailing. It's been too long."

"I'd like that," Sterling answers. "I'll set something up for you and the guys soon. By the way, go easy on the Bucannons. They're good people."

"Man, are you getting soft on me? I'll see what I can do. Later, mate!"

Lisbon, Portugal (63° F / 71° C)

Cautiously sitting in a corner due to his PTSD, Smack Daniels scans the small coffee shop in Lisbon through dark glasses. Reassured of his anonymity, he relaxes and carefully sips his steaming americano. His team of elite operatives all know to update him regularly as they execute scenarios similar to the one in Palo Alto. A yellow alert scrolls across the lower inside edge of his HOLO-LENS, eliciting a satisfied nod and a wry smile. *Four to two. I'll take it.* Four of the six startups have been neutralized in a similar, unsuspecting manner.

Unfortunately, the other two required a heavier hand. In one case, simple blackmail achieved the desired outcome. It's a tale as old as time. Mr. So-and-So didn't relish the idea of Mrs. So-and-So discovering his fondness for other Such-and-Suches, especially with a little So-and-So still at home in the nest.

Sadly, the CEO of the most developed operation became resistant to the point of belligerence, resulting in his unnecessary and untimely death. It wasn't the neatest takeover—failed brakes in the Rockies—but in the end, they got the job done.

He closes the spreadsheet, sends a brief HOLO-EM to Merton, and tells the man that the project's been completed—on schedule and under budget. *Now, how often does that happen?* After Merton's image dissolves, he raises the coffee mug and nods at his reflection in the window. *Cheers! Now, let's head home.*

Spring 2060

Kilkenny, Ireland (93° F / 34° C)

Noah and Shea straggle into the last class of the day. Janice says something indistinct from behind her designer mask as they enter the room. The school's air purification system is down again, forcing students with environmentally compromised diseases to wear nanofiber masks. The girls' harassers, true to form, sit in the back row and make crude animal noises as the two girls move toward the front. Gil, as usual, avoids eye contact by looking anywhere but in his sister's direction.

Their student teacher, Mr. Wilde, is standing in the front of the room with his back to the students, where he dictates an assignment on the HOLO-BOARD. Science is Noah's favorite subject, but having it at the end of the day dulls her interest. She slumps in her seat, eyes wandering as she waits for class to begin. They eventually come to rest on the young teacher. He's well over six feet and has a medium, well-proportioned build. Sitting up straight now, Noah half-smiles and admits to herself, *He's actually kind of cute. In a nerdy sort of way.* She's found herself looking forward to the weekly service days he's organized for the school's Sustainability Club, especially the ones when she's gotten to talk with him while picking up trash.

Shea elbows her and motions with her fingers to keep her eyes on the board, not his backside. Noah can't remember ever having feelings for any of her teachers before. *Well, I guess there was Mr. Plunkett in third grade—but that doesn't count!* She shakes her head and tells herself that she just needs a break after everything that's happened this last year.

The bell rings, and the chatter in the room trails off. Mr. Wilde turns and pans the class with his earnest, dark chocolate eyes. His wavy brown hair and boyish good looks make him look less like a teacher and more like a college student. As his eyes come to the front of the class, they rest on Noah briefly before he begins.

"We're coming to the end of our section on botany today. I realize that this has been a dull slog for most of you. Photosynthesis, pollination, stamens, seeds... all the living stuff that used to be so commonplace it was barely noticed. Until now. Because it's vanishing.

"I hope you better appreciate the fact that life on our planet rests on all the green stuff that surrounds us. As a teacher of mine once told me, 'Patrick, everything begins with plants and bugs.' The ecosystem that undergirds all of life builds from the ground up, right where we stand."

As Noah listens, she nods. Somehow, she knows these things—more than that, she *feels* them. *But the science helps reinforce the things I already know.*

"I want to end this section with a peek into what's happening *beneath* the soil's surface. Anyone want to guess what's down there besides worms and tree roots?"

"Dead bodies," someone mutters loud enough to be heard.

"Pirate booty!" another quips—the class snickers. Noah snaps her head around and stares at the gang—cheeks flushing. For some reason, she feels protective of Mr. Wilde, but he shakes it off easily.

"Good one," he banters back, unflustered—his mentor teacher, Ms. Maloney, snickers, observing from the corner. "There's probably a few of your dirty diapers buried there too, huh, Colin?" The boy's face darkens at the comeback.

"Ooh..." the class croons in unison. Mr. Wilde chuckles and then continues.

"I'm sure all that's there... but what's really interesting is the vastness of all the fungi down there. You think you know what fungus is, don't you? Slimy, moldy green stuff that smells like rotten tripe. Fungus has gotten a bad rap. What's down there is a true miracle of nature; a huge fungal network is underground."

A HOLO-VID of a vertical slice of a forest floor emerges in the front of the room.

"It's an expansive subterranean network... think HOLO-NET. It exists within the soil of forests and other plant communities. It's made up of an endless expanse of incredibly tiny threads that wrap around and even bore into tree roots. This living network connects individual plants, helping them transfer water, nitrogen, carbon, and other minerals. By some miracle of nature, plants and trees can sense disease or other threats, and then shift resources to protect or heal one another.

"Current research now shows us the trees, the plants, and the fungi all demonstrate a form of consciousness... an advanced capability like spatial recognition, memory, and even intelligence. But don't imagine human consciousness. Picture sentience without words... a truly organic form of intelligence."

Noah is glued to Mr. Wilde's words. Her heart speeds up—she *knows* all this—not with the terms he's using, or the science. She knows it because she's tapped into it before—she's *experienced* it.

Gone is her fatigue. She's fully awake now—her eyes are focused, her face serious—absorbed in what she's hearing. Something in her shifts into place. Like a giant puzzle, her whole life has felt like someone—or maybe *some thing*—has been carefully putting the pieces together inside her. She has no idea what exactly the pattern is, but it's there. She knows it. She's sensed it, she's felt it, even if she couldn't explain it.

"So, for your final assignment," Mr. Wilde continues, "I'm not going to have you write another paper or take another exam. All I want you to do is take a walk in the woods. That's it. Two hours... by yourself. Can you do that?"

The class exchanges puzzled looks with each other.

"When you find a spot you're drawn to, I just want you to sit down... put your back against a tree and just be there. Try to imagine what it's like to *be* that tree. Try to visualize what's happening under the soil, between the trees. Don't make things up—just open yourself up to the tree and see what happens."

Despite the cynical smirks and raised eyebrows from several students, Mr. Wilde keeps going.

"The other part of the assignment is... I want you to find a partner and tell each other what you experienced—what it was like for you. I'll have you report back on what they tell you next Friday. Any questions?"

"What if all we imagine is pirate booty for two hours?" Colin quips, and several around him nod and snicker.

"I know, I know... just do your best, class. I realize this is outside most of your comfort zones. All you have to do is try, and you'll get an automatic A. How's that sound?"

The class can sense the bell coming. Their chairs scrape. They noisily collect their books and rummage around the floor, slamming everything into their backpacks, ready to make their getaway.

"See you next week, everybody. Have a good weekend," Mr. Wilde shouts over the din of students making plans for Friday night.

Shea waits for Noah to stand up. But Noah's hand motion shoos her friend toward the door. Noah slips quietly to the front of the room where Mr. Wilde is putting books and papers into his blue sling pack. He looks up absentmindedly, a lock of brown hair falling into his eyes. Surprised to find her watching him, he startles slightly—then quickly recovers—returning her gaze.

"Oh! Hi, Noah. Didn't see you standing there." He pauses as if trying to remember something. "Hey, I really liked your last HOLO-POD. The one where you listed all the ways human warfare has accelerated the extinction of our vulnerable species. Another good reason for being a pacifist, eh?"

"Thanks," Noah responds, blushing slightly at the praise. "I still can't believe how many under-reported ecological tragedies there are."

"So true... and sad." He waits a beat and then asks, "So, got any big plans for the weekend?"

"Not really. Probably just hanging out with Shea. Maybe head out to the Nore up by Barnhill Woods. We like going up there, reading a bit, foraging, maybe do some swimming."

At the sound of her voice, he feels his hands quiver. *That's weird... hope I'm not coming down with something.* Trying to get a grip, he looks down and sees her golden-red hair reflected on the desk's glass top.

He hopes she doesn't notice the tremor. He doesn't feel nervous, but there's this strange vibration he's felt before. He looks up and sees her studying him. *Something about her presence puts off a kind of... energy. That's not exactly the word for it—a buzz. That's it.*

He shakes his head and realizes she's saying something to him.

"Mr. Wilde, I love the assignment. Everything you said today was brilliant. It rings so true to me... it sheds some light on the most beautiful moments of my life. I can't wait to see what happens when Shea and I do the assignment."

He smiles at her as he listens, flattered by her enthusiasm. "Now you have *me* intrigued, Noah. I'd love to hear more sometime. It sounds like you've had some pretty incredible experiences. Well, I've got to get going. Say hello to the river for me."

He walks—head down, lost in thought—out the door and across the parking lot. The buzz is still there when he finally sits down in his car. Not as intense, but lingering. He closes his eyes and slowly shakes his head. *I need to watch my step here.*

Laois County, Ireland (90° F / 32° C)

Noah and Shea finish packing the boot of her ma's Peugeot 404 hybrid, sweat already soaking through their thin T-shirts. She wishes they owned an EV, but they can't ever seem to afford all that their conscience prescribes. *It's so damn frustrating to be caught in such a broken system,* she thinks to herself—not for the first time.

The car's not much to look at, but it's been carting her family around for almost two decades. The girls' kayaks barely fit on top of the small car roof, but they manage to secure them to the rack after scraping what's left of the flaked blue paint from the hood of the old car.

Noah drives out of town, getting on the N77, and then eventually gets off the highway and takes a series of narrow side roads. After a few twists and turns, they pass the sign for Garrendenny Forest. When she enters the forest's shade, Noah rolls down the windows. A mild breeze plays across her skin—her shoulders relax—she takes a deep breath and savors the fresh, clean scent of pine and juniper.

Driving on an old logging road for half a mile, she soon spies the grass turn-off that looks like it hasn't been driven on for years. Driving under a long bank of low-slung ancient trees, they finally come to a clearing where a small berm hut sits. Noah marvels at the utter hiddenness of the place. *It would be impossible to find if you didn't know where to look.*

The girls get out of the car and stretch their cramped limbs. Shea heads into the woods to relieve herself, then returns to sit on the car's warm hood.

Noah walks toward the hut and calls out, "Da! You in there?"

A grizzled yet good-looking man in his forties steps out from the shadow of an open door. He's wearing homespun khaki shorts, sandals, and a well-worn carpenter's apron. As soon as he recognizes his visitor, his dark eyes burst wide with surprise.

"Well, look here! What good fortune pays a visit to this old man today? Look at ya'! This is the best thing that's happened to this old Greenling in a month. Let me get something to drink for you and yer friend Shea over there, too."

Noah nuzzles up to her da, who towers like a tree over her. He puts his burly arms around her and wheels her around, just like he did when she was little. She buries her face in his chest and takes in his scent. He smells like pine, peat, sweat, and leather.

She takes a step back, brushes her hair from her face, and looks into his eyes. The smile is there, like always—his joy at simply being alive, of living in a world surrounded by so much beauty and vitality. But she also senses the emotions he conceals—his sadness at not being with Ma and his unfulfilled desire to spend more time with her and Gil.

He sees her studying him, quickly lightening the mood with his thick brogue.

"What brings ya' by here on such a fine spring morning, my dear, lovely daughter?"

Noah blinks rapidly as she returns to the present moment. "Oh, not much, Da. Shea and I are on our way to camp for the weekend, and since I knew we'd be up this way, I just thought I'd drop in to say hi."

His crinkled eyes and broad smile feel like sunshine to his daughter. "Well, I'm glad ya' did, Noah. I haven't seen yer ma in a couple of weeks. I love the solitude up here, but I miss her enormously. You and yer brother, too. How's he getting along? He seems to never make time to come see me anymore."

"Oh, you know," Noah purses her lips—trying to decide how much to tell her da. "We seem to just get under each other's skin. He's been hanging out with Colin and his gang. He seems... umm... meaner, too. At least toward me. Honestly, I think I'm looking forward to when we don't live under the same roof. Pretty sure he feels the same way. Who knows, maybe it'll be easier then. We're just *so* different. With him, it's all cars and tech stuff. And me... well, you know me. I'd be content living out here like my da does."

Shea approaches the two, lingering as if waiting to be invited into the circle the father and daughter have drawn around each other.

Aiden notices her standing there and enthusiastically welcomes her. "Come on over, closer now, my dear Shea. Don't be so shy," Noah's da motions to three chairs on the porch, where they all sit down.

They spend several minutes catching up on Shea's folks and brother, school, the herb shop, and the weather. When the conversation lulls, Shea tentatively asks her friend's father what it's like to live out here in the woods by himself.

He looks at her, then takes a deep breath and then looks down at his rough, dirty hands.

"Shea, I love it here, but if I had a choice, I'd be in town with Noah and her ma and her brother. I tried that once, ya' know. Haven't I told ya' the story?"

"I don't think so, Mr. Greenling," Shea responds inquisitively. She glances at Noah, who knowingly smiles back—both having heard many tellings of what's to follow.

"Noah's ma's a Calhoun, ya' know. They come from good, choice stock. But me, there's something about my being in the Greenling's line... our DNA and all, that makes us a bit... well, odd. I don't know if there's anything to the tales my ma was told by her ma. But the story came down to me when

I was a wee lad—from God only knows how many generations—that we descended from the green children of Woolpit. Who knows if those little greenling buggers even existed?

He snickers, more to himself than the girls, and shakes his head. "Anyway... whatever the reason... when I'm in town or around human-made things for too long—things like cars or building materials, especially anything that runs on electricity—I break out in an awful rash. Then I start to have trouble breathing; I wheeze and cough until I almost pass out. Noah's ma made me get tested even though I told her it was no use. After being poked and prodded for all kinds of poisons and pollutants, nothing of use came back from any of it. It's a curse, to be sure." He pauses, and his dark, sad eyes rest on Noah. "But I've made my peace with it. I just hope I haven't passed it on to you, Noah. You're still alright, aren't ya', girl?"

Noah listens to the familiar story, reassuring him with a nod of her head. She's made her peace with it, too. It's normal to her and her ma now. But she's not so sure about Gil.

Da finally breaks the spell and abruptly gets out of the chair. "Noah, I almost forgot. I've got something for yer ma." He turns and heads to the door of the bermed hut. When he returns, he's holding several brown bags that appear soaked with water and soil.

"Can ya' take these back with ya'? I've found a few things for the shop. There's some comfrey root, meadowsweet, and a couple of small batches of vervain and water mint. Tell yer ma I wish there was more. I'm not sure what the problem is, but it's getting more challenging than ever to find some of these plants. Especially the ones she says have healing properties."

Noah reaches out and takes the bags. She smells the familiar scents she's grown up with, activating memories of her childhood. Down to Earth is like a second home to her. *I love hearing the stories from old-timers who come in and talk about the days when it seemed like nature's magic filled the area.* She remembers helping her ma dry and hang herbs, mixing them according to secret recipes and sealing them in apothecary jars. *It always makes me feel connected—to ma, to the community—even to the earth itself.*

She sees her dad watching her, a crooked smile on his face that makes her wonder if he can read her mind. "Da, we're going to have to get going. Sorry it's such a short visit. I'll come back soon. Shea and I want to set up our campsite before it gets dark."

"That's alright, dear one. It's always good to see ya'. Both of ya'. I'll walk ya' out to yer car."

They slowly stroll side by side. Noah hesitates after a few steps, uncertain about what she's about to ask. Her da stops and looks at her, raising an eyebrow in a question mark.

"Da." Noah takes a deep breath. "Graduation is coming up... and I know you probably won't be able to make it... I wouldn't want it to be bad for you or make you sick, but if there were any way you could come, it would mean so much to me. And I'm sure, to Gil, too. It will be outside if that helps. Think about it, please?"

The sadness returns, written on his crumpled brow. "I will, dear one. I will... and ya' know I'd be there if I could. We'll see. Goodbye, Shea. Keep an eye on Noah. Ya' know how she can be when she goes off the grid," he says, winking at her friend.

After the girls each get a warm, earthy hug, they get in the car and manage to turn around without getting stuck. Da waves at them as the old car creeps through the packed dirt. They slowly drive back through the thick, low branches, hearing the whisper of the limbs brushing over the kayaks. As they look behind them, it seems the forest has closed a giant green door, shutting the rest of the world out of her father's private paradise.

Tinnaslatty, Kilkenny County, Ireland (88° F / 31° C)

The foggy glen between the River Nore and River Barrow is shrouded in thick, early-morning grayness. The two tributaries and their companion, the River Suir, were named the Three Sisters by the ancients and revered by the Elizabethan poet, Edmund Spenser—*so flowing all from one, all one at last become.* The trio were the lifeblood of the forested lands, nourishing lush grazing grounds for the once-massive red deer. It was these majestic creatures that eventually gave rise to the original name of those who dwelt there: *Orgaige—People of the Deer.*

Within the late afternoon's misty fog, seated on the low, u-shaped branch of a large wych elm, a human-like form all but merges with the tree's greenery. The hair and face are covered in moss-colored leaves and branches. His legs are long and slender, swinging under him, his head cocked to one side—listening.

"Táimid ag faire, ag tacú, agus ag soláthar dár ndeartháir beag ón gcéad lá..." a rich, feminine voice intones. The vibration surrounds the Green Man. The source is invisible, but she is tangible in everything around him—his Mother and the Mother of all—Mother Earth.

"My son, you, above all others, know how we've been watching, how we've been supporting and providing for our little brother, ever since the first day he stood up on his scrawny little legs and took those first uncertain, unsteady steps. You were there as we cheered him on, as proud as parents. We've done this from the beginning – from *his* beginning in *our* garden." The voice releases a long exhale that sets the leaves to trembling. "Even when he forgot us, or became indifferent or self-serving toward us, we have been as patient as a mother raising a toddler through childhood into adolescence."

The Green Man's eyes glimmer in the shadows. Golden flecks seem to spiral in and out of the depths of his irises. He nods, a knowing half-smile within the tangle of vegetation surrounding his lips.

She patiently pauses as a doe, and her tiny fawn wanders into the clearing. As they graze, the Mother's tone becomes somber, her words full of frustration and grief.

"Our concerns began to mushroom during their so-called industrial revolution. At that inflection point, they found new and increasingly dangerous ways to break away from us—to wrestle control from us—to alter the careful balance we have guarded over so many millennia."

She sighs and continues, a slow fierceness building in her words' cadence. "Nature is generous, even sacrificial, you know... but we should never be viewed as *nice*. Nor are we inert and forever passive, accepting man's injustice or his dangerous human-centrism. They have forgotten.

We, too, can have fits of outrage. And we are not mere props in humanity's universe to be rearranged while he takes center stage... while he disregards all others in his grand performance."

Amid the swirling mist, a clearing blossoms, gradually expanding until it's slightly larger than a doorway. The Green Man peers into the opening's center, a puzzled twig playing on his brow. An image soon materializes. A young woman stands before him, her golden-red hair framing her lightly freckled face. The Green Man jumps down from the branch and stands face to face with the lifelike image shimmering through the opening. What he sees charms him as no human has before. Her green eyes glisten, moving back and forth between joy and sorrow. She's crying. Or is she laughing?

"Her name is Noah. What do you think of her?"

The words take shape deep within him—words from the Mother.

"She is my chosen one."

Barnhill Woods, Laois County, Ireland (92° F / 33° C)

Noah pulls the car off the road's tight shoulder to unload their kayaks and gear by the Tallyho bridge. Shea then jumps behind the wheel and drives to the other side, where there are a few spots to park in a small turnabout. She writes a note and puts it on the dashboard.

Camping for the weekend. Be back Sunday.

Back across the road, she joins Noah, who has tied on a green bandana covered with dancing frogs and is busy dragging their kayaks down the steep bank to the River Nore. The sky is partly cloudy, but the temperature still sets a record for this time of year. In silence, they both ready their dry bags in the boat's hatches. The river resembles pea soup, and is a full meter lower than just three years ago. They slip their boats into the water, barely making a ripple. Noah leans back and gazes straight up into the full, white clouds. It feels glorious to slice through the gently flowing water.

Both girls have taken off their camp collar shirts, and are now in shorts and sports bras—their matching pine marten tattoos glisten as the sweat on their forearms reflect the hot sun. Noah stops paddling and looks at her friend, pretending to straighten something at her feet. As Shea passes her, she doesn't notice the crooked grin on Noah's face. The next moment, Noah sprints up on the left side of Shea and splashes her with several paddle-fulls of river water. Shea squeals and almost tips over, trying to avoid the deluge that keeps coming. Noah stops, leans her head back, and laughs loudly at Shea and her black hair, now drenched and dripping. Shea flashes a mock scowl, then chuckles along. Noah makes an 'I love you' sign with her right hand. The girls grin at each other for a moment; then Shea puts her paddle in the water and races ahead.

They settle into the task of pressing forward and concentrate on their paddling. The wind has picked up, and they struggle forward, muscles beginning to feel the welcomed challenge. Near a gentle curve in the river, the girls duck their heads under several willow trees and slip into the hidden oxbow they discovered last year. Before the inlet curves back toward the river, they power their kayaks up into the dark, slick mud. On the bank, they help each other carry the boats up and then turn them over behind a large, fallen black alder, covering each one the best they can with leaves and dead limbs.

Once finished, they shoulder their packs and trek into the woods— boots now heavy with mud. They stumble across an abandoned game trail that seems to have been forgotten even by the foxes and hares. They follow it and, after hiking for another twenty minutes, step into a virgin clearing surrounded by a copse of scots pines.

They toss their packs to the ground and fall, exhausted, onto the soft pine needles. The scent is fresh, woody, and invigorating. It's been a long day. The tree's fragrance greets them like an invitation, like a host bidding her guest to rest. Yawning as they look at each other, they let the earth receive their shared fatigue, rolling over and resting their heads on their packs to take a quick nap before dinner.

When Shea wakes, the evening's shadows have already started to deepen. She has no idea how long they've been asleep, but time seems to have quietly ignored them as it strode by. Looking over at Noah—her friend's mouth gently forming rhythmic puffs that escape from full lips—Shea marvels at their deep bond, a connection she's unsure she could ever live without.

Finding a twig with soft pine needles, Shea tickles Noah's upper lip. Soon, Noah begins to stir, rubbing her nose and looking at her through half-opened eyes.

"Ummm. That was deee-licious," Noah purrs—sitting up and letting her spine slip into place, one vertebrae at a time. "It was like being rocked to sleep by these big pines." Noah reaches up and stretches as she yawns. "Did you feel it too, Shea?"

"I'm not sure about being rocked, but I definitely needed whatever it was." Shea looks up at the gentle movement of the needled branches, inhales deeply, and then closes her eyes, her face still pointed skyward. "It's so quiet, so private here. I feel like I could say anything or do anything and feel nothing but complete acceptance. No guilt. No shame. No fear." She inhales deeply, then sighs. "And you know, for *me* to say that, that's saying a lot."

Noah—flashing an expression of mock skepticism—stares at her friend, trying not to laugh. "Shea, you crack me up! You know one of the reasons I'm glad you're my friend? I can always count on *you* to feel guilty for me, even when I should, and I don't!"

Shea's expression clouds over. "I know... It's stupid, it's just—never mind."

Noah's smile softens, and her voice lowers. "Go on... say it."

Shea swallows and then exhales deeply. "I feel... different. Like *you* feel different, but yours is sort of... cool. Unique. Me? I'm just a plain Jane. Never had any real boyfriends or even girlfriends... other than you. No one really pays attention to me. Not even Ma or Da."

She looks down at her muddy sandals and shakes her head. "They're consumed with Donny... ever since his accident. I feel like I don't even exist most days. And when I do, it's because they're correcting me, or warning me to be careful with my brother or telling me to be quiet or... So I just sort of creep through our house on eggshells. I guess I do the same thing in life, too."

Noah pictures the day her friend ran up their driveway, wailing in grief and fear. Her brother, Donny, wasn't allowed to jump on a neighbor's trampoline. But that didn't stop him from trying a backflip when no one was looking. Shea—charged with watching her younger sibling while her parents were away—was inside taking a shower. The fall broke his neck and instantly severed his spine, paralyzing him for life. The thirteen-year-old has been bound to his wheelchair ever since.

Shea wipes a tear from her eye, smudging her face with a trace of dried mud. Noah tears up, too. Her gentle smile reveals a genuine sadness, a grief not just *for* her friend but *with* her. Compassion, more than pity. She moves beside Shea and tenderly puts her arm around her, not saying anything, but just sits there. Her presence conveys more reassurance than words ever could.

"Thanks, Noah. It feels good to say it out loud. I don't know what I'd do without you."

"I feel the same, friend. I'm here for you, and we'll get through it. I promise"

They lean on one another for several minutes.

Eventually, Noah breaks the mood's silence. "I'm hungry. How about you?"

"I guess I could eat something," Shea answers.

They root through their packs to find something to eat. Shea brings out some canned sardines, cheese, and crackers. They're not gourmet but they're her favorite staple when there's no heat to cook with. Noah fishes out a couple of squashed peanut butter and honey sandwiches and peels back the wax paper clinging to the sticky, slimy ends. She licks off the paper, wads it up, and puts it in a sack to carry out when they leave.

"Well, here we are, friend. And good timing, too, with Mr. Wilde giving us his wonderfully strange assignment," Noah says.

"Yeah, I know. Do you believe in coincidences? I mean, we planned this weeks ago. Meant to be, I guess." Shea raises her eyebrows and shrugs her shoulders.

Noah stares back, biting her lip as she nods. "Okay, I don't know about that, but here's what I think we should do. To get ourselves in the mood, why don't we pitch a camp apart from each other tonight? You choose the direction you'd like to go, and then I'll go the opposite way until we both find a spot that we feel drawn to. We can spend the night alone. Come back here in the morning for breakfast and tackle Mr. Wilde's assignment tomorrow. What do you think? You feel comfortable being out here by yourself?"

"It sounds a little weird, but why would that surprise me coming from you? I guess it feels pretty safe out here." Shea pauses, a serious look on her face. "Unless yer meanin'—them killer hedgehogs!" Noah wonders for a moment if she's serious. Then, the two girls look at each other and break up with laughter. After they quiet down, Shea makes a loud clap of her hands.

"Let's do it!"

The girls hug each other good night. Shea heads toward a slight rise that she sees in the east. Noah watches her friend push through the pines—wondering for a moment if splitting up was such a good idea—then picks up her pack to head west as the evening's shadows continue to thicken. The slope falls sharply into a ravine, forested with old growth and vines as thick as her legs.

At the bottom of her descent, Noah encounters a small stream that seems stuck. It's not exactly putrid, but it's not fresh either. *Hmm... not here.* She quickly crosses it, balancing on a flat rock, and follows its curving cut a quarter mile upstream. Just as she's pushing through a final knot of thick undergrowth, her feet suddenly skid out from her in mud. Frantically grabbing onto a sapling, she barely has time to stop herself before slipping feet-first into a small pool. On her side now—breathing heavily—she looks at the sandy hollow. Her cheek rests on the soft mound of carpeted moss—puzzled by the creek's water, now clear and clean. *That's it! Better stop right here and call it a day.*

She hangs her pack on a limb about six feet off the ground to keep it away from the hungry curiosity of foxes and stoats. Then she unrolls her small, lightweight sleeping bag next to the same tree and sits on top of it. The last rays of daylight seem to have been blown out like candles on a birthday cake, leaving a trail of curling wisps that dissolve into the twilight.

Time moves as if it, too, were blinded, adjusting to the state of not seeing. Alone and in the dark, Noah feels the complete detachment from anything human—gradually surrounded by the forest's proto-awakenings—its nocturnal citizens coming to life.

Sleep tempts an escape from the teeming, invisible life that surrounds her. At first, she resists the tug from her fatigue—not wanting to miss what weak, human eyes so rarely see. But soon, she gives up—crawls into the dark-blue sleeping bag. She waits and waits, and finally drifts off into what her da calls 'the arms of Morpheus.'

In the blackness of the woods, Noah enters a dream world. *Or is it?* she wonders as she watches the surreal scene unfold. Beneath the tree she's lying under, she sits up, hearing someone or *something* approaching. Turning toward the sound, she sees a silhouette walking out of the dark shadows. As it draws near, she spies an upright, human-like form. The moon melts over its face, and she sees a man. A green man, whose skin shifts with whorls of color—sage, emerald, fern, chartreuse, jade, apple—who keeps moving closer.

Noah's shadowed countenance reveals her initial alarm—ready to crash blindly through the forest. She forces herself to take a deep breath. She considers what she's witnessing. Her shimmering, green eyes widen with wonder and curiosity.

A crown of ivy and holly rests on his head. His wet, golden eyes lock onto hers. They seem generous and gentle. They stir in her a wave of compassion mixed with something else. Awe? Desire?

Her eyes travel down his bare trunk, over knotted arms to his hands, holding something—palms cupped together—extending toward her. She watches, mesmerized, as something that lies in his hands slowly uncoils, and then suddenly billows to unfurl, revealing it to be a waving green fabric. He quickly grabs a corner of it and gives it a sharp flick of the wrist. She gasps, like a child entranced by a practiced sleight of hand from a master illusionist.

A verdant gown magically unfurls. Looking at it closely, Noah can see it's made of small quilt-like patterns—delicate patches of moss interwoven with wisps of heather pressed into a graceful design of living fabric. Their eyes lock on to one another, briefly, as they both appraise each other. A mischievous smile suddenly takes shape on the man's handsome green face. He then motions to her. *Rise up.* As she does, he carefully drapes the quivering garment around her. A shiver runs through her as she senses the confinement of her clothes somehow magically absorbed into the gown's soft lining. She overlaps the fabric's opening around her, watching him as he draws nearer and gently sets a circlet of lavender and shamrocks on top of her head.

Having clothed her, he leans down and softly kisses her on both cheeks. She shrinks slightly in retreat, uncertain what to do or what will come next. The man also steps back and shapeshifts, transforming into a two-meter-tall sequoia. He slowly grows, shooting higher and higher up through the canopy of trees surrounding her.

As he expands beyond reach, she senses a gentle movement near her. She looks down and quietly giggles. Up from the dark earth beneath her, tiny, thread-like filaments of mycelium weave their way up and around her arms and legs, then onto her torso and up to her neck, pulling her to the ground. The movement, though gentle, tickles her as it wends around her.

Suddenly, the circlet of lavender and shamrocks floats from her head into her lap. It, too, has sprouted mycelium-sized rootlets. She cautiously picks it up and places it back on her head. As she does, she gradually feels the same vibration she's often felt. But this time, it's different. The vibration somehow reaches down into her ear canals. It's as if a million vegetal voices whisper in unison. A slippery, verdant chorus—now inside her.

"It's you who is chosen. Yes. You! You, Noah. We've been waiting, always waiting. And we will keep waiting until you are ready. Until you are ready to face all that is to come."

Who knows how dream-like visions end or why? Noah drifts back into the cradling arms of the earth beneath her. She dozes comfortably for the rest of the night, moving back and forth between deep sleep and a drowsy consciousness. When awake, part of her wonders if it was all just a dream or whether it was something even *more than real*—a reality beyond any she's known before.

The flute-like bird trills are the first thing Noah hears the following morning. Eyes still shut tight, she smells the damp dew on the moss and earth surrounding her. Unzipping her sleeping bag, she slides out to sit up, and as she does, she blinks away the sleep and looks around. Filtered morning light gently bathes the scene around her. She vividly recalls last night's dream. As she remembers it, she notices a shift in her chest, but can't yet name what's different.

Her eyes drift to the ground, and a circlet of lavender and shamrocks is lying next to her. *That's strange. I don't think that was there last night when I went to bed. Was it?* She bites her bottom lip as she shakes her head. *The whole thing's about as mad as a box of frogs—a green man, moss capes, giant sequoia. And those voices—still stuck in my head!*

She gently picks up the circlet and carefully slips it into her pack, still wondering if she just made the whole thing up. *How in the world am I supposed to unravel what's real from what's a dream?*

Noah sweeps the pine branches out of her way and ducks into the clearing—
her friend is already there, seated on the ground, arranging her gear.

"Hey, Shea—Morning. You're an early bird. How'd you sleep?"

"Morning, Noah. Well, I didn't end up as bear food, if that's what you're
asking."

Noah drops down next to Shea and reaches out to pull a small twig out
from Shea's dark tangles. The girls catch up for a few moments. Noah says
nothing about her dream, unsure if she's ready to revisit it in the day's new
light. Or with Shea.

They decide to head out and forage for breakfast. Meandering through
the woods for the next hour, they come across a hazelnut tree and load up
their rucksacks with several handfuls of small, green nuts. Although alone,
Noah has a strange sense that they are being watched and supported—
guided by birds and small paths that appear out of nowhere. Along the way,
they find wild strawberries, bilberries, and raspberries—more than enough
to round out their modest meal.

Back at the thicket of pines, they squat down and spread their meal on a
large yellow-and-blue napkin Noah's ma made for her. Noah looks up to the
sky and takes a long, deep breath. She's not an overtly religious person—nor
a praying one. But at this moment, her sense of gratitude overwhelms any
inhibitions she might have felt up to this point.

"You know, I feel like we should... umm... give thanks for the earth's
goodness to us. I'm not sure if we should thank whatever Mystery made it
all or just the earth and its kindness toward us."

The two girls hold each other's gaze for a moment. Shea then shrugs
and looks around. "Noah, what's it matter *who* or *what* we give thanks to.
I'm sitting here with you. And in spite of how simple the food is, I couldn't
be more content. And yes—*grateful.*"

Noah mirrors Shea's earnest smile. "Good. I'm glad you feel it, too. Well,
here goes."

Looking skyward, they take hold of each other's sweaty hands as Noah searches for words that match what's in her heart.

"Shea and I just want to say, *thank you*. We feel at home here. We feel protected and nurtured here. And we feel... delight... and appreciation for everything you've done for us this morning. We hope you have a good day and that we bless you in some way like you've blessed us."

The girls sit in silence, still holding hands. A quiver ripples in the atmosphere around them—the woods somehow seem delighted, too. *I think it's showing us its joy—that we're here—that we recognize it and don't take it for granted.*

৯৯ ৳৶ ৯৯ ৳৶ ৯৯ ৳৶

Noah lets go of Shea's hand and jumps to her feet.

"Hey—I've got an idea! Before we tackle Mr. Wilde's assignment, how about heading back to the river to cool off?"

Shea gives a nod, and the girls hang their packs in a tree and retrace their way back to the bank where they landed their kayaks yesterday evening.

"Shea, remember when we went skinny-dipping at Lough Cullen? I know we just did it as a lark. But today, I just feel like I want to be touched by everything—held by the water—nothing coming between me and good old Mother Earth."

Shea looks at Noah and giggles, a coy smile forming on her smudged face. "I kinda know what you mean."

Noah jumps up and takes off her clothes—shedding yet another layer of the human species' self-consciousness. Standing naked now, she suddenly feels alive—so close to the life surrounding her.

Shea regards her friend, envious of her freedom, and slowly follows Noah's lead, unleashing what's left of her dogging inhibitions. For a moment, she feels the familiar snarl of guilt and shame that always snaps at her when she thinks about breaking out of the mold. But she just lets it be. The shame-filled yelping soon quiets—paces around like a junkyard dog—

and eventually flops down and goes to sleep.

In the water, Shea lets herself float—she leans back, her dark hair drifting around her upturned face. Her exposed skin feels the gentle river's flowing playfulness—the sun's radiant caress. And then something deep within her dissolves. *Or is it being washed away?* She wonders. *Or purged? Who knows? Who cares?*

An innocent smile blooms on her wet, young face, and she begins to weep silently. But now, the tears are not ones of pain or sorrow. They are tears of relief, of joy, of freedom.

❧ ❧ ❧ ❧ ❧ ❧

Heading back to their encampment, they decide to split up for their class's science assignment. Shea, her dark hair still wet and shining, again heads east. Noah smiles and tilts her head as she watches her friend stride away without looking back. *Shea seems... different. More self-assured.* After Shea disappears, Noah turns and follows the descent of the previous evening to the west.

Slowing down, she begins to pay attention, not only to what she passes, but how she reacts to each sapling, each limb, each tree's trunk. It's as if she floats down the ravine, not walking, but swept along by an invisible current. Mr. Wilde's words come back to her. *Find a tree you seem drawn to.*

When she reaches the first small pool—its contents yesterday, dark and swampy—she notices that now, its water is clear and gently flowing. *That's odd. It didn't rain last night.*

She finds herself curious about what might be downstream. So she lets her wondering pull her along. After several bends in the creek bed, she's halted by an ancient wych elm that has somehow grown over the stream. Its trunk is split a meter above the flowing water—its roots shooting off from either bank. The place arrests her, pinning her feet, stilling her breathing. *Is this what being 'drawn to' feels like?*

She circles the dark, fissured trunk, gazing up at the tree's massive crown, then jumps across the creek to look for a spot to sit. There's a curved arch where two roots—each about her size—separate, and between them lay a rich carpet of olive-colored moss with tiny flowers. She sits down gently, not wanting to disturb the site any more than she has to. The combined scents of fresh water, damp humus, and florid greenery flood through her like a forgotten memory.

Noah's rich red hair glows, reflecting the dappled sunlight. She turns her head slowly from side to side and then up and down, locating herself in the present moment. Here. Now. And gradually begins to acclimate to her surroundings. She takes a deep breath, remembering her teacher's instructions. *Be present with the tree. Don't try to make anything up. Just be curious about what it's like to be this particular tree.*

She leans further back into the tree's archway, her gaze softening, and quietly whispers,

"Who are you?"

Pause. Silence.

"And how are you?"

Pause. Silence.

"What's it like to be you?"

Pause. Silence.

Then, she waits. Patient as a tree waiting for the next rainfall—desperate for water, but not in control of if or when it will come.

While she waits, her shirt and shorts absorb the sweltering heat and humidity. The pores of her skin respond in kind and radiate small trickles of sweat. As she loosens her collar, she catches a whiff of her own human scent. Her sweat, for some reason, reminds her of the earthy smell of her da's hut.

She drifts farther and farther away from herself—or is it farther *into* herself? In this trance-like space, she sees herself suspended between two worlds: one, a mercurial world of red-blooded creatures like hers and her humankind, and the other, a Venusian paradise of endless green rootings and spireings, the entire planet filled with verdant possibilities.

The widening breach in her heart finally breaks open, hanging between what appear to be two kingdoms. She feels divided, torn—as if somehow she's being asked to choose one or the other. Or maybe one to be *subservient* to the other.

"I can't choose." Noah refuses, then declares. "Or if I must—I choose both!"

The pull from the differing directions relaxes, releasing her from the tension's hold. Still held between two worlds, though gently now, she looks down. Her feet appear to have become two roots, burrowing into the soft, dark soil. Her arms solidify, slowly lifting up toward the sky. Human limbs have become bark-like, beautiful as a beech tree's smooth, gray skin.

She considers for a moment whether she should be frightened. *Of what?* she wonders. She feels at home, at peace in this new, more solid state that has overtaken her.

Then she hears an ancient chorus vibrating her leaves, soaking into her soul.

"We're coming for you, Noah. We're coming. Because we need you... just like you need us. But be patient... for it's not time yet. Soon, though, Noah. Very soon."

Noah gradually returns to her senses, her human senses. *Time for what?* she wonders as she blinks away the vision. Or whatever it was. She then looks down and examines her arms and her feet. They're flesh again—human flesh.

She sees a trio of tender shamrocks springing free from the damp, green moss beside her legs. *Were those there when I sat down?* She can't remember but doesn't think so.

She reaches down and softly touches one of the three-lobed leaves. The now-familiar vibration courses through her, but it's more potent this time. When she looks down, the leaves seem to weep, clear droplets forming on top of them. She lets out a small gasp, and as she does, a shower of the tree's pale cream and magenta seed petals swirls through the air, dancing in the streaming light and blanketing her and the ground around her.

On the drive home, the girls easily vacillate between long stretches of silence interrupted by giggles and light-hearted chatter. Their sidelong glances at one another convey an agreement—they aren't yet ready to talk about what happened back in the woods.

After Shea merges onto the N77, she turns up the volume of some Irish prog-rock band on the HOLO-SOUND. The soaring guitar, flute, bodhran, and fiddle blend naturally with the singers' soulful voices.

As they approach the town's outskirts, they decide to stop off at the Hole in the Wall on High Street. The pub is housed in the oldest surviving townhouse in Ireland—the 1582 Archer Inner House.

Sitting outside in the patio's corner, they're surrounded by high, rough stones that guard the empty courtyard. They kick off their boots and sip their drinks in silence for several minutes until Shea breaks the spell.

"Well, want to flip a coin to see who goes first?" Her eyebrows rise, detecting her friend's hesitancy.

Noah shifts uncomfortably, cradling her drink, head down. Still feeling uncertain, she nods toward Shea, inviting her to start.

"I'm not sure I have much to say, but okay—I'll go. I found a small hill in the woods... it was sunnier than the rest of the woods, and I sat under a black alder. I guess my main feeling was... I don't know... peace, I think. But the longer I sat there, the more I started to feel something else... sort of anxious... and flustered, I guess.

"I tried to push the feeling away and asked the tree something like, 'How are you feeling today?' For a long time, I didn't sense anything. I wasn't surprised... I didn't really expect much to happen anyway. But then, a new feeling, or maybe an image, drifted into my mind. All of the trees, not just this one, seemed tired of being ignored... devalued. Like they have so much more they'd like to share with us, but all we want is their wood or their fruit. I wonder... I don't know... I'm probably making all this up, but it hit me that they have some kind of ancient wisdom they want to give us. But instead we just keep looking past them, not seeing... or I guess... not *knowing* them as actual, living beings."

Shea's shoulders sag as her head drops, revealing a sudden lapse of self-confidence. *How crazy does that sound?* She's seen firsthand how Noah's been ridiculed for talking about these kinds of experiences—even though she knows her friend would never dishonor her in that way. She studies Noah for a moment, who's been leaning forward the whole time she's been talking.

"Wow! That's incredible, Shea. Can you believe it?" Noah's green eyes expand until the entire iris is visible. "You actually heard something. You heard *them*. All of them! So... did you ask them about the wisdom they have for us?"

Shea's face brightens with surprise. *I did hear something!* But then her eyes quickly fall to the ground in disappointment. Disappointed in *herself*.

"No, I didn't. Damn it! I was so amazed by what they were saying... that they were saying *anything*, I just kind of... went blank. And stopped interacting. You know how I can be. Just fade into the background. I'm sorry, Noah."

Noah looks at Shea with earnest understanding as she reaches out and puts a strand of dark hair behind her friend's ear.

"Why are you apologizing to me? Believe me. I get it. It kind of overwhelms your whole sense of what's real, like... I don't know... like a whole other dimension opens up."

After a few moments of savoring Shea's experience, Noah launches into her story. She starts with the dream of the green man on Friday night, leaving out none of the strange details. Then, she goes on to describe the startling messages she heard while she was sitting under the wych elm in the morning.

As she's talking, Noah looks up over Shea's head and sees a jay sitting on the wall, its head cocked toward her. There's something odd about it. Its face is completely white, and its intelligent eyes look as if it understands what's being said. She shakes her head and returns her attention to Shea.

When she finishes, the two sit in silence again, holding hands. They want to fully appreciate what's happened to each other and not break the spell. After a while, Noah notices her friend's perplexed expression and grins.

"Come on, silly, finish your drink before it gets warm! We told our mums we'd be back for dinner."

The girls say goodbye to the barista and then head toward home. Unnoticed by them, the jay from the courtyard flies above the car, easily keeping up, until it veers off and lands on the rough branch of the wych elm outside Noah's bedroom window—its white head cocked to one side. Watching. Waiting.

⚓⚓⚓⚓⚓⚓

Noah parks the car next to the small detached garage behind the house. She sees Gil inside the open garage door with his head under the hood of a rust-covered Range Rover. Where he got the money to buy it, she can't imagine. More than that, where does he find the *patience* to keep working on it?

Noah scrapes her feet on the driveway, trying not to startle him. "Hey, Gil. What're you up to? Still can't get that piece of junk to run?"

"Oh, just stuff it! You and I both know that you wouldn't even know how to put staples back in a stapler." He lets a long breath out through pursed lips, wiping his greasy hands on a rag. "For *your information*, I'm replacing the gaskets on the water pump. After that, she should be ready to fire up for a test run."

Ma hears them talking and sticks her head out the back door.

"Dinner's about on the table, you two. Noah, you come in and set the table. Gil, you're filthy. Wash up out back, and then go change your clothes."

The two teenagers exchange mock frowny faces—even though they can't stand each other, when Ma orders them around, they suddenly find themselves on the same side again.

Noah runs up the stairs two at a time to brush her hair and put on some deodorant. *Dang. I forgot to take my boots off. Ma will slay me if I brought mud in.* Looking behind her, she doesn't see any incriminating evidence. When she goes into her room, she looks around and takes in her various collections. There are several small terrariums, a microscope on her desk, and a pair of binoculars hanging from the bedpost. Framed posters of mushrooms and an antique map of the earth's magnetic fields hang over a bookshelf with titles like *The Forager's Guide to Wild Foods* and *Neurotransmitting in Plant Signaling and Communication.*

As much as she loves her room and the way it makes her feel at home, her trip this weekend has made it seem smaller, too insulated. *Where's the mystery? I feel safe here, but also... imprisoned. I wonder... is this what Da feels when he leaves the forest?*

She starts to unpack her clothes and the trash she brought back, and finds the circlet of lavender and shamrocks on top. Carefully removing it, she turns it slowly around in her hands, drinking in the woodsy sweetness before putting it on the shelf. As she does, she turns her head and notices a jay out her window. *That's weird—it has the same white face as the one at the pub earlier.*

The following week drags on as the girls anxiously look forward to sharing their experience in the woods for Mr. Wilde's science class. The night before the presentations, the air is muggy as Shea steers her bike to Noah's. Fireflies speckle the yard as the two friends walk side by side along the driveway. They sit on the damp grass behind the garage, where no one will be able to listen while they rehearse one another's stories for tomorrow.

Shea wants to be clear on what Noah wants her to say tomorrow—since the assignment is to tell each other's account—and more importantly, what she *doesn't* want her to say.

"I'm not sure, Shea. What do you think? Part of me thinks you should just let it fly. Blurt the whole weird thing out for everyone to make fun of. A lot of them have already written me off as a freak from another planet anyways."

She's holding the circlet and turning it around as she thinks. "But... I don't know. I don't want to put you in the middle of anything, either. I know you'd do it if I asked you to. But it seems... personal. Private. Like it's just for me. And for you, too, of course." Noah looks directly at her friend, who holds her gaze. "I'd lose my mind, Shea, if I couldn't tell you my secrets. All of them."

Shea puts her hand on Noah's arm, her eyes communicating her devotion. "Noah, I'm up for saying whatever you want me to. And don't worry about what they might think of me. I just don't want you to get hurt any more than you have been."

Noah shakes her head, staring at the flashing yellow pinpricks in the night's blackness. "I know... believe me. I know *too* well. Thanks, friend. Feel free to say whatever you want. Just leave out... oh, never mind. I trust you... and your judgment. Okay?"

"Alright... if you're sure," Shea says, the tilt of her head still conveying uncertainty. Finished, they stand and hug each other, both unaware that Gil has snuck out of the house and crept to the other side of the garage to spy on them.

He shakes his head, a misshapen grin twisting his thin lips. Hearing his sister describe this scene—a green man, a mossy gown, a living crown— triggers in him a shotgun of emotions. Disgust. Jealousy. Agitation. Arousal. All these swirl together in his overactive, adolescent brain.

Noticing that he's been holding his breath, he exhales dramatically. *Finally... even Ma will have to agree... she's gone too far this time.*

❦❦❦❦❦❦

Mr. Wilde stands in front of the class, his beard's rough stubble disguising the fact that he's only twenty years old. His brown eyes scan the students' faces for a few moments before he speaks.

"Well, it's Friday. Last class at the end of the week. Are you all ready to complete the assignment I gave you and present your reports? Who will go first?"

Any noise suddenly stops. No one moves a muscle or dares to look up, refusing to even glance in the teacher's direction. After several moments of awkward silence, Noah slips her hand up and volunteers to go. She walks to the front of the room, smooths her scattered hair from her face, and then describes in rich detail what Shea shared with her. It's an accurate, though slightly embellished account that she hopes both honors and protects her friend's image with their classmates.

As she sits down, Shea anxiously stirs and offers to go next. Opting to stand next to her desk, she begins, eyes moving back and forth between Noah and the floor. In a quiet voice that makes the telling all the more mysterious, Shea weaves a beautiful account filled with imagery that makes the class feel like they are there. She is just wrapping up and—enjoying the attention more than she usually would—gets carried away by her story's climax.

"And then, if you can believe it, a green man takes her clothes and exchanges them with this amazing living gown..." Murmurs begin to ripple around her. She presses on, oblivious. "So, there and then he places a beautiful circlet of lavender and shamrocks on her head, leans in... and kisses her."

The spell is quickly broken. Shea, confused for a moment, soon realizes what's causing the hubbub—she's said too much. Mortified, she turns to her friend and mouths, *"I'm so sorry."*

Colin doesn't miss a beat and snipes, just quiet enough so the teacher can't hear, "I didn't know we were supposed to take magic mushrooms, or I would've taken it more seriously!" Others quickly launch in on the two girls.

"Man, what a pair of lesbo psychos," Keelin mutters.

"Noah, you're totally batshit crazy, you know that?" someone else whispers.

Colin leans over to Gil. "Thanks for the heads up, bro. I hope one of ya' spanners recorded that on your HOLO," he says, looking at those around him. Gannon nods as he lifts his HOLO in the air.

Shea sinks into her chair—shocked—feeling like someone's knocked the wind out of her—totally deflated for betraying her friend's trust. *How will I ever face Noah? How can I even face myself?*

Noah sits, staring blankly into space, an overwhelming sadness imprinted on her face, pressing her shoulders and head onto the desk. *I'm just sick and tired of it all—tired of this school—tired of these kids.*

She's never felt more isolated from her peers. But she's also aware of a growing despair that seems to stem from everything she's experienced—the messages from the trees and her dreams, the impact of what she's tried unsuccessfully to communicate, and the intractable ignorance of those who used to be friends.

Mr. Wilde's eyes sharpen their aim. His stern voice attempts to regain control of the class. "Quiet down, people! That's enough!" Frustrated with the snarky group huddled around Colin, he presses on. "We still have the rest of your presentations to get through. Now, if you can bring your attention back up here, who wants to go next? Do you *really* want me to start calling on someone?"

That night, Patrick Wilde sits alone on his small flat's shabby, green-and-gold sofa. His wavy hair is carelessly tousled, mirroring his tangled-up mood. He pours a second glass of Bunratty Mead. It's an acquired taste after growing up in South America, where his young palette was formed by the intense complexity of Argentinian Malbecs from the Mendoza region. The simple mead, however, is a straightforward drink that doesn't distract him from his spinning thoughts tonight.

"What a day!" he grouses to no one as he arches his back—a futile attempt to straighten out what seems coiled inside after the episode in class earlier. *Sending that damned bully and his mates to the headmaster's office will do about as much good as flunking the lot of them. Nothing.*

As he gradually moves beyond the drama that took place, he begins to ponder what he heard from the girls. He was so hacked off by the gang's cruelty that he missed the beauty and wonder of the things the girls had experienced.

Something about what Noah told Shea makes me wonder—what do we really know about interspecies communication—especially between plants and humans? Still mulling over the question, he remembers a study he'd read once that examined how plants and trees communicate. Opening his HOLO, he hunts for it.

What was the title of the article? It used phrases like 'vegetal intelligence'... 'organic will'... 'mutual generosity.' It takes him several minutes until the title comes to mind. *Here it is! "Plant Bioacoustics."*

A number of credible sources in the academic report provide well-documented findings of plants creating ultrasonic waves. As he continues reading, he's astounded by the mysteries science is just beginning to grapple with—how the latest research illuminates just how complex these common life forms are. The material on the vibrational aptitude of plants is especially intriguing to him.

He pauses, looking out the small window at a holly bush. *Did Noah and Shea pick up on these vibrations?* Growing up in the Amazon, he knows firsthand that if someone attunes to nature through imagination and openness, they may experience something like a mystical encounter.

That's why he gave the assignment: to help shift his students' perception of the world from the left to the right hemisphere of their brains. He believes that did indeed happen to some. But Noah and Shea experienced something different, something tangible. Something *interpersonal.*

Pouring a refill of the honey-colored mead, he continues his investigation. He comes across many unconventional researchers and pioneers—scientists whose botanical experiments convincingly demonstrate a world-altering view of the nature of life on this planet.

Eventually, he comes across a HOLO-VID interview with a white-headed Dorothy MacLean, one of the three founders of the Findhorn Monastic Community. Patrick's gaze turns inward—a panged expression drifts across his face. He's heard of Findhorn, but because of its painful association with his past, he's chosen to ignore it.

Shaking himself free of old ghosts, he brings his attention back to his HOLO. In the grainy interview from 1978, he listens as this small, unassuming woman describes her earliest encounters with the sentience of plants.

"My first contact arose from my attempt at my own inner attunement. It all seemed like a very silly idea, but I went ahead and chose a vegetable. You see, we were trying to grow a garden, and we didn't know anything and desperately needed help. You see, you can only attune to something you are somewhat familiar with. So, I chose the pea plant. I knew all about it—its taste, shape and color, what it was for, and so on. I loved it.

"Eventually, I tried to imagine what the essence of this plant was. To my surprise, I got an answer—an intelligent response. It just said it was going about its business when I came straight into its awareness. It then went on and said it wished that other human beings would do the same and realize that we could work together. That was it. And in that first contact, I got the whole essence of the spiritual nature of all things."

Patrick looks up from the HOLO. He runs his finger slowly over the rim of his glass and sips his lukewarm drink—letting her words sink in. *She seems pretty batty to me. Correction. She's way off the map. And yet... science now seems to be headed in a similar direction as the old woman. Is it possible that science is just playing catch up to what these nature-mystics already know?*

His mind drifts to Noah. *Could she share some capacity similar to this woman's?* Her sensitivity and assuredness seem to go way beyond her years or training. He leans back and closes his eyes while his thoughts linger on her for a while. He imagines her in the woods. The scene plays before him—her being embraced by the ground's richness, a shared vibration passing between them—like he's felt from her.

Patrick is aware that he's nursing a complicated ache. Visions like this aren't something new—the familiar longing to experience a vibrant connection with *something*... with *someone* who will complete him.

He releases a long, low exhale—the empty glass teetering on the edge of the coffee table—uncertain what to do with all the feelings pulsing through him. After unlinking his HOLO, he turns off the lights and sits in the dark, wondering. As he replays Shea and Noah's words, he can't help but think there's something more. *More than what? More for who?*

Unable to come up with an answer—his eyes too heavy to resist—he curls up on the sofa, where he drifts into sleep's welcome pause from this long, strange day.

Rising earlier than he needs to—the sofa too short to really stretch out on—Patrick shuffles into the kitchen and makes a cup of strong, black, Kenyan coffee. After the second cup, the caffeine starts to kick in. Almost awake now, he grabs his binoculars and wide-brimmed safari hat and heads out for Kilmacoliver Loop to birdwatch and clear his head. There's something about the throaty bird songs on a misty morning that helps him lose himself. And then, somehow, he winds up finding himself again.

As he walks, he chooses to listen to the surrounding birds' sounds rather than make an effort to look for them. The sun is just starting to burn off the morning's haze as he turns and then strolls along the faint hint of a game trail. There's a piping call that keeps pace with him. A jay finally hops down on a branch next to him and gives him a curious look—as if questioning why he's here instead of somewhere else.

For some reason, he starts to think about Noah again, gradually admitting what he's tried to deny—he's starting to feel some kind of pull toward her. *Whoa... really? A student?* He shakes his head and then chuckles, remembering his former girlfriends and how things always seemed to end. At some point, they would tell him he's either too serious, or too intense, or too preoccupied with anything that didn't put them squarely in the center!

This is crazy, he chides himself. Shaking his head, he keeps walking toward a sign pointing in the direction of the trailhead. When he gets back to the car, he gets behind the guidance screen and struggles with what to do. He instructs the car to switch on, then quickly tells it to turn off. He abruptly generates a HOLO and then shuts it. A long sigh passes over his lips—his hands rubbing the stubble on his chin. He hesitates another moment, then quickly launches his HOLO and calls up the class roster. There's Noah's picture and contact info. He chooses the messaging icon and hesitates.

His voice falters, but instantly, his words are transcribed into a message.

> Hey Noah, it's Patrick.

He deletes it and starts over.

> Hi, Noah, it's Mr. Wilde. Just checking in to make sure you're okay.

Send.

He closes the HOLO, wondering what in the world he's thinking. Or, more accurately, what he's *not* thinking. A few seconds later, his HOLO chimes.

> Hey, Mr. Wilde. Thanks! I'm fine. How are you?

His heart rate picks up its pace.

> Doing okay. Yesterday's class was pretty rough on you. Wanted you to know that I thought your and Shea's presentations were great. Would love to hear more sometime.

Waiting.

> Thanks! It was pretty amazing, and it made me think about my life and where I'm headed after school.

"Okay," he mutters, remembering what his Uncle Seamus would always say. *'In for a penny, in for a pound!'*

> Hey, I'm headed over to the Hole in the Wall. If you're not doing anything, want to join me and tell me more? If you're free.

Man, that sounds lame, he tells himself. He waits—she seems to be thinking about it. Finally, the HOLO-EM pops up.

> Sounds fun. I can be there in thirty minutes.

He lets out a long breath and replies with his signature icon—a jaybird flashing a winged thumbs-up.

❦⁊❦⁊❦⁊

Patrick, still wearing his hat and safari vest, is waiting in the courtyard, hands cupping his mug, when Noah arrives. He can't help but notice her youthful, natural beauty—walking toward him in cutoff jean shorts and a paisley halter top. She smiles as she pulls out a chair and sits across from him.

"Hi, Mr. Wilde. Isn't this place grand? I mean... in a charming, broken-down kinda way."

He chuckles. "Yeah! That it is. Good to see you, Noah. Thanks for joining me. Want something to drink? My treat."

"Well... the Irish coffee's pretty good. Is that what you're drinking?"

"Umm... Yep. Let me get you one." Patrick offers, still wavering—uncertain whether she's even old enough to drink legally.

A few minutes later, he returns with her drink—a faint trace of patchouli in the light breeze registers as he approaches. Noah is looking up at the tree behind the wall. The sun casts swaying dapples of warm light on her face and skin, her hair a loose twist of shining, gold-and-red curls. Watching her, he feels that same mild vibration again, causing his heart to accelerate slightly.

"Thank you," she says, turning her dimpled face toward him and taking the mug from his hands.

"Penny for your thoughts. What were you thinking about just then?" he asks, still trying to recover his composure. Noah takes a careful sip of the hot drink, then searches his deep brown eyes.

"You'll probably think I'm being childish or making it up, but I was looking for something. When Shea and I were here the other day, a jay was in that holly tree," she says, her raised eyebrows and nose pointing up over the wall. "Later, when I got home, I went up to my room, and a jay with the same markings was sitting on a limb outside the window. I was... I don't know... it sounds silly to say it. I was wondering if maybe it would show up again. Like a sign or something."

Patrick nods, his smile reassuring. For some reason, though, he chooses not to tell her about his own encounter with a jay that morning.

"I don't think that sounds so far-fetched, Noah. If we're open to it, birds carry all kinds of meanings for us. Just last week, I was hiking and spotted a white-tailed eagle in a tree branch above me on the trail.

"The white-tails disappeared in Ireland about a hundred years ago. They were hunted and poisoned... persecuted into extinction, really. Then, a group of conservationists imported a few dozen from Norway and released them into Killarney National Park. And now... it's really quite impressive. Now, they've taken root and are starting to thrive again.

"I've only seen two or three before, but when I do... I sense my life is about to shift. At least that's what it means to me... kind of like when an eagle finds lift from the rising and falling air currents."

He pauses and offers an embarrassed grin, realizing he's gotten lost in his own explanation. "Now I'm the one who sounds featherbrained. *Pun intended!*"

Looking up, he catches Noah studying him. Her green eyes searching, probing, as if she were able to peer into his soul.

"Oh no, that's a lovely story," she says. "It sounds like... like something I'd say. Thanks for telling it to me, Mr. Wilde," she says, her voice soft and halting. He clears his throat as he prepares to ask for something.

"Noah, would you mind calling me Patrick? It just seems so... formal. Mr. Wilde makes me feel like you're talking to my da." There's a pause as he looks at her, his eyes revealing both his uncertainty and hopefulness. "We're really... not that far apart age-wise, you know... I'm twenty. What are you? Seventeen... eighteen?"

"I turned eighteen a week after Earther's Lament Day, on October 29th."

"Well, see... there are just a few years difference. I feel like we could be good friends if this whole teacher-student thing weren't there, watching us like some blundering football ref."

Noah snickers at the image, which makes him smile back. They sit quietly for a few moments—their hands circle the steaming mugs—both aware that once the step is taken, there's no returning to before.

Finally, Noah breaks the silence.

"Okay, Mr. Wilde, I mean *Patrick*," she says in mock deference. "That's the way it will be then." She nods her head and reaches over to give him a friendly pat on the arm, letting her hand linger there.

Suddenly, the moment is interrupted. The piercing sound of a jay above them jeers mockingly. "*Haasch. Haasch. Haasch.*"

Noah looks up and spots the white-faced bird with its head cocked as if it's looking toward the door. Removing her hand from Patick's sleeve, she shifts her attention in the direction the bird is now focused and sees her brother, Gil, standing at the counter, grabbing a to-go cup of coffee. Their eyes meet for a few seconds. He glares back and shakes his head, then abruptly snaps about-face and walks away.

Here we go again, Noah carps to herself—miffed by what she imagines her brother is thinking. *Why can't he just mind his own effing business?*

She sits up straight, a determined look flashing in her emerald-green eyes, emboldened by Gil's reaction. She turns back toward Patrick, who looks a bit bewildered at the twin's non-verbals.

"So, you say you'd like to hear more about what happened last weekend?" Not waiting for an answer, she launches in, holding no detail back, vividly describing the entire experience.

Patrick listens in silence, his eyes narrowing in concentration, as he tries to absorb everything she's telling him.

"Holy mackerel, Noah! That's massive, and... it sounds like a really confusing experience to take in... to make sense of. And then, to top it all off, you had to put up with Colin and his gang. I'm really sorry I didn't do a better job of stopping them. It was bloody awful..." His words trail off as he looks down and rubs a tightened fist.

Noah smiles faintly at him. She feels seen and heard in ways she's only felt from her best friend.

"That's alright, Patrick," softly saying his name as if they've been close friends for years. "I've gotten used to it. It's harder on Shea, though. We've talked it out and... you know, we've weathered a lot over the years. We seem always to find some way to stick together. But... it's hard to watch her torture herself. She feels responsible. It's horrible for her." She takes a long sip of her coffee while casting a thoughtful look toward him.

"You know, I'm actually kind of glad it happened. It's made me more resolved to break free. To follow my own path. I know they're just a bunch of ignorant little snots, but if something doesn't change... well, they'll all just grow up and be a bunch of stupid old men and women. That's what makes me think I need to do something... something big. Or at least bigger than I can do here. I just don't know what it is yet."

"I get that," he says, then waits, letting the silence lengthen for a moment. "Hey, you got time to take a walk? I'd like to hear more about what you'd like to do."

She nods her head and downs the rest of her drink.

As they walk along the narrow alley, he leans toward her, listening closely as she talks about her future, about what she feels drawn to after school. After she's finished, he asks if he can offer an idea.

"My uncle, Seamus, is a professor at the University of Toronto. He heads a transdisciplinary program focused on global science, environmentalism, and political affairs. Pretty mundane stuff, huh?" They both chuckle before he continues. "Anyway, he also sponsors an eight-week summer immersion program in the Amazon. I just talked with him a few days ago, and he mentioned that a few spots are still left. I immediately thought of you and told him about you—"

"You did?" she interrupts

"—and he asked me to run it by you and see what you think."

She waits and looks at him through lowered eyes. "Oh... thank you. I just can't believe you'd think of me."

Patrick notices a brief flicker in her wide eyes—a spark of curiosity playing beneath her words of gratitude.

"Listen, I'll send you a HOLO that will give you more details, but... I think it would be really awesome for you to get away. A chance to get a new perspective on things as you figure out what's next."

Their conversation returns to more casual topics as they continue to meander around the small city park. There's a comfortable ease that's settled between them, present even as they move in and out of silence. Eventually, Noah looks up and notices the same jay from the pub peering down at her from a branch overhanging the sidewalk. *There you are again, little buddy. Whatcha doin'?* Beside it is an antique street clock announcing it's afternoon. She's a bit flustered at how much time they've spent together.

"Patrick, I think I need to head back now. Thanks so much for this morning. And the drink. It was all... umm... lovely. And you've given me a lot of new things to think about."

As she turns to leave, his hand gently reaches for her arm and stops her. He smiles warmly, his kind eyes resting on her as he searches for his words.

"Thanks for... for trusting me, Noah. I know it can't be easy after... you know... the way others treat you." He pauses, searching her face for reassurance. "I've really enjoyed today. Thanks for hanging out. And let me know if I can answer any questions about my uncle's program. I really do think it could be an amazing experience for you. Give it some thought. Okay?"

"I will," Noah answers, aware of his eagerness to help open this door for her.

"Well... see you in class," he says with a wink.

"See you in class, Mr. Wilde," she answers with a coy smile and then walks away. *I wonder what's ahead... what's behind all the other doors I'll have to choose between someday?*

Later that afternoon, Noah goes up to her room, which feels surprisingly cool—probably from the shade of the wych elm's broad, jagged leaves—

so she grabs a light sweater to put on. She looks at her unmade bed and regrets not making it that morning, then sloppily pulls the quilt and pillows up. Flopping down, she props herself at the head of the bed and signals her HOLO ring so she can read more about the Amazon study program Patrick told her about.

As she studies the program's aims and values, she notices she's nodding along. The short HOLO-VID is narrated by Seamus, Patrick's uncle. It's both inspiring *and* depressing. With his self-deprecating Irish humor combined with a playful way of delivering bad news, Noah finds herself opening up to the man, feeling a sort of trust in him. *Maybe it's because he's Patrick's uncle... but I think there's something more to it.*

She's heard that the Amazon serves as Earth's natural climate protector—but sitting here in her safe little room, she realizes how little she comprehends its importance.

Her mind wanders to her sensitivity to plants and trees. *I wonder how it would be activated there. Or is it an Irish thing—something about my connection to the land or my da's genes? It would be cool to see what happens somewhere so biodiverse.*

Dissolving her HOLO, she sits and looks out the window, lost in her thoughts. *Is this mine to do?* Other than her quick trip to Virginia with Journi, she's never traveled outside Ireland before, let alone to the other side of the planet. *Am I crazy to even think about this? But what if everything's been leading up to it?* She stares at the wych elm, its leaves gently rustling, whispering, as if offering its assent. *I mean, what is there really for me here? Do I want to just take over Ma's shop and spend my life repeating her life?*

In answer to the question, her body takes over. *Enough thinking about it.* She then quickly sends a HOLO-EM to Patrick.

> I'm in! All I have to do is convince my ma and da.

Immediately, a reply comes through.

> That's grand! Let me know how it goes. I might have to
> see if my uncle needs an assistant!

She giggles and replies.

    By the way, you didn't tell me your uncle is the good-
    looking one in the family;)

He responds with a colorful pyrotechnic display of exploding *thumbs-down* icons.

☙❧☙❧☙❧

Noah bounces downstairs, looking for her ma. She soon spies her on the wicker swing that hangs from the big wych elm—the air flutters, releasing breaking waves of the tree's playful spray of winged seeds. The sun warms half of her ma's face, the other half hidden in shadows. She looks content, though her eyes look distant.

"Hi, Ma. Sorry to interrupt. Can I sit with you? I want to ask you something."

"Of course, dear one," she replies, patting the cushion as she scoots over to make room. "I'm your ma. You can ask me anything."

Noah leans in, so their arms press together. "You know that I love everything you've taught me since I was little. And I love the herbalist's craft and the shop... I don't think I'd be who I am without it all. But... I need you to listen. I feel like there's more for me. More for me to do... more to experience that I wouldn't be able to if I stayed here. I know I'd planned on staying and helping you out more. That could still happen, but I want to get out... to try some things before I settle down."

Noah's ma looks at her, gently nodding as she takes in her daughter and who she's become, who she's becoming. She's known for some time that this was coming—that it *needs* to happen. And although she feels the soon-to-come vacuum already pulling her heart down, deep within the love and understanding, she also has to let go.

Noah's eyes flash with excitement, her words fast and animated. "So here's the thing. Mr. Wilde, the student teacher in my science class... his uncle is a professor in Toronto. He runs an eight-week immersion program in the Amazon. It's for kids like me who want to learn more about our planet's ecosystem... about how desperately it needs our help. They've got a couple of spots open. And they've asked me to consider joining. I know I'm springing this on you, but... do you think there's any way I might be able to go?"

Ma looks at Noah and smiles. Her soft, hazel eyes are beautifully cradled by familiar laugh lines. Time slows as they take each other in. It is times like this when they feel like more than mother and daughter. *More like soul sisters*, she tells herself.

Ma slides her arm around Noah's shoulder and pulls her close. She slowly strokes her long red hair the way she always did when Noah was a little girl. Leaning close to her ear, Fina quietly says, "I think it's a splendid idea. I'm so grateful there's still a spot for you. Thank Mr. Wilde for thinking of you. Can you send me the HOLO so I can get some details? I'll talk to your da this evening when I go up to see him. After that, we can talk about the practicalities. How's that sound?"

Noah pulls away and looks at her ma for a moment, her mouth half-open, and she smiles with relief.

"Really? Ma, you never fail to surprise me. I didn't even have to talk you into it! Thank you. Thank you so much. I've gotta go tell Shea. Okay? This is going to blow her mind!"

Noah kisses her ma on the cheek and runs into the house, leaving Fina sitting alone in the afternoon sun. She can't help but let a tear slip from the corner of her eye, even as the slight curve of her mouth turns up in a subtle, yet envious smile.

After Fina leaves to visit Aiden, Gil slinks around the corner of the kitchen. Noah is eating a salad of bibb lettuce, sliced egg, Dubliner cheese, beets, and asparagus, unaware of his presence. He stands there for several moments, watching her, his feelings conflicted.

Her eyes are focused on a recent study projected from her HOLO that reports the pace at which the Amazon rainforest is disappearing, having already shrunk to half its original size. She looks up, melancholy blooming in her gut as she considers how different life will be in just fifteen years—for her, for her family, and for her community. "My God," she says to herself. "I'll only be thirty-five... younger than Ma."

Gil slips into the room and stands over her. Sensing his shadow, she turns toward him. "Oh, hey, Gil."

He scowls at her, feeling the same complicated cocktail he's always felt for her. Protective. Jealous. Love. Disdain. Envy. Repulsion.

"I saw you today, you know." He spits the words out as if they were barbed arrows. "And I know you saw me, too. What is effing wrong with you? He's a damn teacher, Noah!"

"Student teacher," she shoots back.

Ignoring her comment, he presses on. "What would Ma say? I bet you'd be grounded until after graduation! You've put me in a tricky position here, you know."

Noah glares back, an icy silence hanging between them. *Who the hell does he think he is to have an opinion about what I do... or who I do it with?* She breaks eye contact and swallows hard, trying to rein in her anger. *Anything I say will just set him off... but oh... how I'd really like to give him a good punch in the nose.*

After a moment, she looks back at him, softening her expression, and says with practiced remorse, "Gil, I know... but believe me, we're just friends. Really. Shea and I have had some really great conversations with him at Sustainability Club. Today's the first time we've ever met up like that. I'm sorry if it bothers you. You know, Patrick... I mean, *Mr. Wilde* and I both share an affinity for—"

Gil breaks in. "Patrick? Patrick! Even if he's a student teacher, since when do you call a teacher by their first name or talk that way about them? I don't care about your cock-eyed *shared affinities*. You're coming off the rails, girl. And as for him... what kind of teacher holds a student's hand or takes them out drinking? Huh?"

"And just why do you think you know what we were drinking?" Noah snaps back. "I suppose you snooped around and chatted up the barista or—"

"You're damn right I did! You better watch yourself, Noah. This little... whatever it is... is not going to end well. It's a good thing it was me that saw you. I'm still your brother, you know. I just can't believe how stupid you can be sometimes. Maybe I should go ahead and tell Ma before this whole thing gets out of hand."

He stands there and waits a few beats—daring her to say more—then turns away and heads toward the door. Noah quickly jumps up and puts herself in front of him.

"*Please*, Gil. Don't say anything—"

He waves her off and, not even looking at her, steps around her and leaves.

Noah returns to the table and sinks down. Her fingers grab strands of wild red hair, tugging at it as if pulling weeds. She feels the prospect of her Amazon adventure withering in front of her, slowly dissolving, just another half-hatched fantasy.

She sits in dreadful silence for several minutes. The evening's shadows begin to replace the late afternoon glow coming through the kitchen window. She starts to get up, and her HOLO chimes with a message. It's from Ma.

> Da is in! Now, we just have to work on finding the money. He's asked me to reach out to his family to convene a council meeting to present the idea. They have a trust fund for this sort of thing. You know the Greenlings! All for one and one for all. We're shooting for this Friday. Be home tomorrow.

It's well past dark. The only sounds are the scratching chirps of bush-crickets and a soft duet from a couple of long-eared owls. Gil is in the garage with a pair of utility lamps pointed under the hood. A HOLO diagram of the engine floats next to the rusted Range Rover's fender. His irritation is palpable as he grunts and swears, his head buried under the hood.

"I must have torn the damn gasket when I cranked that last turn… or it's a piece of junk, just like the truck," he snaps as he slams the wrench into his tool box.

He's sweaty, and the mozzies are swarming around, biting him on the back of his neck. He keeps smacking them with oil on his hands, then smearing the grease up into his hair.

His HOLO interrupts his misery. It's Colin.

> Hey, bro. HOLO SHIT! Just got your message. You really scored with this one! Or was it Wilde Man that scored?

Gil doesn't bother to reply. He disconnects the HOLO, suddenly unsure if telling his friend about Noah and their teacher was such a good idea.

"Oh, well—Karma's a bitch. Whatever happens, it's on her, not me," he mutters to himself.

He's too tired to finish up. It's after midnight, and besides, there's school tomorrow. He reaches up and unscrews the lightbulbs, cussing as he burns his fingers. As he walks out of the garage into the starless night, a long-eared owl that's been watching him from the wych elm launches off the branch. Its wings softly clap as it brushes overhead, so close that he feels the gusts of air. Throwing both greasy arms over his head, he swears at the darkness, stumbling toward the back door.

Noah and her ma arrive as the sunlight slants golden through the sessile oak, cherry, and spindle trees. She flashes a nervous smile at her ma.

"You've got this," Fina mouths back, offering an encouraging nod. The butterflies in Noah's stomach aren't so much at the outcome of the

evening—her da has assured her the gathering is just a formality—but
at the anticipation of seeing so many Greenlings in one place, many she
hasn't seen since she was a little girl.

As they walk up to her uncle Liam's long, low berm house in Fhaltaigh
Millennium Forest, she sees the leather door folded back, pegged to
the turf overhead. Her da's handmade wooden bicycle leans against the
small stone well in the front, sporting his signature swept-back walnut
handlebars. Arm in arm, they duck their heads as they enter and smell
the smoldering peat fire in the far corner. Mismatched hedge chairs made
from ambrosia maple are placed in a relaxed, casual circle. The rest of the
furniture is pushed to the outer walls.

Across the low-slung room, they see Da and Uncle Liam facing each
other, engrossed in a loud, lively debate. Fina calls out to the two brothers
as they approach. "What are you old woodchucks talking about? Don't you
have a proper greeting for us two lovely lasses?"

Aiden flashes a chastened expression, then leans forward to kiss Fina.

"My apologies, Fina," Uncle Liam says, touching his hand to his
forehead. "Your other half was trying to correct this older brother's
recollection of some of the finer points of the Greenlings' charter. I was
reminding him that anyone who lives in a hut made of that soft soil from
up north where he lives is the one with a soft head. But enough of that.
Greetings, my fine ladies." He bows with a humble flourish of his birch
bark cap.

They spend a few moments catching up on family news and juicy
Greenling gossip. As they talk, others start to arrive. The round, low
room quickly comes to life, voices buzzing like bees in a hive. Distant
cousins, aunts, and uncles enter and glide around, creating a bohemian
kaleidoscope of earthy, hand-made fabrics. They greet each other, grateful
to be given an excuse to reunite.

Noah sees her cousin, Bridget Grace, laughing at something their
uncle Ronan has said, pointing at her da and Liam. Knowing the gathering
is for her—feeling shy and conspicuous—she retreats to an unoccupied
place against the wall where she can watch. Among the group, there are

even ancient great-aunts and grizzled great-uncles Noah has only met once or twice. *And here they are,* she marvels, *coming together... for me. I've never realized until tonight just how vital these connections are.*

The room is quickly getting warmer. Noah notices a few small trails of sweat on her temples and the back of her neck. Even the hard cider she's holding has lost its chill. The men begin to take off their shirts and stand bare-chested. The curly hair on the broad trunks of their torsos is a deep golden bronze color and is as thick as ancient moss. The women, too, shed their outer blouses, revealing honey-dipped skin laced with lovely pale freckles. Without inhibition, the Greenling women continue to mingle with each other in their tulle cotton undershirts.

When a natural lull settles in over the warm gathering, Liam's voice rings out. "Welcome, you Greenlings! It's good to see you all. Please, find a seat to sink your rear ends in, and we'll get started with the business that brings us together tonight."

There's a brief shuffling movement as the elder Greenlings are offered seats and the others shift to fill in the remaining spots.

"As we all know, our mas and mamos, our das and grandas—as far back as any of us can remember—have contributed out of their modest means to the Greenling Wisdom Trust. Many of you, as well as your bairns, have been shaped and formed, have learned crafts and trades because of its generous provisions. Am I right?"

As he surveys the circle, heads nod. Several of the Greenling mas and das turn to look at their young ones, putting an arm over a shoulder or patting a knee.

"But times are different now. We all can see it—right in our own woodlands and bogs—that the Emerald Island is becoming less and less vital with each new season." Liam pauses to find Noah and extends a hand toward her. "My brother's daughter, Noah, feels drawn to do something about the situation... to try to better understand a problem that's not just affecting us but the entire planet.

"You know, we've all managed to stay concealed in the safety of our solitude all these years. It's been a good life, if not a lonely one, for us and those who came before us. But maybe we've avoided a responsibility that was ours for life as a whole. Who knows? Either way, it seems this way of life is coming to an end."

Heads move back and forth, glancing at one another. Their concerned faces acknowledge the undeniable losses and changes they see.

"Noah here wants to bring some of what we know... what we love... what we care about, to these dire days. Who knows? Maybe she can help do what we've failed to do for the greater good. The reason we're here is that she's been invited to go to the Amazon and learn what the rainforest has to say to her. My brother tells me she has a strong gift—that the Greenling blood flows strongly through her. I, for one, think this opportunity may contain more than meets the eye. Who knows? The Great Mystery itself may be calling her for such a moment as this. So, what do you say, my brothers and sisters?"

A wave of heads nod, punctuated by quiet whispers from those around the circle. No one speaks up; they just hum murmurs of approval.

Liam waits and then calls out, "Are we one then, Greenlings? Will we send out Noah as our own?"

"We are one, though we are many," the women in the room reply in chant.

"Though we are many, we still are one," the men, in unison, respond in kind.

In the silence that follows, Liam motions for Noah to enter the circle's center. As the big man puts his arm around his niece's shoulder, a single tear begins to trail down her cheek and then mingles with the hopeful, earnest smile of youth.

After a few moments, the Greenlings quietly rise to their feet and begin knocking their fisted knuckles together. When the muted sound ends, they approach her one by one. Without speaking, each one either shakes her hand or gently embraces her, then moves toward the door and walks into the night. The silent goodbyes are poignant; no words are needed to convey their love and their blessing.

Noah's eyes glisten with joy and relief. Without the Greenlings' funds, her dream would never become a reality. Her young heart swells with gratitude for these people of the earth, humbled by their unbounded generosity. She feels a growing determination. *I'll do my best and not let you all down or... let the future down... whatever that means.* A new weight of responsibility seems to have settled on her, and she can't help but wonder what's ahead.

As they walk out the door together, Da puts his arms around Noah and Ma, pulling them in close, their heads almost touching.

He whispers to Noah, "I'm so proud of you, dear one. No matter what happens next, your clan's here for you. We're as knotted together as a tightly wound vine. You're a part of all this, you know. You and your ma both."

He kisses them both on the forehead, releasing them to return home. Noah's eyes glisten as she holds her da's warm gaze. After a few moments, he breaks the spell.

"I'm spending the night here with Liam. It's been too long, and we have a lot to talk about now that both of our families' chicks are flying out of the nest. I'll ride back to my berm tomorrow," he says, pointing to his bike by the well's now-dark outline.

It's not unusual to find Colin Deegan waiting outside the headmaster's office. What's remarkable is for him to be there for anything other than a teacher's frustrated plea for backup. Yet here he sits, looking not exactly angelic but like the bearer of some important news.

The door opens abruptly, and Mr. Hawkins looks down at him, scarcely hiding his perennial impatience with the boy.

"Come in, Colin. This is quite the surprise. What's this about, son?"

Colin takes a seat on the other side of the metal-gray industrial desk and then launches in. "Okay, Mr. Hawkins. I feel really awful about telling you this. I mean... I know I've been here to see you because of some of the stupid things I've done. But, well... you know, I'm just a punk kid. And you kind of expect it from us, don't you?" The boy stops, his innocent expression one of feigned regret.

"Alright. Just spit it out, then. What's going on?" The headmaster's frown conveys his lack of patience—urging the boy to get to the point.

"This is sort of hard to talk about, but, well... here goes. You know Mr. Wilde, our science teacher?"

"You mean the student teacher? Of course I do. Now, get on with it. What's he got to do with anything?"

"Umm... well, I think he and Noah are, you know... seeing each other."

"What do you mean, 'seeing each other,' boy?"

Colin looks down at his feet, acting uncomfortable and embarrassed. But inside, he's amped up, ready for the kill.

"You know, like *boyfriend* and *girlfriend*."

"What in the world are you talking about? Where did you hear this? If you're making this up, I swear to God, you will be finished here, Colin. And I'll make damn sure you never graduate from this school!" the headmaster warns, leaning over his desk.

"Um... I really shouldn't say. Maybe I shouldn't even have bothered you with all this. I just... don't want to get anyone else in trouble—"

"—That's not your concern here," Mr. Hawkins interrupts.

"Alright... alright, I'll tell you, but please don't tell anyone." Colin pauses as he flashes a sidelong glance over his shoulder. "Noah's brother told me. He seemed pretty upset about it, too. I don't think he knew what to do. Just seemed like he wanted someone else to know in case... you know... if somebody in charge should know about it."

The headmaster leans his big frame back in his office chair and looks down at the stack of reports, barking for his attention.

"Colin, you did the right thing, coming in to tell me. Now here's what I want you to do—leave it to me. Just keep it to yourself for now. We don't need to get ahead of ourselves here, okay?"

Colin bobs his head up and down. "Sure, Mr. Hawkins. I feel a lot better now that you know. Thanks for... for, you know... believing me."

The boy stands and quickly moves to walk out. As he reaches the door, he turns and catches Mr. Hawkins still studying him.

"Remember what I said, boy," the headmaster growls, his voice flat and authoritative. "This better not turn out to be one of your mudslinging pranks."

❧❧❧

Colin quickly makes his way outside to the street and jogs away from the long two-story building. When he's beyond range, he fist-pumps and hoots a weird victory cry. "Hoo... Hoo... Hoo!" He turns into an alley littered with trash, calls up his HOLO, and messages Gil.

> It's done. What a way to finish! Just left the head-masturbator's office. I should get a BAFTA award for acting. You should have been there.

❧❧❧

Walking home ahead of his sister, Gil hears his HOLO and opens it. When he reads the message, he stops suddenly. Standing in the middle of the sidewalk, he nervously starts to rub the back of his neck as if there's a spot of grease on it.

"Oh, God," Gil mutters to himself. "Shit! No! No! Oh, shit. What have you done, you idiot?"

Noah's head is buried in her HOLO as she walks, and she plows into him hard, almost knocking them both down. She's been messaging Patrick and didn't notice her brother planted in front of her.

"What the...? Sheesh! Watch where you're going, Noah," he snaps, rubbing his arm where she ran into him. Dazed, she shakes her head and stares at her brother—a puzzled look passes between them.

"What's wrong with you, Gil? You almost tripped me! You're not the only one on this street, you know."

Surprisingly, he softens and gently replies, "I know... sorry. I didn't... I wasn't paying attention."

She studies him for a beat or two, then steps around him and walks on.

He watches—his foot nervously tapping the ground—making sure she's out of range and then shoots off an angry HOLO-EM to Colin.

Noah stops half a block away and looks back. Gil is slowly turning around and around, both hands in his pockets, staring up at the sky. She looks up, too, seeing nothing but the clouds' ash-gray. Deep within her heart, though, a wave of sadness emerges and settles heavily in the foreground of her awareness. Her head bows as she releases a long, loud sigh. *What have you done, Gil? What have you done now?*

Patrick rambles home after his brief meeting with Mr. Hawkins, occasionally stooping down to pick up a scrap of litter. The thirty-minute conversation was cordial and professional—thankfully, Noah's name was never spoken. He was told by the headmaster that his termination wasn't because of a "capital offense" that needed to ruin his career—it was, however, a gross failure of good judgment.

When the meeting was over, the young student teacher's embarrassment dogged him down the long hallway and out the school door, his shoulders hunched, head focused on the floor's worn tiles. Fortunately, he didn't bump into any students or teachers, leaving him to ruminate alone as he walked.

Whatever shame he initially felt gradually begins to dissipate. *Sure, it's a blow to my ego. And I know I'll spiral down—compiling a list of coulda, woulda, shouldas. But right now, being unemployed feels more like a gateway than an ending. It's strange how life can seem lighter after choosing a new fork in the road—or, in this case, chosen for you.*

Although he knows he'd be a good teacher, there's also something that still feels unfulfilled in him. He doesn't know *what* it is, but he recognizes the void.

He walks up the steps to his flat, unlocks the door, grabs the mail, and walks in, throwing his bag on the floor. In the kitchen, he opens the fridge and sees the beer he bought last night. *Better not—not today. I'll drink the whole six-pack if I get started.* After pouring a tall glass of cold water, he moves to the sofa, where he settles in and opens a HOLO for his uncle. After three chimes, Seamus answers—his image displays a surprised smile as he walks under a canopy of trees.

"Hey, Laddie. Surprised to see your name pop up. You caught me heading to a meeting in a few minutes. What's up?"

Patrick apologizes for calling in the middle of the day. Then, he tells his uncle what just happened. "The headmaster was understanding... actually, sympathetic. He says he'll give me a good reference, but I'd crossed a line... and if it came out, it would look bad for him... and for the school. I get it, but it sucks... I've never gotten canned before."

Seamus slows down and spots a rustic park bench to sit on. He knows how hard his nephew has worked to get to this point. "Oh, man... this makes me so sad for you... and for the students. You've had such a great year with those kids. I'd like to come over there and cuff a few of those young sods for you."

Patrick laughs and heads back to the fridge for one of the beers. "You've always had my back, Seamus. No, I'll be alright. I was just stupid. Even though it was completely misconstrued—I should have known it would bite me—and done more to keep it from being misinterpreted. I just found myself torn... between common sense and... What can I say? I just dropped my guard. And let my radar get jammed." He takes a long draw from the bottle before going on. "That's not exactly true... I think I just turned the damned thing off."

Seamus smiles at his nephew's metaphor. *He's more like his ma than he knows!*

"Actually, I'm sort of relieved... I've been having some doubts about being a teacher for the next forty years. It's good work... and I think I could make a difference, but I don't know... there's something missing too. Like I'm made for something else, something bigger. Like you. Like Ma was. Both of you have always been about changing things... making things better."

"Patrick, you need to know—you've been making a big difference in those kids' lives. I bet you're their favorite teacher. And not just because of your good looks, either. Which—I'll have you know—you got from me! Seriously, though, you have a way of inspiring folks with your stories... with creative ways to engage them with science. You make it more personal, more relatable."

Patrick nods as he listens to his uncle's effort to encourage him. "Thank you. I think I needed to hear that... even if it's all over."

There's a long pause before Seamus speaks again. When he does, his tone is more measured. Serious. "I honestly didn't see this coming, Patrick. And I'm not entirely prepared for what I'm going to try to say next. Your ma and I tried to steer you down a parallel, but safer path than ours. But maybe we were wrong. Who knows? I'm really not sure."

Patrick waits, his expression puzzled as he tries to decode what his uncle is saying.

"Listen... I've got some things that I've become aware of that I could use some help with. After the summer program in the Amazon's over, how about coming to Toronto? It's been way too long since you've been to visit me. We can talk then, after the dust has had a chance to settle a bit more for you. How's that sound?"

Patrick brightens at the idea, momentarily forgetting his uncle's mysterious allusion. "Now you're talking. Could be just what I need. I haven't been back since graduation... and I'd really like to—" He's about to wind down the conversation and say goodbye when Seamus interrupts.

"There's one more thing, Patrick. Now, don't say anything right now... and I know you don't want to be told this... but I think it's time for you to see your da. I know all the hurt you've carried, losing both your ma *and* your da. But he's still here. Even though she's gone, he's not. I've seen him a few times over the years, you know. He really is a changed man. At least... give it a thought, will you?"

"Hmm..." Patrick murmurs as he slowly shakes his head—his guardedness visible in the creases of his frown. "I'm not sure... it's been a long time. Too long, maybe. He had his chance. But I'll think about it, Seamus. It's something I think about from time to time... but it's hard to sort out my feelings. Maybe you're right... I'll see.

"And thanks for listening. You know, ever since Ma left us... never mind. It's good to see you. Let me think about your offer, and I'll get back with you. There are still a few things *here* I need to see through before I can think about what's next."

They say a quick goodbye and disconnect. Patrick sits in the silent aftermath, finishing the rest of his beer, just listening. He listens to the traffic noise, the sound of the wind outside, and the ticking of the clock on the desk. But most of all, he listens for a voice in the depths of his soul—his ma's voice.

Way leads to way, Patrick. You can count on it.
Way... always... leads... to way.

Noah wakes early—earlier than she needs to. Rolling over, covered by a thin white sheet, the sun filters through the wych elm outside her window. The morning light shimmers around the room, strobing across her golden-red hair like fireflies. Her gaze lands on the ancient tree, and she considers how it's always been there, always watching over her. *It's funny that I've never tried to connect with it before.* Feeling nostalgic, she continues her wondering. *Why is it that the things and the people most present to me... seem to be the most invisible? Like this tree... or like Ma... or Shea.*

She sits up in bed, leans over to open the window, and then faces the opening's dappled light. With eyes closed, she tilts her head back, feeling the sun's gentle warmth on her skin. After a few slow, deep breaths, she whispers to the tree.

"Good morning, old friend. How are you today?"

Silence. Her breath seems to join with the wind and caress the tree's green leaves. And then, without announcement, a vibration with no sound blooms—first within her, then around her. She detects meaning... emotion. She perceives that the tree is glad to see her. It's happy to *be seen*.

For a few moments, they just seem to enjoy being together. But soon, Noah senses that the wych elm is growing weary, burdened by all the changes in the world. Noah feels the weight, too. Then, all at once, something awakens in her. She feels *known*. The tree conveys hope, not in the future, but in her part in it. Not wishing the connection to end, she becomes aware of how blessed she is. She sinks further down into her thoughts—grateful for life, *her life*, and all she loves.

Noah gently smiles. She's unsure *how* the tree knows her, but she knows it does. Addressing it with spoken words, she speaks out loud.

"I'm sorry I've ignored you. I've been so caught up in my life that... I've forgotten how much you mean to me. Thank you... for always being there. For watching over me. For filtering out some of the harshness of the world. For witnessing my tears... my growing up. I wouldn't be the person I am today without you."

The tree grows still. The breeze playing in its branches ceases. Then, a scent Noah's never encountered breaks into the room. It carries memories—not her memories, but the tree's and its kin.

Suddenly, Noah becomes aware that the trees are grateful, too. Thankful for her, for her people, the Greenlings, whose coexistence with the woodlands has helped the forest flourish, even during these dangerous times.

What's that? The hairs on her arms tingle. Gooseflesh stands alert on her pale skin. Like an alarm call, she's jolted by something she can't quite name—then, it comes to her. *Urgency!* That's what she's picking up, the trees' urgency. *But why?*

The answer, when it comes, is like an irresistible undertow. *The trees are changing things—the quiet care of the earth is no longer enough.* An overwhelming awareness quickly envelopes her—a time is coming when she must leave to join, not what *has been*, but everything soon to come.

Noah breathes deeply, almost panting now. The torrent pulling at her instantly stills. Soon, a gentle, tender notion returns. She feels content... wanted, and cared for. She sighs, bowing her head, and then opens her eyes, facing the ancient elm.

"I love you," she whispers. In return, she hears a million verdant voices whispering.

"We love you too, Noah."

Gil looks across the seat of his truck at his sister, their green graduation gowns folded neatly between them. She's wearing a dressy, dark-turquoise jumper, her golden-red hair swept loosely back in double braids. He's wearing a loud, kiwi-green dress shirt that's painfully mismatched with Noah's outfit.

"We're one, but we're not the same..." U2's acoustic version of the song *One* is in mid-play. *"Well, we hurt each other, then we do it again."*

As they drive away, he offers a brief but natural smile. Noah mirrors it, wondering at his willingness not only to give her a ride but also to swing by and pick up Shea. *He seems weirdly accommodating*, she thinks.

After arriving at Shea's house, the two girls move to the back seat and sit scrunched together, just like they did in primary school. Gil glances in the rearview mirror and sees his sister crying, pale tears tracing her cheeks.

Shea lifts her hand to Noah's cheek and brushes away a remaining tear, smoothing her friend's makeup at the same time. Noah catches a glimpse of Shea's new tattoo—a gallery of extinct species forming a colorful sleeve—a blue-eyed lemur, a pangolin, a vaquita. The girls lean toward one another, whispering, but Gil can only make out Noah's words.

"So, what do you think of Patrick, Shea? He's pretty awesome, isn't he? I feel like he's sacrificed something for me. I just wish... I don't know... I wish things could have gone on the way they were before."

Shea nods, a sad smile written on her face.

"Sorry. We're here," Gil gently announces, aware he's interrupting something private. "I'll go ahead so you two can finish up." Without looking back, he jumps out of the truck, puts his cap and gown on, and starts walking toward the school's football field. He quickly merges with the growing crowd as it also snakes its way through the busy parking lot. In the distance are neat rows of folding chairs set up in front of a small elevated stage, where a HOLO background animates the antics and accomplishments of the class of 2060. On either side of the field are bleachers steadily filling with parents and grandparents, family and friends.

Shea shakes her head as she watches Gil slowly move away. "Is it my imagination, or has someone swapped out your brother for a new and improved model?"

Noah chuckles under her breath. She's wondered the same thing. After Patrick was fired, she and Gil had the mother of all blowups. But unlike their other conflicts, when the dust settled, Gil was subdued—contrite, even. Since then, she's noticed that he's been more helpful, more kind, and less reactive—definitely less reactive. He even offered to take her to Dublin to shop for some gear she'll need for her Amazon trip. Over the last few days, a mishmash of all kinds of feelings have been bubbling up inside her toward her brother. Relief. Curiosity. Guardedness. Even affection. *But... I think I need to wait and see what happens. Forgiveness just doesn't feel like part of the mix yet.*

They exit the car, weaving in and out of the crowd as they run to catch up with Gil. At the edge of the field, the two girls hug each other and split up. Noah and her brother move through the congested aisles and find their seats on the brown folding chairs on the school's football field. They feel silly in the green caps and gowns, but the fact that everyone else is wearing them softens the indignity of it. Not saying anything, they both keep scanning the crowded stands. Ma sits alone, looking slightly overdressed for an outdoor school event.

But where's Da? Gil asks himself.

Noah asks herself the same thing—*He all but promised he'd be here.*

The two exchange a look, as if hearing each other's thoughts. They wear the same quizzical expression and share their first openly genuine smile with one another in ages.

The high school choir takes its place on the rickety risers and begins singing an old Irish blessing. With everyone now seated, the headmaster commences, welcoming the students, their families, and their friends. As he continues, Noah keeps glancing up to the stands to see if her da is there. *Come on, Da. Where are you?* She's only half listening when she hears Mayve Moran, the class valedictorian, speaking through the HOLO transmission system.

"So, friends. Let's not waste the time ahead. Even if we fall short of our dreams, what better way to spend our short time on earth? And let's be real, there are dark days ahead. But no matter what, remember, we are always greater than what we must suffer."

Noah's surprised to find her attention return to her classmate's words. *These speeches always seem so over-the-top. Scratch that, cheesy! But this... this isn't too bad. Kind of inspiring, really. That's weird.*

Looking back at the stands, she sees her ma still sitting alone—a familiar, solitary image—the empty seat gapes beside her. The headmaster's instructions interrupt her wandering thoughts. Students in the rows ahead of them are called by name and walk to the stage to receive their diplomas. The twins, still seated, continue to scan the crowded stands.

Their row is eventually invited to stand and line up by the stairs. When Noah hears her name called, she walks onto the stage and pauses, self-consciously listening to what Mr. Hawkins has to say about her.

"Noah has been this class's unelected north star. Not only has she excelled with exemplary marks, but she has also been an unwavering compass for our school. Her passion for our planet's many crises has inspired all of us to consider what we might do to help the Earth heal. Thank you, Noah! And congratulations."

Mr. Hawkins extends his right hand and shakes hers, followed by Ms. Cunningham, who hands her a green-and-gold leather folder containing her diploma.

"Gil Calhoun," the headmaster announces. Noah turns to see her brother walking toward Mr. Hawkins. Over their heads, she sees their da now sitting with their ma. *So he did make it… and just in time.* She smiles in their direction, raising her arm at the elbow to give a quick wave.

"Gil shows a strong aptitude for the world of mechanics and engineering, along with a special knack for various practical applications, according to his homeroom teacher, Mr. Tully. We hope to hear more from you, Mr. Calhoun. Congratulations, young sir!"

The twins return to their seats and listen as each of their classmates walks across the stage to receive tangible evidence of their graduation. Mr. Hawkins serves up a brief but flattering remark about each one, including Colin and Keely—something that Noah finds beyond the call of duty!

After the benediction by Father O'Rourke, the graduates toss their caps in the air and twist through the knots of young bodies. Many embrace, slapping each other on the back. Some exchange a final laugh or shed a tear with those they've known for their entire young lives. Soon, each one is joined by mas and das, grandparents, and siblings who repeat the ritual of well-wishings.

Noah looks up and sees *her* ma and da weaving through the crowd toward them. The two look at the twins, beaming with broad smiles and eyes glistening with pride. Ma steps forward first, gives Noah a long hug, and whispers something in her daughter's ear meant just for the two of them. Da moves beside his son and leans his head toward Gil so he can be heard.

"I'm *so proud* of you, son! Having a daughter who's becoming a woman… and a son who's becoming a man… I can't tell you what that means to me." Da locks eyes with Gil and puts his big hand on his shoulder. "I know I'm your da, and I'm supposed to have it all figured out, but… you know, you're gifted in ways I could never hope to be."

Aiden wipes his eye with the back of his hand before regaining his humor. "I'm still bigger than you, though," he says with a quick wink. "So don't be getting any mad ideas in your head! But seriously, I hope you know how much you're loved."

Gil looks into his da's eyes and feels the man reaching out to him, offering his heart the best he knows how. Rather than letting himself feel embarrassed or pushing his da away to assert his independence, he instead softens and relaxes into the moment. Feeling there's nothing else to be said, Gil turns to face his da and gives the man a big bear hug.

"I love you too, Da."

❧☙❧☙❧☙

A few minutes pass before the four become aware that someone is standing near the family's quasi-boundary. They all turn in sync and see Patrick Wilde—a sheepish expression on his face, his posture unassuming.

There is an uncertain moment or two as Aiden and Fina exchange glances before looking back to the former teacher. Gil takes the lead and steps toward him.

"Hi, Mr. Wilde. Well, we finally made it."

If Patrick knows anything about Gil's part in his termination, he doesn't let on. He reaches out to shake hands, and they both regard one another and then release their grip.

"Indeed you did, Gil. Indeed, you both did. Congratulations!"

Noah moves next to her brother, her green eyes soft searching his face for a clue—uncertain as to whether something has shifted in him—like a combination lock slightly out of alignment.

"Thanks for coming. I didn't know if you would... you know, with everything that's... oh, never mind. Hey, I want you to meet my ma and da." She touches his arm and steers him toward the center of their circle. "Ma. Da. This is Mr. Wilde. Also known as *Patrick*," she says with a wink toward him.

He steps toward Noah's parents, displaying a contrite grin while he apologetically shrugs his shoulders.

"Hello, Mr. and Mrs. Greenling. It's so good to meet you. And congratulations on raising two amazing human beings. You should be very proud."

After exchanging another quick glance, Aiden and Fina extend their arms toward the young man to shake hands.

"And it's good to meet you too," Noah's da offers. "I know firsthand these two can be quite a handful. The crossfire from some of their epic spats will leave you maimed if you're not careful," he jokes, conveying his characteristic warmth and generosity.

Fina nods her head and smiles. "That's right, Mr. Wilde. We're glad to finally meet you. A bit overdue, don't you think?"

Another awkward pause hangs for a moment, and then Patrick answers, "Of course, Mrs. Greenling."

"Here's what I think we should do," Aiden says to everyone, not really asking. "I think Mr. Wilde should join us back at the house for a bit of lunch and some cake to celebrate the big day. That way, we can all get a little better acquainted and get you out of those ridiculous outfits." He gestures to the twin's green gowns. "Sound good to you all?"

Patrick looks at Noah, who barely nods her head in his direction and gives him a subtle, sly grin.

"If it's no trouble for you all," Patrick responds. "I wouldn't want to get in the way or interrupt your family's celebration."

"Not at all. We'd be happy to include you, Mr. Wilde," Fina answers.

"Please, call me Patrick, Mrs. Greenling. Actually... Gil, Noah, now that you're done with school... you call me Patrick too," he says with a crooked grin.

"Okay, *Mr. Wilde*," Noah says in mock deference. "How about we call you Patsy—or maybe Paddy—or—"

He raises his hands, cutting her off. "Definitely not!" They all laugh and begin to make their way to the parking lot.

After a few steps, Stephen Deegan swerves to intercept them—Colin awkwardly trails a few steps behind. The man approaches the small group unsteadily, as if his two legs aren't heading in the same direction. His burgundy tie, cinched around his neck with what looks like a square-knot, hangs from the collar of a dirty-yellow, short-sleeved seersucker shirt.

"Well, I'll be damned. Isn't this the wee, happy family? It's a flock of Greezlings, ain't it all?" the man says in a loud, slurred voice. "And with the young gobshite his elf. I, for one, am glad they corked your spunky ass sir," he sputters as he weaves toward Patrick.

Caught off guard, Patrick quickly recovers and tries to intervene. "Okay, Mr. Deegan, you've had your—" But the man ignores him and totters toward Fina.

"And ain't it the queen of Kilkenny herself, looking all happy and gay-like." His rheumy eyes circle around her, as unfocused as his drunken mind. Fina takes two steps back, her nose scrunched up as if walking through pig slop.

"Ya' know, ya' should've just kept to your little roots and magic cures, leavin' the real work of helping this town to us men folk. But no, ya' just had to muck it all up," he says and spits at Fina's feet, tottering unsteadily.

Aiden scowls at the man and takes a step forward, fists clenched, ready. He smells the whiskey and sees his bloodshot eyes, his purplish drinker's nose.

"Give it a rest, Stephen. Get on home, and let us be."

Colin steps forward and grabs his da's arm to steer him away. But the man just shakes him off and leers toward Noah.

"An' you, little Miss Muffet. You oughtta be ashamed of yourself. I knew me son was too good for ya' when ya' ditched 'im way back."

A tattoo of a drunken sea monster winks from underneath his shirtsleeve. Something tickles Noah's memory. *What is it?* she wonders, and then recalls something—a writhing image from a photo the Garda showed them after her ma's shop was vandalized. Her fists are balled, ready to explode, when she's interrupted.

"That's enough, Da," Colin says, finally getting his dad's unfocused pupils to turn toward him. The boy's expression betrays a pitied concern Noah's never seen in him before. "Let's get going. Ma's waiting in the car.

Just leave it alone. Yer in the crapper deep enough, ya' know. They ain't worth it, remember? That's what ya' always told me."

Stephen looks at his son as if seeing him for the first time today and pats him on the shoulder. "Yer right, son. Yer right. Let's leave 'em. See ya' *Greezlings!*"

Colin struggles to turn his da around as Noah's family watches the two stumble toward the parking lot.

After a few moments, they exchange knowing glances, shaking their heads. Aiden's big form slumps, the day's joy suddenly drained out of him. Gil's face is sour—crumpled in disgust and anger—uncertain whether it's directed toward Colin, his drunken da, or himself. Noah's ma looks tenderly at her daughter, trying to gauge how she's holding up.

Noah finally breaks the silence. "Hey, let's get out of here. I'm burning up. This stupid gown feels like a sauna." She doesn't bother to wait for an answer, but turns and starts walking away. Gil nods, pulling at his collar as he moves behind his sister and heads toward the parking lot. The remaining three look on sympathetically, and then move along in silence.

❦ ❧ ❦ ❧ ❦ ❧

Noah and Patrick drive together in his car. She looks at his profile, noticing a nick on his neck where he cut himself shaving. When she inhales in the closed space, there's a musky scent of cedarwood and something else from his aftershave.

"Are you sure you know what you've agreed to?" Noah teases, raising both eyebrows.

"What do you mean? They seem great."

"Oh, they are, but just wait. They've got this rich habit of turning small talk into something else... you'll see."

They get to the house first and go inside. A few minutes later, the other three show up and walk through the front door.

"My, *you're* a rather snappy one, Patrick," her da says with a wink.

Patrick looks a little sheepish and says something about hitting the lights right.

Aiden interrupts, "Never mind all that. I'm just pulling your leg. Come on. Join me. I need to head out and park myself under some trees. Being bombarded by the toxic haze back at the school has started to catch up with me."

Fina's voice rings out from the kitchen. "Go out back and find a place to sit, everyone. We'll eat outside. I'll be right out with the food. Gil, get everyone something to drink. Noah, come and help me. I've made some Irish egg rolls, corn beef puffs, and cheesy potato cakes."

They all move to their stations, leaving Patrick alone with Noah's da. Aiden studies the younger man, his dark eyes hard to read.

"You know that we know what happened, don't you, Patrick?"

"Yes. Noah told me. Listen, Mr. Greenling, I'm really sorry for all the trouble I've caused. If I could—"

"*Trouble*? You're the one who caused trouble for yourself."

"And I know that. I want you to know... I take complete responsibility for everything... But I just—"

Aiden motions to Patrick to pause while Fina and Noah return to set out the plates. Gil steps forward and passes around five ice-cold Harp Lagers.

"*Sláinte*," Aiden calls out, then tips his bottle toward each of them.

"Fina, I was just starting to tell Patrick that in our day, it wasn't others' responsibilities to guide their young ones; it was the family's duty. Fina here was three years younger than me when we met. She was seventeen, and I was a mature, experienced twenty-year-old!"

"No, you weren't. Let me tell this right—" Fina corrects him, a playful glint in her dark-blue eyes.

"I was too—" he interrupts.

"What I was going to say was, yes, *of course*, I was seventeen, and you were twenty. But I know firsthand that you were neither mature *nor* experienced!"

Everyone grins, enjoying their easy banter. It's been too long since they've shared laughter, food, and drink like this. Even Gil seems relaxed, not looking for an excuse to be somewhere else.

"Here's what I'm trying to say, if *Mrs. Greenling* will let me finish. We met when she was seventeen, and I probably waited until she was at least... oh, let's say... *eighteen* to steal a kiss."

"Yeah, right," Fina says, rolling her eyes. "You tried to kiss me on our *second date*! Remember we were—"

"Well, alright, if you say so... but let me go on, woman. Things were different back then. We were rural folks. Growing up started sooner for us. We were married when she was just nighteen, and by the time she was twenty, Noah and Gil were tussling like Isaac and Jacob inside her. Or is it Jacob and Esau? I can't remember—"

"What he's trying to say, Patrick," Fina says, picking up the conversation when Aiden loses his point. "What *we're* trying to say is that we understand. Noah's assured us that you didn't abuse your position or act out of line with her. We can see that you're young enough, even though you've graduated secondary and started your student teaching. We've already talked this all out with Noah." She glances over at her daughter and continues. "Like we said to her, we know what the school says and what they have to do. And we actually agree with it. Noah's told us everything, and if she says you're trustworthy, it's good enough for us, unless—"

Aiden interrupts. "Unless you're a large, fine wolf in sheep's clothing. If I find that out, I'll come back to haunt you for the rest of your days."

"What you see is what you get," Patrick says, not quite sure if Aiden is joking but trying to assure them that there's no duplicity in him.

Seeming satisfied—at least for now—Fina invites them to fill their plates. Soon, their eating is only punctuated by a chorus of satisfied 'mmm's' and 'ahhh's.'

The conversation soon steers to Noah's Amazon trip. They want to know more about Seamus and his background, as well as the rest of Patrick's family.

"We were a fairly typical Irish family—just ma, da and me," Patrick begins. "My ma, Erin, was the real leader of the family. What she said was law. Da and I both knew not to cross her." His cadence slows as his voice lowers. "She did her best to keep us all in line and connected... until they divorced. She's gone now, though."

He pauses. His eyes briefly gaze into the tree arching over them. "You see, it's hard to describe. Her absence hasn't ever really been filled. I doubt if it ever will be... or can be. And as for me and my da... we just sort of drifted apart. I haven't seen him in years."

Fina and Aiden exchange a subtle glance, empathy evident in the softness of their eyes. They have questions they'd like to ask, but know it's not the right time, so they just continue to listen.

"I called Seamus and told him what happened with my job at the school. He's invited me to go to Toronto after the Amazon intensive. He says he might have an opportunity for me to do some work for him. I'm not sure what he has in mind, or even if I'd be interested. But putting some miles between myself and this place will probably do me some good."

Noah studies him, unable to read his subtext. *I wonder if I'm part of that need to get away—to figure things out.* Suddenly, she's also glad to have a reason to put some distance between herself and her life here. She wonders if that life includes Patrick. *Do I really want to get involved... to be tied down, right when I'm launching into my own future?*

"Who wants another beer?" Gil asks, standing up and looking around the circle. Everyone raises their hand and passes him their empties. After he returns, the conversation continues along other lines until, eventually, Patrick senses it's time to excuse himself. He thanks Fina and Aiden for including him and then turns to head home.

Noah walks around the side of the house with him. Their shoulders brush against each other as they walk toward Patrick's car in silence. When they reach it, she reaches out and catches his hand as it moves for the car door.

"Patrick, thanks for coming over. It means a lot to me for my ma and da to meet you after... everything that's happened. It took some spunk to face them."

He turns and looks into her eyes, seeing her concern, her questions, as well as her hopes.

"They're great, Noah. Really. I can see a lot of them in you. I hope to have a chance to get to know them better. And I hope I didn't scare them off."

"Scare *them* off? I hope they didn't scare *you* off!" They both chuckle. "I'll HOLO later after I see what the plans are for the rest of the evening. Want to meet up? Or... I could just drop by your place? I'd like to see what a science teacher's den looks like." She puts a finger to her chin, pretending to imagine.

"You mean *ex*-science teacher," he quips. There's a pause, and he looks at her wistfully. Not knowing what else to say, Noah leans in and gives him a quick hug.

"Goodbye, Mr. Wilde."

A week later, Patrick's home alone—HOLO surfing—neither paying attention to the images that parade around the room nor finding anything of real interest. He feels stuck and knows it. Now that school's finished, he and Noah have been able to spend more time together. Tonight, though, she's with Shea, having some "girl time." Sitting alone in the dark this evening, mindlessly wasting the hours, sheds some much-needed light on his life and how much he's avoided thinking about what happened. *Or more honestly*, he tells himself, *unwilling to consider what's next.*

While he is lost in his thoughts, the doorbell rings. Whoever it is keeps pressing the buzzer obnoxiously. *BRONG... BRONG... BRONG.* He compresses the HOLO with two fingers, looks around to make sure the place isn't a complete wreck, and goes to open the door.

"I'm coming. I'm coming... geez! What's the matter with you?" he mutters in a perturbed voice as he opens the door.

"Hey lad, don't you know not to talk to your elders that way?" Looking a bit rumpled, his uncle Seamus pushes the door open and drops his bag in the hall. "Don't you look a proper mess, son?" The older man puts a hand on his nephew's shoulder and then pulls him in for a long, hearty bear hug.

Patrick angles in and then slaps his uncle's back, feeling the brief scratch from their unshaven faces as he steps back.

"What are you doing here?" Patrick's mouth hangs open, still surprised. "I would have been over to see you in a few months. Did you miss me that much?"

"*Me*? Miss *you*? Nah... I missed old Eire... and a properly poured Guinness."

"Good to see you too, old-timer. Let me grab my wallet, and let's head down to the Brazen Head... that should remind you of what home tastes like."

They walk through light rain to the neighborhood pub and find a dark corner, removed from the spirited shouts and cheers. The Brazen is one of the few bars that's fiercely ignored progress, employing friendly female bartenders instead of the faux-fem server bots.

The two catch up, their conversation leisurely, both enjoying their pints of dark beer. After they order a second, Seamus leans in closer toward his nephew. His countenance shifts, his tone more somber.

"Patrick, I'm not just here because I miss you—which I do. Or because I miss Ireland—which I certainly do." The man shifts in his seat and pauses to take a long, thoughtful drink, then wipes both corners of his mouth. "There are things in my world... or more accurately, the whole planet, that are happening faster and faster. I've got things I need to tell you. Things about your ma. About me. About the future and how you might fit in."

Patrick looks down into his beer and bites his lip. Previously discarded uncertainties about the nature of his ma's research resurface.

"Listen. You don't know the whole truth," Seamus continues. "You barely know any of it, really. Your ma and I went to university together. While we were there, we were shocked by what we learned about the degrading health of the planet... the illusion of democracy... the corrupt power and limitless greed of the one percent of the one percent. We immersed ourselves in our research and were overwhelmed by grim statistics and models that have now exceeded the predictions."

Seamus scans the buzzing crowd, shaking his head, his smile carrying a now-practiced cynicism. "We were young then... and at first, idealistic. We believed in the potential for eco-advocacy to help shape global political and economic strategies. We gave our early energies to being part of the solution. Hell, I'm still trying to be part of that effort."

Patrick nods as he waits—his open expression conveys understanding and sympathy. Seamus examines his nephew, his pupils large, his expression cloudy. His gaze sweeps the lively pub, music blaring and voices raised—satisfied no one's listening.

Before continuing, he takes another long drink, then presses the sweating glass against his temple. "But here's what you don't know. Your ma and I... we both recognized... that tactics needed to change. Research and rhetoric would never be enough to reverse the tide. So, with her background in biochemistry and my connections in the Amazon, we set out to develop a kind of bio-arsenal.

"She discovered several bio-compounds in the Amazon's reptiles, insects and plants that could be used to trigger, or even mimic, a wide variety of lethal or near-lethal health events. The beauty of the plan was how these compounds could be delivered: Trojan-horse style, targeting individuals like corporate and political criminals who top the planet's 'most wanted' list."

Is he actually plotting to assassinate these people? Patrick's head spins, less from the second beer and more from his uncle's revelations— confessions, actually. "Are you fucking serious, Seamus? Shit this is crazy. Not to mention dangerous. And, oh yeah, illegal!" Patrick pushes his chair back and puts his arms behind his head—the volume of his words rises, causing a few heads to turn. "And here I thought you were just my eccentric uncle."

Seamus signals with his hands to calm down. "Son, that's what I wanted you to believe. The whole 'professor' thing is just my cover now."

Patrick sits, silent. Dazed. Unable to keep up.

"But the real tragedy... the unknown tragedy to *you*, is that there was an awful accident in the lab one day." Seamus stares into his beer, his eyes suddenly mournful. "I'm not sure how it happened, but your ma came in contact with a viral agent that hadn't yet been assigned a human exposure limit—"

"Hold on!" Patrick interrupts. "Are you saying she died because of something you were making?"

Seamus ignores the question and continues. "Her histamines went wild, and they triggered a full-body anaphylaxis spiral. We did everything we could for her, but it left her... compromised. You were just new in college... she didn't want to distract you. I'm so sorry, Patrick."

Seamus tentatively reaches out toward his nephew's arm but then pulls his hand back. The older man's remorse, his regret, is palpable. Patrick—shaking his lowered head— tries to stay focused, but his emotions keep piling up, making it impossible to absorb everything his uncle has been telling him.

Softer now, Seamus continues. "Afterwards, she recovered, but she had long stretches of confusion and made small mistakes. Maybe you remember some of them. Anyways, I've often wondered if her hang gliding accident could have been prevented—that she shouldn't have flown by herself that day. Who knows, really? I've had to live with the possibility every day of my life... along with my choice to mislead you. I'm sorry, son."

Patrick leans forward, squeezing his beer as if he's about to shatter the glass. His face is red. A dark mood has quickly settled over him—his fury aimed not only at the news about his ma's condition but also at what she and her uncle were really pursuing.

Before his nephew explodes, Seamus quickly interjects. "Patrick, your ma is a hero. She made the ultimate sacrifice. She made it for all—"

"I don't give a shit, Seamus!" Patrick shouts. Heads pivot from a table a few feet away. "She's gone. That's what matters. And you lied to me... and what's worse... it sounds like you could have prevented it."

Seamus answers his nephew's glare with grief-laden eyes. "I know... I'm... I'm so sorry. It's unforgivable."

The people at the nearby table return to their drinks and storytelling.

Patrick and his uncle sit in silence for several minutes, staring at nothing across the noisy pub, enveloped by the familiar buzz of rowdiness.

Eventually, Patrick expels a long, loud sigh. "It's just... a lot to digest. I need some time, Seamus... maybe a lot of time. I don't understand everything, but... I always felt there was more to your and Ma's work together. Whenever I was around, there seemed to be a screen, or... a door she would skillfully close whenever I'd ask about certain things. But, shit... what you're talking about is... radical, extremist talk. "

"I know, son. Believe me, I know."

Patrick peers at his uncle, his eyes narrow and wary. "So, why are you telling me this now?"

Seamus returns his nephew's inspection and says, "It's time, son. Your ma anticipated something like this, you know. With you in transition and with things with me rapidly evolving—or rather, *devolving*—I'm finding myself in need of help from someone I can trust completely. Nothing central for now, maybe some communications or courier work—I'd want you to stay unobserved, on the periphery. All this might not sit too well with you, but that's it... that's the score."

The two sit in silence, staring into their drinks. The atmosphere around them still masks the heaviness of the moment. Patrick's thoughts bounce around—raging... rationalizing... disputing... agreeing—as he tries to process everything he's just heard.

Eventually, he looks at his uncle—some of the hostility on his face gone, replaced by an unreadable expression. "I'll think about it. I've got to get away and take some time to clear my mind anyway. It's just too soon for me to make any commitments. But I promise I'll think about everything you've told me."

Seamus nods. "Of course, son. Take all the time you need. And you have the freedom to send me packing if that's what you decide. Okay?" Trying to lighten the mood, he waves the barmaid over toward the table. "Now, enough about all that, how about another round on me?"

They continue catching up, drifting into the usual subjects, even though the prior conversation hovers like a dense cloud of cigar smoke. As the night continues, Patrick gradually relaxes. *It's good to see the old man but... holy shit. He's not talking about some game. What the hell am I supposed to make of it?*

Then, for the first time in years, a question bobs up out of nowhere—*I wonder what Da would have to say about all this?*

PART FOUR

Episode 22: Extinction is Forever
HOLO-POD Hosted by Noah Calhoun-Greenling

"With the China Sea decimated by overfishing, Chinese fishing trawlers cover every square kilometer of coastal water—not just feed the People's Republic of China, but to keep its gargantuan economy on life support. The insatiable demand for seafood worldwide continues to soar, even as suppliers strain to keep up with it.

"However, the real impact is not our rising grocery bills, but rather, a collapsed food chain in which humans have been overconsuming for decades, eating the sea's bounty faster than it can reproduce. Sharks, tuna, salmon, rays, marlin, swordfish, skate, even the lowly sardine and anchovy are teetering on total species extinction.

"What's for dinner, you ask? I'm not sure, but it won't be fish!"

Summer 2060

Fort Meade, Maryland, USA (93° F / 34° C)

B.B. pushes the Chief in his wheelchair past the security checkpoint at NSA headquarters. The Chief knows there are rover-bots that could shuttle him around, but he prefers the statement the old chair makes. *I want any unfortunate bastard who has to deal with me to know I've survived four fuckin' generations. Who says age can't intimidate?* B.B. backs the wheelchair into an elevator; the twin oxygen tanks attached on either side mimic a pair of sidewinder missiles ready for battle.

An invisible, androgynous voice addresses them from overhead. *"Welcome back to the Puzzle Palace, Mr. Cartwright. I've been assigned to elevate you and your companion to the twelfth floor today."* Neither man speaks as the doors close and the lift begins its rapid ascent.

Exiting the elevator, B.B. smoothly steers the Chief to the right, ignoring the AI's offer to guide them to their destination. Despite the maze-like hallways, they've been here often enough that there's no need for a HOLO-ESCORT. After they make several turns, they come to a nondescript door with a placard that reads:

JEREMY BARGES
DEPUTY DIRECTOR
NSA: BIO/ECO-TERRORISM

B.B. doesn't wait to knock. He shoves the door open and pushes the Chief into the large office. The stocky man behind the desk jerks to attention—startled by the unannounced interruption. He scowls over his black half-rimmed readers, but when he notices who it is, his square jaw eases, and he stands to move toward the two men.

"Don't get up for me," barks the Chief. "I sure as hell wouldn't get up for you, even if I could."

The deputy director smirks. "It's good to see you too, Charles. B.B., pull your boss's chariot over here where we can sit."

Small talk is not either of the men's forte. They've known each other for over fifty years, but whenever there's a favor to call in, they go through the same old song and dance to meet face-to-face instead of by HOLO. Both know there's less risk of being compromised that way. Plus, neither has any real friends. The nature of acquiring such great professional power has surrounded them with a revolving door of "yes men" and subordinates, making the lack of friendship inevitable.

"What in the world is so important that you'd feel you had to come up here, Charles? I can't believe you'd leave that wannabe republic of yours unless it was something especially important to you... or personal. Is that it?" Barges leans forward, head tilted.

"That's the damn truth, Jerry. This string of attacks on me—not to mention *my* people—is *extremely* personal. You know how much I hate it up here." His face scrunches like an English bulldog. "But you federal bastards have wasted so much of my good money on worthless real estate here to ever pull up stakes and move down to civilization. Maybe if it keeps flooding, you'll all come to your senses."

The Chief looks around the office, glowering at the framed commendations and requisite photos, making no attempt to hide his disdain for everything his eye lands on. "Here's the deal. I think I was... no, I *know*... I was poisoned. Everyone, including my staff, the politicians, the media, hell, even my wife, thinks I had a heart attack. Come to find out, it wasn't my old ticker. It's some fuckin' new bio-weapon. And I'm pretty sure some eco-maniac is behind it. Same can be said for some of our goddamned top people, too. "

The deputy director listens, his steel-gray head nodding as he bites his bottom lip. "I was sorry when I heard everything you went through. It sounded awful, Charles. It's good to see you up and—"

"Don't treat me like I'm some snivelin' invalid, damn it! I could *still* kick your ass with both arms tied to this fuckin' wheelchair. That's not why I'm here."

"Okay, okay. Shit, Charles. You're just as high-strung as ever. So tell me, why are you here then?"

"I've deployed some of my own resources to a number of sites where this damned cocktail could have been developed. We'll see what they find. I can take care of the sites. But I want *you* to take care of those responsible for it. This is startin' to get out of hand, and I want your resources to get on board. It used to be that all these eco-hippies would just strap themselves to a redwood or set a piece of equipment on fire. But now, I know of at least eight other CEOs who have suffered health attacks similar to mine this year. I tell you, they're getting bolder."

The Chief's eyes narrow as he continues, his words measured and deadpan. "Remember, I own you, along with your whole damn NSA operation. You may even want to brief the President so little Madam White House can feel like she's a part of the crusade. But don't forget: our interests are your interests. Not the other way around. You read me?"

Jeremy is well acquainted with the Chief's point of view. In fact, it's why he has his position as deputy director. And they both know it.

Their imbalanced history traces back to their days at Rice University. Jeremy has often reflected on his indebtedness to the man. Without Charles, he wouldn't have been offered a bid from their fraternity, gotten his first interview with the National Security Agency, or been fast-tracked to a directorship. Over the years, he's witnessed his powerful friend open seemingly closed doors—either with ease or by force. All that was required in exchange was to perform as expected, like any other useful business asset. That arrangement has never deviated, even as their lives branched on divergent paths.

"I'll see what we can do, Charles. Anything else? You got time for lunch?"

"B.B., get me out of here," the Chief barks, not even acknowledging the invitation. "Storm's a-brewing, Barges. Mark my words. It's been too easy for too long."

The deputy director opens the door for B.B., who pushes the Chief into the hallway and back through the maze toward Dallas.

Noah's yawn sounds like a cow giving birth. She's still waking up ridiculously early. Because of the time difference, she's wide awake at four in the morning. And that's after a restless night, staring at the tent's thin, green fabric at one o'clock... two o'clock... three o'clock. *I'm done. I'm so sick of just lying here,* she tells herself as she quietly slides out from her sleeping bag and sits up on the aluminum cot. Four feet away is her tent mate, Sylvie, a white-haired nineteen-year-old from Fresno, California.

"No trouble sleeping there," Noah murmurs under her breath. The slender Nordic princess burrows deeper into her sleeping bag and gently snores, seeming to practice her humming bee breath while she dreams.

Noah grabs a clean T-shirt, shorts, and underwear, stuffs them into her backpack, and slips out of the tent. Carefully zipping the tent back up so nothing can slither in, she heads away from the camp toward the shower station. Although she wishes someone else had gone ahead of her to scare off any giant insects or poisonous reptiles, after three days here, she's started to adapt, maneuvering around the deadly inhabitants with care and respect.

After her less-than-lukewarm shower, she carefully folds and puts her dirty clothes into her pack. *They're not too grubby... and who knows? I might have to rewear them if I can't figure out how to do laundry.*

Fully awake now, she squints as she picks her way through the darkness toward the tent that serves as the canteen to heat some water for tea. She shifts on her feet impatiently, waiting for the kettle to boil. Lost in her thoughts, she doesn't hear the quiet footsteps approaching from behind her. Not wanting to startle her, Seamus clears his throat to register his presence.

"Sorry to interrupt. I'm usually the only one up at this black hour," he says with a wry grin.

"Well, looks like I beat you to it, Dr. Wilde. Seems I've come down with a bad case of jet lag. What's your excuse?" Noah relaxes as she takes in the casual way the rugged academic carries himself. *I really can see the family resemblance,* she admits to herself.

He pulls up a chair beside her as she lowers a bundle of Lyons tea bags into the kettle to steep. They both stare at the steam rising for a few seconds. Just before it starts to feel awkward, he speaks softly, almost reverentially, as if considering a rarely-visited memory.

"I've not always been such a poor sleeper. Five hours of sleep is only about half of what I would settle for when I was nineteen. Sorry. Don't try to do the math. It's multivariable calculus!" Noah's wry grin and raised eyebrow show she doesn't get the joke.

Seamus takes a deep breath and then slowly exhales. "When we first set up the camp, I could sleep through anything—even the howler monkeys. I didn't need earplugs, and I didn't have your fancy silence-bots back then. No, I would sleep like a wee one then."

He trails off, seeming to lose himself in his memories. Noah quietly pours two cups of tea and hands him one.

"So, what happened? Your bladder shrink? That's what my da says stole his nights from him," she says, trying to lighten things up a bit.

"Nah, though there's some truth in what your da tells you. I wish it were just that. Then I suppose I could just wear a man diaper and be done with it," he says with a wink. She chuckles softly.

He lets out another long breath and then continues in his quiet, reflective way. "When we started the camp, it was just me and my sister, Erin—Patrick's ma. Has he mentioned her?" Noah simply nods before he continues. "She was a dedicated leader and courageous activist, as well as a brilliant biochemist—always willing to do whatever it took to make a difference."

Not wanting to interrupt the man as he reflects, Noah sits still, continuing to nod along. *Patrick's not said much about her... she died in an accident... she divorced his da... but that's about it.*

Seamus takes a sip of tea and leans back, stretching his legs in front of him. "There's a small plaque at the foot of a giant kapok tree about three kilometers east of camp. I put it there after Erin died. According to the jungle's ancient legend, the kapok tree cradles the soul of the forest and connects Earth to heaven. You might want to walk out there and have a look sometime."

"I'd like that," she answers, smiling. "And that legend... it all sounds rather lovely."

"Patrick tells me that *you* have a gift that helps you connect with trees back home." He looks at her for a long moment. "You see, this tree's quite a special one, at least to me. I scattered my sister's ashes around its feet after she was cremated. I know that's what she would have wanted—even though we never discussed it. She would have liked the idea that she was somehow nourishing life even after she was gone."

Noah feels a bit exposed by what Patrick's told his uncle, but she nods along. *I can imagine wanting the same thing when I'm gone.*

He sinks into his private thoughts again, shifting to sit up while he looks into his cup. "I'm not sure why I'm telling you all this. Maybe it's because, in a way, you remind me of her. She would have liked you."

Noah's countenance reflects her youthful earnestness, even though she feels self-conscious about what's been said about her. "You honor me, Dr. Wilde. Thank you for telling me about your sister."

"There's so much more to say about her... how she helped set the trajectory of this program... and, if truth be told, my own life's work. But enough about that. I've been way too down in the cups for this early in the morning. *'Death leaves a heartache no one can heal.'* I usually only slip into my Irish melancholy after a few shots of Jameson."

Quickly throwing back the last of his tea, he flashes Noah a sad smile and heads out into the jungle's surrounding darkness, the growing cacophony giving birth to another dawn.

The morning's field excursion takes Noah and a small team of students down the Itaquai River in search of some of the Amazon's most deadly wildlife. Over the next few hours, they carefully pick their way through the river bank's mud and dense undergrowth, spotting several Brazilian wandering spiders, a swarm of bullet ants, two dart frogs, and even a large pit viper.

Before they set out, Dr. Wilde announces how his unconventional approach to safety works—introducing the students to these predators in their habitat so they can recognize them before they make a lethal mistake. Noah has learned from Patrick that much of the proprietary research undertaken at the camp's laboratory focuses on these natural assassins—the deadly mystique helping to keep unwanted eyes away from the more secretive aspects of the Amazon project.

At noon, when they trudge back to camp—the humidity hovers at 95%—Noah feels hot, slimy, and famished. Grabbing two peanut butter and honey sandwiches, she finds a table and sits down. Over her shoulder, she hears someone call out in broken English, "Hello, Noah, can I join you?"

She turns her head and sees Yoshi waving at her. His short, round body and straight black bangs, brushing against his large-framed glasses, make him look like a cute little beetle. He seems almost to skip toward the chair beside her and then waits to be invited.

"Sure. Help yourself." Noah nods to the empty seat as she removes her tye-dye bandana and wipes the sweat on her forehead. "But I'm not sure I'll be much company. That hike—on top of not getting much sleep—is really kicking my Irish butt."

"Mine too." He grins. "I mean my Japanese backside. For me, it's exact opposite. When we get up, I need to be going to sleep."

Noah smiles back. A comfortable silence settles between them. Neither one seems uncomfortable eating quietly together. It seems to her that a subtle yet growing bond between them already exists. Deep in her chest, she feels a gentle, slow vibration humming. She glances sideways at this wisp of a young man and wonders, *Is it coming from him? And what is it?*

Too exhausted to think about it, she pops the last bite of her sandwich in her mouth and licks the honey off her fingers. "Yoshi. I've gotta go take a nap. I'm so tired that a pit viper curled up on my cot couldn't keep me awake. Good having lunch with you. Let's do it again," she says, then performs her signature gesture, knocking her two fists together.

He bows his head and offers the same motion in return, saying nothing.

Noah quickly falls into a deep sleep. The combination of sleepless nights and hot, humid days takes over like a drug. After a couple hours, she forces herself to sit up—her T-shirt clings to her sweaty torso as if pasted there by unseen hands. Half-open eyes blink away the drowsiness that still shrouds the periphery of her vision. Her hair, a wild, tangled nest, cradles her slender nose and freckled cheeks.

For a moment, she considers studying for tomorrow's quiz. But after this morning's field trip, she feels the jungle's many dangers and names have burned themselves into her brain. Instead, remembering her early morning conversation with Dr. Wilde, she decides to take a walk to see the giant kapok tree.

Following the small trail that leads east of camp and into the jungle, she passes the low-slung structure that houses Dr. Wilde's research labs. She pauses, sensing she's being watched. There's a sudden, palpable silence now—as if someone muted a HOLO-VID. After a few moments, peering into the jungle's shadows and seeing nothing, she shifts her attention back to the building.

A vibration emanates from inside. *It seems empty, but I don't think it's exactly uninhabited.* The secretive nature of the place, combined with Seamus's reluctance to discuss the work that goes on inside it, arouses her curiosity. She looks around for something to stand on and finds a rusty fifty-gallon drum. Still partially filled with some thick liquid, she struggles with the barrel's weight but eventually manages to wheel it under a high, narrow window. Scrambling on top of it, she raises up on her toes to look in. As her eyes adjust to the darkness, she suddenly becomes aware of something, or rather, *several* somethings inside that seem to be reaching out for her.

Her eyes widen. Her jaw slackens in bafflement. On long tables are hundreds of glass cases stacked three or four high, filled with deadly amphibians, reptiles, and insects—many she had seen earlier in the jungle. Most, however, she only recognizes from watching HOLO-VIDs. It's as if a giant, exotic pet store has been compressed into the small space.

A shiver begins along her shoulders and streaks down her spine. Her thoughts are unable to keep up with what she's feeling. Adrenaline. Excitement. Anticipation. A burst of life-preserving cortisol explodes from her middle and courses through the rest of her body. However, it's not fear that's driving her primal response. It feels like something's *preparing* her. But preparing her for what?

She watches the deadly menagerie as they move in unison to the side of their cases nearest to her. *What's happening?*

The cases of yellow scorpions and vipers near the window look directly at her. With dark, unblinking eyes, they convey that they are ready. Ready for her. Ready to receive their orders.

Instantly, she knows. *I'm being prepared to lead. To lead an army... or if not an army—a revolution.*

Noah walks the three kilometers slowly, head down, trying to digest what's just happened. She's often experienced vivid connections with trees, some plants, and even birds back home. They've always seemed benevolent, motherly even. But this was unlike anything she's felt before. *I've gotten used to feeling... different. Strange even. Yet, I never lost sight of what was normal. But now, the lines between what's ordinary and what's extraordinary seem to be merging.*

Suddenly, she feels alone, isolated. She misses Shea. Her friend has always been there to listen, a safe place to be herself and express her doubts. *And Patrick. I wonder what he's up to? It's weird to be here without him.*

The sun settles in the west behind the jungle's thick foliage. She senses again that she's not alone, that she's being watched. *That's not it... it's more like I'm being watched over.* Soft light slants at an angle overhead and dapples the path and its surroundings like a verdant zebra. *There! What's that?*

Fronds of plants rustle in motion while a thick, humid mist swirls upward. A break in the clouds sends a shaft of golden sunlight that suddenly reveals the brilliant patches of a spotted feline. *A jaguar. A pair of them.* Their amber-colored eyes gaze flatly toward Noah. She becomes aware that she's been holding her breath. She exhales deeply, never looking away, their eye contact transmitting some mutual primal intelligence. Feeling more awe than fear, Noah nods her head toward the pair of powerful cats. As if in return, the two simply yawn and paw the ground with their long claws, then slip silently back into the shadows.

Sensing the encounter is over, she turns and begins walking again. *Why don't I feel afraid?* she asks herself. Not finding any good reason, she loses herself in the simple rhythm of walking, mesmerized by the mysterious beauty that surrounds her.

Eventually, the path she follows abruptly turns, opening into an expansive clearing. The space is nearly fifty meters in diameter—a perfect circle, as far as she can tell—ancient yet organic. But most striking is the mammoth tree standing in the center, dwarfing her and everything else. *The giant kapok!*

Her eyes travel slowly from the ground upward toward a small, blue ring of heaven, then outward to muscular limbs reaching out to the jungle wall, but not touching it. She feels as if she's standing within a roofless cathedral—enclosed, covered, yet also accessible, open to all possibilities.

Reverentially, Noah walks around the circle's perimeter and then spirals toward the center as if led through an unseen labyrinth. As she approaches the tree, she thoughtfully steps over large, exposed roots. But when she gets closer to the trunk, she has to scramble using her hands and feet. She climbs over mammoth tendrils that have become a tight, growing weave, completely entwined now in their parallel explorations of the earth around them.

She feels the vibration she often feels when encountering, or rather *being encountered*, by such ancient giants. But this time, something's different. She sits between two giant roots that curve into the trunk, almost disappearing into a small cavern of bark and moss. As she does, she senses another presence—one that's not made of wood and sap but rather bone and blood. There's a sudden pulse of energy in her brain—something about it reminds her of the energy she picks up in Patrick—and she knows.

"Oh my God. Erin," she whispers. *"You're still here, aren't you?"*

Laois County, Ireland (93° F / 34° C)

It's been over a year since Gil's been out to see his da. He hasn't strictly been avoiding him, but he's not felt any real connection with the old man either. He figures today's a good day to let his truck run for a while and see what kind of shape it's in. *A trip to Da's berm hut sounds just about right.*

He backs the truck out of the garage and turns toward the road. Too bad he hasn't installed a HOLO-SOUND yet, but he's low on cash. As he heads out of town and gets off the main roads, his mind wanders to the future. *I wonder what's next. Moving away—that's for sure. But to do what? And where?*

His engineering teacher, Mr. Tully, is encouraging him to attend Technological University in Dublin. He's told Gil that they have a dual studies program in biotechnology and sustainable energy. On top of that, if you're accepted, they place you in a paid internship on day one. *Maybe I could get that new sound system then. And maybe Da would see some of the value in my skills.*

He misses the turn into the woods where the berm hut is and has to backtrack. The entwining tree branches and undergrowth make the pathway's tight passage unrecognizable since he was here last. Then, about halfway in—the ground still showing tire tracks from Noah's recent visit—

it starts to look familiar.

When he shuts the truck engine off, he steps out into the absolute silence of the woods' shadowy denseness. Not exactly silence. Harriers overhead, buntings on the tree limbs, and grouse in the underbrush. *How do I remember all this?*

The boy in him hasn't felt this way in a long time. But the independent adolescent in him warns him to have nothing to do with any of it. He looks up when he hears the gentle wind stirring the trees' branches; he watches them sway back and forth as if sweeping the sky clean. Gradually, he starts to notice something else inside him—he still feels drawn to this place, to the earth and the values his ma and da planted in him.

He moves slowly to the two *súgán* chairs by the front door. *Da's workmanship has improved,* he observes, running his hand over the smooth, gentle curves of the oak wood. Sitting down, he feels glad he came. He's pleased with his truck—that it didn't give him any trouble, even on the rough trail. Rocking on the chair's smooth rockers, he silently wonders, *Maybe Da and I still share a few things in common.*

After several minutes, he hears whistling. Growing up, he remembers how his da would always be humming or whistling an obscure Irish tune composed by some forgotten, ancient bard with a surname that began with a Mac, or Mc, or O'. They were all inspired by some woodland fairy—or more likely from one too many single-pot whiskeys.

His da—tromping into the clearing—does a quick double take, taking in the car and his son sitting there. He lays an armful of hardwood branches on the ground, then pauses, before cautiously approaching to sit in the other chair.

"Hi, Gil... good to see you, son. Everything okay?"

Gil nods, extending a warm half-smile. "It's all good, Da. I've just been working on my new truck and wanted to take it out on a test drive. It felt like a good day to come up and see you. How've you been?"

Despite the moments they shared at graduation, the same old awkward distance between father and son soon returned, filling the void left by Da's absence. They continue to catch up—their weak connection, hard to ignore. Finally, Gil risks speaking into the vacant space between them, his brow focused and resolute.

"Da, it's not a surprise, you know... but I'm different from the rest of the family. I'm not much like Ma. And Noah... she's got something you all share. But I'm not like her. Or *you*, either. So... where's that leave me, huh? I just—"

"Don't, Gil. It's not like that—" The big man shakes his head, his curly brown mane falling across his brow.

"No, let me finish. I need to say this. Can you just listen to me for a minute?" The boy's tone intensifies. Aiden chews his lip, listening. "I'll be headed out on my own soon. And I haven't felt like I fit in here for a long time. It's made me feel... I don't know... less of a son or something like that. And like you've felt... to tell you the truth... less of a father to me. I'm not sure either of us has tried like we should. I know I haven't, but you living out here and me trying to figure things out without anyone's help... it just... it's just made me feel like I'm all on my own. Like I don't really matter to the family. Noah always comes back happy, telling me how good it was to see you. But for some reason I know... if I come here to see you, I'll just leave feeling worse than I did before."

His da looks at him, his walnut-brown eyes quickly welling with tears called forth by the depth of the hurt and isolation his son has suffered. The guilt he feels over their separation presses down on his shoulders, burdened with its unbearable weight.

Finally, Aiden breaks the silence. "Phew... that's quite a load you've been carrying, son. I'm so, so sorry." Gil stares back, his eyes neutral, and waits for his da to continue. "I don't expect you to understand, let alone *accept* this strange life that's been dealt to me. It's been mine to bear, but it's also been yours to suffer. I *see* that. I *feel* that." The big man sniffles, then wipes his eyes. "Every single day, I have to face the ache... my longing to be with you and your ma and sister. It's harder on you than Noah—I know that. She's got your ma. But look... like you said... who do you have? Some freak who can't even live with his family. I don't blame you for not coming out here anymore. Seeing me is probably... one more reminder of all the things you never got."

Gil looks away. It's uncomfortable to watch his da speak like this—more honestly than he's ever heard from him before. But he's also relieved. He's always assumed that the distance between them meant there was something wrong with *him*. Something missing in *him*. The hurt he's carried remains, but there's something else. Something new. *Compassion.*

"Da. Listen. I'll be okay. You probably did your best, even when it felt like you couldn't. And I get it. As much as I hate to admit it... Noah *is* special... she's special in ways I can never hope to be—"

"Son, that's not true," Da interrupts.

"No, it's alright, Da. I'm just not like you... or her. And I'm able to accept that. I'm more attracted to man-made things—cars, engines, technology—all the things that you can't be around. And that's hard. I hate it that we can't share some of that. But I just hope you can accept that *that's me.*"

"Accept it? I *love* all those things you can do, Gil. And I love who you've become. I'm so proud of you, Son. Honestly, I'm intimidated by you sometimes—I have no idea how you do the things you do." Da smiles, his lips quivering. "I look at you, and I just can't believe that someone as remarkable and talented as you came from me." Da suddenly breaks down, finding his own unacknowledged grief, released now in a stream of tears lodged in the depths of his soul. Aiden blindly reaches for his son's hand and envelops it in his large, calloused fingers.

Gil watches as his father openly sobs, then allows himself to be pulled into the big man's chest. There, he also begins to cry as he hasn't since he was a small boy, knowing that something out of place in both of them has shifted back into alignment.

Kilkenny, Ireland (92° F / 33° C)

A month later, Gil steers his Land Rover down the gravel driveway and onto the street. He looks at the gas gauge to make sure he has enough petrol to get to his da's. *Should be fine.* The frequent visits to the berm hut are becoming something he looks forward to.

As he rounds the curve on the narrow road east of his house, he's listening to some classic rock from the early 2000s on his new HOLO-SOUND system. The band U2 is one of his and Da's favorites. Sometimes, on days like today, he's quickly lost in the beat, the monotony of the Edge's guitar, counterbalanced by Bono's open-throated fire breathing. Not just lost—able to *find* what he's lost. The music makes him *feel* what he's lost—helps him name the feelings and emotions buried inside.

For the first time in a long while, Gil finds himself singing along. *"I have held... the hand of a devil... But I still haven't found what I'm—"*

Suddenly, a car shoots out from a side road, dead ahead of the Rover—brakes squeal. Gil yanks on the steering wheel to narrowly avoid the collision. His heart hammers like Larry Mullen's rim shots on *Sunday Bloody Sunday*. He's pulled off the road at a forty-five-degree angle on the left side. The front bumper completely plunged into the hedgerow—his truck tilts, almost in the ditch.

When he finally collects his wits and looks out the side window, he expects to see a little old lady, lost in senile confusion. Instead, he sees Colin smiling from inside a rusted copper-colored Volkswagen Golf. Gil's adrenaline flips—the jolt of a nearly fatal collision replaced by a boiling rage at his friend's stupidity. Jumping out of his car, Gil storms up to Colin's open window.

"What the fuck are you doing? You could have gotten both of us killed, you wanker!"

The other boy looks up and just smirks at him. He shoves Gil's hands off the window's edge, then unwinds himself from the small car. He's eight centimeters taller than Gil and ten kilos heavier. *I really don't give a shit right now*, Gil tells himself, squaring off. Ready.

"Calm down," the bigger boy says scornfully. "Nobody's hurt. Shite! Ya' think I'd let ya' hit old Grinder here?" he says, slapping the hood of the idling junker.

The two haven't seen each other since graduation. Colin ghosted Gil after the scene his da' made there. And before that—after Gil found out

Patrick had gotten canned—he tracked Colin down at his hangout in Jenkinstown Wood. Gil showed up, ready to rip his ex-friend a new one, but dialed it back when he found Colin holding court with his little gang.

"That's really grand coming from you," Gil fires back. "Don't get off telling me to calm down. What's wrong with you? You know I only told you all that stuff about Noah so you could give her a hard time—like you usually do. You weren't supposed to twist it into some full-blown affair and ruin that poor sod's life. What the hell were you thinking?"

Colin snickers dismissively. "Hey, ya' mucker. You gave it to them as much as I did. Come on, grow up... grow a pair, will ya'?"

The two glare at each other for a few tense beats. Gil is boiling—both fists clench with rage. The guilt and anger swirl inside him.

"Want to know a little secret, mate?" Colin's voice escalates as he carries on. "I've never cared a thing for either of you... you or yer sister. Ya' know why?" He snickers and then throws his head back, looking down his nose at Gil. "Yer just two of a kind—two sad little Greezlings. We're *nothing* alike! Ya' hear me? Nothing!"

Gil's eyes narrow, his voice becomes accusatory. "You're damn right we're nothing alike! You and your drunkard hooch of an old man. If I know you, you'll grow up to be just as shit-faced as he is."

"Watch it! You don't talk about my da like that. Ya' hear?" Colin's eyes and voice go flat as he presses on. "All this was just a little payback for what yer ma did to our family... back when she stuck her little *hippie nose* in the town's business and got me dad canned. Ya' know, she ruined a pretty sweet life for us. Getting that stupid science teacher canned and dragging yer snooty sister through the mud was just some of yer own medicine. Ya' read me?"

Colin spits a large glob of phlegm on the pavement between them, a nasty sneer on his face. Gil, his fists and jaws working in unison, starts to walk toward the bigger boy, then halts when Colin launches in again.

"Did ya' know that it was me da and his cronies that busted up yer ma's shop? I was told they did a pretty good job, too. But I never got to add *my* boot to yer family's pathetic little neck... at least not until now. Go on!

Get yer little Greezling ass out of here before I—"

Suddenly, Gil springs at the other boy, catching him off guard, and slams his knuckles into his mouth.

Colin howls with pain. Blood trickles down his chin. For a moment, Colin looks at him, stunned that Gil actually stood up to him. Then, his bravado quickly returns.

"Ya' fuckin' better get out of here, ya' hear? I guess you owed me that... ya' tool. But here's what I'm gonna do... I'm gonna count to five... and then... if yer still here, I'm gonna beat the shit out of ya'. One... two..."

Gil glares at him, then dismissively turns his back on Colin—half of him tells himself it's not worth it—the other half hopes the boy will grab him from behind so he can satisfy his hunger for revenge.

"...three... four..."

As he walks to his car, he feels Colin's eyes on him, mocking him for how easily he was able to manipulate and use him.

Gil jumps in and starts the engine, jamming the transmission into reverse. The tires bite into the soft earth and throw mud from under the truck's chassis onto the Volkswagen's side panel. Colin's face turns dark with hatred as the soil ricochets onto his jeans. As the truck accelerates, Gil's middle finger snaps out the window. In the rearview mirror, he catches sight of Colin—one hand repaying the gesture.

That was stupid, Gil chides himself. Then, he remembers the shocked look on Colin's face. He smirks to himself as a rush of satisfaction courses quickly through him. *But shit that felt good. I thought he might actually wet himself after I landed that punch.*

Terra Nova, Vale do Javari, State of Amazonas, Brazil (101° F / 38° C)

More often than not, Yoshi and Noah find themselves paired together on their daily expeditions. The two have developed an easy, comfortable way of communicating that reminds Noah of her friendship and bond with Shea.

This morning, they were challenged to identify as many birds as they could see or hear within four hours. After Dr. Wilde had paired the students for the competition, he sent them into the forest to track their sightings.

Later—after a few hours of searching—Noah and Yoshi rest on the stump of a giant Brazil nut tree and share a drink from her canteen. With a practiced flourish, Yoshi dramatically pulls out two crushed peanut butter and honey sandwiches from his backpack and extends one to her.

Noah grabs one and says, "You really know how to wine and dine a girl, Yoshi."

He takes the bait and plays along. "Is this a date, then, Noah? I thought we were just boy-girl teammates." After a quick wink, his eyes—black as midnight—linger.

Is he flirting with me? Noah wonders what Patrick would think of her new friendship. *It's not like Patrick and I are committed or anything... more like an unspoken understanding... whatever that means.*

Yoshi clears his throat, bringing her back to the present moment. "Okay, I count thirty-seven birds so far—if we count the motmot and the horned screamer, which we only heard, but didn't see. You okay with that?"

"Yep! Totally! Dr. Wilde told us it's okay to count birds we heard but didn't see *if* we were ninety percent sure. I can't think of what else it could have been, can you?"

"No. I'm good with that," he quickly answers, nodding his head. His almond-shaped eyes remain fixed on her, and he asks, "Did you have a favorite, Noah?"

Her eyes narrow, and she gently surveys the space over his head as she considers his question. "That's hard to say. So many of them were so incredibly gorgeous—the toucans, the hummingbirds, macaws, and parakeets. I'm blown away at how endless the beauty is here—it's everywhere!" She pauses, as if replaying a scene in her mind, and then continues. "But if I had to choose, I'd go with the laughing falcon. Seeing it catch that coral snake... wow. Can you imagine the courage it takes to attack something that deadly? I mean, why take the risk when there's so much else to feed on?"

Yoshi slowly nods as he listens to her, his black eyes dancing above round cheekbones. "That's a good choice, I think... for you, Noah. For me, it was definitely the hyacinth macaw. Did you see that wingspan? Over a meter and a half. And its bright blue color! Fantastic!"

Noah smiles, then wipes her hands on her shorts and stands up. "Hey, let's get going, mister. I want us to get at least forty on our list before time runs out. I know you're not the competitive type, but I want to see what they've cooked up for the prize."

As they turn to walk down the trail, a laughing falcon dives onto a low-hanging limb above where they were sitting and watches them leave.

"*W-hah... hah... hah... hah.*" Yoshi and Noah spin around when they hear its eerie, human-like call. Held between its sharp talons, a dying coral snake squirms, soon to be just one more meal for the hunter's three hungry fledglings.

At one o'clock, each pair of students filters into the canteen. There are twenty in all. They begin to find seats next to each other, sweaty and smeared with brown soil or stains from who knows what. Several down gulps of cool water, dehydrated after running out of water on their hunt. Noah and Yoshi sit silently, heads together, looking over their list.

After a few minutes, Dr. Wilde steps into the tent's center. "Well, I see you all made it back. I'm not sure what happened this year... we usually lose a few on this challenge. The ones that survive are grateful for the extra food left by their disappearance." Everyone groans good-naturedly. "Let's check in to see how you did. Samuel, you and Clare go first."

Each pair reports their sightings and final tally. Eventually, it's Noah and Yoshi's turn to present. Yoshi stands silently beside Noah as she announces their results.

"We recognized forty-three different birds, Professor. Four of them were just from their songs."

"Very good, you two. Well done," Dr. Wilde says. "And last but not least, how about you, Sylvie and Jean? How did you do?"

Sylvie, her white hair in braids, stands up, looks at Noah, and frowns as she mouths, *"I'm sorry."* She clears her throat and then faces the professor. "We were pretty lucky and identified forty-five birds by sight... and two by song... so that gave us forty-seven. Jean, he was amazing—"

A female voice yells out, "I bet he was!" The group snickers.

Sylvie flushes, then continues. "Jean was *amazing*... because he found five different hummingbirds and recognized the songs of a capped heron and a cream-colored woodpecker."

Another student whispers loudly enough for everyone to hear. "Wow! Did she say a cream... colored... wood... pecker?" Everyone guffaws at the heckler's wisecrack. Now it's Jean's turn to blush as Sylvie—hamming it up in mock disgust—scoots further away from beside him.

"Okay, okay! We've had our wee bit of fun," Dr. Wilde says loudly, trying to corral everyone's attention. "But seriously, that's a new record, you two. Well done! Very well done! The highest count before today was two years ago at a whopping forty-two. The two of you, as well as Noah and Yoshi's team, have both broken their record. But... there's only room for one winner. Jean, Sylvie. Congratulations!"

The students clap and whoop. Enjoying the attention, Sylvie flourishes a deep, full-body bow next to Jean, who awkwardly curtsies, unleashing a fresh wave of whistles and laughter.

Dr. Wilde's voice eventually breaks in above the ruckus. "And for their heroic work and outstanding contribution to science today, they will each receive... drum roll please," the Professor announces, as if he's the emcee on a cheesy game show. "A second go at the shower!"

The students slap the pair on the back, whistling and high-fiving each other. Sylvie and Noah's eyes soon find each other amidst the racket. Noah grins widely at her tent-mate and then points with two fingers at the couple, mouthing her encouragement. *You go for it, girl.*

As Noah walks into the canteen later, Jake, the part-time cook and full-time intern, is setting dinner out. She spots Sylvie and Jean in the corner, both with wet hair, laughing at some private joke. Noah scans the makeshift cafeteria until she finds Yoshi. She slips in line to join him. After picking up their food, they find a spot where they can sit by themselves. *As if we haven't already been together enough today,* she thinks to herself.

But she's noticed how comfortable she is with him; something natural and organic has grown between them, without the need for words. She breaks the silence and leans closer to him so no one can overhear her.

"I went to see the kapok tree I told you about last week. You know, the one Dr. Wilde told me about... where his sister's ashes were scattered." The moment reminds her of how she feels when she confides in Shea.

Yoshi turns toward her, his head leaning in, almost touching hers. "You did? How come you not mention it before?" he whispers, sounding mildly perplexed as his brow scrunches over his eyes.

"Yoshi," she begins and then halts, weighing whether to continue. "There's something I need... that's not right. There's something I *want* you to know about me. I didn't tell you before because it's part of my... identity... and in a strange way... sheesh, this is hard to admit... it makes me feel *special.*"

She pauses, but before there's time to gauge his reaction, she presses on. "But it's given me a lot of grief, too... and conflict. It's created problems with my friends and classmates... even my family. I thought maybe here, I'd be able to leave it all behind me. But... it seems to have followed me here."

Yoshi leans away, a puzzled expression on his face. "What do you mean? You confuse me sometimes." Noah takes a deep breath and looks back at him, searching his black, almond-shaped eyes. *Can I trust him?*

Taking a deep breath, she launches in. "Yoshi, I sometimes have a connection, a vibration that passes through me with... certain trees. I've had it since I was little, but it seems to be growing. It seems like it's becoming more... I don't know... *vivid*. More *sentient*. I guess that's it. There are times I've seemed to experience a sort of verbal connection. Almost like I'm being addressed, *called* even, by these giant green sentinels. Are you sure you can handle this without writing me off as nuts?"

Yoshi gently smiles at her and nods his head. His wordless affirmation registers as he shifts his posture toward her.

"So," she continues, "the other day, when I went to the giant kapok tree, I sat down, and as I was sitting there, I had an overwhelming sensation. Something I'd never felt before. I didn't just sense the energy of the tree reaching out to me, but I felt a *human* energy. And I imagined... no, I *knew*... I knew it was Dr. Wilde's sister, Erin.

"Yoshi, it seemed like she was still there. In some mysterious way, she was there... in the tree's sap, or its fiber, or leaves. There wasn't any interaction, I just... I don't know. I just had a definite awareness. And I think I need to go back. I feel like there's something more for me. That's not quite right. Something... for the future. I don't know. I just know I have to go back."

Yoshi looks at her earnestly and waits for a moment, then says, "Can I go with you, Noah?"

She tilts her head, looking back at him through her shimmering green eyes, and wonders, *Who in the world are you? Who might you become?*

Not coming up with an answer, she responds, "I'd like that, Yoshi. It would be good to have the company. And I'd really like for you to see this amazing clearing the tree has somehow formed. It's like a natural cathedral. Back home, we call a place like that a thin place—where the veil between the spiritual and physical almost disappears. You know... a holy place. A place that makes you want to take off your shoes."

"Noah, in my culture, we take our shoes off whenever we go into any house, no matter how nice or not nice. But I get what you say," he says with a knowing smile.

Later that night, Noah and Sylvie catch up while lying on their cots in the dark.

"Thanks for the nudge earlier," Sylvie says. "It made it easier for me to admit how I feel about him."

"I'm not sure I'm following, Syl. What do you mean?"

Tentatively, Sylvie answers, her words slowly drifting through the darkness between them. "It's like... you gave me permission. Like it was okay to follow my heart. To not overthink how I really feel about Jean."

Noah winks, even though she knows Sylvie can't see her in the dark. "Well, you're welcome. I'm not sure I've ever had much luck as a matchmaker." After a lull, she continues. "You know, you kind of remind me of my best friend from back home, Shea. She's always needed me to help her learn to color outside the lines. But then, she eventually snaps back and feels guilty about it."

"That sounds about right." Sylvie agrees. Both girls chuckle and then lapse into the quiet.

"So, tell me about Jean," Noah asks. Sylvie answers with a dreamy description that makes them both giggle girlishly. They carry on like that late into the night—embarrassing secrets, private hopes and heart-breaking tragedies entrusted with one another—until they give up and gradually drift off.

It's after two in the morning when Noah wakes from a deep sleep—her heart racing for some reason. As she shakes the fog away, she hears gruff, raised voices coming from somewhere outside in the distance. *Is that Dr. Wilde? He sounds... upset.*

She lies still a few moments, unsure of what she should do. Unable to ignore the professor's distress, she slips quietly out of her tent and follows the sound of the altercation, leading her toward the canteen. As she creeps through the blackness, she senses dark movements just out of sight, matching her pace on both sides of her. A faint trace of musk signals another's presence. *The jungle has a thousand eyes, she tells herself,* trying to reassure herself.

Not wanting to be noticed, she approaches the voices quietly and stands in the shadows. Professor Wilde is backlit, standing in the doorway to the canteen. Another figure in camo gear stands inside the tent. Between them is a life-sized HOLO image of a man in a dark suit.

Dr. Wilde's voice suddenly thunders, thick with resentment, "Merton, I'll ask you again, what the hell's going on here? And why, in God's name, is one of your hired guns creeping into my camp in the middle of the night? I could have shot him, thinking he was, I don't know... *you!*"

The voice from the HOLO is arrogant. Rough. Condescending. "Wilde, is that any way to treat an old friend? In case you haven't noticed, it's a jungle out there." The man chuckles, seeming amused at himself. "Shit, my associate could have fallen into a pit full of piranhas."

"Now there's a thought, you goddamned son-of-a-bitch," Dr. Wilde spits out.

Noah shivers despite the heat, her perspiration chilling her gooseflesh. She's disoriented by the way the professor is speaking to the man, uncertain if she's ever heard him raise his voice, let alone swear before.

Unnoticed by her, two sets of amber-colored eyes appear on either side of her. They stare into the tent's light, suspended in mid-air like four copper marbles.

Noah sees the man in camo move to one of the canteen's chairs and sit down. After a few beats, Dr. Wilde also enters the tent and sits down, turning a chair backwards and straddling it.

"I've heard a lot about this camp of yours, Wilde," The man in the HOLO says, trying to sound natural. "It's good to see it, even from Dallas. I bet it looks even more impressive in daylight."

"You still haven't told me why you're here, Merton! Or why your lackey just shows up unannounced," the professor snarls at the image, barely controlling his spite for the man.

"Well, we're just doing a little scouting for some potential projects. *Big* projects—ones that could change a lot of lives down here for the better.

And if done correctly, make some of us a lot of money." There's a pause, and then he continues. "By the way, I'm sorry I didn't make it to Erin's wake. I wasn't sure I'd be welcomed. *And* I was a bit preoccupied with other things."

"At least *then* you knew when to stay away. I'm sorry you forgot the lesson so soon."

"Come on, Wilde, I just wanted to stop by and pay my respects. Even if it was several years ago. It was a hang gliding accident in Rio, wasn't it? She always was a thrill seeker. I remember the stunts she pulled when the three of us met and hung out on spring break. Remember that time when—"

"Merton, just shut up!" Wilde interrupts. "We were never friends! You know that. Even more than me—she couldn't put up with you and your two-faced brown-nosing."

"I know, I know. Shit, just calm down, Seamus. But still, it's a damn shame what happened to her." He pauses as if waiting to set the hook. "You would have expected her to have been more careful with her equipment that day. I heard... what, three fasteners failed on the left wing somehow?"

Seamus studies the man, his scowl brooding with suspicion. *That's impossible! Besides the paramedics, I'm the only one who knew the details of the accident.*

"How do you know about that, Merton? Is there something you need to tell me?"

"Oh, sorry. No, not really. I was in Rio at the time of the accident. Strange thing, you know. I bumped into Erin the night before it happened, and we chatted a little. She was really looking forward to the next day's flying. I'll tell you what, she was a lot friendlier than you. Damn shame, though. I've been to that site where she launched from. Beautiful vista. I mean, if you had to make your exit, you couldn't—"

Noah hears Dr. Wilde knock his chair over and turn toward the figure in green camo.

"Get up, you dirty son-of-a-bitch!" he screams. He pivots back to the HOLO. "Are you just trying to get in my head? Or are you saying you had something to do with the accident?" Wilde faces the man with him in the tent. "Get out. Get out! And Merton, if I ever find out you had something to do with her death, I'll hunt you down, drag your sorry ass up the highest peak and throw *you* off. Whatever this is all about, we're done." He glares at the man in camo. "You. Get going. Now!"

The figure moves toward the doorway as Merton's HOLO image drifts along behind the shadowy courier. "Alright, Seamus," Merton says. "Alright. Man, you've gotten a lot pricklier than you used to be. Maybe that Preston bitch needs to come down here so you can get laid." The man in the dark suit evaporates as his needling fades into laughter.

Noah quickly slips away and moves silently back to her tent. Whatever invisible presence that had shadowed her before is now gone. As she lies on her bed, her suppressed breathing gradually finds its cadence, and her heart slowly throttles down. Questions without answers seem to chase elusive tails until she finally falls into a dark, fitful sleep.

Noah anxiously looks for Yoshi the following morning—her concern mounts whenever she remembers what she witnessed last night. *What if Yoshi bumped into the guy wearing camo? He seemed dangerous... unpredictable.* The boy's not in his tent, and Jake says he hasn't seen him around the canteen. She nervously circles the grounds, hoping to bump into him, asking everyone she sees if they've seen him. No one seems to know where he is.

She sits down near the burnt embers of the campfire, waiting. All of a sudden, she feels a sharp poke in the ribs.

"Gotcha," a voice squawks from behind. She spins around and sees Yoshi grinning. He's pressing a stunning purple-and-white passion flower toward her. "For you. For when you cannot sleep. Sorry if I frightened you." Noah takes the flower from him. She closes her eyes, puts it under her nose, and inhales, long and deep. The scent is calming.

"You didn't scare me," she lies. "I was just worried about you. Where in the world were you?"

He shrugs as he sits down beside her. "I went east of camp and followed the sunlight, hoping it would take me somewhere special. I found this passion flower in a small clearing. It was alive with buzzing insects and hummingbirds. They were singing your name to me. Not really singing, but vibrating something in me like a song." He pauses, his smile apologetic. "Sorry if my little prank ruined the gift for you."

Noah looks at him, taking in the young man and feeling a tug, a strong pull toward him. *Is it brotherly affection or something more?* She ignores her question and puts her arm over his shoulder, softly speaking into his ear.

"Yoshi, I've been thinking. I'd like to show you the kapok tree and the clearing today if you'd like to come with me to see it." She leans away to look at his reaction, and he's smiling, his eyes sparkling.

"Lead on, my *bijin*!" Noah looks at him, her brow raised. "Oh. Sorry. *Bijin* means 'beautiful woman' in Japanese." After the words come out, he quickly blushes and then chuckles at himself.

Noah laughs along, ignoring his awkwardness. "Come on, my *bijin* boy!"

For some reason, Noah takes a trail *around* the laboratory she discovered on her hike the other day. She wonders why—*I feel like I'm intruding… but I also feel like something's drawing me too*—then quickly dismisses the thought. Walking through the jungle, they fall into a leisurely pace. At times, they talk about their lives back home, their families and friends, but eventually, they slip back into a comfortable silence.

The scent of the rainforest is multi-layered, enveloping them in the smells of fresh leafy greens, tropical fruits, aromatic blossoms, and base notes of moss and wood. She imagines that she's inhaling an exotic, sensuous perfume that only exists in the wild—a fragrance that could never be bottled.

As they near the opening of the clearing, Noah puts her hand out and places it on Yoshi's chest to stop him. Her deep green eyes shimmer like living stones. She looks at him as if preparing to share a private secret.

"Yoshi, I feel like we're crossing a threshold here for some reason. I'm not sure into what, but just... something's shifting. This place, the clearing, the tree feels... um... *sacred* to me. That's the only word to describe it. And my returning to it with you means something, too. I don't know what. I feel nervous, *and* I feel excited to share it with you."

He stands perfectly still, his gaze merging with her earnest, searching eyes. "Noah, I feel it, too. Here, take my hand, and we enter together. Okay?"

She takes a moment, then reaches down and holds his hand, sweaty palm to sweaty palm. They duck beneath the door-like, sculpted lianas vines and enter the clearing.

Instantly, they are surrounded by a spiraling kaleidoscope of brush-footed butterflies. They gasp in wonder, spinning around. Their arms wave around in the air like little children—the tiny winged miracles brushing against exposed skin. It's as if each of the six thousand varieties of this one simple species has arrived to greet them. When they finally emerge from the dancing swarm, they see the giant kapok, its trunk cloaked with hundreds of large, blue morpho butterflies. The pulsing indigo sea ripples as a host of paired wings open and close—they wave to their two guests, inviting them to come nearer, to enter the center of the circle.

When they are within arm's length of the giant tree, Noah squeezes Yoshi's hand and leads him around its base. Climbing over the enormous roots, they soon reach the other side of the tree.

Noah suddenly stops, startled. Yoshi senses her alarm and leans in close beside her.

Seated on the ground is a middle-aged man with tattoos of scorpions, snakes, and butterflies on both cheeks. He is bare-chested, and a simple loincloth covers his hips and front. The man looks at them with a toothy grin and points to himself.

"Tucano tribe. My name Cubeo. Sit. Chew," he says, offering them a leaf.

The pair look at each other, nod, and sit down on either side of the man. Noah studies him. He smells of sweat, fish, and grease. *The man kind of reminds me of Da. I wonder if he's a father.*

Cautiously, she reaches out for the leaf he's extending toward them. *Hmm? I wonder if it's safe? I don't want to offend him, but...* She chooses to override her apprehension and tentatively puts it in her mouth. Yoshi does the same. The man smiles again and makes a motion with his mouth to chew.

"Cordoncillo," he announces.

As they begin to chew, they notice their mouths feeling numb. After a while, they have to wipe some saliva from the corners of their mouths, as if they had been to the dentist to fill a cavity. They look at each other, grinning, and the man grins back, giggling as if sharing a secret joke. They laugh with him, not exactly understanding his sense of humor but still amused by the absurdity of it all.

After they finish chewing their leaves, he stands and picks up a bundle of large leaves and hands it to Noah.

"You keep. You need. Bad things soon."

With that, he bows and knocks his knuckles together, just as Noah often does. She bows her head toward him and makes the same gesture. He takes a moment to return her gaze, then turns toward a narrow seam in the clearing's perimeter. Somehow, the leaves and limbs move on their own and open a path for him, revealing a pair of jaguars lounging on the ground, waiting. He then quickly disappears, slipping through the dark, dense undergrowth.

"What was that all about?" Yoshi asks, his eyes wide in confusion.

"I'm not sure. He almost seemed like he was expecting us. Waiting for us. And what was that about 'bad things soon'?" Noah shivers as she repeats the words.

Both sit in silence for a few moments. Yoshi moves closer to Noah and reaches out for her hand. She entwines her fingers with his and takes a deep, long breath.

"Yoshi, I think we've been led here. That man. The butterflies. This tree. The sacred sense of wonder here. I feel... overwhelmed. Transported. Grateful, even. I'm not a person who prays much, but I feel like we should say something."

"I feel it too, Noah," he replies, displaying the most serene look she's seen on his round, open face. They lift their eyes to the distant edge of the kapok tree's canopy.

"We're glad to be here," Noah says. "We're honored to share this ground, this moment, this shade, this rest with you and each other. Whoever you are, thank you for all these gifts. If you will allow it, we wish to linger here, to just be with you and hear what *you* think—what *you* feel—what *you* want."

Yoshi squeezes her hand and says, "Yes."

Noah sighs deeply and says to him, "I'd like to sit by myself for a while. Would you be okay sitting here by yourself, and I'll go to the other side? I want to be alone with whoever or whatever is in this place."

"Of course, friend. Good idea."

Noah settles in between two enormous roots. Her forehead muscles relax, her jaw slackens. She feels as if she is cradled between her mother's thighs, looking up into the eyes of pure love. Soaking in the deep sense of wellbeing, she closes her eyelids and descends into a sleep-like reverie. Deeper and deeper she floats, feeling like the roots are absorbing her into the wet sap that flows within its ancient fibers. Then, she feels as if she is drifting upward briefly, followed by a sense of gently moving downward into the black soil, where tiny root hairs touch living things and small caches of life-giving minerals. Up, then down, she is being moved by the very life breath of the tree.

At one point, the process pauses. A warmth radiates from a branch. She is drawn into its slender, feminine-shaped crook and stops. Resting there, she waits. *What is it? Who is it?*

Noah senses, not with her ears, but deep within her flesh, an energy like Patrick's, a woman's presence.

Erin. Patrick's mother. Dr. Wilde's sister.

"Hello," Noah whispers. "Can you hear me? Can you see me?"

Noah waits. She opens her heart and her mind as wide as they will stretch. A vibration gradually escalates from the tree's center. A panorama of ancient history begins to be funneled into her own human core:

Last century's tragedies.

Plans worked and reworked.

Dreams dreamt and promises broken.

And then a vision of war.

Death, destruction, and the many collateral losses that are yet to come.

Then, peace.

All that was necessary.

Everything changing.

Nothing untouched by what has again become possible.

Suddenly, she hears the murmur of a multitude: *"We are with you, Noah."*

With that, she gently returns to earth and back into her body. As she descends back toward the ground, she becomes aware of another.

Yoshi? she whispers in her mind. Immediately, the words bloom inside her: *That was incredible, Noah! I met Erin.*

When she awakens in her body, she shakes her head and opens her eyes. Still alone, she stands up and walks around the tree to where she left Yoshi. He's still there—eyes half-closed, a broad smile on his face as if he's lost in a gentle, all-encompassing euphoria. She walks directly in front of him and sees that he's been crying. He shakes his head as if shivering, seeming to return from somewhere both near and yet remote.

She reaches down with both hands and pulls him to his feet. They embrace for several moments. Then, he steps back and kisses Noah's forehead.

"You are our leader, Noah. Erin told me so," he says.

She looks at him, puzzled. They stand in silence—a sense of mystery still surrounds them.

"What do you mean?" she asks, her voice measured with uncertainty.

"I don't know. Can't you feel it?"

Noah shrugs. Not knowing how to answer, she bends down, picks up the bundle of Cordoncillo leaves, and stuffs them into her backpack. As she throws it over her shoulder, a cerulean-blue morpho butterfly dances over her head and lands gently on her golden-red hair. Several moments pass— they savor the experience as if standing at an altar. Then, the kaleidoscope of butterflies takes flight, spiraling over their heads. The large butterfly on Noah's head joins the others as they ascend into a pillar that guides the two of them forward.

Together, Noah and Yoshi walk hand in hand back through the pirouetting palette, out from the shimmering clearing, and into the dark jungle, where night is preparing to claim its daily due.

Walking along the darkly shadowed path back to camp, the pair sense they are somehow different from who they were when they stepped into the kapok's clearing that afternoon. Yoshi keeps casting bemused glances toward Noah. When she notices him looking at her, she shrugs and shakes her head. As they amble along, they move in and out of silence, and the few words they speak, a tangle of possible explanations of what just happened.

When they are half a kilometer from camp, Noah decides to tell Yoshi what happened when she looked in the lab's window—how the wildlife turned in their cases to face her. Fully trusting him now, she describes the entire experience, including what the animals seemed to communicate.

"Do you want to see it?" she asks as they approach the fork in the path that will lead them there.

"Are you kidding? I'd love to see it!" Yoshi quickly answers. His eyes are wide and gleaming.

"Okay. Let's stop talking now. I'm not sure why, but I feel like we're crossing an unmarked boundary with Dr. Wilde. He's not exactly told us to stay away from the lab, but it seems like he hasn't told us about it for a reason."

Yoshi nods and hurries forward. Soon, the clearing comes into view. The low building's silhouette is as black as the deadly scorpions inside. Noah's pace slows, and she lets Yoshi run ahead of her. *I'm bushed! Think I'll rest. I'll catch up to him.* She drops her backpack and sinks to the ground, watching Yoshi approach the window. As soon as she sits, she hears footsteps crashing through the jungle on the far side of the lab. She frowns. Was it an animal? The hairs on the back of her neck shoot up—a warm glow grows inside the windows, and a whiff of pungent gasoline wafts through the humid, night air.

She jumps to her feet and starts toward Yoshi to warn him to stop, but it's too late. He's already climbing up on the large barrel to see inside.

"Yoshi, wait—!" *BOOM.* Her cry of alarm is immediately cut off by a loud explosion that shoots the window's glass outward.

She shuts her eyes just in time, turning her face away from the bright flash. The blast hits her like a drum in her chest, knocking her to the ground. When she opens her eyes, she sees Yoshi on the ground, cupping his eyes and rolling from side to side. Without warning, a second detonation erupts through the roof. The red-orange heat radiates around them while roiling smoke begins to blind all vision.

Despite the loud ringing in Noah's ears, she still hears the serpentine screaming from within. Her heart reaches out in grief, in confusion, in anger. Watching the fire spread, it's obvious that someone sabotaged the lab and whatever Dr. Wilde is doing here.

Noah's adrenaline spikes—her rage quickly blooming. For a moment, she looks toward the jungle on the other side of the lab, ready to pursue whoever she heard running away. But then her attention snaps back to Yoshi, who is now whimpering—his moans low and guttural. She stumbles toward him and slowly kneels to the ground, gently placing her hands on his shoulders.

When Yoshi feels her touch, he removes his hands from his face. Forcing herself to look at him—the fire casting erratic light—Noah sees that the skin around his eyes is wet and red, covered with small blisters. There are several bloody cuts on his forehead and cheeks.

He tries to open his eyes, then whispers in a scratchy, panicked voice, "I can't see, Noah. I can't see. What's happening?"

On the other side of the lab, they hear someone yelling, angrily crashing into the jungle. "You bastard! I know you can hear me!" It's Dr. Wilde—his shouts are obscured by the roaring fire and quickly fade as he runs. "You tell Merton, if I ever catch him, he's a dead man. You hear me? *Dead!*"

Noah calls out for help, but her cries fall empty into the darkness. *What do I do?* As soon as the thought forms, she looks up and sees a pair of jaguars emerging from the jungle. They silently slink toward her and then stand on either side—tails flicking with nervous energy, seeming to wait for their instructions. Noah nods her assent—*Yes! Go!*—releasing them for the hunt. They bolt into the blackness as if shot from a rifle.

Turning her attention back to Yoshi, she brushes his hair from his forehead and whispers reassuringly, "I'm right here, buddy. It's okay. You're safe now." In response, a weak smile forms on his smudged face.

His blindness might only be temporary, she tells herself, but she has a sick feeling it may be a lie—an empty comfort. After helping him to his feet, he sways unsteadily for a moment, and then they slowly follow the trail back to camp. Yoshi tightly clings to Noah with each step. From time to time, he stops to catch his breath and then nods to her to continue. At one point, he stumbles over a tree root, nearly pulling them both to the ground.

Somewhere in the distance, a man screams in terror. A pair of raspy roars rip the night wide open. The man's howling sounds like part of some macabre duet, subsumed by the predatory, bass-like bellowing. Noah shivers as the horrific sounds amplify and then abruptly cease.

Yoshi's head lolls against Noah, seemingly oblivious to the brutal night noises. They slowly push on until they make their way back to their base. When they reach the camp's perimeter, it's pitch black, and everyone seems to be asleep. Noah pauses and considers waking the others up, but then—knowing how private he is—decides to get Yoshi inside where she can assess his injuries. Walking through the dark shadows, she soon finds her tent and enters quietly. *Where's Sylvie? Probably with Jean again.* In the dark, Noah guides Yoshi to her cot and then carefully lowers him to the edge. She fumbles with the lantern, finally getting the light to sputter to life. Yoshi sits there hunched over, forcing himself to take several deep breaths, and then begins to cry quietly.

"The tears sting," he tells her.

"I know, Yoshi. I know. But they also might rinse out whatever it was that flew into them."

"Okay. Okay, Noah."

Adrenaline still floods her body. She takes a moment before speaking, trying to slow her racing mind. *Breathe. Just breathe.*

Finally, as calmly as possible, she asks, "What do you want me to do, Yoshi? Do you want me to find Dr. Wilde?"

For a long time, Yoshi is silent. Eventually, he says, "I'm beginning to see a small glow of light. Nothing is clear." He pauses and then continues. "Do you remember what the man in the clearing said? He said... keep the leaves... that something bad would happen... that we would need them."

Noah had forgotten the Cordoncillo leaves she'd stuffed into her backpack. She grabs the pack and opens it. The small, tightly wrapped bundle of leaves is still intact. For a moment, she's taken back to the time her da got some giant hogweed in his eyes. Her ma made a paste of Irish eyebright and pasted it on his eyes. After he lay down, the swelling and blisters quieted down. Eventually, his eyesight completely returned.

"Yoshi, I've seen my ma use something like this. I can't promise it will work, but if you want, I can grind the leaves into a powder and mix them with some salve from the emergency kit. Then, just let them soak your eyes and rest. Or I can go find Dr. Wilde. Tell him what happened and have him contact the medical clinic to airlift you out. It's your call."

He takes his time and considers his choice for a moment. "I want to try the leaves, Noah. And then, go find the Professor."

She nods, a concerned frown on her face, then spends the next several minutes preparing the leaves and paste. When it's finished, she brings it back into the tent and smears it on both of his eyes.

"Yoshi, I'm turning the light off now. I want you to lie still and just rest until I tell you to wipe it off. Can you do that? I'll be right next to you in Sylvie's cot. Okay?"

"Okay, Noah," he responds, his voice weak.

Exhausted, Noah lies down. Her body tells her unambiguously that she needs rest. *I'll just close my eyes for a few minutes... then go and find Dr. Wilde.*

She tosses around for several minutes, her mind unwilling to cooperate with her body's needs, replaying again and again what's just happened. After sifting through her memory of the explosion and Yoshi's injury, her thoughts turn to what happened next. The jaguars. Her desire for retribution. The screaming.

Did I cause that? Did a man just die because of me? She begins to weep. Layer upon layer of emotion pile up inside her. Guilt. Anger. Fear. Power. Regret. Love. Shame. The weight she feels soon sinks her, forcing her to release everything as she succumbs to a dreamless slumber.

Arlington, Virginia, USA (101° F / 38° C)

Journi Preston rolls over in her queen-sized bed. It's been a fitful night. The sheets are a tangled mess. Her T-shirt is soaked with sweat. Another fire dream haunts her—a vivid nightmare of global conflagration with her in the middle, unable to contain it.

The HOLO chirps and pulls her out of the clinging terror. She bats her eyes open and glances at the violet-colored numerals floating above the foot of the bed—three twenty-seven a.m. Struggling to shake off the dream, she pushes herself up and leans back, answering the HOLO.

"Hello. Seamus?" she answers, her heart galloping in her chest. "Why in God's name are you waking me up in the middle of the night? This better be worth the crow's feet it will cost me."

Pause... The only sound she hears is heavy breathing. Even with his HOLO's poor lighting, she quickly sees how haggard he looks.

"Sorry. Are you alright?" She says softly, sensing something is wrong.

"No, I'm sorry to wake you. I just... I just didn't know who else to... or what to do." His words are chopped and confused.

I've never seen him this uncertain before. He sounds... fragile.

"Are you alright, Seamus? What's going on, dear?"

He takes a deep breath and then launches in, his voice rising as he recounts last night's events. "It's Merton. One of his goddamned hirelings showed up in the middle of the night yesterday. He opened a HOLO, and Merton started talking about some new venture here in the Amazon. Can you believe it? I sure as hell don't. It all seemed like some weird ruse. And then, to top it off, he not-too-subtly implied that he had something to do with Erin's accident. I don't know if he's making the whole thing up or just taunting me."

Fully awake now, Journi's hands ball into tight fists. "That fucking weasel," she snarls, her skin crawling at the sound of his name.

Seamus continues, his words softer, more thoughtful. "And that's not all. The lab's gone. I mean, it's still standing, but there was a massive explosion a few hours ago, and it's all blown to hell. Erin's research is in safe-keeping in Toronto, but her equipment is useless, and most of the wildlife... are all dead. I'm pretty sure *that* phase of our operation is over."

"Holy shit! I'm so sorry, Seamus. What kind of scumbag would do something like that?" She frowns as her shoulders sag, feeling all the weight he's carrying. "You really think it was a bomb?"

He shakes his head and shrugs, saying nothing in response. She eventually breaks the silence, the tenderness in her voice reaching out to him. "What a huge loss. I know how close you felt to your sister there. How are you holding up?"

She sees tears of frustration, grief, and exhaustion beginning to pool under his heavy lids. "It's like losing her all over again. Whenever I'd go there, I could shut my eyes and see her sitting behind her equipment, handling her ugly little creatures. Something about the space made me feel... close to her, even though I knew she was gone. I'd locked it up and made it off limits, you know? The animals were still cared for. But now... they're all dead too." His words trail off, not concealing the catch in his voice.

After a moment, Journi asks, "So, you really think Merton's behind it?"

"Of course, he's behind it! We've both watched how he outsources the Chief's dirty work. It has his bloody signature all over it."

"Every time I see that bastard, I feel sick. He's dangerous, Seamus. You need to be careful."

"I know. I know. But if I ever see him again, I don't think I'll be able to stop myself."

Journi pauses, letting him vent, then asks, "So, what's next?"

He lets out a long exhale before answering. "I've decided to wrap up the program here early. Besides, there are just three days left. I can't put the students in danger. It's not worth it. It's just too great a risk."

Journi nods as she half-listens—in her thoughts, she dreams up bloodthirsty scenarios of taking Merton down. *My blue spiked shoe on the Texan's throat.* A shift of energy in Seamus' voice interrupts her dark fantasy, bringing her back to the conversation midstream.

"...sick about the loss. But it may be time to pull up stakes here and close the whole thing down. Anyway, I think we're entering a new phase. I've managed to recruit five of the students to join me in Toronto. And I want to talk with Noah next. She's the youngest of the bunch, but a natural leader, and her own person."

Journi watches him slowly pace back and forth, releasing the final drops of his adrenaline-fueled emotions. "Well, at least that's something to show for everything you've been through. Is there anything I can do, Seamus? What do you need?" she offers and then pauses. "I'm going to go to work and see what media levers I can pull to put some pressure on him."

"Nah, I don't want to suck you into all this, Journi. You've already done more than enough. I'm okay. Well, not exactly, okay... but I've been through worse. I just needed to tell someone. Since Erin's been gone, you've become my closest confidant."

"Is that *all* I've become to you?" Journi says in a low, throaty voice.

He hears her slow breathing, imagining he's feeling it on the skin of his neck as she sleeps next to him.

"Well, you've also become my favorite eco-journalist. And I've known a few over the years," he teases.

"You watch your back, Seamus. I'll see you up here in the States sometime soon, okay? Something's shifted with what's been happening... and I don't mean just between you and me," she hints. "HOLO me if there's anything I can do."

He grins at her HOLO image and releases a low chuckle. "I'm sure there's *plenty* you can do. But that will have to wait. Goodnight, Journi. Get some sleep... I know I woke you up. And thanks for letting me ramble. I feel better now. See you soon." He waves and then ends the connection.

Journi's nostrils flare as she takes a long, deep breath. Fully awake now, she props herself up with an extra pillow and squints at the dark scene outside her window. *Game on, you little prick. By the time I've finished with you, Guantanamo will look like a fucking church camp!*

Terra Nova, Vale do Javari, State of Amazonas, Brazil (95° F / 35° C)

The morning light filters in through the tent flap. Low voices mingle and begin moving through the camp as students get up and start their day. The sounds finally register in Noah's semi-conscious state. *Oh, shit. I fell asleep,* Noah scolds herself, shocked to find herself still lying on the cot.

Her guilty feelings fade slightly as she refocuses on what she tried to do for Yoshi. She rolls over onto her side and studies the sleeping young man through worried eyes. *I'm not sure we did the right thing, but... I was supposed to find the Professor... I just couldn't wake up.* Torn by her self-recriminations, she watches the steady rise and fall of his chest. His round, pale face appears contented. Serene, even with the goop oozing around his eyes.

Not wanting to disturb him, she just waits. *He looks so vulnerable just lying there... vulnerable to what? To me? Or something else? Devotion? I wonder—has he become too attached to me?*

He lets out a long yawn that brings her attention back to their present crisis.

"Yoshi, can you hear me? It's Noah," she whispers.

"Hello, Noah. How did you sleep?" His voice is low and groggy.

Noah shakes her head. "That's not important. How did *you* sleep? How do your eyes feel?"

"I sleep pretty good. I don't know about my eyes. How do I look? They feel sticky right now."

Noah comes beside him and kneels by the cot. After she gives him a drink of water, she asks if he's ready to see what the leaves have done. He quivers, then nods—nervous to find out.

"Okay, here goes," she says, slowly wiping off some of the dried paste from around his eyes.

"Ouch!" He winces and reaches up to grab her arm. "That's sticking to my skin. Don't rub it too hard."

She strokes his hair as she extends a compassionate frown he's unable to see. Then she continues, more gently now. Layer after layer, she carefully peels off the hardened paste. First one eye, then the other, until they are completely exposed. His skin has turned a purplish pink, like the color of a wailing newborn. The cuts already show signs of healing, leaving fine pink trails crisscrossing both cheeks.

Noah takes a deep, uncertain breath and leans back. "Okay, Yoshi. Whenever you're ready. Open your eyes. Let's see what you can see."

As she watches, she's reminded of a HOLO-VID of a blind girl opening her eyes for the first time after surgery. Yoshi's eyelids slowly rise, revealing two ebony irises. Yoshi carefully blinks and then gazes up at Noah.

His grin answers for him. "I see you!" He tries to wink, then cringes. "*Wow!* That hurts!"

Noah throws her arms around him, tears of relief streaming down her face. Something about this experience has opened her heart even wider toward him. She feels something she's never felt before. *What is it?* she wonders, feeling his chest rising and falling under her embrace. *Maternal? That's it! I feel motherly,* she suddenly acknowledges, kissing the boy on the forehead.

The sun's first light barely sneaks through the dense, dark foliage surrounding the compound. The canteen's large iron bell rings out with mounting insistence, calling everyone to attention. Students still in their tents look at each other, wondering what could be so important to wake them up this early.

There's still a strong, acrid smell of smoke from last night's fire. Most notice it but assume it's the campfire's smoldering rubber tree limbs. Some begin to shuffle around, looking for semi-clean clothes to put on. Others roll over, covering their heads with anything they can find to muffle the bell's pounding. Eventually, they give up and wind their way past the others' tents into the canteen, where they find a growing group seated around Dr. Wilde.

Noah trudges toward an empty bench in the canteen, still beating herself up. *I still can't believe I fell asleep. I said I'd go find him, but I don't know... he's so attached to the lab... maybe he'd blame us.*

Dr. Wilde looks haggard, as if he slept in his clothes. There are smudges of soot on his forearms. His hair is a tangle of salt and pepper. He's holding a small stack of notecards, lost in whatever is written on them. Jake sits next to him, frequently flashing a concerned glance at his mentor. As the last of the group arrives, they take a seat, too. The students exchange looks and puzzled expressions, silently asking, *What's going on?*

After a few moments of silence, Seamus looks up and takes in the small group of bright and dedicated students surrounding him. He looks at them through sad eyes, longing to have better news to deliver. Clearing his throat, he launches in, stuttering,

"Um... sorry, uh... to wake you up so early. I know... uh... this was going to be your free morning. But... Well, I don't know how to say this. There's been an incident... an accident, actually... last night."

He pauses while the students, stricken with worry, look around, silently counting heads to see if everyone is there.

"Everyone's alright. It's not that kind of accident. Last night, a building used as a research laboratory caught on fire and collapsed. I'm still trying to find the exact cause, but... how do I say this? It looks like it was caused deliberately by someone who snuck into the camp, poured gasoline on the building's roof, and then lit the match."

Several students expel low murmurs of disbelief. Noah looks at Yoshi, who is now seated beside her. She arches an eyebrow as if to ask, *Should we say something?* He reaches over, taking her hand, and shakes his head—his answer obvious.

Seamus glances at Yoshi, his eyes lingering on him for a moment, and then presses on. "I know... I know. I'm still in a bit of shock myself. The building housed the life's work of my late sister. It's not exactly off-limits— more a personal memorial of mine to her and her legacy. It also housed her stunning collection of venomous creatures that comprised the core of her research. Tragically, other than a handful of scorpions and vipers, they all seem to have been lost in the awful blaze. I can still hear them screaming..."

Tears slowly move down Seamus's cheeks as he remembers them. "You see... they weren't just animals to her, but hand-chosen representatives of the staggering diversity of this place."

Heavy silence envelopes them all. Even though none of them met his sister or saw her collection, they understand how remarkable a place this is, and feel the incredible tragedy of this loss of life.

Taking a deep breath, he continues. "So, I've made the difficult decision to conclude our time together—" Several students start to butt in, objecting to the announcement. Confused and frustrated, they talk over each other and push back.

Seamus says nothing as they express disappointment. After a few minutes, they notice his silence and gradually settle down, determined to be fully present to whatever's left of their time together.

"The program's been a brilliant success. Each of you should be very proud of what you've accomplished. I know I am." His watery eyes glisten as he scans the group. "You've experienced in a wee, short time more than most of your peers will tackle in a lifetime. I'm just sorry it's coming to such an abrupt and unplanned end, but for safety's sake, I can't in good conscience risk anyone's well-being here—"

Seamus smiles faintly, as if to rouse himself out of his own heaviness. "I typically end the program spouting off some amazing facts about this incredible ecosystem we've called home these last few weeks. But in light of what's happened... since you're the last cohort I'll ever bring here... I want to give you the last word and finish our time together and simply read what *you've* said the rainforest has come to mean to you."

He picks up the first card and starts to read.

I heard somewhere that 'beauty will save the world.' Now I believe it. I know it's saved me–saved me from myself. I wish everyone alive could experience the colors, the multi-dimensional wonder, the scents of this place. I want to bring its beauty to light and inspire people to change. Not out of fear, but because of love. -- Jean

---

The trees are like giant brothers to me. At home, there are few really ancient, big trees. Having so many living monuments to connect with and be protected by and provided for makes me realize how gifted I am. My life isn't something I can manufacture on my own; it's given to me from the ground up. -- Yoshi

---

I've always felt connected, addressed even by nature. But in this place, I feel a deepening kinship that is changing my fundamental identity. I am no longer an I, but I am becoming a We. From now on, I no longer want to just fight for nature. I want to fight alongside nature. -- Noah

He continues to read each student's card. When he finishes, he raises his head and slowly looks each student in the eye. His gentle smile temporarily erases the fatigue and grief. When his gaze falls on Noah, their eyes hold one another for a long moment.

Noah feels a vibration welling up from the earth, urging her to rise. And in response, she stands and knocks her two fists together. The other students feel it too and follow her lead, performing the same motion in sync with hers. The vibration soon calibrates with *their* rhythmic movement, reminding them that they have literally been living inside the planet's huge lungs.

❧ ☙ ❧ ☙ ❧ ☙

As the group begins to slowly disperse, students hang around, knotted in the perimeter with cups of tea or coffee, murmuring while they wait for breakfast to be set out. A few—who noticed the pink lacerations on Yoshi's face—circle around him, intently listening as he recounts what happened last night. Seamus casts a puzzled glance toward them and then walks over to Noah, who is quietly talking with Sylvie.

He clears his throat. "Sorry to interrupt. Noah, can we talk for a few minutes?"

"Sure thing, Dr. Wilde," she answers.

Sylvie shrugs her shoulders, raising an eyebrow slightly.

"Great. Grab a cuppa for both of us, and meet me in my office."

The man quickly leaves the tent. Noah stands up, looking at Sylvie for reassurance. "I feel like I'm back at school, and I've just been called to the headmaster's office. Do you think he knows Yoshi and I were at the lab last night?"

Not waiting for an answer, she gets two cups of tea and then walks over to Dr. Wilde's *office*—really just a sleeping tent partitioned with a gray and gold cotton blanket.

They both settle into simple wood chairs, cradling their drinks.

Eventually, Dr. Wilde looks up from his tea, focusing all his attention on her.

"Noah, you've been a vital part of this program this summer. I know you didn't have much time to prepare beforehand, but you've shown real grit and leadership. Everyone here looks up to you, even though most of them are older than you are."

She relaxes some but still feels unsure where this is heading. "Thank you, Dr. Wilde. They're a great group. Each one's so gifted and dedicated. It's been a real privilege to be part of it all."

He looks at her, some of the old spark returning to his gray-blue eyes. "Well, I think Patrick was right. You *did* need to be here. I've seen firsthand what he sees in you and why he's so fond of you."

She feels a tinge of shyness creep up her neck as he steers the conversation toward Patrick and their relationship.

"Noah, what you wrote on your card really struck a chord with me. I'd like to hear more. What did you mean when you said 'fight *with* nature'?"

Noah has given a lot of thought to this but hasn't verbalized it to anyone. She waits for a moment to find her words, then says, "It seems to me that those of us who care the most about the planet aren't really making much of a difference for all our efforts and activism. I've seen it in my own efforts. HOLO-POD after HOLO-POD, students say they're standing with me... with the planet's crisis, but then—Poof! Nothing really changes. I think I've been fighting *for* nature... it feels like I'm just too small to actually bring about any meaningful change."

She pauses and takes a long sip from her cup, remembering the part the two jaguars played in last night's events. "So, what I'm wondering about is whether we need to *listen* to nature and take our lead from *its* wisdom, from *its* sense of what needs to happen today. In other words, to fight alongside it and *with it* as a partner. Sort of like two nations who join forces to defeat some unstoppable totalitarian regime. We've seen that happen with human alliances. Why can't we form some kind of human and non-human alliance?"

Seamus gently nods as Noah speaks. After a pause, she quickly adds,

"The non-human beings on the planet have as much to lose as we do. Maybe more. So I wonder, why wouldn't *they* want to be part of the solution?" She stops, out of breath, and realizes she just aired her teenaged speculations to one of the most respected environmentalists of the twenty-first century.

Seamus takes what feels like a very long minute before speaking. He's moved, inspired by the girl's passion. He knows firsthand that she's right. The old ways—whether it's the pursuit of policy reform, the push for greater accountability, or the use of environmental scare tactics to develop a new economy, or even appealing to people's conscience to form new habits—they're all just *too damn slow*."

In the long run, they make total sense. But the plans will likely fail in the short run as the doomsday clock runs down. That's why he and Erin initiated Operation Hail Mary. But a surgical approach with the limited manpower and resources he has simply won't be enough, or soon enough.

"Noah, I'm really intrigued with your line of thinking. I've also been disheartened at how little progress we've made. Having spent my life fighting the good fight, I now wonder if it's been a fool's errand. We need young, new thinkers. Like you."

He savors a sip of tea—his gaze toward her pensive. "Patrick's probably told you about the program I chair at the University of Toronto. It's a rather off-beat composite of academic disciplines—environmental sciences, public affairs, political and social theory, economics, even spirituality. Each year, I have a limited number of scholarships available to award. Several of the other students were offered a spot before they came. But I've held one place back to see who stands out from our summer program."

He raises his arms and folds his hands, looking appraisingly into her eyes. "Noah, I'd like to offer it to you. I think you're *exactly* the kind of student we need if we're going to get out of the box and make the kind of big changes we need to make before it's too late. I know it's a lot to toss out, especially right before you head home. But what do you think? How's it strike you?"

Noah just sits there, stunned—a deer blinded by an accelerating headlight—completely lost for a moment. "Wow! Dr. Wilde, I don't know what to say. I have a million questions, but right now, all I can think is... are you sure? I mean, I'm just a simple girl from a small Irish town. I've barely dreamed of going to college, let alone that far away. Of course, I never dreamed of coming to the Amazon for something like this, either." She shakes her head and tries to catch her breath. "You really caught me off guard, you know. Can I think about it? I'll have to talk to my ma and da."

"Of course you can, Noah. I realize it's a big decision. And I'm sorry for just springing it on you. Just so you know, Sylvie, Jean, Desmond, Ged, Raven, and Anvi have all agreed to join the program. So you'll at least know a few others if you decide to come."

Noah studies him closely as he speaks and notices Patrick's features mirrored in the older man's face. More weathered and gentler in some ways, yet fiercer, too. *I hope Patrick looks like that when he gets older.*

"Okay," she answers, reaching out her hand to shake on it. "We have a deal. I'll talk with my parents and get back to you as soon as I can."

He smiles broadly. "Great! If you sign on, that will make *seven* of you—enough to make my *week*! Get it?"

"Ugh," she moans, slapping her forehead at his jibe. "You're starting to remind me more and more of your nephew. What you two won't do to get a reaction!"

Dallas, Texas, USA (118° F / 48° C)

Noah is seated at a small table against the wall in a coffee shop at the Dallas Fort Worth Airport. Already worn out from the first leg of her trip, she can't wait to see home. On top of her utter exhaustion, she now feels heartsick after her HOLO with Yoshi. His tearful voice telling her about the aggressive return of his mom's cancer only added to her melancholy.

She wanted a cup of tea but settled for a large black coffee instead. *These clumsy Americans still can't figure out how to make a good cuppa.* While lost in her thoughts, looking at the floor's black-and-white marble tiles, she becomes aware of someone approaching—a sudden glimpse of long, slender legs in black stockings and the edge of a short black leather skirt catches her eye. Looking up, she quickly spots the fake smile and false eyelashes of Marta Stennheiser. She's wearing a short, cropped leather jacket and vermilion lipstick, attempting—in Noah's opinion—to look older and sexier than she is.

Their relationship, if it can be called that, has always been public—never personal. However, Marta's commentary always seemed to make *everything* personal.

"Can I join you, *meine freundin*?" Marta asks in her deep German accent.

"Listen, Marta. I'm beat. I've been traveling all day. Maybe another—"

"I'll just be a minute," Marta interrupts, pulling up another chair. "Promise."

After talking about air travel, where they've been, where they're headed, the conversation quickly turns from these niceties to their conflicting perspectives on the environment.

"You're actually kind of kooky, Noah. I mean... that's probably what makes you endearing to your followers. And it's why the mainstream media doesn't know what to make of you." Marta looks down her slender nose at Noah, cooly regarding her like a cat playing with a mouse.

Despite her fatigue, Noah's adrenaline kicks in, perhaps too much. "The reason the media doesn't fawn over me like they do you is because of your daddy's bent friends. They *own* the news and just follow along, reporting the lines given to them by the corporate bosses. It has nothing to do with me, my approach, or my mental state!"

Noah takes a breath, her voice more measured as she continues. "You know, Marta, I think you should start putting *my* name in the list of credits for your show. I'm the one who's the inspiration for you. Whatever I produce on *Extinction is Forever*, you just come along and say the opposite. It makes me wonder why you can't do anything original."

They stare at each other over their drinks for a few beats before Marta smiles and replies, "Oh, I've got something *original* in mind. I'd actually like your comment on it. I've learned, and pardon me if it's too personal, but I've done a bit of digging into the Greenling's history. And oh my. You come from quite an odd family tree, don't you?"

Noah's face scrunches in a puzzled expression. "What do you mean?"

"You know... all these weird claims, these strange behaviors of yours—the ones most people think are unnatural or a sign of mental illness—come to find, they run as rampant as weeds in your family. Oh yes... the Greenlings are a *very* strange brood indeed. Aren't they?" Marta waits a beat and then deepens her voice as she head-bobbles mockingly. "*We are one, though we are many!*" She snickers, glaring at Noah, daring her to lash out. "Here's what I think. I think your relatives are part of some backwoods, wacko clan that says it suffers from all kinds of fabricated *allergies.*" She makes air quotes with her fingers. "That's where you get your strangeness from, isn't it? I'm surprised you're not all allergic to yourselves!" Marta's snigger makes it obvious how much she's enjoying herself.

Noah's face flushes. Since she was a little girl, she's always felt protective of her da—and now, she also has growing worries about all the Greenlings. *They're so innocent... so vulnerable... I don't know what I'd do if anything...*

Her words become exact, confrontational. "Where in God's name did you come up with all this?"

Marta responds, her words cool and unhurried. "Oh, I've tracked down a few of your cousins who got out of your Greenling cult. Very interesting the things they've told me. In fact, they've given me loads of juicy details. My viewers will just gobble it up. I'm so excited to produce a whole episode about *you.* You're welcome for the heads-up, dear Noah. How's that for *original.*"

Noah's anger boils over as she pushes herself up from her chair. "Marta, that's not the whole story! And you know it. You can spin it however you want, but my followers will see through it."

Marta reaches over to put her hand on Noah's arm and replies in a soft, patronizing tone. "Darling, how cute of you. How naive you are. We shall see." She quickly stands up, blows Noah a kiss, and whispers, *"Auf*

Wiedersehen Freund." When Marta brushes past her, she bumps her entire cup of coffee, spilling it all over the table for Noah to deal with.

Dublin, Ireland (88° F / 31° C)

Arriving in Dublin mid-morning is a shock to her system. Maybe it's because of her body's rapid rebound from the temperature swing she went through eight weeks ago. On top of that, the flight from Dallas to Dublin was delayed twelve hours, upping the total trip to just shy of thirty-six hours.

With an *Extinction is Forever* sweatshirt draped over her shoulders, Noah slowly exits the Dublin Airport, exhausted. She indulges herself by renting a carrier-bot and heads for the lower level, where she stands at the curb. Patrick sent her a HOLO-EM yesterday and told her he'd pick her up and have a "little surprise." *I just hope he got my message about the delay.*

She starts to settle on a bench next to two other passengers from her flight but then looks up and sees Gil's Range Rover pulling up. Patrick jumps out of the passenger side, a wide grin beaming. He rushes toward her and gives her a hug that envelops her like a warm blanket. She collapses into his arms, inhaling the familiar cedarwood, and suddenly starts to cry.

Is it because I'm exhausted? Relieved to be home? Or something else? Something about being with Patrick again?

"Noah, I'm *so* glad you're home," he whispers in her ear, still holding her close. "This has been the longest eight weeks of my life."

She slowly finds her words, realizing just how absorbed she's been in her program and how overwhelmed and drained she feels now.

"I missed you too. It's been such a long flight. I can barely stand up."

"Of course, let's get you home," he says, throwing her bags in the back.

As she walks around the car, Gil opens the door, grabs her shoulders, and says, "Welcome home, sis. I missed you. Missed having someone to argue with other than Ma." He snickers, then adds. "She's been kind of edgy with you gone."

Noah looks at her brother. *He seems older. Gentler. More open.* "Hey, Gil. I missed you, too," she says, wishing she didn't just half mean it.

Patrick and Noah get in the backseat, while Gil jumps in the front and heads toward the M50. "I bet you're surprised to see the two of us coming to get you," Patrick says.

"Nothing surprises me when it comes to either of you, but *together*, that might be a bit much," she says, managing a crooked grin.

"Ah, come on, sis, can't you feel the love?" Gil quips.

"I'm starting to, *bro*. What's this *sis* stuff anyway? You haven't called me that since we were kids."

Gil tells her about his trips to see their da over the summer and then tries to explain what's happened. "I don't know, Noah. Maybe it's graduating and looking forward to something beyond home. Or maybe it was screwing things up for you and Patrick and then living with the guilt. I just feel like... I want to be done playing the asshole."

Gil catches Noah's eye in the truck's mirror. Both search the other's face for clues. His expression displays a pleading desire to be understood and forgiven, while hers conveys a guarded reluctance.

Sensing all that's unsaid between the two, Patrick gently breaks the silence. "Noah, Gil sent me a HOLO after you left and said he wanted to talk. So we met up, and he told me about his part in what happened with Colin. I was pretty pissed—especially about how he leaked some of the stuff about your experience in the woods to the jerk. I wanted to punch your brother in the face. Not because I lost my job... more because of all the nasty stuff they said about you."

Noah, wide awake now, listens to every word, not totally sure about what she's hearing.

"You see, I've done some pretty stupid things too, Noah," Patrick continues. "As I sat there listening to your brother, I saw his remorse. I know what it's like to get twisted around inside and take it out on others. When my ma died, at first, I was just withdrawn, distant. But pretty soon, it soured inside me... it turned into biting sarcasm and mad flailings at whoever tried to get near to me. When Gil finally told me what it was like not to have your da at home, I understood a bit more of what was going on with him."

Not wanting to disrupt the moment but unable to stop herself, Noah teases. "Gil, do you have a *man crush* on my boyfriend?" As soon as she says it, she puzzles over her word choice. *Hmm... That's the first time I've called him that.*

Patrick and Gil look at each other through the rearview mirror. "Well, what if I do?" Her brother counters.

All three of them snort in laughter. Noah can't believe what she's witnessing. She'd given up salvaging anything of her and Gil's relationship, and there he is now. Acting like a grown-up.

She catches his eye in the mirror and mouths, *"Who are you?"* He simply grins and keeps driving toward home.

Kilkenny, Ireland (89° F / 32° C)

The house is empty when they get home. Ma is at the shop. They dropped Patrick off at his apartment, so it's just the two of them, sister and brother. The quiet reminds Noah of how peaceful she feels here. It's like a warm bath, soaking into her pores, gently relaxing her. She's also aware that several years of animosity between her and Gil seems to be dissolving. *Will I know how to be with him if we're not fighting? Can I forgive him? Not just say the words... really forgive him?*

She senses her brother watching, waiting. Automatically, her guard goes up. "Gil, I'm really beat. I know we need to talk, but honestly, I just can't right now. You've probably been waiting for us to do this. But I'm sorry... I've got to get a shower and some sleep. Okay?"

She sees both sympathy and disappointment in his face as he answers. "Sure, Noah. I understand. When the time's right."

She reaches out and puts her hand on his arm. "Thanks, Gil," she says, feeling a warmth toward him she hasn't felt for a very long time.

With heavy footsteps, Noah plods upstairs, then down the familiar green hallway, and heads to her room. She opens the door and stands on its threshold, taking in her collections, artifacts, books, posters—all her favorite possessions. She's missed this private little sanctuary. She thinks how strange it is that these few odds and ends that belong to her somehow ground her. Slowly, something deep inside starts to unwind, gradually loosening the intensity of emotion she's recently experienced.

She skips her shower, too exhausted to turn on the water or even walk to the bathroom. Instead, she slips out of her sweatshirt, takes off her boots, and gets under the blanket on her bed. Closing her eyes, she feels like her body is still moving, churning. Her mind tries to keep up, but eventually, it gives up. Sleep soon overtakes her and pulls her into its irresistible descent.

"*N-O-A-H*," the dream voices whisper her name several times in a slow-metered, vegetal harmony. "*You know how long-suffering we've b-e-e-n... how giving we are... in spite of everything... we still belong to one a-n-o-t-h-e-r... nature and human nature... know this, Noah... you and your brother b-e-l-o-n-g... to one another... you began together... you may even e-n-d together... we need Gil t-o-o... be like us, f-o-r-g-i-v-e... don't let the past destroy w-h-a-t... c-o-u-l-d... b-e...*"

The last phrase—"*what could be*"—reverberates, then recedes like an echo back into silence. Noah is now alone. Emptied. Waiting to be filled. Slowly, Patrick walks up to her, both hands behind his back. She can't see what he's holding. He looks fiercely into her eyes and then brings his arms to the front, offering her something. It's a small wooden box with a sprig of mistletoe tied on its top, one of her ma's favorites. She reaches out to take it, and when it's in her hands, Patrick is swept away in a hazy mist. Her heart sinks.

"*Did I do something wrong?*" she asks. Confused by what just happened—frustrated and uncertain of what to do—she finds herself weeping. "*I don't know how. I don't know... I just don't know.*"

Hesitantly, she removes the mistletoe and then opens the simple box. It looks like something her da would have made. Inside, she sees two halves of a beautiful scallop shell. They are deep purple with sunburst yellow swirls moving from side to side. The two shells are still firmly connected by their shared ligament, protected by a strong, invisible muscle.

"*Gil*," she murmurs, tears streaming down her face. "*We belong to each other. I forgive you*," she whispers, meaning it in every fiber of her being. "*Nothing... nothing you do... nothing I do... will ever separate us.*"

She gradually wakes up and lies there for several minutes, mulling everything over. On her cheeks, she feels the coolness of her tears. But she also feels a radiance gently kissing her face. As she opens her eyes, the afternoon sun plays over her, reflecting its golden light on her rich, copper hair. Looking out the window, she sees the same jay that she's seen before watching her. It cocks its white head—a curious look in its tiny black eyes—then launches toward the woods and flies out of sight.

❦ ❧ ❦ ❧ ❦ ❧

After she showers and puts on clean clothes, Noah starts to feel more like herself. The vivid dream remains with her—an unambiguous invitation from somewhere beyond. She walks down, hoping to find her brother. The house is quiet. Emptiness, instead of peace, fills the space. She goes to the fridge and gets herself a glass of cold water. *Where could we have gone so wrong?* There's a sudden ache to find him, to see him, to hear his voice.

"We belong to one another," she whispers. She steps out the back door onto the concrete stoop. Her clean, bare feet feel the rough sand and stone underneath. The gentle breeze blows over her arms, raising goosebumps on exposed skin. And then, she catches sight of her brother walking around from the back of the garage. She steps down onto the grass and feels the damp earth on her toes. Feeling grounded, she moves quickly toward him.

She halts when he turns and notices her. They stand a few meters apart and, for several moments, simply gaze at one another, soaking in who they are and who they're becoming.

"Noah, I just want to—" Gil begins. But Noah quickly moves toward him, putting a hand up to cut him off.

"Stop," she says, a little too firmly. "I mean... you don't have to say another word, Gil. We've both made mistakes. In case you haven't noticed, I'm not the easiest person to have for a sister. But whatever we've done to each other... whatever we do in the future... we belong to each other."

Gil's eyes are tender, yet also pained as he listens. "But... Noah, it can't be that easy. I feel like I owe you something. Like I need to *do* something to set things right."

She studies him, taking time to think before answering, sifting through past injuries. *Is it safe to trust him... to be vulnerable?* She weighs her decision, listening to her heart as well as her common sense. *It's all about trust... otherwise, we have nothing.* The desire to be known is deeper than any potential misgivings.

"Gil, there is *one* thing you can do. And I'm not sure it will be easy for either of us."

"What is it?" he asks softly.

Noah takes a deep breath as she looks up, searching for the words. "I'd like to be completely real with you. I'd like to be able to tell you about these weird encounters with nature... no matter how strange they might sound. Do you think you can handle that? Can you try to give me that?"

He takes his time before answering. "Noah, I can try. I want to do that for you. I think I've actually envied you and these connections of yours. Who knows? Maybe, if I try to listen to you... if I'm more open... maybe I'll start to feel something too."

Noah takes his hand and pulls him onto the grass, where they sit side by side. She then tells him about her recent dream and the jay outside her window. He listens well and asks a few simple questions as she shares. Feeling safer than she's felt for a long time with him, she goes on, recounting from beginning to end each of her past nature experiences— leaving nothing out.

When she finishes, they sit quietly, staring into the woods behind the house. After several moments, Noah breaks the silence.

"Oh, and there's one more thing, Gil."

"Sure. What's that?" He asks.

"Stop calling me *sis*! It makes me feel like I'm six years old," she playfully scolds, punching him a little too hard in the arm.

"Ouch! That hurts!" he whines.

"Sorry, *bro*," she responds with mock contrition before changing the subject. "Hey, I don't suppose I could borrow your car? I'd like to head into town to see Ma now."

"Feel free to use it whenever you'd like. But how about if I take you? I'd like to be part of your big homecoming."

Noah pauses to absorb Gil's newfound sincerity, smiling warmly at him. She's grateful to have her brother back.

"Great! Give me five minutes, and then we can head out. And... thank you. I'd completely given up on us."

"Me too, *sis*," he answers, drawing her in for a long-overdue, brotherly bear hug.

⁓ ❧ ⁓ ❧ ⁓ ❧

It's after five o'clock when Noah and Gil walk quietly into their ma's shop. She's tidying up from the day, putting the apothecary jars back on their shelves. Her hair's a bit undone—it looks like the day may have gotten the better of her. She stands in front of the glass case and notices the two blurry forms reflected there. A thought flashes in her mind: *I'd recognize my children's presence even if I were blind and deaf.*

Spinning around, she hurries over to Noah. "Oh my God, you're here! What a beautiful sight for this old woman." Her ma gives her a long, warm hug. Noah lets herself melt into the woman's body. *Now I feel home,* she tells herself. The scent of the herbs linger around her mother, as if she were a fragrant vine wrapping herself around her daughter.

Noah's eyes drift around the shop's perimeter, soaking in the familiar sights and smells. *Is it my imagination, or has the place shrunk? It seems a lot smaller now. Maybe a place like the Amazon changes your perspective.*

"Both my children, together again," Fina says. "Do you know how happy that makes me? Gil, come over here." Fina wraps him in her arms—

though careful to show him a bit of restraint—the way mothers hug boys who are now young men.

Noah smiles, watching the two, but then her excitement quickly boils over. "Ma, I can't wait to tell you all about my trip. There's so much to catch up on. I don't know exactly where to start—"

Noah's ma holds her hand up, gently interrupting her. "There will be plenty of time for all that, dear. I've been getting ready to have you home for a few days and brought some things along for dinner. I thought we could go out to your da's place and catch up there." She hesitates, turning her attention back to Gil. "Are you free too, son?"

"Sure, Ma. Wouldn't miss it. Want me to drive?" he offers, not missing a beat.

"That would be grand." Ma grins at both of them, then practically runs to the storeroom to gather this much-anticipated homecoming meal.

Laois County, Ireland (89° F / 32° C)

Ma and Noah heat the food they brought over an open fire. There's smoked salmon, boiled bacon and cabbage, along with boxty—a fried, crispy combination of mashed and grated potatoes—her da's favorite. And, of course, enough soda bread to feed the forest.

While the two of them get the table on the hut's porch ready, Gil and Da amble along the paths outside the hut. Noah would usually have been annoyed that Ma asked her to do "womenfolk's chores," but seeing her brother and Da engaged in conversation makes those past squabbles seem petty. She's thankful that the two of them seem to be growing closer.

During dinner, Noah recounts her experience in the Amazon rainforest. She tells her family what she did every day, what she saw, and who became her friends. She decides to test Gil's openness and describes her mysterious encounter with Erin and the kapok tree. She even describes the lab's dark menagerie of insects, reptiles, and amphibians who seemed to look to her for some kind of direction. Gil listens thoughtfully, offering his sister encouraging smiles and nods.

"Oh my. That Erin sounds like a girl after me own heart," Da says, piling a third helping of boxty onto his plate. "Will you do something for me when I'm gone? And I'm serious here. When my time comes, I want you to sprinkle me ashes all around the giant wych elm to the north of the hut. You know the one I mean. It's over four meters around."

"Let's not get ahead of ourselves, you old Greenling," Ma says. "We've got to get these kids out of the house so I can come out and civilize you again." Ma winks at her burly husband. "I'm afraid you're stuck like glue to me for another five decades. *Then* we can start talking about you feeding the wych elm with your big bones."

Gil and Noah glance at one another, exchanging an amused expression. *How's it going to work out when they actually live together after all these years?* Noah wonders.

After her ma and da are finished sniping, Noah wraps up by telling them about the last day's tragic events—about the paste she made from the Cordoncillo leaves and Yoshi's body's incredible response.

Ma gazes into Noah's eyes. She knows her daughter is special. But this? Her curiosity is fully aroused now.

"Noah, I know plants, and I know their amazing power to heal. But I also know that they take time to work—more time than that paste was on Yoshi's eyes. I don't think the paste was the only thing at work. I know you have many gifts, but this one seems new... like a new sprout on a tree with deep roots. I've never seen this in you before."

Noah's brow stretches with skepticism. If Ma notices, she doesn't show it. Instead, she continues on and narrates a tale of Airmed, the goddess of healing. "According to Irish legend, when her brother Micah died, she went to his grave and cried until her tears soaked the earth where he lay. Later, out of the ground sprang up as many herbs as days in the year—three hundred and sixty-five—one for each joint and sinew in her brother's body. Those herbs, so the story goes, then became the rootstock of all the healing arts." Fina pauses as she studies her daughter. "It seems to me, Noah, that the spirit of Airmed is strong in you too."

They all sit in silence. Noah suddenly feels awkward taking up so much space and being the center of attention, especially with Gil there. Looking at her feet, her face flushes. *I wished Ma would stop with all these old legends. I'm confused enough.*

As she glances up at Gil, she sees him smiling at her. *What's with that expression?* She wonders. *Admiration? Maybe. Brotherly pride? Could be. Love? I hope so.* Then, an interior awareness blossoms so vividly it shocks her. *Adoration.*

Feeling totally uncomfortable now, Noah abruptly shifts her attention back to her mom. "Slow down, Ma. I don't think I exactly believe all those old tales anymore. Let's just leave it at this: the plants and my quick thinking helped Yoshi recover his sight. Who knows, maybe his injuries weren't as bad as we thought?"

Ma considers her daughter knowingly, a gentle smile playing on her lips. "Of course, Noah. We can leave it there. All I meant is that your wisdom and skill as a healer seem to be growing stronger."

Da breaks in, sensing the need to steer things toward shallower waters. "Let's go in and gather 'round the hearth. I have some Guinness I've been cooling in a bucket out in the well."

As he retrieves the beer, the others push chairs around the fire. Gil prods the glowing embers until they become steady flames.

"Here you go," Da announces as he passes open bottles around.

"*Sláinte!*" They say in unison, tipping their bottles toward one another.

After Noah's parents take some time to catch her up on what they've been up to, Gil eventually clears his throat to announce he has something to say. "Ma. Da. I think I know what I want to do, or at least what I want to study. There's a new program at Trinity College in Dublin that integrates both computer and environmental sciences. There's a professor there researching how AI may be able to connect with trees, and possibly even interact with them.

"It's way outside the box, but it seems like it could bring together some things that I'm interested in. I have an interview next week. The program is in the very early stages of development. Maybe that's why I've got a shot at getting in."

He shrugs as if to say, '*Who knows?*' But they all know he's far brighter and more ingenious than his grades demonstrated.

"Gil, that sounds amazing!" Noah's voice is enthusiastic and genuine. "I've never heard of anything like it. You'd be incredible with something like that. I hope you get it. I'd love to learn more about it myself."

His head tilts as she speaks. Her generous affirmation touches him; he can't remember the last time he's felt respect from her.

"Thanks, sis. I'll keep you posted."

After expressing their excitement and approval—peppered with a few practical questions—their parents turn their attention back to Noah.

"And what about you, dear daughter? Any update on your plans?" Ma asks.

"As a matter of fact," Noah says, "that's the other thing I wanted to talk to you about." Noah tells them about Dr. Wilde's invitation to study at the University of Toronto, along with a few other students from the Amazon project. She outlines the interdisciplinary program he chairs as best she can—finally adding that she would receive full tuition, room and board, and a small stipend—hoping to satisfy any practical concerns they might have.

"Noah, this sounds grand," Aiden says. But as she watches, her ma reaches for her da's hand, nodding as he continues. "It's just *so* far away. I know you have to fly the nest, young one, but so far?"

Noah feels a sinking sensation in her chest. "Honestly, I've had the same doubts... and yet..." She goes on and tells them how torn she's felt—how one moment she imagines how great it will be. And then the next, she wonders if she's cut out for any of it. And then again, she reminds herself of the other risks she's taken and how they've turned out. Her parents listen, nodding along, communicating their understanding.

"Oh, well." Da finally sighs. "I guess that's what we get for raising such a strong, independent daughter. It sounds great, Noah. Really, it does. Perhaps *this* is what going to the Amazon was all about."

She stands up and races over to her da, throwing both arms around his thick neck. "You two are so great!" she says, looking over his broad shoulder at her ma. "Thank you for always trusting me and supporting me. And besides, it's not that far away, is it? At least it's not Brazil!"

Kilkenny, Ireland (92° F / 33° C)

On the way home, there's an easy, expansive silence. Gil and Noah share an occasional glance, tender smiles passing between them. When they enter town, he drops her off at Patrick's. Before getting out of the car, Noah leans over and gives her twin a long hug.

"Thank you, Gil. I feel like I've got my brother back. I've missed the way we used to be together, like some Irish yin and yang."

"Me too, sis. Which one am I? Yin or yang?"

Noah lets go of him and chuckles. "Yang. Definitely yang!"

She pokes him in the ribs and jumps out of the truck, wearing the same silly grin she used to flash at him when they were kids. He studies her as she walks up the steps to the apartment, feeling something new. *I feel... protective.* His pondering is quickly interrupted as she turns back toward him, giving him a quick wave.

Noah slowly enters the half-opened door. "Hello! Anyone here?" she sings out.

"Come on in," a muffled voice calls out from the rear of the flat.

Noah enters the dark hallway. There's a gentle glow coming from the back room. The flickering light on the wall seems to be coming from warm, open flames. She then recognizes the scent—a combination of gardenias and cedar wood.

"Back here," she hears Patrick call out.

As she enters the room, she notices how the candles softly shimmer on the gray-green walls. On the coffee table, in front of the sofa, is a chilled bottle of wine, alongside a tray of cheese and crackers.

Patrick rises from the couch, his hair gently tousled from lying on it while he waited for her.

"Not bad for an ex-science teacher slash bachelor, huh?" He says, gesturing to the spread he's laid out.

"Not bad at all. And you look pretty delicious, too," Noah blurts out, then kicks herself. *Slow down, girl. Let's not get ahead of ourselves.*

They move toward each other and embrace in a way they were unable to yesterday. *Now THAT makes me realize how much I've missed him!*

He invites her to sit down and then pours two generous glasses of Gewurztraminer. The delicate peach color glistens in the candlelight. They tilt glasses together, creating a brilliant, crystalline ring.

"To the future," he announces.

"To the future," she echoes, as they each take a sip of the cool, bright wine.

"So tell me, what's it like to be back in our humble little country after your travels to the other side of the world?"

Noah releases a low chuckle, almost a sigh, while she puts a few nibbles on a plate. She shares what it feels like to be home—about her surprise at the shift in her brother and the repair happening in their relationship. She describes her dinner with her parents and how good it was to see them—how much she missed them.

He then asks about her time away, inviting her not only to recall the experiences but also to process them.

"When did you feel most alive, Noah? The most... like yourself?"

She describes her time in the kapok's clearing, the butterflies, the jungle's ever-present smells and sounds.

Patrick listens until she finishes, then arches an eyebrow and says, "You seem... I don't know. Different. How do you think the time there—the time away— has changed you?"

Cocking her head, she pauses, surveying him. "You're pretty good at this, you know." She pours a second glass of wine for them.

"Good at what?" A sheepish expression spreads across his unshaven face, telling her he knows *exactly* what he's good at.

"Seriously, when I'm with you, I feel listened to, pursued. Like, you really want to know what I think, what I'm feeling. Thank you. It helps me sort through what's happened. Or maybe, what's happening *to* me."

He nods, and she continues to share both the material elements of her summer as well as the more private, mystical ones. Patrick loves being given a window into these personal encounters that Noah experiences. He's felt inspired by the ones she's shared with him over the past few months, even praying that something similar would happen to him.

She pauses, her green eyes peering into his. "I have one more thing to tell you. I didn't know if I wanted to—or needed to. But if we're going to trust each other, I know I *have* to."

"Okay," he says, biting his bottom lip. "You're starting to worry me."

Noah finishes her last bite and then pushes on. "While I was on the project, I started to have feelings for someone."

"What do you mean, *'feelings'*?" He asks, leaning away slightly.

"I mentioned Yoshi to you earlier. We spent a lot of time together. It was like having a little puppy at first. It was kind of sweet how he would follow me around, trying to please me. But... I don't know... being away from home, from everything familiar—it all seemed so distant there. I found myself... umm... *curious*. I think that's it. I wanted to know if I could feel about someone else the way I'm starting to feel about *you*... about *us*. Nothing happened—I mean, physically—between us. Well, that's not exactly true. We sort of leaned on each other... and I took care of him after his accident. But I felt something for him I've never felt before—"

Patrick crosses his arms, looking like he's preparing for the inevitable punch in the gut.

"—I felt *maternal*. Does that make any sense? I've had close friends, like Shea. And I've had a few boyfriends. But I've never felt this kind of tender concern and protectiveness for someone other than my family. I sometimes felt like a mother to him—even though we're the same age. That bond feels like it's still there. Especially now that his mom's cancer is back. I'm just not sure what to make of it." She pauses, out of breath now. "But I'm not sure I want it to end either... just like I don't want my connection with you to stop." She finally ends in a flurry. *What on Earth is he supposed to make of all this?*

After several agonizing moments, he starts to laugh under his breath. "Woah... you had me worried. I thought you were setting me up. I could have sworn you were getting ready to dump me for a Mario Kart character."

Noah lightly punches him in the arm and then leans toward him, pulling him close. "Don't tease me about this. I wasn't sure if I could tell you how I feel about him. It's different from how I feel about you—you mean so much to me, Patrick. It's just, I don't know... I have so many *other* feelings, too." She pauses. Their breathing is magnified by the moment. "Can you handle that? I never want to hurt you. But I also never want to lie to you either."

He gazes into her earnest eyes, wondering how she musters so much courage. "I believe you, Noah. And I'll do my best to follow your lead. But you do know—I'm not some puppy following you around. Although it seems you do hold my leash." Noah laughs, playfully reaching out for his collar and pulling him closer.

Before losing momentum, she presses on, her tone signaling that she'd like to spare him from what comes next. "Okay... there's one more thing, Patrick—"

"*You're pregnant!*" he interrupts teasingly. Noah gives him a hard elbow to the ribs. "Shite, girl, that hurt!" he whines, wincing as he rubs his side.

"Listen, this is important. Your uncle, Dr. Wilde—"

"You mean Seamus?"

"*Dr. Wilde* sat down with me on the last day and offered me a full-ride scholarship to come study with him at the University of Toronto. I think I'd like to go." She pauses and searches his face, hoping he won't burst her bubble or get sulky. "I know it would mean we'd be a long way from each other again."

Patrick offers a reassuring smile. "Seamus sent me a HOLO-EM yesterday and told me the news. I'm happy for you. Really. Proud of you, too, Noah. This opportunity seems like the right next step. I don't know where the future's headed any more than you do, but I can tell you this: *this* is what's next for you."

He turns and looks out the window for a moment before continuing. "It looks like I won't be around here much longer either. My uncle seems to have plans for me, too. We're still working out the details, but he's told me a few things about his and Ma's project that are new to me. I think I might like to help continue what she was so passionate about. And I'm also thinking about taking some time to get off the grid and do some backpacking."

Noah smiles, mirroring his enthusiasm. "That sounds grand. I think you should do it. All of it. Who knows, maybe all this is leading somewhere, some new, grand purpose? Eh?"

She pauses—uncertain whether she should tell him about her encounters with his ma. When she makes up her mind, she lowers her voice and looks directly into his kind, searching eyes. "Listen, Patrick... I really don't know how to say this. I left something out earlier. I don't know why. I guess it sounds... kind of crazy. What's new, huh? But when I went to the clearing where your ma's ashes are scattered, I felt your ma. Sensed her... like she was still alive, or somehow still present in the giant kapok."

Patrick stares at her, his face displaying his growing puzzlement. "What do you mean, 'felt her'?"

"I can't explain it. Somehow, I knew it was her—there was something familiar about the energy, it was like *your* energy—and she was united with the tree. Then her words—not exactly her words, the tree's and nature itself—poured out this overwhelming impression, a look into the past and the future."

Once spoken, her words quickly fall into the silence that envelops them. They sit, not speaking for several minutes.

"What are you thinking?" Noah finally asks tentatively.

Patrick's eyes are closed, as if trying to awaken an image. He takes a deep breath and opens them. They glisten with emotion. Love. Sadness. Longing.

"I believe you, Noah. A year ago, I wouldn't have known what to think. I'd probably have written you off as crazy. But now everything seems different. I think I'm different too." He pauses, earnestly holding her with his eyes. "I'm glad it was you she spoke to. It makes me feel closer to you. I just wish I could have experienced her like that for myself."

Patrick continues telling her what he remembers about his ma. As he describes Erin and shares his memories of her, Noah feels the connection again—gently vibrating within her—to this woman she's never met, at least not in the flesh.

Somehow, I do know her. Know her within the kapok tree. And know her within this beautiful man sitting next to me.

ઉ⁂ઉ⁂ઉ⁂

Shea's fiddling with a colorful deck of cards; extinct animals correspond to the card's suit and value. Playing solitaire with actual cards instead of virtual ones is her attempt to temper her simmering impatience. Suddenly, her HOLO chimes. She fumbles with the cards, dropping them to the floor, and accepts the HOLO-EM she's been waiting for.

"Oh my god! Noah? You're home, right? I wanted to give you some space, but I haven't been able to think about anything else, knowing you were probably here. How are you? Have you seen Patrick?"

"I'm fine. Good. Really, I'm great, Shea." Noah answers, thrown off by the barrage of her friend's questions. "A lot has happened... uh... a lot *is* happening. Listen, I want to tell you all about it. And I want to hear about *you*, too. You up for a little camping trip? I think I need to go back to the site of that famous—or was it *infamous*?—science experiment. There's something I need to see. I don't know... I just feel like that place is where I need to be right now. Going there with you would be just what I need right now."

"Me too," Shea agrees instantly. "Let's do it!"

After disconnecting the HOLO, Shea bounds up the stairs of her house two at a time to pack her knapsack. From the kitchen, her ma half-whispers and half-yells. "Shea, don't wake your brother!" But she's too excited to slow down.

This has been the longest the two of us have ever been apart. I wonder what it will be like to be back together. I can't believe how dull life was without her... even for eight weeks.

As she stuffs her gear into her pack, she thinks about their brief conversation. *Something in her voice sounded different. Happy? Yes, but also sad. I don't know. Both, maybe. I'm probably just making it all up.* Still, she has a strong sense that their individual futures, as well as their future together, are rapidly changing. *Is this the last time we'll feel like our girlhood selves?*

She hopes she's wrong, but she is starting to face the fact that it's all out of her hands.

Arlington, Virginia, USA (94° F / 34.5° C)

Journi takes a deep breath—but not because of recording tonight's program. She's done that for so long she doesn't even break a sweat under the set's hot lights. Instead, her mind races because of the message her assistant, Simone, just sent her.

Journi rushes out of the studio and heads to her office. Dropping into her chair, she signals her HOLO to connect with Noah. After almost a minute, a tired, disheveled version of the young redhead accepts her contact.

"Um... Hi, Journi. Sorry. Just waking up. What time is it?" Noah yawns. Eyes still closed, she asks, "How are you?"

Journi notices a background of dense forest and insects buzzing in the HOLO's light. "Hi, Noah. Sorry to wake you. Where are you?"

"Oh... Shea and I are just camping. I'm still trying to get over my jet lag. And Shea... well, she can sleep through anything."

"Okay, I'll keep this short. I'm sort of walking on air right now."

Noah is gradually waking up now. She slips out of her sleeping bag and traipses to a log on the grove's perimeter, not wanting to wake Shea. Looking over her shoulder, she sees her friend curled up like a baby, breathing deeply with her mouth wide open.

Journi smiles, feeling a little guilty for calling so early. "Listen, I know you're beat and probably just need to sleep for like a month. But I think we need to talk about what's next. There's some significant momentum right now, and we don't want to waste it."

Noah blinks away the remaining cobwebs, her mind finally slipping into gear. "Okay... what exactly did you have in mind?"

"You know Marta Sennheiser, right?"

Noah huffs. "Of course I do. I just crossed swords with her in the Dallas airport a few days ago."

Journi's brow furrows. "I'm curious to hear more, but that will have to wait. As you know, she's the new darling of the far-right, their poster child for climate change opposition. She's funded heavily by multi-billion-dollar corporate sponsors—no doubt because of her dad's seat on the board of the Trans-Natural Economic Coalition.

"Anyway, I want to host a series of HOLO-NET roundtables with you and Marta—sort of like a debate, but more of a conversation. I think it could be big. Really big! We could start with a few smaller virtual events and then, next winter or spring, go global. I've unofficially approached Royal-Net's Samantha Erskine with the idea of co-moderating, and I just heard back from her—she likes the idea. I think we'd get stronger interest if our two rival networks co-sponsored the events."

Journi finally takes a breath and notices Noah's eyes glaze over. "That's it. Don't answer right now. Go back to sleep. Take a shower and eat some breakfast when you get home. Then think about it. But not too long. And then... say yes. *Please*?"

Noah runs the sole of her bare foot over the cool, damp moss, attempting to digest everything Journi's said with limited success. She yawns uncontrollably and then blinks with heavy eyelids at the other woman through the HOLO. "Okay. Will do. But right now... I can't think about anything except going back to bed. And, Journi... thanks for thinking of this."

Noah's HOLO image evaporates as they disconnect. Left alone, Journi turns off the table lamp and looks out the office window. It's long past twilight, and darkness hovers over D.C. She notices star-like pinpricks shimmering for several miles off into the distance.

Journi stands inches away from the large window, studying her

reflected image, feeling like she's eyeball to eyeball with herself—or is it the
of her that she sees in Noah? *She'll say yes, won't she? I would have. She's
way too invested to say no to something like this.*

Kilkenny, Ireland (92° F / 33° C)

The weather has been perfect for Noah and Shea to camp and hike, giggle,
and even cry together this one last time. The previous twenty-four hours
have rushed by much too quickly for both of them. Wishing they could
make time slow down—or better, reverse itself—they sit across from each
other on the kayak decks, parked on the river's bank, ready to launch for
home.

Shea leans forward and looks deeply into Noah's eyes. "I have
something I want to show you before we leave. I hope you're alright with
it," she says shyly as she stretches her baggy T-shirt over her left shoulder
to display a new tattoo over her heart. Looking up at Noah, she nervously
waits.

"Another? What's this?" Noah says, moving closer to examine the
colorful details.

Across Shea's pale chest is an artful miniature scene of an ancient boat.
Two silhouetted figures stand in the foreground, arm in arm, sandwiched
between a leopard and a snowy owl. Above the scene is a vibrant rainbow,
cradling a soaring dove.

"Noah's ark!" Shea announces, regaining her confidence. "Now I'll be
able to carry you with me wherever life takes us."

Noah sits, her gaze moving back and forth between her friend's
glistening eyes and the work of art inscribed in her flesh. Unsure of what to
say, she starts to cry. After a moment, she finds her voice again.

"It's perfect! Shea, you never—and I do mean *never*—fail to catch me
off guard. You silly girl. Thank you. Thank you *so much* for always being
there for me... for being such a devoted friend."

The two break down and embrace, crying tears that carry their many
joys and memories, along with their griefs and expectations. There's no

need to say anything more. They're completely spent from the exhaustion that comes after a good cry. They turn toward their kayaks and prepare to slip them into the water.

As Noah's back is turned, Shea slips a small, brown, kraft-wrapped package into her friend's backpack—struggling to suppress her excited giggle.

PART FIVE

Episode 35: Extinction is Forever
HOLO-POD Hosted by Noah Calhoun-Greenling

"At last, something that feels like good news. The growing green movement of island nations has ratified an agreement to form a global alliance, which will grant Eco Nation status to its members and provide a pathway for other emerging environmental states to join. This coalition is designed to publicly differentiate itself, both in policies and strategies, from what it calls the repressive 'Petrol Nations' we are currently controlled by.

"Several battered coastal regions and states have even begun to take the unprecedented action to draw up secession plans; ready to sever their current national ties to join forces with the growing list of those facing similar climate threats to their populations and lands.

"It appears a battle line between David and Goliath is forming. It makes me wonder what sling or stones the shepherd boy might find to take on such a massive giant. Even if it's too little too late, it's inspiring and should remind us all to never give up."

Fall 2060

11,000 Meters Over the Atlantic Ocean (23° F / -5° C)

As her plane takes off from Dublin Airport, Noah feels the familiar guilt that comes from the unavoidable complicity of modern travel: jet fuel, petrol for cars, diesel gasoline for trains or buses. It seems to her that necessity, as well as humanity's impatient need for expedience, lead from one regrettable compromise to another.

"I'm sorry," she whispers to the green-and-blue planet beneath her. "Goodbye, my Emerald Isle." Her own green eyes reflected in the window, she gazes down—her homeland disappearing beneath the brilliant, sunlit clouds that envelope their ascent.

Grateful to have the tiny air-pod to herself, she opens the brown wrapped package Shea must have snuck into her backpack. A handwritten note falls onto her lap as she pulls out a turquoise journal tucked inside. She brings it to her nose and smells the sweet scent of the cactus leather. Seeing her friend's neat cursive lines on the note loosens a gentle wave of nostalgia in her. She imagines Shea's crooked block letters in second grade, now transformed into an artist's practiced script.

My dearest Noah, I really can't believe that our time of growing up together is over. We both couldn't wait to be set free, out on our own, exploring what's next. Well, now that it's here, I'm already missing it. Missing you.

The letter goes on—Shea shares memories of their childhood adventures, their deeds and misdeeds, crushes and heartbreaks. Noah laughs out loud one moment, only to have tears rolling down her cheeks the next.

You've been there for it all, Noah remembers, feeling a flood of gratitude for Shea and their history together. Her eyes return to the letter, and she keeps reading.

> *I guess what I want to say—what I've always wanted to say but never had the courage to say is—I love you! Not just in a friendship kind of way—you know that already. And not only as a sister to me—we will always be that to each other. But I feel a love for you as the woman with whom I've shared everything. Almost everything. I'm sure you would have known exactly how to handle my attraction—you always know what to do. But telling you always seemed too risky. I never wanted to do something or say anything that would get in the way of all we have. But now that you're going so far away, I'm not sure. I've kept this one last secret from you, and now it seems too late. I wonder how things might have been different if I had told you how I felt.*

Noah's heart quickens at Shea's declaration. She's occasionally felt a similar attraction herself. They've shared so much that it sometimes felt like their friendship *was* something more. She feels flattered but also saddened. Confused, too. *Yes, how might things have been different, friend?* Several moments pass—Noah daydreaming as she stares at the bright clouds below—before she finishes reading the letter.

> *Well, there, I've said it—or rather, written it. I hope and pray this doesn't change everything we have as best friends. No matter what, you are my guiding star. You always have been. Always will be. I don't know where I'd be without you. You've given me courage and awakened in me the desire to live, to really live my life. Whatever happens between us from here on, I want you to know my life has been changed by you.*

> *All my love, dear Noah.*
> *Shea*

Lulled by the steady drone of the aircraft, Noah's eyes soften, half shut, and she loses herself in a kind of reverie. She's surprised that this far away from her familiar trees, she can feel such calm. What is it? What is this feeling?

The simple words drift into her consciousness: *You are loved, Noah. You are so very well loved.* She wonders where they are coming from. From Shea? From the Earth beneath her? From some sacred, invisible spirit?

Looking out the window at the bright sunlight reflecting on the tops of soft white clouds, she easily soaks in everything.

Hmmm... I am loved. That's what matters. Noah smiles, feeling certain at how greatly favored she must be.

Toronto, Ontario, Canada (91° F / 33° C)

Noah fiddles with her HOLO ring as the taxi-bot pulls up to 109 Brunswick Avenue. The ring's green Connemara marble reminds her of home; her precious Emerald Isle containing everyone she loves. A sudden pang of homesickness, of nervous uncertainty, is exhibited in her slouched frame.

There's no driver to thank. She's on her own to get her bags out of the trunk that pops open. After she gets everything out of the car's boot and stands on the sidewalk, she takes a deep breath and looks up. The sprawling plaster and brick house is three stories high, shouldering five dormers. The roofs' sharp, angled lines point toward the sky like five arrows ready to be fired into the heavens.

Walking up to the central doorway, she now sees the house has cracks and other evidence of run-of-the-mill neglect. *I kind of like the grit and imperfections—it adds a bit of charm.*

When she gets to the steps, she sees a hand-painted sign with blue-green letters above the door: THE GREENLING HOUSE. She raises an eyebrow, confused to see her name above the main entrance. She timidly knocks. *I wonder if anyone's here?*

The door is instantly answered by a white-haired sprite. Sylvie stands in the opening and flashes a warm, welcoming smile.

"Noah! Oh, it's *so, so good* to see you!" she squeals as she wraps Noah in her pale, lithe arms. "We've been waiting all afternoon for you. Come in!

Welcome to your new home."

Behind Sylvie stand six others; one of them is Dr. Wilde. Soon, they all swarm forward and surround her. There's Jean, Desmond, Ged, Raven, and Anvi. But no Yoshi. Noah's heart sinks, remembering how quickly his mom declined at the end. *I miss you, buddy… I really wished you were here.* The clamor waiting for her quickly snaps her back.

"Noah, you made it!"

"Here, let me take your bags."

"Come on back!"

"We were just having some wine and cheese. Are you hungry?"

"How was your flight?"

She looks at them through dizzy eyes. Seeing all her rainforest friends in a civilized setting feels disorienting. Yet after all they went through together, there's also the ease of reconnecting with old friends. Gradually, she slips from the group's center and finds herself becoming just another member of this warm, comfortable circle.

She breaks in after a few minutes—cracker crumbs clinging to her chin. "Okay, I have to ask about the sign over the door. We all live here, right? So why is *my* name up there? Is it a 'welcome to your new home' gesture, a joke, or what?"

The students pass secretive looks to each other and then turn to Dr. Wilde.

"Noah," he says, "you see, none of the others have names that align with the aspirations of this program. No offense, everyone. Can you imagine what the neighbors might think of Gupta House or Balogun Manor?" There are a few snickers and ribs elbowing among the students.

"None of the others sounded quite right. And besides… honestly, Noah… none of the others have your notoriety. You have a brand, you know. Like it or not, you're kind of a role model. But more importantly, everyone just really loved the idea of naming the house after you. I hope you don't mind. We can change it if it makes you feel uncomfortable."

Noah blushes slightly and looks down. She's aware that others look to her and look *up* to her, but she never really wanted it; it just happened. And now it's happening again. *Oh, well, it's just a sign. It is kind of cute,* she thinks to herself.

"Okay," Noah finally says, panning the group. "I'm resigned to it—get it?" Groans fill the room. "I'm okay with it as long as I can teach you how to say it *properly* with an Irish brogue. Like this: *'Grāynling.'*" They all begin to snicker as they unsuccessfully attempt to imitate her.

"Wait a minute," Jean interrupts. "Everyone remember gremlins—the little tech tricksters? Maybe we should change our name to the *Grāyn Gremlins.*" A few of the group chuckle, and then Jean starts chanting, "GO! GO! GO! GO! *Gr-ā-ā-ā-ā-y-n* GREMLINS!" The rest—including Noah—join in, ending the cheer with a riot of hoots and howls.

Whether from the wine or the laughter, her shoulders start to relax—apprehension giving way to anticipation—as she gradually begins to feel at home with the Professor's eclectic new cadre.

So this is it, she tells herself. *I'm going to do life with these clowns for the next four years? What a blast!*

Seamus gives the group the next three days to settle in and get their bearings. On the fourth day, he schedules one-on-one conferences with each student to outline their course of study for the fall semester.

At eleven o'clock, Noah knocks on the ten-foot oak door on the first floor of Sidney Smith Hall. Cracks in its frosted glass not-so-subtly divulge the building's age.

"Come in! It's open," she hears the Professor shout from inside.

The door squeaks, and she looks in. "Hello, Dr. Wilde. Is this still a good time?"

"Of course. I've set the whole day aside to help the Greenling House choose their coursework." She swerves her way through several stacks of books on the floor and takes a seat in a simple chair facing a large burl oak desk. "So, how are you finding your new home so far, Noah?"

She pauses before answering, running her fingers over the desk's well-worn edge. "Well... the city is so much bigger and more alive than little Kilkenny. I had no idea a place could pulsate with the kind of energy that's here in Toronto. I like our house. Except the hot water runs out pretty fast. We're all racing to get there before Jean. If he gets there first, it's just a splash of cold water on your face until afternoon." Noah chuckles to herself. "But that's alright. The group's great... though it's different living together in civilization instead of in tents in the jungle. We're still figuring things out—how to do groceries, meals, and house chores. But that'll come."

Seamus listens, nods occasionally, and then promptly gets down to business.

"Here's what I'm thinking for you, Noah. I'd like you to consider taking a full load to get your mind engaged in the subject matter." He slides a piece of paper written in neat cursive writing in front of her and then continues, reading the list.

For Noah:
- *Economic Theory in a Transitional World Order*
- *Biogeography*
- *Organic Semiotics and Linguistics*
- *Paleo-Virology*
- *Environmental Activism and Law - Successes and Shortcomings*
- *Nature Mysticism in Ancient and Recent History*
- *The Practice of Disinformation in the 21st Century*

He looks at her over his half-rimmed readers, gauging her reaction. "They're all three-credit-hour classes. So, it's an overload of twenty-one credit hours. All of these courses are upper-level. A few are taught at the graduate level. You'll have access to my graduate or doctoral tutors if you need any help.

"We're jumping over a lot of traditional learning steps here, Noah. I realize it's a lot *and* that I'm throwing you into the deep end. But given the current level of crisis, we really don't know how much time's left. Hell, I don't even know if education is a luxury we can afford right now. There's just so much that's falling apart that needs immediate and swift solutions." He waits a few moments as she looks over the list of classes, then asks, "So, what do you think?"

Noah blinks a few times at the paper, then nods as she swallows hard. "Dr. Wilde, these all sound incredible. I'm not sure I know what some of them mean, but they all sound amazing. If you think this is where I should start, then I'm good with it. Thanks again for... I don't know... seeing something in me and inviting me here. I'll give it my best. I promise."

Seamus looks at her and feels a gentle vibration in his midsection, moving up to his chest and then coming to rest in his heart region. *Who on Earth is this girl?* He wonders, feeling from her—or is it toward her?—what his nephew Patrick must have sensed.

"Well, that's settled then. And Noah, please call me Seamus. We're not too big on formalities here. There's a battle we're waging here, and we won't win it by being polite."

"You sound just like Patrick when you say that. Okay. Game on, *Seamus.*" She parries with a wink, then raises her hands, knocking her knuckles together.

The next few weeks are filled with big adjustments for Noah. There's a new schedule, filled with classes, reading, studying, and writing papers. Then, there's figuring out transportation and getting around campus. There's also the cooking, cleaning, and the practical parts of doing life in another country. And, of course, the roommate relationships and accompanying drama, conflicts, and conversations.

It's Sunday morning. Noah finally finds herself alone in her room, with literally nothing to do for the first time since arriving in Toronto. She picks up the clothes scattered on the floor or hanging over the chair and puts them in a cardboard box she uses for dirty laundry. After changing her sheets, Noah sits at her desk and puts her books on the shelves, straightening up piles of paper and half-used paraphernalia.

She notices the journal Shea gave her when she left. *Man, it's been so long since I've written anything about myself to myself.* Picking it up, she flips it open, and the letter from Shea falls to the ground.

"Ohhh, shit. I totally forgot about this," she says out loud, cursing herself and her thoughtlessness. Retrieving the small envelope from the floor, she then carefully unfolds the note inside. After re-reading her friend's words, she mulls over how she wants to respond. *Should I write a letter? Send a HOLO-VID? Initiate a conversation? And more importantly... how do I really feel about what Shea said?*

She decides to send a letter by mail. It feels proportionate. Safer, too—so she doesn't say something she'll regret. She begins with a lengthy, heartfelt apology for failing to respond sooner. She acknowledges she's tempted to use her schedule and course load as an excuse, but that's not true. She just forgot. *Or maybe,* she wonders, *I didn't write back because I honestly didn't know how I felt or what I wanted to say.* As she continues to write, she searches for the right words—ones that are clarifying, honest, and understanding.

> I am so, so humbled by your love and friendship, Shea. Besides my ma and my da, you know you have the first and deepest place in my heart. And you always will. These feelings you have for me—in my own way—I share them, too. They just aren't exactly the same as what you feel. I'm sorry. There are just so many things that I'm still trying to figure out.

Noah puts her pen down and looks out the window—drops of rain etching the dusty glass. She immediately pictures Patrick—his chocolate brown eyes—and how she feels around him. The sound of his voice, his nerdy enthusiasm, the fragrance of cedar in the air when he's nearby. *Where does he fit into all this? I know where I* want *him to fit in. What Shea wants from me, I want from him.* The sound of footsteps on the stairs brings her back from her daydreams, prompting her to finish writing.

Can you be patient with me? Can you still love me even if your love for me is different from my love for you? I wish you were here right now so we could go camping and really talk about all this. Hey, that's an idea! What if you come to Toronto sometime? Anyway, I love you, dear friend. And I always will, no matter what.

Constantly growing in love,
Noah

She re-reads her words a few times. *Did I say enough? Did I say too much?* Still not entirely sure of her feelings, she folds the letter and puts it in an envelope. As she addresses the letter and writes Shea's name and postal code, an unexpected homesickness rises in her. *Will I ever go back home? Or is home here now?*

The following day, Noah slowly walks along the creek that winds through campus. A gentle ease rests on her face, in her movements. The air is crisp, but the sun is brilliant, shining through overarching trees half-filled with colorful maple leaves. As she walks, she ponders one of her class's recent lectures about the new research on telepathic communication in nature. It reminds her of Dorothy MacLean's experiments at Findhorn that Patrick told her about.

Is that what I feel, what I experience? she wonders. Her communications are often without words, or at least, without the use of her physical ears. Yet she does clearly hear something, or some*one*.

It's like I'm being invited into some ancient conversation, but also, some new way to be human. Maybe that's why I feel so misplaced—I just don't fit into the old ways of being human.

She shakes herself to let go of her wonderings and continues walking east, toward Saint Michael's College for her class, Nature Mysticism. Having never considered herself religious, it still feels strange to be here among many who have devoted themselves to a particular faith. Walking up the steps to the chapel, she experiences something usually reserved for when she's near an ancient tree or in an old-growth forest.

She senses a sacred silence that reaches out to welcome her, to hold and help her. Suddenly, she feels her eyes mist over, a subtle sadness emerging into the foreground of the present moment. The sensation quickly passes as she's jostled by hurrying students and swept into the chapel's narrow nave.

The rows of sturdy pews seem lit from within by a kaleidoscope of colors pouring down from the surrounding stained glass windows. The sun's angle seems perfectly attuned to the direction of the walls, the windows, and even the roof and floor. *Or is it the other way around?* she asks herself. *Is the church carefully designed to greet our planet's star, the source of all life?*

While mulling over these questions, Noah strolls toward the front and sits next to three other students in the first pew. A few minutes later, a beautiful older woman with braided white hair and brown skin glides down the center aisle. She's carrying a satchel made of woven sweet grass. Her expression conveys both nobility and humor. And her eyes sparkle with magic and mischief. Noah has come to quickly fall in love with this woman.

On the first day of class, she introduced herself as a member of the Ojibwe tribe known as the Mississaugas of the Credit River. Her indigenous name is Waatese. She explained that traditionally, Waatese is a masculine name and means "there is lightning." But now, she rejects the gender conventions of her people, feeling she has transcended all human stereotypes. To her students, she simply goes by Tessa.

Her earthlike voice calls out with its mixture of Ojibwemowin and French intonations. "Welcome back. We never know if the Great Spirit will give us tomorrow, but when It does, we are grateful. And I am grateful for each one of you. You are a blessing. *Never* forget that. *And* you are loved. Never doubt that, either. Never depart from that knowledge, for it is part of your sacred responsibility always to remember."

She launches into the subject of today's lecture—the universality of mysticism. Noah listens more with her heart than her mind, doodling and drawing in her notebook instead of writing. There's a picture of a mother bear hovering over her vulnerable cubs. Another of a fierce bobcat climbing a mountain, looking for a den to weather winter. And still another of a pair of eagles soaring over a lake in search of something to eat.

"If we think of mysticism—not only nature's mysticism but any kind, formal or informal—if we think of it as simply an experience of communion with Ultimate Reality, then we have a fairly good definition of the mystic encounter.

"We do well at this point not to introduce the term or conventional idea we often label 'God.' My people call this Ultimate Reality 'the Great Spirit', but this too can be problematic, for not all people feel comfortable with these terms. Often, this discomfort is rooted in personal or even communal trauma and abuse. That's why 'Ultimate Reality' is a neutral term for building a useful description of these universal, mystical experiences and encounters."

Tessa walks over to a tall stool and sits—her beaded turquoise moccasins now visible from underneath the long, fringed white gown. She pauses to take a drink of water and then continues. "You see, it's not just the religious or those who possess certain ideas and terminologies who can claim this mystical phenomenon. *All of us,* regardless of our spiritual, cultural, or intellectual affiliations, have likely experienced, at one point or another, a moment that could be described as overwhelming, limitless belonging—a moment that is perhaps best described by the idea of 'Universal Communion.'

"The people we call 'mystics' aren't really any different from the rest of us. They merely give to these experiences the attention and honor they deserve."

She steps down from the stool and walks to the top of the steps, her hands extended, palms up. "Listen, my children. It's not the frequency or the intensity of these experiences that matters—it's the *influence* we allow them to have on our lives. When we are open and accept these mystical encounters—including what they offer, what they demand of us—then each of us will become the kind of mystic we were meant to become."

Tessa takes a long moment and pans the students through fierce, loving eyes. No one except Noah can return her gaze. Tessa continues, speaking in a low voice, never breaking eye contact with Noah.

"A mystic isn't a special kind of human being. No! That's a myth. That's a lie!" She lifts her right hand and slowly points her crooked finger to each student, speaking in song-like tones. "A mystic is not some kind of special kind of human being, but *every human being* is a *special kind of mystic.*"

The group sits still and remains silent. Noah has a feeling that Tessa is speaking to her directly. *I wonder if everyone else has that same sense or if she's singling me out in a unique way.*

She smiles back at Tessa, feeling stirred with appreciation and—more than that—overwhelmed with a sense of affirmation. *Mystic.* She realizes that being so misunderstood her whole life, she has never had a name to help her understand herself.

Overcome with gratitude, she stands, takes both fists, and knocks them together several times. To her surprise, the students on either side of her stand, glance sideways at her, and then begin knocking *their* knuckles together. Before long, there's a wave of others rising to their feet and imitating the simple gesture.

Tessa focuses her gaze on Noah, then pans the entire gathering, smiling radiantly even as her eyes fill with tears. Soon, she also raises her fists and echoes the movement, bowing her head toward Noah.

Noah rides her bike to the Native Canadian Centre. The sun shines, though there is light fog from the wet pavement and chilled air—the atmosphere creates a magical mixture of glowing shafts of light in the gray, swirling mist.

The bike rack is half-full. She points her bike into an open slot, not bothering to lock it. *If someone wants it, they can have it.* She quickly walks up the few steps to the building and enters through carved, ancient doors.

Immediately, she's met with the smell of wood smoke, wet leather, and something earthlike, the scent of musk and sweat. There's a small sitting room to the side of the main foyer with two high-backed chairs in front of a low fire. Tessa sits in one of the chairs, staring into the glowing embers. The low, gold-and-red flame is reflected in her chestnut eyes.

Noah pauses and takes in how striking the woman is. She looks regal in the most natural sense of the word. The woman's lips are gently curved, giving the impression that she's somewhere else, enjoying some timeless reverie that she alone has access to.

Hating to break the spell, Noah softly announces her presence. "Hello. Tessa. Sorry to interrupt. Is this still a good time?"

Tessa slowly turns her head and then stands to welcome Noah. "Of course, my friend. I've been waiting for you. My soul is warmed by your presence. Please, sit down. The message you sent so intrigued me. Would you like anything? Some tea, maybe?"

"That would be lovely—if it's not too much trouble."

Tessa walks to a small tea station and prepares two burled-wood mugs filled with the steaming brew. Noah takes a cup and inhales the vaporous fragrance.

"This smells delicious. Like walking in the forest. What is it?"

"It's an ancient blend of white pine, sweetgrass, and sage. My people believe that it increases vision, communion, and clarity. May it bring these gifts to us today, my young friend. Now, what's stirring in your heart, Noah? Tell me. What can I do for you?"

Noah waits to speak while she sets her cup down. "Tessa, your class has meant so much to me. It's hard to put into words. I've been living with... a paradox, maybe? I think that might be it. I've been living with a paradox my whole life—trying to resolve it, trying to understand it. If I'm honest, sometimes I've wanted to shed it like the skin of a snake."

The older woman listens, gently nodding as if to draw the younger one into the soft light for a closer look.

"I've felt different from my friends and classmates for as long as I can remember. I've had this kind of *earth sensitivity*, a sense that seems to always pull me out of *their* world and into another world, one that's not normal to them. I try to keep it in. I try not to talk about it and am careful about what I say. But eventually, it comes out, and then I'm... I can't tell you how many times I've been bullied or made fun of because of it. I'm used to it now. So here's the paradox. I'm actually glad I'm not normal. That I'm different. Does that make sense?"

Tessa takes her time, holding her sense of Noah's spirit for a moment.

"Ah, indeed it does," she finally says. "It absolutely makes sense. I'm sorry you've been so misunderstood. That's painful, isn't it? But you have a gift, don't you, Noah? A gift that sometimes seems like a problem. But also, one you treasure, that gives to you a deep sense of who you are and what matters in this world of ours."

"Yes, I think it does that," Noah answers. "Not being like everyone around me has given me a pretty good idea of what does and doesn't matter—of who I am and who I'm not. It also makes me want to know how I can make a difference in the world. I've had a couple of these roundtables with Marta Senheiser—you know who that is, right?" Tessa nods, smiling back. "It's pretty nerve-racking, but I think I'm actually kind of good at it."

Noah turns and stares at the fire. The pensive furrow above her dark green eyes now smooths as she takes a long, deep breath. Tessa waits. Her loving gaze holds the young woman, who soon looks back through her wide, earnest eyes.

"That's what I'd like to ask you," Noah says. "You seem like you feel at home in your own way, in your own soul, like you fully embrace what you're passionate about, that what you sense matters, and that it's enough. At least that's what I feel whenever I'm with you, whenever you speak, or even whenever you're silent. It just seems to radiate out from you."

Tessa releases a low chuckle as Noah continues.

"What I want to ask is if you would ever consider being something like a mentor to me. I'm not sure I've ever known someone who seemed to understand the road I'm walking. Someone who has traveled a similar path."

Tessa takes several moments. They seem held by something surrounding them—something tangible, yet ephemeral—something just outside the periphery of sight—a slender thread weaving their hearts together while also tethering them to the sacred Other.

"Noah, Dear. I'd be honored to serve you in this way. The Ojibwe word *wiidookodaadiwin* means 'we help each other.' There's no exact word in our language for your English word, 'mentor. ' With our people, I would be also a mutual learner. You have gifts to give me, as I have gifts to give you. With that in mind, I choose to say yes to you. I will give to you whatever it is I have for you. And I will receive what you have to bring to me. Is that what you want?"

Noah's face beams with affirmation, rocking back and forth in an unsuccessful attempt to bridle her enthusiasm. "Oh, Tessa, that sounds just like what I need. Even the way you name it, the way you understand it, gives me so much to think about. You've already been doing this for me, you know. Thank you. Thank you so much."

Tessa takes a few slow breaths as she looks into Noah's eyes, then says, "I have my first gift for you. Okay? While I was waiting for you, watching the fire dance, I received something for you. You don't know this about me, but one of the gifts I have been given is the discernment of *bineshiinyag manidoo* for women who have been given a strong, good purpose in the world. And you, Noah, have quite a unique and potent mission ahead of you.

"I sensed it when you first walked into class, before we even met or spoke. I saw it in your eyes, as well as your soul, as it hovered around the space you sat in. *Bineshiinyag manidoo* is best translated as *avian spirit* or *spirit bird*."

Noah's heart beats faster as she listens, wondering what Tessa might tell her next.

"For instance," she continues, "my spirit bird is the snowy owl. As my hair has turned to snow, this seems more and more fitting, but even as a young girl, I was already an old soul. I already had early signs of my hair changing from black to white. Throughout my life, I have often found myself lost, confused, or in great need. Just then, my spirit bird would arrive in its own time and the place of its choosing to assure me."

"Soooo…" Noah says, as if she were a child waiting for a special treat from a grandparent. "Are you going to tell me what *my* spirit bird is?"

"Patience, young one. Yes, I will tell you. As I looked into the fire before you came today, I saw a fierce, young peregrine falcon. It was diving with wings drawn back, sleek and fearless, toward a much bigger, much stronger bald eagle. I immediately knew it was your *bineshiinyag manidoo* by the earnest, knowing way it looked at me."

Noah becomes still, staring into the fire as Tessa continues.

"Did you know that the peregrine falcon is one of the few birds found on every continent? But above all, they are incredibly swift and powerful. They use their extraordinary speed and agility to catch their prey off guard. Without question, they are the fastest creatures on earth, capable of diving at speeds over 320 kilometers an hour. Their speed and fearlessness enable them to protect their young from predators much larger than themselves. That's what I sensed as I watched your *bineshiinyag manidoo* slam into the bald eagle."

Noah has never considered herself fast or fierce. *But maybe that's why my spirit bird is both—to help me when I'm uncertain or afraid—to help me when I need courage.* Noah remains still for a moment, then quietly says, "Thank you. Tessa. I'm not sure what you or the bird saw in me. But thank you. It's a treasure I will carry with me always."

"Don't thank me, Noah. Thank the Peregrine Falcon. It's the bird who chooses its companion, not the other way around. Here's my advice for you. Release it now. Don't try to clutch what I've told you too tightly. Your spirit bird will show up when you need it. You don't have to cling to it. It knows how best to watch over you."

Noah nods. She's learned this from the tree's messages to her. They are sacred, living things beyond control or ownership.

Tessa smiles and then laughs at herself. "Oh, I almost forgot. While searching the fire, I saw two other birds—a magpie and a jay. Both are very intelligent and loyal birds, you know. The jay's face was completely white. The magpie appeared less distinct but exuded a fiercely protective energy. I'm not sure why they were there, but I sensed they belonged to two people who are close to you and love you very much. Stay alert to these two birds as well. Who knows? They might also have something to bring you that you will need someday."

Noah lets out a long, deep breath. They both turn their gaze toward the fire's glowing embers and sit in silence for several moments. Noah then reaches over and puts her hand on top of Tessa's—her brown skin soft and smooth. Noah feels the woman's strong, steady pulse through her fingers. She returns her hand to her lap, letting the rhythm of her own heart synchronize with her newfound mentor's.

Winter 2061

Dallas, Texas, USA (105° F / 34.5° C)

Brett Colfield, Seamus Wilde's young assistant, saunters across the large, luxurious lobby of the Dallas Omni Hotel. His youthful good looks and perfectly tailored blue-black suit enable him to blend in easily with the affluent clientele. Being careful not to stare, he notices an attractive young woman with raven hair in a smart, olive-green suit seated on one of the leather wingbacks. Her slender legs emerge from a raised miniskirt, betraying a calculated disregard of the professional, buttoned-up look preferred by others. Their eyes meet briefly—hers widen, revealing her silver-blue irises—an eyebrow lifts to suggest her curiosity. He returns her gaze. A crooked smile begins to form just before he recognizes her. *Ooh… be cool, son… bad timing. That's Marta Sennheiser.*

He's only seen her on the HOLO. Thankfully, he's never met her in person. Not slowing down to look back, he continues walking, hoping she won't give the exchange a second thought. He makes his way to the bank of walnut-and-gold-trimmed elevators and rides to the twenty-second floor. Trying to shake off the unexpected encounter with Marta, he takes a long, deep breath, refocusing on the task at hand. As the bell announces his floor, he glances at the mirror and notices a smirk on his face as he exits; his accelerating heart rate announces his readiness for the strike. *I'm starting to look forward to these little forays Seamus dreams up for me.*

Although most of the guests are busy attending TNEC's annual round-table summit, he cautiously glances both ways to make sure no one else is in the hallway. *I don't know how Seamus does it, but being hired as Helmut Sennheiser's conference liaison for the week is a perfect cover.*

He walks to Room 2227 and again looks both ways before kneeling in front of the door. Opening the slender titanium briefcase he's carrying, he pulls out a clear plastic container, which he slowly turns upside down and sets on the floor. His eyes narrow with nervous respect as he stares at its agitated contents, who wriggle aggressively in anticipation of their freedom. Sliding the lid slowly across the carpeting, he tilts the small container toward the bottom of the door. A small gap at the threshold is just large enough for the two bio-engineered yellow scorpions to skitter into the room.

❦ ❧ ❦ ❧ ❦ ❧

Vivienne walks into the hotel lobby and sees Marta immersed in her HOLO, holding a small glass of Hefeweizen. The older woman collapses into the chair across from her niece.

"I'm glad that's all done. These time changes are becoming brutal. Food's all steer meat. Sleep's impossible. If the press can't find a way to bury me, international travel will," Viv complains.

Marta nods at her aunt with a concerned smile that says, *I see the price you've paid.* Beneath the makeup and well-preserved beauty, Vivienne's cracks are widening.

"Why don't you go up and rest?" Marta says. "I'll wait here for Papa. Then we can go get a bite of something edible."

"I know I won't be able to sleep, but hmmm... it does sound delicious to put my feet up... close my eyes. Feel free to come up whenever you'd like. I have Merton's room access," she says as the topaz necklace, nesting in her open neckline, projects a spinning HOLO key. "I'm having my luggage brought over this afternoon so you can have our suite all to yourself," Viv titters with a suggestive wink.

With some effort, she pushes herself out of the chair and then reaches for Marta's glass. After drinking the rest of the light-colored ale, she looks at the shimmering image of the key to remind herself which floor Merton's room is on.

"2227—here I come!" She then heads toward the waiting elevators, blowing a kiss over her shoulder in her niece's direction.

It's the middle of the afternoon. Most of the conference attendees have moved from the formal gathering into the hotel's cozy lounge, where they huddle in tight knots of private conversation. The low buzz of inaudible whispers interrupted by forced laughter reminds Merton of the sounds of the jungle. Sitting at the end of the hotel bar, he slowly savors the last few swallows of his Redbreast 27-Year Irish Whiskey. His mom's scratchy voice on the HOLO replays bite by bite what she had for breakfast, then moves on to her culinary commentary on the lunch menu of the posh senior resort at Starfish Point.

"Sounds like you're having fun, Ma. I'll come see you soon, okay? Gotta run now. I'll talk with you tomorrow." Pause. "I love you too." Not typically prone to guilt or regret—except after he speaks with his mom—Merton stares out the heavily tinted window and briefly wonders at his feelings. *Why is it that whenever we're done talking, I feel disappointment? Is it with myself? Or is it from her?* Unwilling to get bogged down in introspection, he waves to the bar-bot and asks for another drink.

Vivienne strips out of her clothes the moment her feet cross the threshold. Her leopard heels and black silk skirt hit the ground before the door completely closes. The red haze outside the window casts a warm, unearthly glow over the room's walls and furnishings. *Warm? Scratch that,* she tells herself. *It's absolutely hellish! Who in their right mind would ever want to live here?*

The dusty glare makes the room feel oppressive, despite the air-conditioning. She catches herself in the mirror and notices the damp glow on her face reflecting the rusty red. Shedding her blouse, she orders her HOLO to close the ceiling-high drapes and then turns toward the bedroom.

On the dresser, she notices two large bolo ties in Merton's open travel kit. She picks up the one with a screeching eagle made of white-and-black mother-of-pearl, surrounded by deeply veined pale turquoise. Rubbing her fingers over the image as if conjuring some memory, she slides it over her head and then moves to the bed. As she glides between the cool, clean sheets—her eyes half-closed in the twilight—she sinks into an irresistible torpor.

In concert with her rhythmic breathing, a static-like hiss soon stirs to life from under the bed. An alien message is exchanged between the two emerging scorpions. They look at each other as if in mutual agreement and begin their clutching ascent up the rumpled duvet.

❧ ❧ ❧ ❧ ❧ ❧

Merton quietly knocks on the door before using his HOLO key. He walks into the living area and grins at the discarded women's clothing on the floor. *I need the Chief to schedule more of these international meetings.*

Noticing the closed drapes and the silence in the bedroom, he moves to the small kitchen and removes the bottle of Louis Roederer champagne he placed in the fridge earlier. He fumbles with the foil and wire cage, then pops the cork. *That should wake her up.*

Silence.

"Viv, I'm pouring you a glass. Want me to bring it in, or do you want to join me out here?"

Silence.

"Okay. Comin' in," Merton announces, carrying two brimming flutes of bubbles into the darkness. As he rounds the side of the bed, his foot bumps something soft. *Must be a pillow or...*

He puts the two glasses on the nightstand and reaches down to grab the pillow. "Come on, Viv. Time to wake up and talk about the dangerous flood waters and the rising..." His words trail off as his hand feels smooth, clammy flesh. "What the fuck? Viv, are you alright?"

He shouts for the HOLO to turn on the lights. On the floor, he sees
Viv lying on her back, her chest barely rising and falling. Dropping to both
knees, he leans over her.

"Viv! Wake up. Come on."

He stares at her pale body. His eyes move to her long, slender neck.
What the hell? There's a patch of reddening skin beneath her Adam's apple,
slowly spreading out in all directions, circling her neck from front to back.
His eyes drift to her midsection, and the same rash moves up to her ribs and
under her bra.

"HOLO! I need an emergency team to Room 2227. Immediately. A
middle-aged female is unconscious and barely breathing."

He leans toward Viv's lifeless form and scoops his hands under her
waist and shoulders to pick her up. As he lays her on the bed, he looks more
closely at the rashes. In the center of the deepening discoloration, he sees
a small, swollen puncture wound, oozing large, amber-colored droplets.
Not sure what else to do for her, he goes into the bathroom to grab a warm
washcloth to clean the nasty gouges that have defaced her soft, smooth flesh.
As he tends to her, wiping the ooze, he chokes in disgust at the rank odor.
Shit! What is that? It smells like rancid meat. He gags, his eyes tearing from
the seeping stench.

❧ ❧ ❧ ❧ ❧ ❧

Marta and Helmut stand next to each other in the hushed hotel lobby. Their
anxious faces watch as the gurney-bot carrying Vivienne wheels itself to
the ambulance to take her to the hospital. Marta's head hangs heavy on her
hunched shoulders. Her papa notices and puts his arms around her small
frame. *A girl still,* he reminds himself. *Not fully acquainted yet with how cruel
the world can be.*

Merton, following the EMTs, breaks rank and approaches the two. An
awkward moment passes between the two men as they match one another's
opaque inspection. Marta studies them, knowing something of their jealous

history, and breaks the deadlock.

"Were you with her?"

"No, not really," Merton says. "I just came in and found her unconscious on the floor."

"I saw her an hour ago, and she seemed fine. Tired, but nothing unusual."

Helmut clears his throat, his countenance toward the other man relaxing slightly.

"You go with her. Marta and I have to be at the closing dinner tonight. But please keep us updated. And if there's anything she needs... just make sure she gets the best available care."

"Of course. You two go on. I've let the Chief know."

Marta examines the man—a mixture of concern and fury written on her face. Merton nods slightly, a deep frown mirroring the young woman's worried expression.

"Well, I better run," he says. "I'll let you know what the doctors have to say when I learn more." He turns and jogs toward the door, heading out into the dusty afternoon heat of downtown Dallas.

❧❧❧

Marta returns to her hotel room after midnight. She kicks her shoes off, flinging one from her foot across the room—the tall, black window reverberates like distant thunder when the heel strikes it. She flops onto the bed, not bothering to undress, and calls up her HOLO.

Throughout tonight's dinner—during the conversations and inept attempts by the Chief's guests to console her—something in the back of her brain was trying to surface. *What is it? Think, Marta. Think.*

She replays the recording of her conversation with her aunt in the lobby—glad for the habit of running her HOLO-CAM when she's in public. *Nothing unusual there.* Staring at the shadowed forms across the skyline, she rewinds her HOLO's memory to earlier. She remembers ordering a drink, the good-looking young man in the lobby, and their not-so-subtle inspection of each other. She leans her head back and closes her eyes. *Too bad he was in such a hurry.* Later that evening, she saw him with Papa. When Helmut introduced him, she was told he had been assigned as her father's conference liaison for the week. She also learned his name. Brett Colfield. *Who are you really, Mr. Colfield?*

Marta has her HOLO perform a facial recognition query from the images captured of Brett in the lobby. In a few seconds, a concise yet thorough synopsis appears. He grew up in Texas. His father was a wealthy oil baron. There were images of Brett protesting corporate greed at his elite high school. Then, a snippet pops up about his plans after graduation to attend Toronto University and study environmental politics with Dr. Seamus Wilde. Finally, there's an image of Brett standing beside the professor with five other students at a Halloween party. They are all dressed in hazmat suits and have signs hanging around their necks that read, "THE NEW GRIM REAPERS."

Toronto, Ontario, Canada (95° F / 35° C)

Returning from winter break, Noah studies even harder than she did in the fall. Every waking hour claims her complete focus—science, spirituality, economics, linguistics, geography, law, even rhetoric. On top of that, there's preparing with Journi for her bi-monthly debates with Marta, including managing her nervous stomach the week before they happen. Then, there are the meetings with tutors when she either hits a brick wall or—more often—finds her curiosity piqued by some esoteric intersection of these diverse subjects. But the best part is the late-night discussions with her roommates, each one immersed in a unique academic portfolio designed to develop their particular gifts and capacities. She simply loves it. All of it.

But tonight, I'm going to do something just for myself, Noah tells herself as she unlocks the front door to the house. Kicking off her shoes, she bounces up the stairs to her room, not bothering to find out if anyone's around. She flops down on her bed—actually, on top of a pile of clean clothes she hasn't gotten around to folding yet.

It's been so long since I've done something by myself that I don't even know what to do, she chides herself. A loud knock at the front door interrupts her attempt to name what sounds good to her. She waits, hoping someone else will answer it. *Sheesh! Come on, will you?*

The knocking continues, forcing her to reluctantly get up. Walking down the stairs, she sees short, wavy brown hair through the transom window. The sidelights reveal a partial view of a medium-sized satchel. The glimpsed images tickle a remote part of her brain, but she doesn't have time to scratch it.

She opens the door and suddenly squeals, "No way! What are you doing here? Why didn't you HOLO me and let me know?" She rockets out the door and throws both arms around him, giving him a warm kiss on the lips.

Patrick doesn't have a chance to say anything. He's enveloped by Noah's energy, by her spirit. As always, she takes his breath away—and now, it seems, his ability to speak, too. Taking a small step back but still holding her, he looks into her smiling eyes.

"I've missed you *so much*, Noah. I wanted to give you as much space as you needed to get settled and start your new life. But, well... I just couldn't wait anymore. It's so good to see you. How are you?"

She grabs his arm and pulls him forward. "Come in, silly. We can talk about all that later. I just want to head back in, open a bottle of wine, and feel you next to me. Unless you've got someplace else you need to be," she says with a playful wink.

He shrugs his shoulders apologetically. "Actually, I do have one place I need to go first."

She pushes out her bottom lip but does her best to take it in stride and not show her disappointment. "Oh, okay. Whatever you need to do, just get on with it. I'll be here waiting for you when you're finished."

He chuckles. "Noah, it's not that. I just need to hit the jacks and take a piss."

Noah grins with relief. "Well, why didn't you say so, *Mr. Wilde*? Do you need a hall pass or something? Go on. Get on with it!"

While Patrick goes in search of the loo, Noah moves to the kitchen to find a bottle of wine. She glances out the window over the sink. A Steller's jay with a white face sits on the low branch of a nearby cedar. It seems to be looking through the window at her with its cocked head and intelligent gaze. *Funny*, she thinks, *I've never seen you there before.* She waves her fingers at it, and it flutters its wings, then makes what looks like a low bow toward her, its tail spreading high above its lowered body.

Patrick returns from the bathroom, interrupting her thoughts. She turns from the window and just watches him move. He slowly meanders through the long, windowed hearth room, his fingers tracing the cobblestone fireplace that dominates the center wall. She smiles to herself and then carefully pours two glasses of the inky Petite Sirah before joining him.

"Nice place! Looks like my uncle's putting you all up in style." He nods toward the room as he accepts the glass she offers. She moves over to the blue denim sofa facing the wooded backyard and invites him to sit beside her.

"To our first Canadian adventure!" Noah says, tilting her glass toward his.

"*Sláinte!*" Patrick replies, touching the lip of his glass to hers.

"Mmm... That's nice," Patrick whispers after taking his first sip. "Better than the Bunratty mead back home. Looks like my uncle's taste in wine is starting to rub off on you."

Noah chuckles softly. "Yeah, he stops by most nights so the gang can grill him as to why we're *really* here."

Patrick laughs along. "He's always got *something* up that old Irish sleeve of his. *'More to him than meets the eye,'* my ma used to say." He takes another sip and continues. "In fact, he reached out to me and said he has some things to tell me—things to ask me. He told me he wanted to talk in person so we wouldn't be *compromised.*" Patrick accentuates the word in air quotes. "He sounded all cloak-and-dagger-like. Next thing I know, a ticket pops up on my HOLO, and here I am, with you!"

She watches him, a smile on her open, full lips and playing around her green eyes. She can't believe he's really here—in her house. *I can't wait for everyone to meet him. Or maybe I just want to keep him for myself.*

"What are you smiling about over there?" he asks when he catches the expression on her face.

She exhales contentedly. "I'm just thinking about how lucky I am. And how fun it is to have you here."

He puts his glass down and jumps to his feet. "Well, if it's fun you're looking for, let's get going. I've spent a fair amount of time in the big T.O.; I bet I can find a few places you still haven't been to yet."

"Well, aren't *you* the big man on campus, Mr. Wilde? Let me go change, and then I'm all yours." Noah smiles coyly as she stands up and then scampers out of the room, humming the sappy old Irish love song, *Red is the Rose.*

When Noah finally gets to bed, she savors how full her heart feels. It was a perfect day—strolling through the bohemian Kensington Market, sipping their way through the Distillery District, and discussing their favorite paintings as they wandered the Royal Ontario Museum. Catching up with each other was relaxed and natural. Being with him reminded her of how much she missed him—his Irish humor, the way he listened to her, how it felt to have his arm around her, even the way his male scent aroused her sense of attraction. *Hmm... I can picture him lying on the sofa... maybe I shouldn't let him be such a gentleman.*

Her mind spins with big questions and new ideas. But she's far too drowsy to stay focused. Feeling more than a little woozy after their two bottles of wine—not to mention the late nightcap—she soon releases her mind's many thoughts and then drifts into oblivion.

She sleeps hard for several hours, until—in the middle of the night— she stirs, sensing someone's presence next to her. Opening her eyes, she sees the Green Man from her dream in the woods standing beside her bed, silhouetted by the soft moonlight. A shiver of excitement shoots through her. She's bewildered at her feelings. *I don't know why... I'm not afraid... I'm... curious.*

He looks down at her with gentle, golden eyes. There's something in his gaze that's both playful and wild. She feels hypnotized by his aura and finds herself lengthening her breathing. *What's happening?* she wonders, too enthralled by what feels like a dream to speak or stop it.

The Green Man reaches down and places a circlet of lavender and shamrocks on her stomach. He winks at her, then vigorously shakes his thick, curly head of hair over her. From deep within his rich mane, a single seed—similar to a little helicopter, but faceted like an emerald jewel—is set free and begins spiraling in mid-air. Faster and faster, it descends, whirling like a dervish, until it hovers just above her womb.

She gasps, not in pain, but in wonder, as it begins to sink beneath her skin, burrowing and then disappearing inside her. The sensation—like the vibration she sometimes feels from the trees she encounters—is pleasant, warm, and earthy.

Her eyes close as she feels the seed stop spinning. For a few seconds, she just breathes. Nothing feels different. The vibration has quieted. She feels relaxed and at ease. Opening her eyes, she expects to see him standing over her, but she's alone. Part of her feels disappointed. She wonders if it *was* a dream.

Maybe, she muses, but she knows better. She's heard far too many Greenling stories to doubt that what just happened was real.

Patrick slowly wakes up the next morning, still in his clothes, sprawled out on the denim sofa. Eyes still closed, he smells coffee brewing. The heavenly aroma carries enough caffeine into his nostrils to pull him upright.

As he blinks his eyes open, he catches sight of Noah backlit by the morning sunlight, staring out the window. Patrick notices the now-familiar vibration he felt the first time he saw her. He can't tell whether it's coming from her or something she's looking at. She's so immersed in her thoughts that she doesn't hear him slip up behind her until he puts his arms around her waist.

"Penny for your thoughts," he says, looking over her shoulder at the scene she's been contemplating.

Noah leans back onto his chest. "Nothing much, really." She keeps the strange dream from last night to herself. "Just how happy I am. How at home I feel when you're around, and how I don't want anything to mess that up. Then I snap back to reality and remember how the whole world is living on a knife's edge."

Not knowing what to say, he simply holds her.

Her mind purrs. *Hmmm... I like this. Just being close. Sometimes, words just get in the way.*

They stand there like that, pressed against each other, letting the minutes pass. Finally, Noah breaks the spell. "Hey, let me get you some coffee." She moves away and pours them both a cup of the steaming black brew. "We had quite the night last night."

"That we did, didn't we?" he answers, taking the mug from her outstretched hand.

Patrick takes a long sip before he speaks. "Hey, I'm off to meet Seamus at noon. Not sure if I'll be around for lunch. You okay with that?"

Noah crosses her arms, making a frowny face. "What do you mean? Of course, I'm okay. I was totally fine eating lunch by myself before you got here. Go. Do what you need to do."

Patrick raises his hands in mock surrender before he continues. "Alright. Okay. He still makes me a bit edgy, you know—even the way he's handling our meeting. He wants me to look for him at some bench in the woods at Queen's Park. I half expect him to be wearing a fake mustache and a trench coat. I need to grab a shower before I go. Okay if I use the bathroom?"

"Go for it. But you better hurry, though. I just heard Jean moving around. There are some extra towels in the closet in my room. You can use one of those."

He starts to move away, but Noah reaches out and grabs his hand.

"Patrick. I'm so glad you're here."

They stand, looking at each other for a long moment.

"Me too, Noah. I've really missed you. I'm not sure you'll be able to get rid of me."

She squeezes his hand. "FYI—I've got class until 4:30. I'll HOLO the code to the front door in case I'm not here when you get back. Feel free to make yourself at home."

She leans forward to give him a gentle kiss on the lips and then ushers him upstairs.

❧☙❧☙❧☙

While Noah heads to class, Patrick walks to Queen's Park. He feels the need to move after yesterday's flight and the layover in Montreal. Besides, it's a beautiful fall day, and the outdoors is calling to him. When he gets to the far side back of the park, he notices that it's empty—even the grounds seem barren and neglected. As he winds through the tall grasses and brambles, he sees a park bench. Someone's sitting on it, their back to him, wearing a Toronto Blue Jays cap turned backwards. *Is that Seamus?*

As he makes his way closer, he recognizes the familiar form of his uncle. He seems lost in some dark thought as Patrick's shadow falls across him. The man turns his face up, brandishing his half-cocked Irish grin.

"Hello, son. Good of you to come. Welcome to my little jungle in the city," he says, as he waves his arms at the bleak surroundings, and then stands to wrap his nephew in one of his signature bear hugs. "Sit down, sit down, mate. How're things in your world?"

Patrick takes a moment to look around, his puzzled expression still written on his face. He takes a seat and starts to tell his uncle about his holiday sauntering through Glenveagh National Forest in northwestern Ireland. He describes the incredible scenery, a fish tale about the big one that got away, and ends his narration with his near-fall while climbing Gartan Mountain.

"Beautiful country, son. Glad you made it back in one piece," Seamus responds, patting Patrick on the thigh. "Living by yourself in the wilderness can be good for the soul, but it sure is hell on the body sometimes. I hope it was a good break for you to sort things out and heal up after what happened at your school." Seamus looks down at his hands, rubbing them with his thumb as if trying to wipe something off. "And I trust you're ready to throw yourself back into something else now." Patrick watches his uncle closely— the man's shoulders sag as the focus of his eyes wander, carried away by some dark secret.

"That's why I'm here, Seamus. You mentioned a few months back that you might have something I could do for you. But, well... you were pretty evasive. Oh, and thanks for the ticket, by the way."

Seamus nods as he turns toward Patrick, studying him through haunted eyes. "Son, I'm not absolutely sure, but I think I might be in trouble. I just—"

"What do you mean?" Patrick interrupts. "What kind of trouble?"

Seamus exhales loudly. "Give me a minute. I'm not sure if I'm ready to tell you everything. But I think someone's been following me, trying to erase our research, your ma's and mine. There's more to it, but that's enough for now. I sure don't want to drag you into this any more than I have to. I'll tell you if you need to know more later."

Patrick nods, encouraging his uncle to say whatever he wants him to hear.

"I'm afraid that with everything that's going on with me, the Amazon project will have to end. There's this corporate son-of-a-bitch named Merton—someone from my past—who made an appearance, out of the blue, at the camp. I'm certain he's responsible for blowing up your ma's lab. I've also found traces of him, or his proxies, prowling around behind the scenes. And on top of that, I'm pretty sure he's enlisted some government agencies to come after me. Hell, who knows? They could drop down on me right here."

Patrick glances over his shoulder, not sure if his uncle is serious.

"Don't worry, we're safe. At least for now." Seamus chuckles quietly and flashes a wry grin. "Anyway, over the years, your ma and I have used the Amazon program to enlist small cadres of dedicated environmentalists that now, secretly exist in separate eco-cells around the—"

"Good God, Seamus! What are you talking about?" Patrick interrupts, nervously rubbing both hands over his unshaven face. "Are you telling me that you've been assembling a global eco-terrorist network?"

"It's all semantics at this point," Seamus counters, his sad eyes heavy and weary. "Unfortunately, our activism will need to morph into more dangerous and increasingly radical forms. Who knows, we may be in the final stage of our struggle for the future. Anyone willing to do whatever's necessary in this battle should be saluted as a hero."

Patrick says nothing, eyeing his uncle warily as he continues. *Is he trying to recruit me? Is Noah part of this now?*

"Listen, I need you to..." Seamus pauses to take a breath. "What I mean is, I want to *ask you* to head down to the Amazon camp. When you get there, I want you to go to the kapok tree where your ma's ashes are scattered. You remember it, don't you?"

Patrick nods his head.

"At the tree's base are three roots that intertwine to form an open cup. If you dig down a quarter of a meter or so, you'll find a stainless steel time capsule. I want you to take it with you and keep it somewhere safe. I don't want to know where you put it, in case I'm... it's just, you'll know what to do with it when the time's right. Inside the box is a list of each cell's location along with its members' names. There are nearly twenty different cells, with five individuals assigned to each. They've been tasked to identify the high-value operations and individuals near their locations and develop strike plans." The older man sits up straight, and his eyes reach out to his nephew pleadingly. "Patrick, we're approaching a critical point in our struggle, and I'm afraid I may not be here to help guide it."

Patrick's heart accelerates as he considers exactly what his uncle has been orchestrating all these years. *How much of a risk is he asking me to take? And what about Ma? What part did she have in all this?*

As if reading his nephew's mind, Seamus interrupts the moment to press on. "There's one more thing you need to know. Your ma was the true visionary, the real leader of this effort. Almost everything I know, everything I've done, has merely been my building on *her* thinking and *her* work. Inside the container, you'll also find the only copy of her Green Book. It's her memoir, her journal, as well as her environmental manifesto and battle plan. You need to read it. More than that, you need to study it. Then you can decide for yourself what to do with it."

Patrick leans back and blankly stares at the withered wasteland around him, suddenly feeling the weight of all his uncle's been carrying, now shifting onto his shoulders. Seamus watches him and then shrugs apologetically. He knows the pressure he's placed on his young nephew—that Patrick never signed up for any of it.

It's seven in the morning, and Sylvie floats downstairs. The HOLO-embedded fabric of her oversized T-shirt moves as it recreates Lucy snatching a football from Charlie Brown. She's up earlier than usual, but not so early that Noah won't have already made coffee. *She's like clockwork when it comes to her morning routines.* Sylvie's noticed that her friend has seemed lighter and happier over the last few weeks. *Ever since Patrick's been around,* she grins playfully to no one. *It's been fun getting to know him. Easy to see where the attraction lies there.* A little giggle escapes as her bare feet leave the last stair.

Turning the corner into the hearth room, the first thing that registers is the absence of any evidence of Patrick. No clothes scattered on the sofa. The now familiar pillows and sheets—gone. No suitcase. Nothing.

As she pads into the kitchen, she sniffs the air. There's no familiar aroma of coffee brewing. The pot still holds yesterday's dark, cold sludge. *What's going on?*

Confused—actually, slightly miffed—she sighs and then cleans out the carafe to get a new pot started. While coffee drips, she wonders if she's missed something. *Maybe Patrick had to take off or something.*

When the coffee machine announces it's finished, Sylvie pours herself a large mug and adds a rounded teaspoon of sugar and a long pour of heavy cream into the steaming brew. She walks back upstairs, still puzzled over what's going on.

When she passes Noah's door, she pauses for a minute. Someone's stirring in there. Then, she hears the unmistakable yearnings of two people making love. *What the...* She smiles a mischievous grin. *Well, it's about time!*

She quietly walks away, leaving the couple alone, relieved that everything seems to be on track. *But I'm still peeved that I have to make my own coffee!*

❧ ❧ ❧ ❧ ❧ ❧

That night, Noah and Patrick head out for a bite to eat at a tapas bar. The conversation is light and friendly as they share the small plates of patatas bravas and croquetas. But as the evening goes on, Noah notices a shift in Patrick—there's a subtle distance between them that wasn't there earlier. *Why does he seem... withdrawn?*

Noah reaches for his hand, her green eyes locked on his as she speaks. "Patrick, what's going on? Are you... I don't know... having second thoughts about us?" She braces herself, waiting.

He pauses as if photographing her face and then shakes his head. "Not at all. Being with you is... it's the best thing that's happened to me in a long time... maybe, ever." He rubs her small, soft hand between his fingers, then takes a deep breath and continues. "I've been putting off telling you this—"

Noah interrupts. "Telling me what?"

"I know I told you the bare bones of my conversation with Seamus, but I didn't tell you everything." Patrick goes on and relays *most* of what Seamus told him, although there are things he still can't make sense of. He finishes by telling her about his uncle's request for him to travel to the Amazon.

Noah listens, relieved that the distance isn't about her or them. But when she finally speaks, her disappointment is evident in her sinking shoulders and head.

"This is really hard to hear right now. I've been waiting to tell you... to show you how I feel about you. And it seemed like we were just starting to find our way, and now you're telling me you want to go away—"

"Noah, I don't *want* to go away," he says, looking at her pleadingly. "You mean so much more than any of this to me. But I need to do this, not for Seamus but for myself. There are things I need to do... things I need to take care of and see for myself."

Noah perceives Patrick's honest anguish—her eyes softening with tears. "I know. I don't like it. And I don't completely understand. But I'll try. Go. Do what you need to do, but if something happens to you, you'll be in big trouble, Mr. Wilde."

He picks up her hand and brings it to his lips, tenderly kissing each knuckle while he gazes into her watching eyes.

Terra Nova, Vale do Javari, State of Amazonas, Brazil (75° F / 24° C)

Patrick looks knackered from the grueling transport to this remote spot south of the equator and three days of birding. His clothes, as well as his sagging eyes and slack lips, betray everything he's endured just to get there. Seamus was adamant that he make the trip look like something other than what it is—a covert retrieval of his ma and uncle's life work. So, they hatched the plan for him to fly into La Paz, Bolivia, then take a bus to Manu National Park in Peru to birdwatch.

The flight alone took a whole day—if he counted layovers and cancellations. Then, on top of that, the potholed bus ride added another thirteen torturous hours to the itinerary. The ordeal made Patrick wonder if his uncle's mounting desolation was being foisted onto him.

Because of Patrick's passion for birdwatching, they felt the trip would be the perfect cover. The park boasts over a thousand bird species—a birder's paradise. After three days, Patrick has managed to spot nearly 250 birds, including seven distinct macaws. *Not a bad few days,* he tells himself. *But not even close to the park's record.* In 1982, Ted Parker and Scott Robinson spotted 331 species in just 24 hours at Manu's Cocha Cashu Biological Station. *Maybe next year,* he thinks, flashing a smug grin at the tiny, red howler monkey who watches him leave.

From Manu, Patrick finds a young Peruvian with a jeep and hires him to transport him to the Itui River. There, he charters a small forest boat that takes him to a drop-off point near his uncle's base camp. As he hikes into the campsite, he feels the ghosts of happy times with his ma and his uncle. *It was like I lived in my own zoo—filled with bird songs and bellowing animals—insects the size of rats. It felt like another planet.*

He looks around and notices other, more recent ghosts, too. The yurts are empty. Shreds of mosquito netting are scattered everywhere. The canteen, its abandonment obvious, has been left to fend for itself against anything foraging for a stray morsel or forgotten container.

He eventually locates Seamus's tent. As he enters and drops his gear, he notices his uncle's familiar smell. Hard to describe but unmistakable. *Sweat and leather, maybe?* His cot is stripped bare. The surface of the small desk is thick with dust—small footprints give evidence that a family of mice has found a new home here. There are a few scraps of paper scattered around, but other than that, it seems as if his uncle had just walked out, expecting never to return.

Exhaustion seeps into every neuron in his brain—like a drug taking sudden effect. He kicks off his boots and lies down on his uncle's cot. For a moment, he thinks of Noah. He tries to imagine what she might be doing, but his thoughts go fuzzy. He closes his eyes, giving in to his body's inescapable need for sleep.

As he sinks deeper and deeper into the depths of unconsciousness, he begins to dream. He's with his ma, still a young boy. They walk along a slippery river bank, sometimes wading, then quickly jumping out, chased by an unseen caiman or piranha. As they continue, his ma turns and scrambles up the muddy slope. He struggles to close the distance between them but keeps sliding back, unable to find a foothold. His ma just stands there on top of the slick bank—her arms crossed, a remote trace of encouragement in her expression, but no hand to reach out and pull him up. He finally manages to circle the bank and climb up the stair-like roots of a giant tree—but his ma has already turned away and is walking far ahead of him.

He calls after her in his small voice. She smiles at him over her shoulder and then gradually morphs into an avian form—an osprey. Wings sprout from her back. Feathers grow from her skin and clothes. Talons replace shoes. She makes two powerful strokes with her broad wings and flies off into the jungle, out of view. Left behind, he runs after her, tears running down his red, chapped cheeks, and plunges into a thick, green wall of darkness.

When he wakes the next morning, the dream is still vivid. The memory of it blurs what's real and what's fantasy. It's been seven years since he's been back to the camp. After his ma died, he went back to school and never returned. Until now.

With no one to talk with, he takes a few minutes before getting up, still pondering the dream. He feels a familiar melancholy—not so much that his ma is gone; he's felt that vacant hole for years, though there are times when it crashes back in, fresh as the day he learned of her death. What lingers more is the regret of never truly understanding her or being able to keep up with her. Growing up, he always sensed it—that she was too gifted, too brilliant. He felt he could never achieve anything close to whatever she was attempting.

But there are other questions the dream brings up. *Why didn't she slow down, or come back, or help me up the river bank? And what was so damned important that she left me all alone? Maybe Da couldn't keep up with her, either.* He sits upright and swings his feet to the ground, staring out through the tent's mosquito netting. *Maybe this is why I never wanted to come back— too many questions without answers.*

He slowly stands and scrunches his shoulders and neck, trying to straighten the kinks left from the hard cot. Rummaging through his pack, he finds his energy bars and a water bottle. He quickly downs his breakfast— if that's what it can be called—then shakes his boots, making sure no scorpions or small vipers have claimed ownership. Satisfied they're safe, he puts them on and laces them up, dons his wide-brimmed hat, and heads out. As he steps into the camp's clearing, he notices a tiny hummingbird on a small limb above him. Because of its dull, drab colors, he almost misses it.

"Huh. A straight-billed hermit. What are you doing here?" he mutters, more to himself than the bird, and then moves on.

Walking east, he takes the path that leads to his ma's lab. Before he gets there, he catches a whiff of chemicals and charred wood. Acrid. Moldy. Like burnt hair. He's shocked at what he sees as he rounds the final bend of the trail. The front windows and doorway are surrounded with thick bubbles of black soot. The back wall, as well as one of the sides, has completely collapsed. Sturdy vines have already encapsulated much of what still remains. They seem to strain with a will of their own to erase whatever happened here. Even though the smell is bitter, he decides to walk through the burned-out door frame. It's obvious that Seamus didn't attempt to put any of the broken or charred items in order.

The most disturbing part, however, is the sight of hundreds of insects and reptiles scattered among the broken glass of the aquariums on the floor. *It's like a war zone. And this is the so-called 'collateral damage'—the casualties counted, while the victims' names and lives remain too painful to report.*

Patrick frowns and shakes his head. It makes him feel sick. He remembers watching his ma working here, totally absorbed in her research. Now, like so many other pieces of his life, it's gone too, broken beyond recovery.

Nothing here, he decides, and moves on, not bothering to go through the doorway, just stepping over the collapsed wall.

Walking the trail toward the giant kapok, he remembers how he would explore the surrounding jungle as a boy. *I can't believe the freedom Ma let me have here,* he realizes now, marveling at how undomesticated her parenting style was. 'Free-range parenting,' he'd heard someone call it before. Now he wonders, *Was I nurtured or neglected?*

He recalls the experience on some naive, childlike level. *It felt like the forest itself was watching over me—even if Ma was busy with her own world.* Either way, having survived so many things that could have turned out badly, he's grateful for what he learned from it all. Besides, he has always felt independent and confident in himself, even back then. *Maybe too confident—too independent,* he considers. *Until Noah.*

When he finally arrives at his destination, he passes through the clearing's opening and is transported back in time by the verdant cathedral surrounding him. When he was here as a child, the circle felt immense, as if it would take him all afternoon to walk around it. Now, however, it is dwarfed by the central figure—the giant kapok, which seems to fill the entire space, pushing back even the sky.

The last time he was here was with his uncle. They came back to honor his ma's wish that her body's cremains would be mingled with the earth in this place. She saw it as her final act of nourishing the lives around her that had always meant so much to her.

Patrick remembers the day clearly. But in his adolescent state of shock, he wasn't able to let himself weep, let alone grieve. Now, the raw emotions return and cling to churning fragments of old memories. Suddenly, he's able to feel everything he couldn't feel on that day. His eyes begin to well with tears as he pushes his feet forward toward the giant kapok.

He navigates the roots the best he can until he's close enough to put his hand on the textured, brown bark of the trunk. He bows his head as tears roll down his face. Sobbing now, he lowers his body to the ground.

"Oh, Ma. Why did you leave me? Why... why couldn't you stay with me and... take care of me, teach me? I've missed out on so, so much," he says—

uncertain whether he's talking to himself, or her, or even the tree.

Sunken between the large roots, cradled by the tree, Patrick loses track of time. Of space, too. Consenting to feel all the emotions he's buried, he descends through layers thick with grief, loss, and something new—intense loneliness. He knows where he is, but it's as if he's forgotten where he came from, where he's going. It's as if his life has just stopped. He's simply—

Here.

Alone.

In the jungle.

Where his ma lived.

Where she still is.

Lost in the heartaches of his private world, he gradually becomes aware of a presence. Watching. Waiting. He's reminded of what Noah feels from some trees and wonders if he's having a similar sensation. Unsure if it's his imagination, he opens his eyes and raises his head.

But when his eyes turn toward the jungle, he jerks at the sight in front of him. A small, barrel-chested man with fierce yet tender eyes is staring back at him. He recognizes the tattoos and clothing—*the Tucano tribe.* The man quickly points to his chest, then two fingers to his eyes, then points at Patrick. Finally, he makes a prayer-like symbol with his hands and bows and then begins to speak in broken English. "My name Cubeo. I watch for Erin's boy. I wait for Erin's boy."

Patrick nods his head and makes the same prayer-like motion.

"Sit," the man says. "You here for what mother left?"

Not sure exactly what he means, Patrick simply nods.

"I dig for you. You sit."

The man scurries quickly to a cup-like section between two roots. Using a simple digging stick with a sharp point on one end, he begins scraping a hole, pushing the rich soil up and over the tree's roots. After a few minutes, the stick hits something hard.

"Oh-wow! Oh-wow! Yes!" The man mouths, excitedly. He continues, carefully digging a few more scoops with the stick, then gets on his knees to finish scooping out the rest by hand.

Satisfied with his work, he looks at Patrick and beckons. "Come. You come."

Patrick crawls over, kneeling next to the man. He sees the top of a medium-sized metal locker. It appears to have once been olive green but now is faded and nicked with age. He pushes his fingers into the surrounding soil on either side, then gets underneath the edge and lifts. It's snug and resistant—as if it doesn't want to be moved—but finally, with a few firm tugs, it breaks free.

The man looks at Patrick and smiles a toothless grin. "Good job," he says, patting Patrick on the shoulder. Patrick looks back and smiles, both knowing Cubeo did all the work. Cubeo's smile softens as he looks deeply into Patrick's eyes. "She love you. Very much. Now I go. I do what she tell me. Now, you look. You see, Erin's son."

They both rise. Patrick senses the man's utter devotion to his ma. *Who are you? And how did you and Ma know each other?* There are still so many things he doesn't know about her. Patrick looks down at the metal container in his hands and, for the first time, wonders, *Could some of the answers be in here?*

Cubeo turns to leave, but before the man moves out of sight, Patrick manages a quick, "Thank you." The man doesn't respond, quickly disappearing through the thick leaves of the perimeter. From there, his voice trails back to Patrick:

"You are good son. Find peace."

"Find peace?" Patrick mutters to himself, pulling the brim of his hat down. "What's that supposed to mean?" He suddenly feels very alone again, uncertain of what he is searching for.

Glancing around, he notices another straight-billed hermit directly above him in the kapok. *Kind of strange to see two of the little guys today.*

He slumps down and leans against the tree, uncertain if he should just go ahead and leave. He decides, instead, to linger a while. As his mind drifts, a reverie comes over him—he feels a closeness with his ma here. A gentle peace settles around him. His senses come alive. He remembers.

How her eyes narrowed when she smiled at me—how she smelled like gentle rainfall, even if she'd been sweating. A burst of forgotten sensations stored throughout his body quickly flood his memories.

The way her hair felt between my fingers as I played with it when I was little. How the scar over her left eye turned white in the summer after her face was sunburned. And then there were her off-key attempts at singing. How did that song go? Oh yeah. He clears his throat and starts to sing. "And the rain it fell... like drops of brandy... till the time and tide were gone."

He abruptly stops—suddenly alert to some unseen danger. *She's warning me.* It's as if she's there, shielding him in the same way she would when he was a boy about to step where a snake might be. Then, in his mind, he hears her voice; he hears the words.

"Be careful. They're watching."

It's midnight when Patrick finally makes his way back to Seamus's tent. He drops his pack and takes his boots off. Then he lies back on the cot, considering what to do next. He's not sleepy, but he's exhausted from all the emotions and memories that have been dredged up. After several minutes of trying to fall asleep, he finally gives up, opens his pack, and takes out the metal time capsule. For some reason, he feels nervous about opening the thing up. *I don't even know if I should open it. But then, why else did I make the trip?*

He moves to the simple desk and sets the case down. A tiny hinged clasp is at the top, secured with twisted red wire. After he untwists it, he takes a deep breath and whispers, "What in the world were you thinking, Ma?"

He slowly opens the stainless steel box. A stale, musty whiff reminds him of the dusty pages of books found in an old library. The contents are neatly arranged, taking up the entire space. There's a manila envelope with his name written on it in his ma's script. Beneath it are a dozen identical, well-worn journals and a small accordion folder with the phrase "Eco-Cells" scrawled on the flap. Lastly, he finds a plastic case that holds a larger, much thicker logbook with a scuffed-up green leather cover. *Not much to look at, considering all the trouble it took to get here.*

His attention returns to the envelope. Picking it up, he takes in his ma's distinctive handwriting. Small, neat printing in all caps. PATRICK. He unwinds the string on the manilla envelope. The glue has disintegrated, so he flips open the flap and reaches in. There are several handwritten pages inside. As he looks at the first page, he feels a flood of emotion. Sadness. Heaviness. Anxiousness. Weariness. Anger. Curiosity. Resignation.

He takes a deep breath and begins to read.

My dear son, Patrick Fletcher Wilde. If you are reading this letter, it must mean that something terrible and unexpected has prematurely separated us. I'm so sorry not to be here with you to tell you these things. Sitting here, writing to you in the future, I find that my imagination fails me. I'm at a complete loss to know what this moment might be like for you.

Patrick's eyes lift from the page. It's incredible how just reading her words makes him feel like his ma's still here—still with him. But at the same time, he's aware of the unmistakable void of her absence. Both impressions strike him as equally valid—holding equal weight.

I'm not sure I can say everything I want to say, everything I didn't have a chance to say, across this distance from where I am resting now. There's so much I haven't told you. Besides this letter, you should have found my journals from the last thirty years. These are private and personal. They were for my eyes only. Since I am no longer "here," they are now also for your eyes. They will help you to better know me at this stage of your life, even in my absence—as well as who I was when I was with you.

The other, larger book is a compendium of all my professional research, my theorizing, conundrums, and planning for the work I have given my life. Carl Jung had his famous Red Book. Well, consider this my Green Book! In it, you will see the evolution of my thinking, the demons I wrestled with, the

*moral dilemmas I faced, and the tragic conclusions I felt inevitably led to
put into motion. It may or may not make sense to anyone other than your
uncle. But I want you to have it. I suppose there's even a chance that its
contents aren't so much for you, but for someone else in your life.*

The pages continue in a reminiscing style, recalling moments from
Patrick's childhood. The year his ma homeschooled him while living out
of a VW van to explore New Zealand's Forest of Hope. Their trip to Dead
Horse Point in the desert of Utah to sleep under the stars and watch the
Perseids meteor shower. His thirteenth birthday trip to Sao Conrado in Rio
de Janeiro for his first hang gliding experience.

A bittersweet smile forms around his mouth as he reads about these
events—now seeing them through his ma's inner experience, her own
reflections and emotions. He sets the letter down and feels something
open—like a fist unclenching—deep inside. Instead of the confused
resentment of actual or ambiguous losses, he now sees how many good gifts
his ma gave him. Wiping his pooling eyes with the back of his hand, he
reads on.

*Patrick, I want you to know what I couldn't admit in my younger years.
My marriage to your father ended not because of him but because of me.
I know that I led you to believe (hell, I led myself to believe) that he was
the one at fault. I thought he was nearly all of the problem then, and my
part was only a tiny fraction. That's what you heard. That's what I wanted
you to believe. The truth is, we were both at fault—with my part being
the greater. Whatever you might think or feel about him, I want you to
reconsider who he was, who he is, and who he might still become to you.*

*If you can honor a dying woman's—or, in this case, a dead woman's—wish,
I beg you: forgive him. He tried to be part of your life, but I shut him out. All
I can say now is I was wrong. I hope you can eventually forgive me as well.
I'm so sorry for the hurt I caused both of you. If you ever find him, please*

don't blame him. He's a good man and would have been a very good father to you if I would have let him.

Her words unleash the venom that's still there, still inside him, unsettling him more than anything he's heard since his ma's accident. His mind grapples to keep up with the unraveling of beliefs he's held about the past. His brain rapidly tries to reframe everything he *thought* he knew about his da, about his parents' relationship and lives—how profoundly *misinformation* has shaped his life and the choices he's made. He feels an erupting force of anger, hurt, and grief pushing up from inside. All he's able to do is sit, shoulders slumped, his head on the desk, and shout, "What in God's name am I supposed to do with all this?!"

The silence is total, enveloping the sound of his heart pounding out his unanswered question. *Why Ma? Why? Why did you push Da away when you knew how much I might need him someday?*

Fort Meade, Maryland, USA (-6° F / -21° C)

Wilson's HOLO announces a priority message. He quickly accepts it and is met with an image of a young agent with a close buzz cut.

"Sir, we've just had a ping from Project Erin in the Amazon."

"Go on," the older man replies.

"Per your orders, a monitoring detail went to the subject's campsite and placed a robo-bird. Earlier this morning, it was activated."

"Keep going."

"The good news is that it performed flawlessly and captured recon for a new target as he moved through the jungle."

"...and the bad news, agent?" Wilson knew there was more from the man's tone.

"Well, sir. The bad news is that the bird was unable to transmit any images that unmistakably identified who the bogey was. However, based on the subject's frame and stature, we can tell he is male—roughly six feet two inches—weighing about 190 pounds. We have a complete list from the project's database of potential matches, but because we weren't able to obtain a solid facial image to map, we won't be able to narrow it down much further."

"So you're telling me all we really know is that *someone* was there? We don't have a damned clue who it was?"

"Yes, sir. Sorry, sir."

Wilson, though not surprised, is still peeved. *Dammit all! These spy gadgets are turning these young agents into high-tech pansies. We would have slept in the mud to grab this intel.* He reminds himself that missions rarely accomplish what their planners imagine. Human or technical error, and it's all the same in the end.

"One more thing, sir," the young agent offers, as if hearing his superior's critiquing thoughts. "We're sending an asset there to see if we can lift some prints. But with the rain, along with the humidity and heat, it's fifty-fifty that there'll be anything of value left. I'll keep you posted."

Wilson doesn't bother to respond, ending the HOLO. He leaves to walk down the hall to his boss's door. When he gets there, he takes a deep breath before knocking underneath a simple black and white sign.

JEREMY BARGES
DEPUTY DIRECTOR
NSA: BIO/ECO-TERRORISM

HOLO SPACE (32° F / 0° C)

The HOLO stage is activated and ready for tonight's roundtable—the third and final installment of the Emerging Voices series. The life-like purple backdrop slowly undulates in a simulation of a gentle breeze. Noah Calhoun-Greenling and Marta Sennheiser appear to stand beside each other on the HOLO's virtual platform—in reality, the two are separated by over six thousand kilometers. Noah wears a caramel-colored Harris tweed jacket over a Down to Earth T-shirt. Her golden-red hair falls loosely around her pale face. Marta, her black hair slicked back, sports a cocoa-colored leather tunic dress. Both girls convey anxious readiness.

Moderator Journi Preston—every hair in place and wearing a turquoise blazer—nods to the two, ensuring they're ready, then looks squarely into the HOLO-CAM. Co-moderator Samantha Erskine turns in the same direction—her blonde hair sharply contrasting with her burgundy sweater dress—a confident smile shows she's ready for the cue.

"Good evening, and welcome to this important conversation on our planet's future. I'm Journi Preston, and I will be guiding this evening's roundtable along with my co-moderator, Samantha Erskine. Tonight, we will hear from two emerging voices that represent widely contrasting viewpoints on climate change and climate action."

"That's right," Samantha says. "We're very fortunate to have Noah Calhoun-Greenling and Marta Sennheiser share the stage to discuss their differing perspectives. Noah, by mutual agreement, you have opted to go first."

As she hears her name, Noah raises her chin and turns her gaze toward the HOLO-CAM. "Thank you, Journi. Thank you, Samantha. It's an honor to be here. Even if Ms. Sennheiser and I strongly disagree, we represent our generation, as well as the millions of life forms that don't have a voice or representation.

"We stand here, in the middle of the twenty-first century, in a year that has seen unprecedented climate challenges, catastrophes, and tragedies. Uninhabitable heat domes. Apocalyptic flooding. Accelerating biological ecocide. A tsunami of human climate refugees. It's been a long and frustrating journey since climate activists like Sir David Attenborough, Bill McKibben, and Greta Thunberg sounded the alarm of our global climate crisis. Unfortunately, because we failed to take action then, the predictions made decades ago have now become our harsh reality—threatening even our own fragile existence.

"The evidence is undeniable: our planet isn't simply facing the next crisis. It's in absolute meltdown. No matter what others, like Ms. Sennheiser and her corporate sponsors, might have to say about it—the science is undeniable. And we *must* listen to it. The time for action isn't somewhere in the future. It's now! If we want to survive, we must face this moment with decisiveness and extreme courage."

"Thank you, Noah." Samantha smiles and then turns to face the other direction. "Marta, your opening comments?"

The HOLO-CAM transitions to Marta—her angry frown swiftly disappearing when she realizes the camera has switched to her. "I'd like to say *danke schön* to my peers who are watching tonight, for caring about our future, and for having the courage to think for yourselves—something that is all too rare today. While I acknowledge the reality of certain climate events and some of the challenges we face, I also believe in finding balanced solutions—the kind of solutions that consider our economic realities and technological advancements.

"And, Noah, come on. Let's be honest," she says, her tone condescending. "We both know that science is constantly evolving, always open to revision. Why do you mislead people by appealing to science as if it's set in stone? This *is* a pivotal moment, and we must navigate these issues very carefully. But let's do it with common sense, not with your radical, extremist methods. Only then can we ensure that the future will be sustainable for—"

"Marta," Noah interrupts—the split HOLO display quickly zeros in on Noah's image—"the urgency of the situation *can't* be overstated—it's neither extreme nor radical. The predictions from the last century and the first half of this weren't exaggerations. They were warnings—warnings we failed to pay attention to for far too long. We're way past the luxury of looking for some balanced approach. It's now a raging, five-alarm fire. The only question is whether we can find the will to prioritize the preservation of the planet over everything else."

The HOLO-CAM zooms back out and returns to the split images of both girls. Marta cocks her head, a mock smile playing on her lips as she nods. "While I agree with my friend that *some* action needs to be taken, it's crucial that we avoid extreme measures that most certainly will harm our economies and people's livelihoods. Don't you care about people's lives and well-being, Noah? What about *their* ability to raise families and put food on the table? We've got to find solutions that ensure both environmental sustainability *and* economic growth."

Noah snorts as she shakes her head. "That's rich coming from you. Of course I care, Marta. How dare you say that I don't? But what you don't seem able to see—or perhaps what you *choose* not to—is there will have to be a planet to *live on* if there's going to *be* a future. That's what this is about."

The HOLO-CAM cuts to Samantha. "Okay. Thank you. I'm going to stop you both there. We have a lot of ground to cover. Thank you, Noah. Thank you, Marta. Let's move on. Noah, what specific measures do you propose as we stand here today?"

Looking slightly flushed, Noah takes a deep breath and taps an open palm on the ball of her fist. "The time for half-measures is over. For one thing, we need a rapid transition to 100% renewable energy sources. We've had over half a century to get there. The technology's there, but it always gets bogged down by government gridlock or bought out by corporate monopolies—"

"It does not!" Marta interrupts.

Noah pushes ahead and outlines earth-friendly transportation, building, and agricultural strategies. "But all these efforts have slowed to a snail's pace because corporate and financial leaders block any real environmental progress that—"

"Come on, Noah. Why do you demonize everyone who—"

"Let me finish. You'll get your chance, Marta. Finally, we absolutely must realign our consumption patterns. Consumerism is literally killing us as it destroys our planet."

"Can I say something now, or do you intend to monopolize our discussion until it becomes one of your dull monologues?"

Noah rolls her eyes. "Oh, come on."

Marta takes a beat and looks down, as if thinking, then returns her gaze to the HOLO-CAM. "While I support a transition to renewables, we have to be realistic about the pace of change. Drastic measures will lead to economic turmoil. We need *evolution*, not the green *revolution* Noah carelessly advocates. That's where innovation and technology will create new solutions that will allow us to achieve environmental goals without sacrificing economic—"

"So, why drag your feet?" Noah looks at Marta, both hands raised up in frustration. "You know as well as I do, Marta—it's proven that a green transition will actually create *more* jobs and bring about an explosion of innovations."

"I never said it wouldn't," Marta interjects, shaking her head, her dark eyes glaring with frustration.

Noah scowls back. "You accuse me of being clueless. The economic argument must never take precedence over the survival of our planet. That's like straightening the deck chairs on the Titanic."

Marta smirks as she snickers. "If you're so high-minded, why don't you do something of value instead of—"

"You want to talk about economics, Marta?" Noah ignores the put-down. "The costs of inaction far outweigh any initial investment that's needed for a sustainable future. We need to learn from those mistakes."

The HOLO-CAM cuts back to Samantha. "Let's shift the focus to international cooperation. Noah, how do you see nations working together to address climate change?

"I've thought a lot about this and discussed it in detail with some of the world's finest minds—"

"Finest minds—my eye," Marta mutters, shaking her head.

Disregarding the jab, Noah stays on script. "We desperately need a global commitment to reduce *all* dangerous emissions. The only way this will happen is if international agreements from petrol nations become legally binding and have strict accountability—"

Marta interrupts again. "Noah, while I agree that accountability is important, we have to respect the unique challenges faced by very diverse nations. A one-size-fits-all approach will—"

"Excuse me. I'm not finished," Noah continues. "The U.N. must step up and show some muscle. Laws that are binding, not voluntary, must be adopted. Nations, whether large or small, need to be proportionately penalized if they violate international law—"

"And who's going to enforce these so-called *binding agreements*?" Marta counters, mocking Noah with air quotes.

"Marta, is it so difficult for you to understand that the climate crisis doesn't respect borders, or that global solidarity is more important than national interests in this fight?"

"No, I get that. Of course, cooperation is essential, but imposing the kind of strict regulations you and your liberal friends propose will actually hinder their growth and development. We can incentivize collaboration while also respecting each country's autonomy and unique circumstances. Instead of big brother swooping in, we should—"

Noah raises her hands in frustration and interrupts. "Why is it that you always revert to name-calling to evoke fear—"

"Ah, and you never do that, do you, *meine liberaler freund*."

Journi sees an opening and steps in. "Okay, let's move on. I want us to talk about the role of technology. How do you imagine technology helping to solve climate change?"

Marta makes a deferring gesture in an effort to appear magnanimous. Noah, in turn, takes a sip of water and then responds. "Technology can play a crucial role in transitioning to a sustainable future—it already does. Advancements in renewable energy, carbon capture, and sustainable agriculture are all essential. Unfortunately, the corporatocracies that have stalemated so much of the development of these forms of technology are only committed to two things: profit and power. Their support of the status quo guarantees that they are the ones that will stay in the planet's driver's seat. And although innovation is important, what's *crucial* is tackling the complex, systemic issues—economies fueled by addictive consumerism, capitalistic colonialism, the erosion of democracy, the unelected cabal of transnational corporatocracies, the global war-making culture, and that's not even—"

Marta interrupts and begins to counter. "This all sounds like socio-cultural engineering to me. Is that what this is really about, Noah? Using the climate crisis to further your liberal-social agenda?"

"You know the major players and sticky problems as well as I do, Marta. To ignore the cultural-political factors would simply guarantee that we'd all be duped, yet again, by those who benefit the most from preserving the status quo—always making promises but never delivering."

Marta quickly jumps in as Noah pauses. "I'd like to go back to the topic of technology. Technology is our single biggest ally in this fight. Innovation can lead us toward a greener future, one with cleaner energy sources and more sustainable farming practices. Best of all, this approach allows us to achieve environmental goals without sacrificing our quality of life—"

"Quality of life? For who?" Noah interjects.

"I'm not sure what you're asking, Noah. Why do you always accuse corporations of resisting innovation in these matters? Look at the progress we've made. A free-market economy combined with democratic principles will always lead to better solutions than imposing the dictates and theories of the elitist—"

"Free market?" Noah interrupts, her face flushed with incredulity. "Democratic? Is that what you call it? Corporatocracies: These unelected, anonymous hierarchies of business oligarchs—not democracies—call all the shots. And who do they listen to? The science? Their shareholders? Or is it their lust for power and control? We can't trust these unelected, often unknown, individuals to do anything other than what they've always done: put profit over everything else!"

Marta's face twists into a wicked grin. "Funny you'd mention this problem of unelected, unknown actors and their use of power. I wonder how much the world really knows about *you* and *your* part in recent reports of ecoterrorism?"

Off camera, Journi flashes Samantha an alarmed expression.

Noah's eyes show her confusion as she snaps back. "*What* in God's name are you insinuating?"

Marta tilts her head back and straightens her shoulders. "Oh, I'm not *insinuating* anything, Noah. Right now, my aunt—Vivienne Stark—is in a coma, hanging between life and death. Do you know why? Of course you do. I've learned she's been poisoned—the tragic result of a carefully planned assassination plot. Well, not too careful, or she'd be dead."

Noah's stunned, unable to find her words.

"That's right—the not-so-unknown but unelected—Dr. Seamus Wilde poisoned her. Not personally—but who knows, it might have been your boyfriend, his nephew—or some other member of your little—"

Noah finally regains her voice and interrupts. "That's ludicrous, Marta. Where do you get off inventing such an outlandish theory—"

"Oh, just save it, Noah—"

"Listen, Marta. I'm sorry for you and your aunt, but I promise you, I had nothing to do with any—"

"These aren't just theories. The National Security Agency has been investigating your Dr. Wilde's activities for months. It's just too bad they didn't arrest him before this cowardly attack on my aunt."

Journi and Samantha glance sideways at each other—their nod conveying agreement that the HOLO-CAST needs to come to a close. Journi quickly regains composure and then ends the program as professionally as possible.

"On behalf of CHN and my co-host, Samantha Erskine with Royal-Net, I want to thank each of you for joining us this evening. Good night."

Journi waits a beat until the HOLO-CAM flashes the OFF THE AIR message, then glares at Marta's image. "What the hell was that?"

Samantha exhales in exasperation. "Marta, we talked about this. And you agreed not to bring any of this up."

Noah shakes her head, rage tightening her reddened cheeks.

"I changed my mind," Marta answers calmly. "If this helps bring my aunt back, then a little embarrassment to *meine freund* is a small price—"

Noah's anger explodes inside. But instead of giving Marta the satisfaction of watching it erupt, she abruptly disconnects her HOLO-CAM. Assured she's now alone, she lets the volcanic emotions flow, screaming at the wall, fists clenched. Her wailing resembles a cornered animal—high, fierce, aggressive, and frightened. As the last of her fury drains out of her, she sinks slowly to the floor—her red hair draped around her like a shroud—and she begins to weep. Her tears are spent as if counting the minutes, and like time, her crying eventually runs its course. The intense emotions gradually recede, making room for her mind to think rationally again. *Could there be any truth in this?* She frowns, replaying Patrick's evasiveness about his meeting with Seamus. *When he got back, he seemed agitated... like he didn't want to talk about it. Is there more going on than I know about?*

Noah eventually rises on unsteady legs. She's been crumpled on the floor for the last hour—emotions flip-flopping between intense anger and irrational fear—thoughts looping with worry and suspicion. *Why haven't I heard from Patrick? I need help to find out what's really going on.* Having expended the flood of internal energy, she is able to force herself to leave her room. The mirror in the hallway tells her all she needs to know. Her eyes are unfocused, and her complexion is colorless. She looks like she's been knocked down in a boxing ring, if not had her lights punched out.

Needing fresh air, she grabs her winter parka and heads out into the frigid night air. Somewhere in the distance, a mournful train signals its crossing—the sound reinforcing her feelings of loneliness. Street lamps haloed by frosty air turn on and off as she passes under them. She wanders off campus and then further along the city's near-empty streets, finally coming to her destination—the Toronto Necropolis. There's something about walking the winding paths of old cemetery grounds that she's always found calming. *It's like I can step out of time here,* she muses. *Or maybe I just don't like being around people. Alive people, I suppose.*

She wanders along the pathways until she finds an old limestone bench carved with grapevines. She sits and is simply quiet for several minutes. A pair of owls break the night's silence—low hoots call back and forth somewhere in the woods behind her. An ancient statue of a large marbled angel gazes down at her—delicate fingers hold a large flower bloom as if offering it to her. Noah smiles, looking up at it. Something about it makes her feel watched over.

Exhausted and uncertain of what to make of the statue's effect on her, she lowers her head and stares off into space—thinking nothing—feeling nothing. She shudders slightly, becoming aware of another presence. *Strange... I feel like I'm in some kind of trance.* At that moment, her thoughts dissolve as if they had been written with chalk, now sluiced away with water.

Around her, or perhaps within her—it's hard for her to differentiate—a stormy yet maternal voice speaks in an ancient tongue. *"Noah, t'eh y traa ayn dy choamrey. Cha nel mooarane traa ain derrey..."* The language is unknown to her, but somehow, she understands it easily. *"Noah, it's now time for us to meet. We don't have much time until—"*

"Who in the world are you?" Noah interrupts out loud.

The presence radiates loving concern. "I'm your Mother. Not your human mother, but your mother nonetheless. I'm the Mother of all that has ever lived and breathed on your planet, Earth."

Noah stops breathing. Although she knows she still sits on the bench in the Necropolis—she feels like she's sinking—being buried beneath quicksand. Unable to hold her breath any longer, she consents to whatever it is that's happening to her and inhales deeply. The gray-brown ooze, as if having a will of its own, rushes in, filling her lungs. Her eyes go wide— shocked that she's not choking or worse. An image quickly blossoms in her brain—she sees the single trunk of her trachea—branching out into numerous bronchia—branching yet again and again into thousands of tiny bronchioles. She stares at a living tree—whether with her eyes or her mind—that now seems to be animated by whatever is in the sluggish mixture. Unable to speak, she waits.

The Maternal One continues in the same ancient language. "Know this, my little Greenling. Our living planet has always sought to give back as much as we needed to take. Often, we provided more than our fair share. But now, we have reached our limit—not just our limit, *THE* limit. For too long, humankind has taken far more than it could ever hope to give back. We have been uncertain how far humanity would descend in its unrestrained grasping. So we began our own counter-preparations. Lacking human intelligence that would have crafted a precise surgical strategy, we were forced to blindly develop more basic means of opposition. And so began the time now known as the Era of Modern Pandemics.

"What your epidemiologists call NOVEL ANAPLASMOSIS 612-B has already killed over 430 million humans. It is delivered by several species of innocuous insects that now easily survive winter due to the rise of global temperatures, making the virus even more destructive. Before that, there was XY ACQUIRED HEMOPHILIA-ZET 219. Over 25 million males from your species have already succumbed to it, not to mention the 500 million birds, fish, reptiles, insects, and mammals who died, imprisoned in the eco-penitentiaries you call *zoos*. And earlier, there was the NOVEL CORONAVIRUS COVID-19, its death toll a trifling 7 million."

"No. That can't be right," Noah mutters. When her protest isn't acknowledged, she tries to shake off the trance-like web—her arms cross over her chest as if protecting herself. The darkness of the night conceals her unseeing eyes, which ricochet back and forth as she tries to shape her thoughts—her reactions reeling from the scale of human loss just described.

"I could continue, going back over the past two centuries, but that should be sufficient. We are grateful these terrible bio-deterrents didn't kill more of our little brothers and sisters. But we felt then, as we do now, the need to prepare for the worst. It seems humanity has left us no other choice. And it's with deep regret that—"

Noah interrupts. "Why are you telling me this?" Her voice is thin, barely audible. "You realize I'm a part of this same humanity too, don't you? And what about my family? My friends? This is way past... it's just so far beyond anything I've ever spouted off about. I'm not sure I can handle this... this destruction. I'm not sure I *want* to be able to handle it. Why in God's name... what is it you want from me?"

Noah is panting now, trying to catch her breath. She hears her heart thudding in her ears. Then she hears the voice respond—soft, yet also strong and determined.

"My dear Noah. I understand how overwhelming all this is for you. I'm overwhelmed by it, too. We all are. You wonder why I'm telling you this? Because although you don't yet realize it, you are stronger than you know.

Because for us to move from where we are to where we have to go, a human one must lead the way. You ask, why you? I've watched. I've waited. There's no one alive... *no one* better suited to direct our non-human forces into the coming revolution. You have the heart, the passion, and the creativity that's needed—if we're to reset the planet—if we're to have any hope of surviving. And if not, then the end truly is already here."

Noah slowly slips to the cool ground, needing to touch something solid beneath her. She imagines she feels the already-dead under its surface. Cold. Unmoving. Unalive. She also senses the Mother is still with her, but silent now, giving her space to consider without offering comfort or reassurance.

Tears of exhaustion stream down Noah's face and reflect the moonlight. *Can any of it be true?* Noah wonders as she gradually tries to collect herself. *Maybe I really am losing it. It's just... too much. Isn't that what Gil always tried to tell me?*

With her eyes closed, she shakes her head in rhythm with the questions gnawing inside her. *Who do I think I am, anyway? Who does She think I am?*

Atlanta, Georgia, USA (37° F / 3° C)

Jackson Schumer's HOLO-POD, *Common Sense for Real People,* has been anti-environmentalism's biggest megaphone for over ten years. Its five hundred million followers worldwide have turned it into an unstoppable sledgehammer for global economic and environmental policy. No one runs a more aggressive show on behalf of the status quo than Jumpin' Jack Flash.

Marta has been on the show several times. She often appears with her aunt; however, she's also occasionally flown solo when bashing her favorite foil, Noah Greenling. Tonight, she's alone, dressed in black as if in mourning. It's the most chaste she's looked in public since Vivienne Stark anointed her as her successor. After the program ramps up, it predictably reinforces the establishment's position on its prize issues and favorite villains—carried along by the usual schtick of exaggerated disgust and snide remarks—Marta pauses and looks directly at the show's host.

"Jackson, can I speak with your audience on a more personal and sober note?"

"Of course, Marta. The floor's all yours."

Marta's dark eyes become cloudy. Her mouth quivers slightly. Something between grief and rage settles over her pained expression.

"Several weeks ago, my beloved Aunt Vivienne—another important voice of common sense—fell ill and still lies in a medically induced coma. Every time I visit her, I read to her, sit and stroke her hair, massage her arms and hands—just like she did for me when I was a little girl." Marta brushes a tear from her eye. "Let me tell you... it's devastating to see her like that—this once-vibrant woman now looking like Sleeping Beauty. I keep asking myself, what happened? Why her?"

Jackson leans in; his forehead ripples in concern. His voice becomes soft and gentle. "What do you want to say to our friends listening, Marta?"

Her eyes narrow. There's a look of cold vengeance in them now as she glares directly at the HOLO-CAM. "I've recently learned that my aunt's tragic illness wasn't an accident but the work of a global eco-terrorist network. I'm not sure how they did it, but reliable sources tell me it's now believed that a group of well-known climate alarmists are responsible."

"Un-fucking-believable!" Jackson mutters, shaking his head. "Seriously? I hope you're all listening."

Marta nods in agreement with her host. "Everyone's witnessed the public exchange Noah Greenling and I have engaged in the past few years. Though she's obviously naive and misdirected, I've always believed she was a decent human being. I'm sad to say I was wrong. I now believe she's somehow part of this insane group of rebels that engineered my aunt's attack."

Marta takes a long moment to wet her deep purple lips with her tongue. "Noah, if you're listening, shame on you! How low can you go, huh? Are you so desperate that you'll resort to violence against anyone who disagrees with you? Shame on you. This is a very sad day for all of us, Noah. And if I know anything about public opinion, you're finished."

The HOLO-CAM returns to Jackson, who leans back in his swivel chair. He waits for a beat, then pivots toward the camera, looking into it with his practiced expression of rageful dismay.

"What can I say?" he says to the camera. "Haven't we told you before? These eco-nutjobs are crazy! Not just illogical, but dangerous. It sounds to me like the whole movement has become unhinged; I mean, they're trying to arm themselves with an actual green militia! Well, let's turn the old red, white, and blue loose on them and see how they fare against real patriots." Jackson waits a moment, then softens his eyes and jawline and returns his gaze to Marta. "Seriously, we all hope and pray for Vivienne Stark's recovery. While she sleeps, you stand watch over her for us, Marta. And the rest of us, let's do our part to make sure justice is cooked up hot and dished out quickly."

The HOLO-CAM switches off as Marta turns to Jumpin' Jack, flashing him with her wicked little grin. "Thanks for squeezing me in today, Jackson. I think it just may help Noah feel a little global warming herself. Don't you?"

"Agreed. The whole piece was brilliant!" He gloats, licking his beefy lips with his thick, dark tongue. "Do you have to run, or could I tempt you with a drink later?"

"For you, I have time for more than a drink," she purrs, a slow, sly blink showing off her long lashes. "Why don't you drop by my room when you finish?" She puts her hand on his shoulder and leans down to whisper. "We can explore any openings you might have for me in this growing empire of yours."

She stands and leaves without waiting for his response, but she feels the familiar energy of male desire radiating toward her exiting form.

Marta's own HOLO-POD features a similar steady drip of smears and accusations for the next ten days. Each episode offers a breaking new development or alarming insinuation. By the time the series is finished, Noah, Patrick, and Seamus have all been tagged as notorious eco-terrorists, deserving to be headliners on the planet's most wanted list.

The students at the Greenling House are enjoying a relaxing evening together. There's plenty of good wine, all kinds of tasty tapas, and lots of laughter. Despite the group's mood, Noah is subdued, more an observer than a participant. They all know how misrepresented she feels by Marta's public accusations and give her the freedom to either talk about it or be silent. She gets a bit weepy at how understanding they all are but tells them that she just wants to be *part* of things—not the focus of attention.

As the evening continues, the conversation turns to more serious matters—ethical conundrums, intellectual curiosities, or global concerns. Desmond is in the middle of a clenched-fist diatribe against speciesism. Sylvie and Raven lean forward, and Ged nods along, all three engrossed.

"It's not a matter of balance," Desmond says. "It's the same bullshit as the colonial enslavement of my people—in fact, it's even worse because it's more pervasive. Devaluing *any* life is completely arbitrary and totally based on—"

KNOCK... KNOCK... KNOCK.

Desmond's words are suddenly cut short. The group goes quiet and exchanges puzzled expressions. Sylvie gets up to answer the door and calls over her shoulder, "But Des, if there's no biological hierarchy, isn't that contrary to what we see in the evolutionary arc?"

Through the patterned glass of the front door's sidelights, Sylvie sees two men in dark jackets, mirrored sunglasses, and buzz cuts. She's usually a trusting sort, but now her radar goes on high alert. Before answering the door, she turns the house's HOLO-CAM on and directs the feed to Seamus, hoping he'll get the alert and watch. *Can't be too careful with everything that's going on.*

She unlocks and opens the door. "Can I help you?" she asks.

One of the men takes off his sunglasses and seems to make an attempt to offer a warm smile. "Hello, hun. How ya doin'? I'm Josh, and this is Tony. Nice to meet you. Listen, my friend and I used to go to school here. Can you believe it? And we lived in this very house. I don't suppose you could give us a bit of a look for old times, could you?"

Sylvie frowns, her arms crossing as she answers. "Umm... some friends and I are hanging out, so it's not really a great time. Sorry."

"Oh, sure. I get it. Hey, there was some older dude that used to rent it out to us. He was a good guy. I'm kind of embarrassed to admit it, but we owe him some money. We sort of skipped out on him, and now we'd like to make it right."

Sylvie can feel the man's will tightening to get what he wants. She takes her time, thinking carefully about how to answer.

"Do you remember his name?"

"Uh... Wilde. That was it. Seamus Wilde—an Irishman."

Sylvie looks down, nervously clearing her throat. "Umm... we rent from an Asian woman. Sorry. Hey, I got to get back to my friends."

The man's expression turns cold. He stares at Sylvie through lifeless eyes as he slowly puts a hand into his coat pocket. She takes a step back, uncertain what he's reaching for.

He fumbles around, then quickly pulls the hand out and sticks a small white card between them. "Here. Take my card. If he shows up, I can make it worth your while... if you know what I mean," he says, awkwardly winking.

Sylvie quickly snatches it from his hand and closes the door, relieved to have them on the other side. She looks at the simple white card and notices the Fort Meade address. *What was that all about?*

The two men walk back to their rental car. Neither says anything as they get in. The taller man directs the car to start as he looks at his partner.

"Something's up there. I could feel the lies coming off her like burnt toast."

"Burnt toast? Tony, you're such a tool. Why do you say such dumb, stupid stuff like that? Do you just sit around and dream this shit up, or what? Of course, she was lying. But it wasn't like any fuckin' burnt toast," he complains, hitting Tony a little too hard on the back of the head.

"Oww! Now, why'd you do that? You'll mess up my hair," Tony whines, running his hands over his shaved head.

As they drive away, a nondescript, dark car—lights turned off—slowly pulls up from the next block and slips into the spot where Josh and Tony were parked. The man inside turns the car off and lights a cigarette. His narrow eyes slowly turn toward the house. Watching. Waiting. Ready.

Seamus knew the day would eventually come, but he still can't help feeling conflicted over Sylvie's warning. Watching the HOLO-CAM replay, however, convinces him that his time has finally run out. He quickly grabs the evac bag from under the bed and takes one final look around the small apartment he rents under the anonym, Stewart Johns.

There's nothing he's leaving behind that he feels especially attached to, and yet he feels his heart sink. He shrugs, a grin twisting his sober face. *All good things must...* He doesn't bother to finish the thought but cracks the door open, pokes his head out, peeking both ways down the dim hallway. Appearing to be empty, he locks the door and takes the elevator of the Selby down the twenty-two floors for the last time. As he steps out, he furtively scans the near-empty lobby. *All clear.* He tells himself, trying to drum up more confidence than he feels. To be safe, he ducks down a narrow service hallway and exits the highrise through the loading bay out back.

He orders a taxi-bot with the untraceable crypto-Zcash he's hidden. Paying the hefty surcharge for express service, his ride arrives within a minute. While the car's door is still swinging open, he tosses his bag in and quickly follows. Grateful for the privacy and the cab's one-way glass, he gradually begins to relax, his mind able to focus on the escape plan's next steps.

After the fifteen-minute ride, he instructs the car to drop him off in the alley, two blocks north of the Greenling House. Walking cautiously in the shadows, he pauses frequently to scan the area. Other than the soft glow from the moon, there are no lights in the large backyard. *Here goes... now we'll see how safe it is.* Still seeing no one, he quickly descends the broken steps to the basement's outer entrance, unlocks the old door, and enters.

He carefully threads his way through the old furniture, dusty crates, and piles of junk past students have abandoned there. At the bottom of the stairs, he takes a deep breath, uncertain what or who he'll find. Aware that time is fleeting and not on his side, he finally walks softly up the wooden steps and opens the door. As he enters the kitchen, he hears the students' voices—laughing, arguing, teasing. *Good... that sounds normal.*

Venturing further into the kitchen, he quietly opens the fridge, grabs a La Fin du Monde, and then steps into the hearth room. When the group sees him, they stop talking. Sylvie moves closer to Jean to make room for Seamus to sit on the sofa. Subdued greetings are exchanged, and then everyone sits in silence for a few moments.

"*Sláinte,*" he says. The group echoes the refrain. Seamus looks each student in the eye. His gaze displays focus, intensity, and something else. Peace. For a moment, the only sound is the faint *whoosh* from the beer's frothing bubbles after he sets his drink down.

"Well, my friends," Seamus says. "As the saying goes, all good things must come to an end." He picks up the bottle and takes another sip. "I'm afraid my second life has caught up with me. If I were a cat, I'd have seven yet to go! But I don't want to go into too much detail here. And it's best for you to know as little as possible right now." The group exchanges baffled looks. Noah's expression, however, is entirely opaque. She and Sylvie take a brief glance in one another's direction. Noah notices her friend's raised eyebrow but ignores the implied question and quickly turns her attention back towards Dr. Wilde. A radiator somewhere in the house clangs, making everyone jump. When they remember it's just the old pipes expanding, the tension lowers a degree.

"The men who came by earlier are probably agents with the United States NSA. They're looking for me in connection with several possible acts of eco-terrorism." Thick silence descends on the group. They exchange puzzled looks—some have entertained other suspicions, but nothing resembling what this new information suggests.

"As a result, I will be ending my tenure at the university immediately. I've already sent my notification."

Bursts of shock, coupled with low groans of disappointment, ripple around the room. Jean's voice cuts through the noise. "This makes no sense. It's not like you've done anything—" Desmond interrupts, "That's right. Surely you can... surely *we* can fight this. I don't understand why you'd just walk away from everything."

They all nod in agreement, staring at Seamus, confusion written on their young faces. He lets out a long sigh. *That's twice I've had to pull the plug on them,* he chides himself. He feels their solidarity—their shared commitment to the cause—even though they don't understand the full extent of everything he's given himself to.

"I know, I know. I didn't want it to turn out this way—for you *or* for me. But here we are. I'll be disappearing in just a few minutes and..." His voice catches, giving him time to breathe before he continues. "I just can't risk you all being any more connected to me and what I've—"

Shaking their heads, the group tries to dismiss his concern for them.

"I'm really sorry. I'm sorry if any of this ever comes back on you. Sorry for bringing you here and then letting you down. On the upside, your academic programs and scholarships are all in place for the next four years. So don't worry; they won't be revoked. It's up to you whether you want to continue or look for another path."

Noah chimes in, speaking for the group. "Don't worry about us or our futures. We're here because of you. We're here for you and—"

"Thank you, Noah." He smiles tenderly, trying to reassure her he'll be alright. "I know what you're saying. But... it's the least I can do, considering everything."

His sad, gray-blue eyes pool with tears once more. He quickly wipes them with the back of his hand and then turns his attention back to the group. "We're all living on borrowed time now, you know. I'm amazed our planet has limped along as well as it has. I'll keep with the same fight I've always been fighting—just from the anonymity of the margins, now."

He stands unsteadily, taking a moment to find his balance, then walks around the circle and extends a fatherly kiss and a long, tight hug to each of them. Low murmurs can be heard. "Be safe." "Thank you." The short phrases create a soft drumbeat of gratitude. Each one has a trail of tears streaming down their cheeks. Noah, Jean, and Sylvie can't hold back and begin to weep openly. Finally, Seamus steps aside and takes one last glance around the circle. "Goodbye, my friends. You have all come to mean the world to me. I hope and pray for the best for you, whatever lies ahead. And please... take *very* good care of each other."

Before he changes his mind, he quickly disappears down the basement's dark stairs and then out into the night.

The man conceals himself within the big oak tree's shadow. The backyard of the students' house is dappled with the soft light of a clear crescent moon. Seamus quickly starts toward the gate by the alley. Suddenly, a man steps out in front of him, blocking his path.

"Well, if it isn't the professor himself," Merton says, sarcasm dripping from each syllable.

Seamus jumps, startled—then glares, his anger quickly skyrocketing at the sight of the man. "What are you doing here, Merton? Are you stalking me? Get out of my way, you son-of-a-bitch."

"Tsk, tsk, tsk... there you go again, getting all huffy on me. Say, where are you rushing off to in the middle of the night, huh? By the looks of those two goons that visited earlier, I'd say you're in a shitload of trouble. You know, the Chief wanted to let the NSA take care of you for what you did to him and those board members... but somehow, things felt more *personal* to me."

Seamus's narrowed eyes sweep the yard, quickly calculating whether he can make a run for it or if he'll need to fight his way out. Seeing no way around the man, Seamus's fingers stretch and then retract into two readied fists.

"You know," Merton says, "since it's just the two of us—and as you're about to go down for *crimes against humanity*—I'm going to let you in on a little secret." Merton's gaze briefly drifts away, recalling some memory while he takes a few slow steps toward Seamus. "You know all that about your sister—you've got it all wrong. She didn't have an accident. Nah, she was always brighter than you are. But on the day she died, she was distracted by some kid playing too close to the edge of the cliff." Merton pauses to snicker, his laugh low and throaty. "It gave me the perfect chance to sneak over to her gear and—*snip, snip*—slice a couple straps—*just enough* to launch her glider, but not enough to hold. Boom! She went down like a rock. Pity you weren't there to—OOF!"

Seamus crashes into the man's chest. They both go down hard to the ground. Not waiting to catch his breath, Seamus throws a punch into the man's face. The blow lands hard on his cheekbone.

Merton lets loose a loud growl, the pain sharpening his focus. Enraged, he flips Seamus underneath him and presses his knee into his chest. He shoves a hand into his coat pocket and pulls out a broad, silver blade. The movement gives Seamus just enough time to react—grabbing Merton's arm—straining to keep the weapon away from his body. They struggle there for several seconds, their rage seeking to settle who will gain control of the long, polished bowie knife.

Seamus grunts and finally shoves Merton off of him with a giant heave. They both scramble to their knees and then bounce back to their feet. Merton circles him with the knife, slowly waving it in between them. Someone watching would feel they are witnessing some dangerous, primal dance.

Just as Merton initiates a convincing feint, ready to go in for the kill, he hears a sound behind him. Distracted, he takes a quick glance over his shoulder. He barely has time for the shadow of a tall, female figure to register. The moon makes her tight curls look like a radiant, gold halo.

Then, the world spins as the large oak limb she swings crashes into the side of his head. He stumbles, dazed.

Before falling, his ears register the deafening, high-pitched snap overhead. The explosive cracking of the oak's massive limb pierces the night like a gunshot. From the tree's canopy, a wooden projectile plummets—aimed perfectly along its forty-foot trajectory—knocking Merton lifeless to the ground's hardened soil.

The previous morning, Journi was able to move an upcoming segment on Toronto's sewage incinerators to the top of her show's production list. The hope was that the news spot would create a credible cover story for her. Seamus—having received an encrypted warning from a high-level asset at the NSA earlier—anonymously alerted Journi with a coded extraction request on the subreddit thread. As soon as she arrived in Toronto, she went to the Highland Creek Treatment Plant, conducted several hard-nosed interviews, and then said goodnight to her show's ground team.

She made it to the alley of the students' house just before things turned lethal. Now, standing over Merton's crumpled body—sprawled on the ground like some blacked-out drunk—she grabs Seamus's hand and quickly leads him out the back gate. No words are spoken as she opens the rear door of a rented van. He slips in with the evac bag and finds a blanket, water, and energy bars. Still shaking from his clash with Merton, he tries to steady himself, taking a few deep breaths. At the sound of the electric engine's whine, his heart seems to get the message: out of danger, at least for now. He takes a long drink of water, then slips under the blanket and does his best to make himself invisible while Journi drives to wherever she's decided to take them.

❦ ❧ ❦ ❧ ❦ ❧

After checking in with false names at the Le Germain Hotel, Journi and Seamus sit across from one another in the olive-green wing chairs in their room. This is their first chance since their escape to have an actual conversation.

Seamus leans forward and takes hold of both of Journi's hands, caressing them gently. His eyes melt with concern and regret.

"Journi, I hate that I brought you into all this. I never wanted it to turn out this way." He looks away, shaking his head. "Erin would have probably stayed to fight in the open, but here I am, running away. I just hope I'm doing the right thing."

Journi reverses their hands and firmly grasps his. Her copper eyes lock onto his—a fierce fire burns within her loving gaze. "Seamus, protecting yourself *is* the right thing. And don't worry about me. You've got plenty else to think about." She lets go of his hands and then continues energetically. "I've got this. Besides, you know how we journalists roll. To be a good one, you just need to find the story and tell it. But to be *great*, you have to think like a spy—then you can find the story nobody wants told. People usually bury the truth, and you only find it by taking risks. Then you cover your tracks as fast as you can."

She pauses, studying him. A strand of hair trails across the side of his face, covering one eye. She reaches out and pushes it over his ear, then gently strokes his beard, searching his face for a hint to his state of mind. "We both have our part to play," she says, her voice low. "And you've played yours very well. Think about it, though. What's to be gained by them catching you? You're not finished." She leans back, tilts her head, and crosses her legs, intentionally letting her skirt rise and reveal her long legs. "And Seamus, you know what else? *I'm* not finished with you yet, either."

He chuckles at the moment's irony. *I'm running for my life, but my heart melts like butter for this woman.* "Oh, Journi. How in God's name did we get here?" He reaches for her hand again as tears pool in his eyes. "I'm so grateful that... that I need you... I just can't imagine—"

She slips to her knees in front of his chair and puts a finger to his lips. "Shh... it's alright. I know. I know you do." Then, tilting her head upward, she tenderly presses her lips to his and kisses him in the same way she remembers their first kiss—long and soft.

Later, as they lie in bed in the dark, they share themselves as if they may never see one another alive again, holding back no fears, no secrets, and no dreams. Finally, exhausted, they fall into a deep sleep, holding on to each other as if they're in freefall.

London, United Kingdom (37° F / 3° C)

The following day, Journi escorts a disguised Seamus aboard her plane, introducing him as an old friend in need of a quick flight to the UK to see a dying sister. After disembarking, he offers a friendly goodbye to her team— his embrace with Journi communicating that they are definitely not "just old friends." He then quickly disappears into the terminal's swarming sea of humanity.

Two days later, her plane is readied for another take off, having successfully chased down another journalistic piece about London's frightening levels of metal and rubber in its atmosphere. Heart and lung issues have soared over the past decade; their public health rating has plummeted to somewhere between a three and a four on a nine-point scale.

Journi looks out the plane's window, her gaze distant, anxious. She's worried that leaving Seamus alone here in London will soon turn dangerous; if he stays on the streets too long, it could compromise both his physical *and* mental health.

As she mentally replays their final exchange, her tear-filled eyes quickly overflow again. Their goodbye was more abrupt than they would have chosen, but she had the HOLO crew waiting for her. So, she put her game face on and prepared to say goodbye to the man she loves as if he were some stranger.

Seamus stood behind her in line at a coffee shop, outfitted in a soiled and sloppy disguise. Journi's crew waited in the van for her. She closes her eyes, re-experiencing the moment. How he gently reaches his left hand beside hers. How he softly intertwines their fingers in a way those outside can't see. They both act as if they are softly speaking into their HOLOs so that no one can hear.

"Seamus, I can't keep doing this. You know that I love you, don't you?" Her voice cracks as she asks it, more a reminder than an actual question.

"Of course, I know," he whispers back, tightening his hold on her hand. "And I love you so very much. I hate this chapter of our lives... if things around us weren't so damn bleak, I'd just let it all burn down... just so I could be with you."

The next few minutes were a blur. She moved to the head of the line, picked up her coffee, and slowly brushed past him, squeezing his arm as she left.

Now, sitting here on the airport runway, her tears of worry easily merge with the tears she cried as she walked out the door and left him behind.

PART SIX

Episode 42: Extinction is Forever
HOLO-POD Hosted by Noah Calhoun-Greenling

"The Inuit people struggle to survive tonight. After living for thousands of years in what we now call Alaska, these small, dispersed tribes are fighting for their lives. Recent estimates indicate that over seventy percent of their population has already succumbed to an unknown and deadly strain of anthrax. It's believed the bacteria was frozen in the Hubbard Glacier near Disenchantment Bay. Due to the glacier's degradation from the earth's rising temperature, the previously unknown anthrax virus has now entered its surrounding waters.

"The Inuits' diet consists largely of harbor seals, which we now know are infected with this lethal bacteria. Currently, there is no known cure."

Spring 2061

Dallas, Texas, USA (102° F / 33° C)

Marta sits quietly in the ICU at Southwestern Hospital. Her tired, anxious eyes survey her aunt's lifeless frame. The sound of hissing oxygen whispers incessantly like white noise. The rhythmic chirp of machines rudely intrudes on the room's sterile oppressiveness. She's been in Dallas for nearly a month, helplessly sitting with her aunt every morning and afternoon. A few days after Viv collapsed, Helmut was forced to return to Bonn to manage some urgent government business, reluctantly leaving his daughter to care for her.

Marta disconnects the HOLO, having read a chapter from her aunt's favorite book, *Atlas Shrugged.* As the screen dissolves, her gaze descends to her hands, noticing how she rubs her fingers back and forth, as if physically trying to solve a complex problem. As she watches the movement, a bitter cast twists her tight lips, distorting her flawless mask.

She steps into the hallway and initiates a HOLO to the Chief. There's no answer, so she leaves a message.

"*Gutten Tag*, Mr. Chief. It's Marta. I'm here with Vivienne at the hospital. *Danke* for stopping by last week. I will let her know you visited when she wakes up. It will mean so much to her. Unfortunately, these doctors don't seem to be making much progress. I don't know if it's their ineptness or if, as I suspect, it's something else. You said I could ask for anything I needed as I care for her. Well, I think I know what I need. But it's a bit... well... sensitive. I'd prefer to discuss it in person. If that can be arranged, I would be ever so grateful. *Danke*, sir. I'm in your debt." She disconnects the HOLO and marches down the hall, her face steeled with determination. *It's time to force these eco-rats out of hiding.*

London, United Kingdom (94° F / 34.5° C)

Seamus rises early after sleeping in a dirty second-hand tent in Waldorf Park. The homeless encampment along the Thames River is occupied by a few hundred others who are all sleeping rough for their own reasons. He knows his lengthening beard and greasy hair have helped him blend in—he just hopes it's enough to keep him unnoticed until he figures out what to do next. He's used to shifting for himself after his years in the Amazon, but this is different. His mounting sense of loneliness and vulnerability these past few weeks is beginning to take root as a slowly-creeping paranoia. Even though he's still in his right mind—more or less—he's tempted to reach out to one of his eco-cells. But as soon as he considers the idea, he immediately dismisses it. *One of us in danger is more than enough.*

As he slogs along a street curb bulging with a decade's worth of trash—his spirit heavy with gloom and hopelessness—for some reason, *Paradise Lost* by Dante comes to mind. It feels like the first lucid thought he's had in days. *That's what's happened,* he tells himself. *No—that's what's happening. We're losing paradise.*

He shakes his head at the absurdity of humanity's recklessness. His brain feels sluggish, fueled only from a bite of cold fish and the few soggy chips he found left in a bag by the curb. After he wolfs down the tiny bits of food—fingers licked, the grease wiped on his pants—he sits down on the curb. Soon, his heavy head lolls forward from bored drowsiness. As he drifts further and further into his inner twilight, two words wink like faint twin stars.

NEW EDEN

Where did that come from? Seamus lifts his head—eyes still closed—and turns the phrase over in his mind. *New Eden... New Eden... New Eden.* He slowly stands and looks up at the dirty London sky, quietly repeating the words to himself. It's as if the phrase is a flare, or a reorienting beam from a lighthouse in the fog—giving him the first flicker of direction since leaving Toronto.

Still uncertain about what the phrase means, he starts walking—his thoughts gradually uncoiling—feeling more energized than he's been for days. Stopping and starting at random spots along the way to catch his breath, he eventually wanders into an alley. Still hungry, he climbs up the side of an overflowing trash bin to look for a few scraps of something to eat.

As he rummages around, he spots a doll, soiled and half-clothed. He picks it up and gently turns it over—her hair is matted, and one arm is ripped off at the shoulder. He reads the words "My Forever Friend" embroidered over the heart on the stained cloth chest.

His hands begin to shake. His breathing quickens. Suddenly, his mind is filled with an image of some little girl delighting at the sight of this humble, broken figure in his hands. Soon, he finds himself lost—carried away—feeling an unbidden connection to the doll.

I wonder where home was for them. He imagines the child playing with the doll in her room, and everything he's lost over the years is suddenly dredged up. Tears spring from his bloodshot eyes and trail down his rough, dirty cheeks.

"That's what I need," he mutters. "A place to call home again."

He jumps down from the dumpster, still holding the doll. For a moment, he holds it close to his face and looks into its sparkling eyes. Eventually, he brings it to his chest and sways back and forth, looking like another disturbed vagrant to those passing by.

He drops to sit on the curb with the small figure in his lap. *New Eden... home... a little girl... an abandoned doll. Does it mean anything?* He shakes his head vigorously. *Maybe I am losing it.*

He sits in silence for several minutes, staring as a pair of mice scavenge for crumbs, and then suddenly disappear, like magic, into a tiny hole. *Hmm...* Something slowly surfaces through his fogbound memory. *The Cradle of Humankind—that forgotten ancient site near the Sterkfontein Caves in South Africa. A cradle—that's where home can begin again.*

He stands up, still holding the doll, and begins to move, smiling to himself as he saunters out of the alley's grungy dead end. "The Cradle of Humankind... my God... how perfect!"

He continues walking, reviewing a strand of memories with Erin that he hasn't thought about since she died. He can see it now, though—like a scene from a silent movie. Beyond the World Heritage Site at Sterkfontein are the seemingly endless rolling grasslands, crisscrossed with innumerable unnamed streams and rivers that still conceal never-mapped caves within the limestone banks and fissures.

When Erin and I explored it, we were still in uni together. She was such a daredevil then—so alive, so free. He shakes his head, snapping himself back to the present. *If—and it's a big if—I can find that one godforsaken cave—it could be an ideal place. Not to just disappear to—it would be the perfect place to retool for whatever comes next.*

Seamus's eyes drift down to the doll in his hands. Her smudged, round face cradles bright eyes that—for the briefest of moments—resemble his sister's. He sighs as if about to form a prayer. *Now, Erin, all I have to do is figure out how to get there.*

Findhorn, Scotland, United Kingdom (79° F / 26° C)

Noah's green eyes pan the distant rocky horizon through the large window of her spartan room. The morning mist rises from the richly colored gardens, releasing an earthy blend of soil, flowers, and vegetation. She rubs her hands absentmindedly on the rocking chair's smooth wooden arms. It wasn't that long ago, but she vividly remembers her body's unexpected announcement—the soreness in her breasts, the sudden nausea, the food cravings that were strange, even for her. It was as if every bodily function instantly understood what her mind would need time to accept.

"I'm carrying a child," she whispers. Her long, slender fingers gently rub her belly in slow, leisurely circles. "Not just *a* child... *two of them*," she says— still trying to convince herself it's real.

Findhorn's organic farm and monastic community has been the perfect place for her to recalibrate after dropping out of school. She's grateful Tessa reminded her of the farm's incredible history. The monks' practice of faithfully tending the land and co-creating with their non-human counterparts has been inspiring. Her memory of watching the HOLO-VID of Dorothy MacLean—Findhorn's foundress—still bolsters her confidence that other humans have also been directly addressed by vegetable and animal consciousness.

She slowly rocks back and forth in the bentwood rocker in her small room, lost in a string of recollections. *Seamus disappearing... Patrick's sudden trip to the Amazon... the Green Man's visitation... Marta's attacks and accusations. I hope I did the right thing... waiting to tell anyone.*

So much has happened in such a short amount of time, and her soul has desperately needed the chance to catch up with her body, to what's now taken root within her. Despite the list of unanswered questions, Noah feels gently nurtured in the arms of this community that Dorothy gave birth to. At night, she sleeps soundly in the simple eco-village. During the day, she strolls through acres rich with fruit trees, vegetable gardens, and colorful flowers.

Surrounded by so much generativity, Noah gradually acclimates to the reality of what's happening inside her, as well as her growing sense of responsibility. Minute by minute, the realization goes deeper: she is on the incredible journey of carrying another's life inside her.

Late one morning, just before the sun approaches its zenith, a silver Land Rover pulls into the gravel parking space in front of Findhorn's community center. The monks are heading in for lunch. The one named Fletcher notices the car and approaches tentatively. He's been anxiously watching for them, reminded of the story of the prodigal son. However, he feels that the moment resembles more the son's return to his prodigal father.

"Hello, pilgrims," he says, greeting the couple with his thick Scottish brogue. "Welcome to Findhorn Monastery." Patrick and Shea step out of the car, stretching their arms and legs. Shea exchanges a warm greeting with the short, middle-aged monk but notices that Patrick's approach is a bit awkward.

"Hello, Da. Bet you're surprised to see the likes of me," he mumbles.

Fletcher turns to face his son and swallows hard. His tender eyes search Patrick's face. "Nah, Noah told me," Fletcher replies, trying to disguise the depths of his emotions. "I've been looking forward to seeing you. Come on in. Here, let me help with your bags. There's someone inside who'll be wanting to have a look at you."

The pair walks through the main hall's large wooden doors. They follow Fletcher's lead and remove their shoes, setting them beside several neat rows of well-worn tennis shoes and boots. Patrick and Shea stand on the smooth dark planks of the floor and look around them—there are groupings of oversized furniture scattered in small nooks, colorful fabric art concealing the old rustic walls. And best of all, the aroma of freshly brewed coffee drifts down a hallway, mixing with the buzz of overlapping conversations and clanging tableware. Somehow, the monks have created a hospitable hominess within the large, functional space. Despite Patrick's mixed feelings about seeing his da, he quickly feels the genuine love of the community that works and lives here.

Noah, tucked into a small alcove looking out over the gardens, reads a collection of Wendell Berry poems. She lingers over a few lines of the one titled "Birth."

> *It's the old ground trying it again.*
> *Solstice, seeding and birth — it never*
> *gets enough. It wants the birth of a man*
> *to bring together sky and earth, like a stalk*
> *of corn. It's not death that makes the dead*
> *rise out of the ground, but something alive*
> *straining up, rooted in darkness, like a vine.*

Her thoughts are interrupted by the sound of footsteps approaching from behind her. Setting the book down in her lap, she looks over her shoulder and sees the two smiling faces she's been waiting for. She jumps up and knocks the book onto the floor, squealing.

"Oh my God, you're here! Finally! I've been sick, just waiting for you to get here." She hugs Patrick first, and then Shea, stored-up tears quickly surfacing.

Shea feels the slight roundness of Noah's middle when they embrace.

She takes a step back and glances down at her friend's belly.

"What? What's this?" Shea whispers tentatively.

Noah half-smiles, barely shaking her head.

Shea chuckles, her eyes dancing as if beaming her blessing.

Noah turns back to Patrick and takes his hand in hers. "Come outside. I have something I want to tell you."

He smiles back, an eyebrow raised. "Okaaaay." He draws the word out, not entirely sure about what's happening. They leave Shea talking with Fletcher about Findhorn's gardens and their guest accommodations.

Noah leads Patrick along the winding gravel path to a well-situated bench in the flower garden. The two plum trees they sit under host a pair of robins and chaffinches. The birds' songs serve as a welcome reminder that despite humanity's persistent abuse, the world still offers its abundant resistance in beauty.

They brush the tree's pink blossoms off the bench and sit beside each other, knees touching. Noah holds Patrick's questioning gaze—her eyes soft but direct—then chooses her words slowly. "So, I realize I've been a bit cryptic when we've HOLOed—"

"A bit?" Patrick interrupts, a slight smirk and a sparkle in his eyes showing that he's enjoying this.

"Now let me finish," she chides. "I've needed some time to accept— that's not quite right... to acclimate to something that's happened. Something that's *happening* to me." Noah takes a breath and then continues. "Do you understand what I'm saying?"

Patrick shakes his head, exchanging his smile for a concerned frown. "I'm afraid I don't. You've lost me. What are you—"

Noah presses on, not waiting for his question. "I really don't know how else to tell you this, but Patrick, I'm pregnant." She halts—full stop— and looks directly into his warm, brown eyes that widen at the sudden announcement. "I mean, *we're* pregnant. With twins!"

She waits, watching as the revelation washes over Patrick's body—his breathing deepening, his expression giving way to wonder, and his sloped shoulders acknowledging the call to surrender.

Finally, he breaks the silence. "Wow. I didn't see that coming." He pauses. Noah holds her breath, anxiously waiting for him to continue. "I actually thought you might have decided to join the monks here. Sorry—not the time to joke. But... I'm a bit speechless. How are you—"

"Don't worry about me," Noah interrupts. "I just need to know how this is hitting you and what you're thinking. I've had time to make sense of it. And I know it's a lot just to blurt out as soon as you get here, but I couldn't wait anymore."

He takes her hands in his and holds her anxious gaze. "No, that's alright. I'm glad you told me straight off. I'm just kind of stunned right now. I don't know what I thought it would be like to be together again, but... well, this wasn't it. I'm kinda feeling like... *holy shit*, you know?" He pauses and looks up at the sky, his jaw visibly kneading its muscles. He runs his fingers through his tousled hair. "I mean, beyond the obvious, how will this affect you and your future? Or me... or us?"

Noah reaches up and brushes a strand of hair that the wind has blown across his face. "I don't know," she responds softly. "What do you want it to mean?"

Patrick looks down as their fingers intertwine again. "I know I told you a few things about Ma's letter to me and her marriage to Da. There's a lot more to tell you, but it can wait. This is about you. About us—you, me and them." His eyes are misty when he raises his head, glancing first at Noah's middle and then at her sympathetic smile. "I feel like I see more clearly than ever what I didn't get. And if.. I mean, *since*... I'm going to be a da myself, I want to do it differently. I want to be there 100% for you and for them. I just hope I'll know how."

Noah's eyes fill with tears as she watches Patrick's questions blend into an earnest resolve to be a good father to their children.

"Whatever we have to learn, we can learn it together," she whispers. "I want you... and I want these two little ones to be my family." She leans her head onto his shoulder and takes his arm to wrap it around her. He kisses the top of her head and closes his eyes, breathing in the honeyed fragrance of pink blossoms.

The following day, Fletcher notices Patrick in the middle of the flower garden, seated on a bench facing a fountain. The birds sing while the bees and butterflies are busy sampling the various blooms and blossoms.

At the same time, Noah happens to be looking out her window and sees Fletcher moving towards Patrick—her breath catches. *Oh, my. Already? I'm not sure Patrick's quite ready for this yet.* She begins to rub her belly nervously as she watches. She's torn. She wants to look on, to stand watch. But instead, she closes the curtain and walks away, letting the two have this moment alone.

Fletcher approaches his son and asks if he can sit down.

"Of course. I was kind of hoping you'd find me here," Patrick answers.

They sit in silence for a while, watching the serene surroundings, both feeling the moment's importance. It's as if time slows down to protect whatever needs to be said or felt between them. A collage of moments glide in and out of Patrck's consciousness—his da's absence felt more than remembered—the baby spider monkey he alone rescued from a green anaconda and raised to release back into the jungle—the treehouse village he constructed in the canelón grove, admired only by himself—the E.A. Robinson medal he was awarded at graduation with no family to celebrate with. Each frame displays a personal milestone in which he is the solitary figure.

"Son," Fletcher says at last. "I don't even know if it's okay to call you that, but... um... Patrick, I want you to know how very, very sorry I am for all the hurt we—the hurt *I've* caused you. Your mother and I loved each other, but we weren't really cut out to be married. That may sound like an excuse—and I suppose it is—but we were married to two different visions then. After you came along, you helped us find a shared vision for a while— caring for you, providing for you. But somehow, it was never enough for *us*."

Fletcher wipes his shiny forehead with a wadded-up handkerchief and then continues. "Your ma was completely sold out in her fight for the environment. Honestly, she barely had time for me." He shakes his head. "It was as if she was part of some secret army that demanded total allegiance from her. And me, well, I was even more selfish. I couldn't help chasing another buck, another promotion, or grand opportunity. As I rose in my company, I traveled more and more, living out of suitcases more than I was sleeping at my own home. For both of us, trying to return to a life together just became too hard, too painful. Frankly, it was just too much damn work. So we just quit trying."

Patrick's been staring at the multi-colored gravel at his feet while his da speaks. Though his face is inscrutable, Patrick forcefully expels the trapped air from his lungs whenever his da says something about his ma.

"Your ma," Fletcher continues, "she was always a better mother to you than I was as a father. So when we decided to divorce, I felt it would be best for you if I just disappeared." Patrick starts shaking his head as his da speaks. "I sent money and birthday presents, hoping they'd make up for my leaving. I know now that was wrong—even selfish—but at the time, I felt like I was doing you both a favor."

A grimace seizes Fletcher's face as he drops his head, squinting his eyes as if praying, or trapping his tears, or both. "I wish I could go back and do it all over. I wish I'd worked harder to get to know you. I was afraid—can you believe it? I was afraid of my own son. I felt like seeing you would force me to acknowledge how big a failure I was." Fletcher stops and wipes his nose. "I know now I was only thinking about myself. But... it felt like if I saw you, I'd just... I don't know... disintegrate or..." His words trail off and become inaudible.

The two men raise their heads, each considering the other. Sorrow twists the loose flesh of Fletcher's face. Suddenly, Patrick's eyes ignite with decades of unexpressed fury.

"Da, that's so stupid!" he blurts out. "You should've known how much I wanted to see you." Shaking his head, his voice drops, quiet and low. "I wish you had thought about how much I wanted to know you, even though I was so pissed at you that honestly... sometimes I wished *you* were dead—that *you* would've died instead of Ma." Patrick takes several deep breaths, trying to keep his emotions in check.

"I know, Son. I know." Fletcher responds tenderly, putting a hand on Patrick's knee and then pulling it back. "Not reaching out to you was... sorry... *is* the biggest mistake I could have made after all my other failures. I don't expect you to forgive me. Hell, I don't expect you'll even like me. But I *do* want you to know how I truly feel about you. *Whew!*" He exhales sharply, shaking his head after straining with the last words, struggling not to let his tears wash away what he wants to say next—what he *needs* to say next.

"Patrick, I'm sorry for not loving you the way you deserved. I can never make that up to you. I just want you to know how much I respect you. Noah has told me a bit about you during her stay here. You're twice the man I ever was. I just hope that, at some point, you'll let me get to know you better."

There's a calm breeze whispering in the flowers. The two men feel it gently blowing their hair out of place. Patrick looks up and closes his eyes, surrendering to the sun shining down on his face. Something inside him starts to melt. Something that was so defended—that mattered *so much* to him as a boy—slowly dissolves as he sits next to this imperfect man, who is doing his best to right his past sins.

Patrick turns and looks directly into his da's eyes. "Da, I can't understand everything about you or Ma, or your marriage and your life. I feel like I've missed out on so much by losing both of you in such different and painful ways. And yet, somehow... I think I'm alright. I guess... I've been cared for, even as I've tried to figure out how to take care of myself.

"I don't want to live my whole life being angry toward you. I've seen that play out in some of my mates' lives. It's just not a good way to go." Patrick pauses and takes a deep breath. "You see, I know what I *don't* want. But thinking about you... or us... I'm not sure what I *do* want. I don't mean that to sound cruel or to keep you at a distance. I just need some time to figure it out. Maybe being here with Noah will help me find out what I want. I don't think it will happen overnight, but maybe... maybe this is a start... okay?"

His da waits a moment and then gently nods, offering a Buddha-like smile. "Of course, of course. That's the way of anything worth waiting for.

Time is on our side now that we've broken the ice."

While Patrick talks with his da, Noah leaves her room to invite Shea for a walk around Findhorn's gardens. She eventually finds Shea by herself, staring out the window in the corner of the cafeteria. Noah watches her friend for a moment, unnoticed, and smiles to herself, although her eyes reveal some uncertainty. Even though they've HOLOed many times since last fall, it's never seemed like the right time to talk about their two letters.

Noah quietly walks up behind Shea and puts her hands on her shoulders. As she leans down, she catches her friend's familiar scent. "Penny for your thoughts," she says, "Wanna go for a walk?" Shea smiles back and nods.

They slowly walk in silence for a few minutes as if they are gradually tuning in to each other. As they climb the small hill behind the garden, Noah interrupts the stillness. "Shea, I know we never really finished what we... what *you* began to say to me. You know... how you feel about me and everything. It's just... we've always been such good friends, and these past few months have been filled with so many new things." Noah sighs loudly and then continues. "I don't know. I've just been in such a muddle trying to figure it all out, and without you here... I just sort of let it all go. I'm sorry."

Noah senses Shea's pace slowing, eventually coming to a complete stop. She turns and looks at Noah, trying to conceal everything she's feeling, but her eyes convey a mixture of hurt and sadness. They stand, studying one another for a moment. Then Shea reaches her hand out. Tears begin to gently roll down her cheeks.

"My dear, sweet Noah. I feel so conflicted. I know you didn't mean to, but... not hearing from you was really hard. I felt so... vulnerable... so scared I'd done something wrong—you know me! I know I was the one to put myself out there, but—"

"Oh, Shea," Noah interrupts as she reaches up to wipe the tears from

Shea's face. "I've made a complete mess of things. I've been such a rotten friend."

The two face one another in silence for a moment. Shea's lips quiver as she takes a few shallow breaths. "Thanks for saying that, Noah. It's been so hard not being together to talk through everything." Shea halts and then continues—her expression earnest, her words measured. "I bear the burden—and it's a fine one to carry. It's just... love. It's just... you've always been there for me. I lean on you—and that can get confusing. But while you were gone, I started to see that you lean on me, too. We need each other, Noah. We both know that."

Noah brushes a long wisp of red hair from her face and begins to cry as well—tears of regret mingled with those of love. And something else—joy. As she studies her friend's face, she no longer sees an insecure teenage girl but a strong and secure young woman. She's always considered Shea her confidant and friend, but now, she feels her weight, equal to her own—a new groundedness in her. *My one true friend. You've always had my back, always stood by me—no matter what.*

Shea stretches her arms out and leans in to hug Noah. "Don't worry," Shea whispers in Noah's ear. "I'll be okay. It may take some time, but we'll figure this whole thing out. We always have. Okay?"

"Oh, Shea. If I lost you, I don't know what I'd do. You've always been there when I needed you. How do you—" Shea puts her finger on Noah's mouth, interrupting whatever she was going to say. Noah gazes back and nods slowly.

Shea slips her hand into Noah's, and they walk on in silence for a long while. Eventually, they stop and sit on a rough-cut bench under an apple tree rich with blossoms. The branches sway in the afternoon breeze. Shea waits patiently—her friend appears lost in thought. Noah closes her eyes and sighs deeply, weighing whether it's the right time to tell Shea about the visitation of the Green Man in Toronto. She's been treasuring the memory; up to this point, she's kept it to herself. *It seems so crazy, but Shea's heard everything else, and she's still here next to me.* Noah takes a deep breath and launches in before she loses her nerve.

"Okay, so something happened in Toronto…"

When Noah finishes recounting what happened—first with her and the Green Man, then with her and Patrick—Shea sits back, looking a bit wide-eyed but still present. Noah continues. "Somehow, I think the Green Man had something to do with me getting pregnant. That's what it seems like, right? I'm not sure. I know it sounds unbelievable, but something tells me I'm right. I think I'll know after they're born."

Shea looks out to the distant garden, the gentle hill falling away from where they sit. "Whew," she whispers, taking time to collect her thoughts. "I know you've had some pretty crazy things happen with nature and everything, but this… this is a whole lot to take in, girl."

Noah chuckles and nods. "I've thought about it, Shea. A lot." She reaches out and takes Shea's hands into her own. "And what I do know is that I'll need help. Lots of it. So here's what I'd like to ask you. I've watched Ma raise twins by herself. I mean, I've been on the receiving end of it. It's no picnic. It's all hands on deck." She stops, her eyes serious and level as she looks at Shea. "So, I want *you* to help Patrick and me raise these little ones. I don't know what it will all look like, exactly. But I'm sure we can figure it out as we go. I think *that's* what's meant to be. I think that's what *needs* to be. And I'd like to do this *with you*. And not just like a godmother or an auntie, but really do this… together… completely." Noah's voice slowly breaks off. "But maybe I've messed it all up. I don't know—"

"Noah, stop it," Shea says. "You and I will be okay. But, *whoa*! This feels big… really big. And complicated."

"Yeah, I know it does. If you need some time to think about it, I get it. I've had a little more time than you to get used to the idea of me being a ma." Noah pauses, her energy quickly rebounding. "But seriously, what do you think? You up for raising a couple of little ones together?"

Shea shakes her head. "What do *I* think? I think you're *crazy*. But what's new, you weirdo?" She pauses, weighing Noah's request. "I do have *a lot* of questions. And there's a bunch of logistical stuff we'll have to figure out. But hey—since I don't have any other plans—I'll think about it." She shrugs her shoulders, a smile playing at the corners of her mouth. "So what will you call me—your *Shea-Nanny-Gan*?" Noah slugs her in the arm, laughing. "Ouch! That hurts."

Noah ignores the complaint. "No, silly. We'll come up with something better than that. How about *the Green Goddess*?"

"Ha! Well, I'll just have to add that to my new sleeve," Shea answers, pointing to an empty spot on her arm next to a rather handsome scimitar-horned oryx. They look knowingly at each other, the hurt and regret gone for the moment. And then the two break out in giggles like the girls they once were.

"We'll figure it out when we need to," Noah says confidently. "We always do." Noah pulls Shea to her feet. Arm in arm, they walk down the hill like they always have: together.

Later that night, after the monks have sung Compline, Noah and Patrick stroll back to Noah's room. He quietly closes the door behind them while she quickly kicks off her shoes. They look at each other and exchange weary smiles that say, *alone at last*. Both drop into one of the low-slung wooden rocking chairs in front of the large open window. A unified sigh escapes both their lungs, signalling how weary they are from swimming in their separate emotional waterfalls—Noah and Shea recalibrating their hearts and lives in whatever this new chapter becomes—Patrick and his da attempting to narrow the physical and relational distance that has widened over the years.

Even though they keep yawning, Noah launches in and tells Patrick about finding out she was pregnant and then coming to terms with it. Patrick listens earnestly, without interrupting. His calm demeanor assures her he's already started accepting the surprise.

When she's done talking, Noah moves from the chair she's been sitting on and lies back on her bed—several pillows propped there for her head. Patrick joins her and sits at the foot of the bed and begins to rub her feet with his strong hands.

"Mmm... that feels heavenly. Don't stop," she purrs. He moves on and massages her ankles and calves while she continues. "You know, I haven't even told my ma or da yet. I've been waiting to tell you first."

He slides up beside her, kissing her rounded tummy, then takes her hand. "Thank you. I never told you this, but I've always wanted to be a da—I just didn't know it would be this soon. Don't get me wrong—I'm thrilled. There are still a lot of questions and thoughts running around in my mind, but those can wait." He quickly props up on an elbow and blurts out, "Hey, let's HOLO-CON your ma and let her know she's going to be—"

Noah turns toward him and puts a finger on his lips. "I love your enthusiasm, really—but it's too late tonight. Let's sleep on it and talk with her tomorrow. Okay?"

Patrick grins at her, nodding his head, and then rolls onto his back. Noah repositions herself to lay her head on his chest. "So, *Father Wilde*—tell me about your big Amazon trip."

"Father Wilde?"

"That's right—has a nice ring to it, don't you think? If I'm going to be Mother Greenling, then you better get used to it!" She turns, raising her head towards his and kisses him playfully on the nose, then lays her head back on his chest. "Your turn. Tell me what happened while you were away."

He launches in, telling her everything he can remember—the journals, the folder of eco-cells, and the letter his ma left for him—only taking a breath to wipe an occasional tear from his eye. Noah's eyes soften with tenderness as she takes in how big this was for him.

As he finishes, he rolls over to sit up and unfastens a satchel that leans against the bed. Noah eyes him with curiosity as he carefully pulls out the Green Book and gently places it in her hands—her small baby bump pressing its edge.

"Noah, I can't make much sense of my ma's writing here. I know how important it was to her. But for some reason, I feel it's not meant for me. I'm not sure, but... I think she meant it for *you*—or someone she imagined being *like* you."

Noah sits up and rubs her fingers across the leather cover. It vibrates faintly underneath her touch. Patrick feels it too, like a frisson between them and what's in the book. She opens it to the first page and thumbs through several more. Erin's artful penmanship speaks to Noah even before she reads the words.

She carefully turns to the last page. The final words are written in letters that look like ancient Irish runes. *I've seen these before. What does Da always say about the old scripts? An image without an image.*

The writing's literal meaning is beyond her, but somehow—just like the vibrations she experiences in nature—she understands what it's saying—the words of some divination taking shape now as words. *The birth of two who exchange differing hearts shall usher in a new epoch.*

She gently closes the book, lost in her thoughts. *Could this be about these two little ones growing inside me?* A crooked pout rests on her lips as she casts a brief, sidelong glance at Patrick. She senses that—at least for now—this knowledge is for her, and her alone.

"This is an unbelievable treasure," she whispers. "You know that, don't you? More than that, it's a... I don't know... a fulcrum. It just might... it *will* help shift what's out of balance." Her fingers continue tracing the book's edges. Suddenly, she doubles over, gasping as a pang of horror drills into her breastbone. She shuts her eyes tight.

FLASH. *It's Erin... oh no... watch out!* In a split second, Noah watches as Patrick's ma launches her hang-glider from a cliff and then falls like a stone—her lifeless body crumpling on the jagged outcroppings below. FLASH. A grizzly scene blankets a darkened, blood-red field. Noah has come to accept the burden of immense grief and striving against non-human injustice. *But... these bodies... they're human.* In silhouette, a solitary, upright figure—surrounded by creatures of all sizes—picks its way through acres of carnage slick from both human and non-human remains.

Patrick's head snaps toward her—alarm written on his face. "Noah! What's wrong?"

When she finally is able to find her voice again, she whispers, "My God, people have died for this book." Noah stretches her eyes open, tears trailing their way down to her chin. She stares at Patrick—her chest heaving with effort to catch her breath—wishing she could unsee the gruesome vision.

"And I'm afraid many more will die because of it."

Laois County, Ireland (89° F / 32° C)

A young woman closes the door of a black SUV and walks alone up a path densely lined with trees. Her purple-and-orange hair falls to her shoulders. A Yankees baseball cap and oversized dark sunglasses conceal her angular cheekbones and delicate features. A fake tan and baggy clothes complete the disordered disguise.

Bird song surrounds her as she approaches the clearing that holds the humble berm hut. For a moment, she pauses and smiles at the joyous cacophony. She hears someone whistling as a hand saw rasps through soft wood. Following the sound around the corner, she sees a big man hunched over a rough table, lost in his craft.

He looks up and flinches, startled to see someone staring at him. He recovers quickly, his open face widening with a welcoming smile.

"Hello, my young lassie. You're a bit off the beaten track. You lost or just out for a bit of a ramble on this fine morning?"

Marta returns his smile and laughs, the sound a bit too forced. "A bit of both, Mr. Greenling. This is quite the little paradise you have here. I'm Noah's friend from uni. She's told me so much about you. I'm just taking some time off to see the sights. When she found out I was going to be nearby, she told me I should drop in and say hi. So, here I am!" She shrugs her shoulders and waits for him to respond.

Aiden inspects her for a brief moment. "Well, I'm glad you did," he answers, putting down his saw and wiping his hands on his pants. "I haven't talked with her for quite a while. I get most of my news from her ma, you see. Come in. Let me get you some tea. Or maybe something stronger—if you'd care to have a wee nip of some Irish whiskey with me."

"Oh, I don't want to bother you, Mr. Greenling."

"Shush, no bother. Time for me to take a bit of a break anyway. And call me Aiden. What's your name, Lassie?"

"Oh, sorry. I'm Judith."

"Well, nice to meet you, Judith. So, what will it be? Tea or a splash of what we Irish call the water of life?"

"How can I turn that down? Just a small taste, please."

She follows him through the low door, watching him duck as he enters. The smell that greets her is a mixture of smoked earth and male muskiness—not unpleasant, but not exactly civilized, either. The whole scene strikes her as a romantic nod to a bygone era.

He rummages around a sparse corner that serves as the kitchen and returns with a bottle and two glasses. They sit in a pair of large rocking chairs. Aiden pours a healthy splash of copper-colored liquid into each glass and hands one to her.

"*Sláinte*," he says, tipping his glass toward hers.

As they raise their glasses to take a sip, three masked men rush through the open door. One shouts, "Get down on your fuckin' knees. Now! No funny business." The tallest one holds a pistol and aims it at the big man.

Marta jumps up—knocking the whiskey to the floor—and steps away, quickly moving beside the others. Aiden looks at her, confused. One of the men punches him in the stomach and then roughly pushes him to the ground.

"Ow!" Aiden grunts. "What's going on?" Gasping for air, he struggles to speak. "Judith... What's this all about?"

Marta sneers back at him, letting out a low snicker as she shakes her head. "You should ask your daughter and her boyfriend."

Aiden looks confused, and then angry. He struggles, trying to rise to his feet, but the two men roughly push him back down, and he lands face-first onto the dirt floor. They fasten his wrists behind his back with zip ties. Marta catches a glimpse of one of the men's tattoos—a faded, squid-like sea monster. She puzzles for a moment over its meaning, but her thoughts are quickly interrupted by the muffled sound of tires approaching the hut—signaling it's time to leave.

The man with the gun jams the barrel into their captive's stomach and forces him to his feet, shoving him toward the door. Aiden groans—still catching his breath after the gut punch—then reluctantly complies, too shocked to put up a fight. As he moves through the door, he looks over his shoulder and sees the young woman and another man battering the furniture he's made over the years. They haphazardly toss about the few books and simple possessions he's stored on shelves and drawers.

Aiden is crammed into the car's backseat, hearing more smashing of wood and glass coming from inside his hut. The car door shuts, and his sad eyes stare out the darkened window, watching as Judith exits the hut, her fists clenched, her mouth scowling with angry resolve.

A Ducati two-seater roars up to the hut, its engine piercing the final remnants of Aiden's peaceful paradise. Marta—not bothering to look toward the car that now imprisons Noah's father—quickly moves to the motorcycle, hops on behind its driver, and they rocket away through the narrow green path.

Dallas, Texas, USA (112° F / 44° C)

Merton steps out of Vivienne's hospital room, where she still lies in a coma, oblivious to everything around her, to accept the encrypted HOLO from Smack.

"Hey, buddy. What took you so long? Everything go okay?"

"Hello to you too, Merton. You're becoming more and more like the old man."

Merton sighs in frustration. "Come on, Smack. You know what it's like—cooling your heels, waiting for a status report. Besides, this one's personal. And you're late."

"Alright. Gotcha. Yeah, the package is in long-term storage. Everything went as planned. Skip found some local muscle—a kid and his old man who apparently had a score to settle. The only hitch was with the kid. After he and Lady M drove off on the bike, he pulled off the road and tried to pressure her into some... unwanted horizontal recreation. Skip got her emergency call, caught up with them, and then made him and his old man walk back to whatever snake hole they crawled out of."

Merton becomes aware he's been holding his breath and lets out a long exhale. "Good work, man. I knew you'd come through. And you know what? The little prick is lucky it was one of yours there instead of me. I'd have made it so every time he reached for his little boy flute, he'd remember me and Mr. Bowie."

"Well damn! Now *I* wished you'd been there." Smack snickers. "Don't worry. We've got it covered. The package isn't going anywhere."

Merton half-smiles at the other man's image. "Thanks. I'll keep you posted. It could be a while. Hell, it could be forever if it doesn't work."

Smack nods. "Cheers, mate. For Viv's sake, alright? I hope this works. Let me know if you need anything else."

The HOLO image evaporates, leaving Merton alone in the hall, rocking back and forth, rhythmically knocking the back of his head on the wall. THUD. *It should have been me, damnit.* THUD. *I can't let this...* THUD. Before the heartache of losing Viv completely undoes him, he closes his eyes. THUD. And dissociates into the vibration and pain his skull inflicts on the wall.

Dublin, Ireland *(89° F / 32° C)*

It's after midnight, and Gil is alone in the phytology lab of the EBI— Exploratory Biotech Institute. He's worked by himself here before, but tonight's the first time he's been assigned to calibrate the lab's complex network of VCI—vegetal connectivity instruments. Gil smiles to himself as he gets started—being entrusted with the task gives his pride a welcome boost.

This revolutionary technology has demonstrated to his team an immense potential to someday create an OI—organic intelligence— interface. There are even conjectures about the development—or, more accurately, the *detection*—of a "Green-Web": a human-to-plant-to-human network not unlike the emergence of the internet in the latter part of the 20th century.

As he walks into the control room and examines the measurements, his eyes suddenly go wide, alarm bells tripping in his brain. *What the—something's wrong. Something is terribly wrong!* The central panel is lit up in red—the multiple rows of numeric displays that measure a thousand plant's electromagnetic output are all signaling the same thing—a sudden and catastrophic energy incident. *How on Earth is this happening?* The system has multiple redundant breakers to protect the greenhouse's vast organic network from any sudden escalation of electricity. *But this surge is massive... and unnatural... it's not coming from outside... it's coming from the plants... and damned if I know what to do about it.*

Gil's knotted brow reinforces how confused and helpless he feels. Glancing up from the panel, he looks out through the room's glass divider. What he sees shocks him—a thousand plants, each rooted in its own VCI motherboard, writhing back and forth as if in labor. As he watches, they appear to undergo a metamorphosis—reshaping their forms as they rapidly grow into something unfamiliar. The once-motionless organic network is now swaying in unison—lit, as if glowing from within by a deep violet aura.

Gil's heart races while his mind threads a needle between terror and awe. *This is incredible! I shouldn't be able to see any of this... but there it is. The plants are somehow converting invisible EM waves into a visible energy that's radiating outward.*

He forces his attention away from the surreal scene to examine the control panel's primary data generator. It's reporting EM levels they've never witnessed before. He turns on what the team has dubbed the PVT—plant voice translator. A message, if that's what it can be called, begins to come to life through the panel's HOLO.

A chill goes up his spine, experiencing the same eerie feeling he's felt before from the PVT's output. *Is this what Noah hears?* He wonders.

The sound begins with the subterranean thrum from the roots of old timber slowly blending with the mid-range and soprano vibrations of the plants in the next room—frequencies outside the limits of the human ear for millennia.

Until now.

The PVT is soon amplified through the HOLO in front of him—the sounds windlike, the voices dark and low. Gradually, he recognizes words, repeated over and over.

"*We wait... while we groan... we wait... while we groan... we wait... while we groan.*"

Gil frowns. Nothing new there. They've been chanting that for weeks now.

Suddenly, the original phrase is interrupted, and a new chant begins.
"*Now...*
the waiting...
is over."

Findhorn, Scotland, United Kingdom (85° F / 29° C)

Noah strolls in the gardens alone. The early-morning sunshine warms her face, and a gentle breeze carries hints of lavender. She pauses and closes her eyes, inhaling deeply, missing home—missing Ma and Da. Opening her eyes, she notices one of Findhorn's monks bent over, weeding the cabbages. *Oh, good... it's Fletcher.* She quietly approaches him on soft, even steps. Hearing the faint crunch of gravel, he tilts his head and then slowly stands, straightening each vertebra, one by one.

On her first night with the community at dinner, he told her his name means "Arrow Maker." Then he looked at her, sizing her up, and said, "You'll do just fine, lassie. You watch. I'll make an arrow out of you that will go straight to the heart of this old world." Then he winked at her like it was all a big joke.

Later, when she asked him about it, he hemmed and hawed, saying he wasn't really sure. "Sometimes," he whispered as he looked around, "things just pop out of me mouth before I can stop 'em... but they usually come about... even if I don't know what they mean."

"Good morning, Brother Fletcher."

"Hello, me fine lady," he replies in the somewhat old-fashioned way he often speaks to her.

"My dear monk," she plays along, addressing him in the same manner.

"I have a question for you. I have a particular appetite to spend the day with the biggest tree near Findhorn. Can you help me find it?"

"Me dear Noah, girl. Let this old man think for a minute," he answers, scratching his chin. "I think the one you are looking for is the Sitka spruce near the bank of the River Findhorn near Forres. One of my favorites, it is. The tree grows just above Randolph's Leap, a narrow gorge that sometimes traps the Findhorn's waters around the tree's roots and base. I've been told that during a flood in the mid-1800s, the water rose more than fifteen meters. It's hard to imagine the tree surviving, but if you go to visit, you'll see it did! It's a rare tree, indeed. Several years ago, I measured its girth, and it was well over two spans. I'd reckon it soars toward heaven well over seventy-five meters. How's that sound? Will that satisfy me lady's verdant craving?"

She giggles and nods. He cracks a wry grin and says, "Or would you rather know where the monks hide their precious single malt?"

She elbows him, then rubs her belly. "You know I can't drink!"

He chuckles. "I suppose you can't, can you?"

"No. But the tree sounds perfect, Brother Fletcher," Noah says, then leans forward and kisses him on the cheek. He smiles as he blushes, acting like an embarrassed school boy—unsure of what else to do, he bends down and returns to weeding his cabbages.

Noah says goodbye and then quickly heads off to the cafeteria. *I hope Patrick will find some way to move toward him.* When she enters the open dining space, she spots Patrick and Shea in the corner, finishing their breakfast, which never changes at Findhorn: hard-boiled eggs, oatmeal, and toast. Noah moves along the counter, where a lanky young monk smiles and hands her a cup of tea. She nods in thanks and then moves to Patrick and Shea's table.

"Hey, you two. Whatcha talking about?"

Not waiting for an answer, she slides in next to Shea and reaches under her friend's arm to steal a slice of toast from her plate.

"Hey, *you*! That was mine," Shea blurts out, playfully slapping Noah's hand. Patrick and Shea both shake their heads at her.

Too excited to be bothered—her mouth still full of toast—Noah plows ahead to outline her plans for the day's excursion.

ॐ ॐ ॐ ॐ ॐ ॐ

As the three approach the giant Sitka spruce, they exchange knowing glances; they know they are nearing holy ground. The resinous pine fragrance overwhelms their senses. It feels as if they are surrounded by an intoxicating elixir, stirred by the rising mist of the river and the wet soil beneath their feet.

Noah has learned that a tree's ever-changing chemical composition—carried by scent—is one of its primary means of communication. Taking a deep breath, she closes her eyes and inhales the complex fragrances as if trying to decode a secret message.

She moves to the Sitka's trunk and sits carefully on its soft, now-browning needles. The other two follow her lead. All three lean back and straighten their spines against the tree's purplish trunk—feeling as if the giant spruce is holding them—as if it has something to say. *As if...* Noah wonders in silence.

The three feel both alone and united with one another. Suddenly, they all hear the same thing—the murmur of soft, buzzing voices that sound like a vibrating beehive. *Chōōōōō... zĕĕĕĕn. Chōōōōō... zĕĕĕĕn.* They snap their heads around and look at each other, searching for confirmation. But it seems clear: they are being summoned. More than that. *Chosen.*

Noah then becomes aware of another presence. Or, more accurately, she becomes aware of *many* others who are also "there"—visible in the space around the Sitka, but also drifting through her mind, registering an immediate sense of their souls in her consciousness.

It's Yoshi—his toes in the ocean! And Sylvie and Jean—walking hand in hand under the stars. She sees her other roommates, now scattered to the four winds. Cubeo, too—concentrating as he hunts piranha with a spear. *Oh, and there's Ma*—refilling jars of herbs at the shop. Even Gil is "here"—in front of a bank of HOLO gauges.

The living images appear as separate panels suspended in the air around Patrick, Shea, and her. There's Liam and the other Greenlings. *Tessa, is that you, too?* She knows it is—the woman is standing in a primal forest, watching a snowy owl on a limb above her. *There's Seamus*—huddled next to a small fire in a cave. *And Journi*—staring out her office window over the D.C. skyline.

But where's Da? A silhouette of someone slumped in a chair comes into view. The room is poorly lit, but she instantly recognizes the form. "Da! What's wrong? Da! What—" Noah gasps.

The emerald orbs of four banshees hover above Aiden—their trailing wisps of shredded fabric circulating something that looks like clumps of tiny insects. And then, another presence—familiar, yet still mysterious—moves through the dimly lit space. *Erin.* Patrick's ma is there with her da too—her arms extending upward through what looks like thick vines of English ivy.

Patrick sees it, too. Tears stream down his face as he recognizes his ma's presence. Other images of unknown men and women float into view. Noah looks at Patrick, confused. He recognizes some of them from summer camps in the Amazon as a boy. Names from his ma's time capsule surface. *Pádraig. Susan. Amir. Min.* Suddenly, like multiple pairs of magnets snapping together, he's able to put names and faces together.

He turns to Noah and whispers, "I'm pretty sure they're the ones I told you about—the members of the eco-cells that were listed." Noah shakes her head as if she can't take anymore.

She looks back at the images surrounding them and notices faint green fibers threading everything together. They slowly pulse with light from within. *What is that? It kind of looks like those technical diagrams Gil's always looking at.* Then, as if a light goes on, her intuition sparks—she sees it. A supernatural green-web; a green-network. And it now seems to have been activated by something. Or *someone.* Whatever it is, Noah, Patrick, and Shea are all connected in a way that none of them has ever experienced. Connected, not just to one another, but to the world itself.

The three of them find themselves in the middle of what seems to be an ancient conversation, one that makes them feel like little children in the presence of ancient elders. Noah turns to look at Patrick and Shea. They stare back, awe written on their faces. Their forms swiftly shrink as the scene surrounding them rapidly expands—upward and outward—filled with giant tress and bushes, plants and mosses.

Noah reaches out to grab hold of what looks like the trunk of a small tree. When it bends, she gasps in realization. *That's not a tree. That's the stem of thread rush.*

The experience is dreamlike and surreal. But her physical senses register the wind carrying the river's mist, the overwhelming smell of verdancy from the supersized flora, the songbirds' ascending counterpoint, and tell her... *it's real.*

Reining in the overwhelming shock and wonder of the scene, they start to breathe again. As their heart rates slow, they hear busy, buzzing voices vibrating in the air around them. The swirl of streaming messages gradually coalesce, enabling Noah, Patrick, and Shea to slowly attune to what's being said—aware that *they* are being addressed—by both the magnificent Sitka *and* by every non-human life form that has ever existed.

Suddenly, a chorus of voices erupts—spanning that immense spectrum of all songs, all sounds, every call, and every vocalization ever made by Mother Nature and all her beloved children.

"*It's time,*" the Forever-Maternal One announces.

"*Yes. It's time,*" replies the panoply of her offspring.

"*Past time, my little ones.*" Her words thunder like a storm.

"*We've all been waiting so long,*" they respond.

"*Time to begin again.*" Her proclamation crescendos.

"*Time to make a fresh start.*" Their words rise with hers in anticipation.

"*Prepare yourselves for all that must come next,*" she commands, as if unleashing a cyclone.

"*We're ready,*" Earth's entire non-human community bellows in answer.

Suddenly, silence returns. There's no wind. No river flowing. No birds singing. Noah feels her utter smallness, her complete insignificance; her temporal sense of self feels like it's evaporated. Staggered by the vision, she slumps forward—speechless—supported by the Sitka's roots. Patrick and Shea, seated on either side of her, cast concerned looks at one other, and together, each drape an arm over her shoulders. Finally, from within the quiet, the Mother addresses her in a low, hushed tone.

"They are ready, Noah."

Unnerved by the sound of her name being spoken, Noah instantly feels the same painful emotions she's felt her entire life—self-conscious, vulnerable, exposed. She closes her eyes and shivers at what she sees—the glowing eyes of trillions upon trillions turning, then locking their unified gaze on her.

Her discomfort is immediately interrupted by their chorus, their declaration—sung to her and her alone.

"We are ready, little sister. We are ready. Are you?"

Laois County, Ireland (92° F / 33° C)

Gil hasn't been out to see his da for several weeks. He's appreciated the renewed connection with his old man, but juggling school and his internship has left him with no time to spare. Today, however, he had an unexpected break in his schedule—it seemed like the perfect day to make the trip.

He pulls the Land Rover into the grassy lane—the frame squeaking as it wobbles over the uneven earth. As his da's hut comes into view, he pulls into the clearing and parks to the side. A long sigh of contentment escapes from deep within. *Coming here feels like a sort of pilgrimage. How'd I miss that before?*

He turns off the engine and gets out of the truck—instantly aware of an empty silence. The birds' songs are absent. There's no sound of his da's usual humming or sawing or hammering. He slowly pans the surrounding trees and feels a growing apprehension. *It's never been this empty.* Walking up to the front of his da's berm hut, he notices the opening's leather covering carelessly flung back—a sweet, putrid smell hangs in the air. *That's strange. Da never leaves the door open.* A gentle light slants through the opening, revealing dust motes hovering in the air.

Walking into the dim space, he quickly gags at the carnage—flies covering rank foodstuffs—the disgusting smell of rot hovers over the room's defilement. Gil's eyes go wide as he surveys the broken furniture and smashed glass.

"What the hell? Da! Are you in here? Da?" Getting no response, he turns and walks outside. "Da! Where are you, Da?" He circles the hut, his eyes darting under bushes and trees, an anxious, sick feeling rising from his gut.

For the next hour, he moves deeper into the forest, frequently calling out as he trudges through underbrush—his voice interrupting the eerie silence. Nothing. Not a trace of where his da might be or where he's gone off to.

When he finally returns to the hut's front porch, he drops into one of his da's chairs. He stares off into space for several moments, trying to make sense of what he's found. Coming up blank, he initiates a HOLO with his ma and his sister and describes what he's seen.

A worried frown pulls the corners of Ma's lips as she climbs onto a stool at the shop's counter. "Gil, I have no idea where he could be. My first guess would be with Liam... but that doesn't explain what you found... how the place was—" She shakes her head and takes a deep breath. "Your da might not be the tidiest, but he'd never leave things—"

"And there wasn't a note?" Noah breaks in—dropping onto the edge of the bed in her room, chewing her lip. "Or anything that gives a clue... not even the sign of an accident? No blood?"

Gil takes a deep breath, sadness softening his features. "No, sis. Nothing. Just his stuff busted up and the awful stench from the spoiled food." Gil suddenly feels very alone, as if a weight has suddenly shifted onto his shoulders. "Ma, can you check with Liam and his brothers and find out if any Greenlings might have seen him? I'll contact the Gardai and tell them what's happened. Maybe they can come out and help make some sense of it."

Noah slumps, and her face turns pale. She can't imagine a world without her da. She feels like she's on another planet—far away, useless.

"Gil, what can I do? You want me to come home? Is there anyone you want me to contact? There's got to be some explanation or... something."

Her brother shakes his head, his mind blank. "I can't think of anything, Noah. Just pray we find him... that he's not hurt or..." He stops himself and forces himself to take a deep breath to prevent his worst fears from taking over.

"Tell you what," Noah says, giving Gil a moment to catch his breath. "I'll contact the hospitals just in case. Maybe they've heard something. Although, can you imagine Da in a hospital?" She tries to sound lighthearted. "He'd be worse off than if he'd stayed home sick."

Ma makes an anxious attempt at a chuckle and then breaks in. "It'll be alright, you two. Your da is the most self-sufficient man I've ever met. Whatever he's got himself into, he'll be okay. Now, let's do our best to find out what we can."

The three exchange feeble smiles—doing their best to reassure one another—then say goodbye.

Findhorn, Scotland, United Kingdom (87° F / 31° C)

Noah anxiously rubs her belly as she stares out the window of Findhorn's small chapel, tears streaming down her pale cheeks. *I really don't know... should I tell Ma, or should I wait? I'm just not sure she should have to face me being pregnant right now.* Three of the chapel's four walls are made of tall, narrow windows, offering a sweeping view of the kirk's landscape. Since Gil's HOLO three days ago, the quiet refuge has allowed her long moments of privacy where she can cry. *Da, where are you? What's happened to you?* Noah puzzles over the same questions she's been asking non-stop. Contacting the hospitals was a dead end—the same as Gil's and Ma's attempts. *Nothing.* They still don't feel any closer to an answer. It's as if her father has just evaporated.

The day is gray and flecked with intermittent spits of rain. She turns away from the windows, grabs her umbrella, and slips outside to clear her head. She finds a bench under a large beech tree and sits, watching the rain. Her HOLO chimes, and she frowns. *Hmmm... HOLO unrecognized?* Usually, she wouldn't accept an unknown contact like this, but given her da's situation, she decides to accept it. Floating before her is Marta Sennheiser, dressed in a low-necked, lemon-colored blouse. Her polished hair and makeup give the impression that she's taking a break from a photo shoot.

"*Gutten Tag*, dear Noah. Thank you for accepting my HOLO. How are you? I've just heard about your father. I'm so sorry." Marta's bent smile contradicts her placating words. "If only I'd known, I wouldn't have come after you so aggressively today."

Noah glares at the life-sized image, unwilling to play her game. *If she thinks I'm a terrorist, maybe I should start acting like one!*

"You're such a leech, Marta. Hearing from you is the absolute last thing I need today. Knowing you, you'll probably record this and use it on your pathetic little show. You've got a lot of gall. First, you smear me, and then you slander Patrick and Seamus—with what? Some juicy, fake journalism?" Noah jumps to her feet and jams her finger toward Marta's placid image. "You make me sick! It's like you just make stuff up hoping to make people believe—What?—that INTERPOL's outside the door, ready to storm in and take us off to be waterboarded?"

Marta's expression mimics that of a concerned friend. "I know, dear. I've been just awful. Will you forgive me? You're under so much—"

"Listen, Marta," Noah interrupts. "Forgiving you is not even—" She takes a deep breath. "Just drop your little act."

Marta's eyes narrow, and her thin lips press together. "Okay, Noah. I'll cut to the chase. I do feel bad about your father. But not nearly as bad as I feel about my aunt. Can you imagine what it's like for me to watch her slide further away from us, not even knowing what's wrong?" Her head tilts to the side as she flashes her wicked grin. "Why, of course, you can. Can't you? Don't you think there's a kind of shared justice—or karma, if you will— bringing us together now, as we both suffer like this?"

Noah shakes her head, her brow scrunched in dismay. "Oh, that's rich. There's no justice in any of this. How can you even think that?"

"Oh, my dear Noah, I believe you *do* know. Deep down. Can't you see? Haven't you put it together yet? I know something about your father's disappearance that I'm fairly certain you'd be quite interested to learn, but—"

"What are you saying?" Noah shouts, cutting Marta off. "Whatever it is—spit it out."

"Now, now. Slow down. Why don't you take a breath and sit back down? I was going to say that I happen to know something about your father. And I believe *you* know something about my aunt."

Noah frowns in puzzlement. "What on earth are you talking about? I'm confused. What could I possibly know about your aunt?"

"Well, to find that out, you'll have to talk to your boyfriend." Marta smiles smugly. "Or, better yet—his uncle. You see, Seamus is the key to helping us resolve *both* these tragedies."

Noah's nostrils flare. Her voice turns shrill. "Stop with the games, Marta! Just say whatever it is you want to say to me."

Marta peers back coldly. When she finally speaks, her voice is soft yet devoid of all emotion. "Okay, Noah. I want you to listen carefully. There is a grave injustice that's taken place. And do you know why? Of course you do. Whether you can admit it to yourself—you, your boyfriend, and all your friends—you're the ones responsible for this mess. You're nothing but a sad little band of eco-terrorists. Ask Seamus. He knows."

"Seamus? What's he got to do with—"

"I've tried to track him down, you know." Marta continues, ignoring Noah. "But he's simply disappeared—just like your father. Well, not exactly like your father; that's another story. Seamus, you see, is the one behind my aunt's near-lethal health crisis. I believe he *also* has the cure—if only we could find him."

She pauses to pick something up—DIRTY MEDS Energy Drink written in bold letters on the can's side—and then takes a long sip from it.

"But I think *you*, my good friend Noah, might just be able to find a way to contact him. Am I right? So, to help balance this cowardly act of injustice—and to provide some incentive for everyone—I nudged things a wee bit to put a little pressure on you and your friends to help... expedite things. You understand now?"

The missing pieces quickly fall into place like giant boulders coming to rest after a landslide. Her anger explodes in her chest.

"WHERE'S MY DA?" Noah shouts. "Marta, so help me God, if you've done anything to—"

A second HOLO instantly opens beside Marta's. Noah stares at the shadowed image of a man covered in ivy and hears something like the buzzing of bees. Her anger settles back into her gut, where it turns sour. Her brow knits in frustration and worry. "Is that him?" she shouts, already knowing the answer. "You dirty little—"

"Settle down, Noah. He's fine. He's probably happier than being in that little hole he calls home."

"You don't understand. If he—"

"No, I *do* understand. Believe me. I'm watching my aunt waste away. So I understand all too well. Now, *meine freund*, you better get on with it. Before it's too late for both of them. Oh, and don't think of going to the *authorities*." She grins, making air quotes. "They've been bought and paid for long ago, should we ever need a favor. Save this HOLO contact, dear. And let me know when you have the antivenom."

Before Noah can respond, the image abruptly atomizes into nothingness. She drops her head and slowly zips her jacket up for protection from the descending showers. As the wind picks up, the rain responds and shifts direction, making the umbrella utterly useless. Suddenly, she feels more alone than ever. Her hands fall to her growing middle, and she begins to sob, uncertain whether her da will live to see his two new grandchildren.

As she wipes her wet cheeks and nose with the back of her hand, a shrill bird call from overhead registers. *KAK-KAK-KAK.* She looks up and catches sight of a peregrine falcon diving toward the earth—on the hunt. *Oh, Tessa. My bineshiinyag manidoo!* A few meters from the ground, its talons stretch out. The bird explodes into a dark gray mass of fur hidden in the brush. It lands, then begins ravenously tearing the rat's flesh with its sharp beak into bloody shreds.

"Thank you," she murmurs to the raptor.

Though still feeling off-balance from Marta's gambit, a new determination settles over her as she watches the falcon tear into its meal.

I'll be the one to decide the outcome of this stand-off, Marta.

Gilford, County Down, Northern Ireland

The third floor of the abandoned Gilford linen mill is empty—except for a rusted shipping container and the sprawling vine of English ivy that almost entirely covers the large room's walls, ceiling, and floor. The inside of the metal box is dimly lit. The only sounds that can be heard are the faint breaths from the lump of a man seated in the middle and the low buzzing of an active swarm of hundreds of bees in the air around him.

Aiden Greenling sits, tied to a wooden chair—severely weakened from the toxic effects of the manmade box. He unsteadily bobs his head from side to side, looking for something to drink or eat—there's nothing there. It's impossible to discern whether he's asleep or existing in some kind of suspended state. A HOLO-CAM in the upper corner silently keeps watch. Soon after his captors left, the tangle of ivy began breaking through the container's floor. Weakened and confused, he rouses himself enough to watch as the vine quickly grows and carefully twists its way around his legs, his torso and both arms, then finally gently encircles his neck and his head.

Strange... I'm still... afraid... but I also feel—

A loud screech of straining metal suddenly focuses his attention—the fibrous climber has wrapped its muscled length around the HOLO-CAM. *CRASH!* Aiden jumps at the sudden noise. With a mind of its own, the aggressive vine hurls the HOLO-CAM to the floor with a smash.

Am I dreaming? Aiden wonders. *Maybe I'm dead already?*

He rapidly blinks his eyes, trying to wake himself up, and he feels one of the tender shoots swirl to the top of his head and then rewind itself down his legs toward the floor. The vine's movement keeps repeating itself—up and then down, again—as if weaving him into a cool, living basket.

A woman's voice—low and thick, like honey—slowly registers in Aiden's sluggish brain.

"Shhh... Be still, Greenling. We're here to protect you."

Aiden, still able to reason in spite of his allergic stupor, mutters, "Who are you?"

There is a long pause—a fresh, slightly bitter scent lingers in the air—before the voice continues. *"Shhh... I once was known as... Erin. But no longer. Now I am... the Keeper."*

"Errr...inn..." Aiden whispers, his shadowed mind casting about in its forgotten recesses.

"Shhh little Greenling... relax now... sleep..."

The words vibrate from the leaves and communicate through his exposed skin. Before he loses consciousness, he hears the sound of buzzing increase. As if in a dream, he senses a single-file parade of fuzzy bees working their way across the vine, onto his face, and past his lips, where they carefully deposit drop after drop of honeyed sustenance.

The last thing he remembers are the Keeper's gentle words.

"Be still, little Greenling. We're here to take you home."

A Few Words of Appreciation

Mega kudos to my original Scotch-Irish girl, Beth McGauhey McLaughlin Booram. For your enthusiasm (and indulgence—when I all-too-frequently neglected "us") as I read drafts of chapters to you on the porch of the Lily Pad. Thank you for the encouragement to "stay at it." You are forever my biggest fan, most careful reader, exacting editor, and honest critic. You faithfully tether me to reality and good sense when things get too far-fetched or too indelicate!

For my two granddaughters, Harper Lillian Booram and Juniper Ann (Booram) Nolan. Your response to the first two chapters encouraged me to write a story that might inspire you and your generation to fight for what's good and beautiful in this world. Your genuine, unfiltered reactions were, and are, priceless to me!

I am grateful for my good friend and talented young-adult fiction author, Tim Byers, and the many moments we spent discussing good writing and good stories. Thanks, Tim, for the energizing conversation—after trimming trees at the Lily Pad—that sparked the flame to write "just for the fun of it."

I want to give a huge "thank you" to all my beta-readers—Cara Chandler, Amanda McLaughlin, Susan Carson, Anne Eschlemann (for being the queen of finding inconsistencies, need for clarity, and confusing conundrums!), Nathan Baker (for your suggestion to include the Family Ties diagram), *Professor* Mark Abdon (for your supportive interest that began with drinking bourbon when we should have been doing other things), Justin Nolan, Dan Sheehan, Mark Condy (my Celtic friend), and Nancy Nethercott. Your over-the-top investment of time, support, and insight says volumes about your love for me. Your contributions made this book stronger, clearer, and more readable.

A special thank you to Janet McCabe—former Deputy Administrator of the U.S. Environmental Protection Agency—for your thoughtful comments on the book and, more importantly, for your tireless service to our country, our world, and its future. Your fact-questioning and prescience of human and planetary life in 2060 were beyond helpful in adding a realistic sense to the story. We can only hope and labor that better days may be ahead for our shared grandson, Remy William Larramore.

I want to especially acknowledge Raina Sternke, who had the unfortunate privilege of being one of the book's initial readers and then subjected herself to meticulously reviewing the manuscript repeatedly as my editor. Raina, you've been more than an editor; you've been my writing coach. Just when I think *I'm almost done*, you kick me in *my* editing butt, always ending your helpful critiques with an impish "*haha.*"! I can only say, "Thank you" and "Where did you learn this stuff?"

For Emma Angell, thank you for your continued artful sensibilities, patience, and enthusiasm after all these years of working with me. I can always count on you to "sweat the details" with the backside of the design, layout, and production process. You know I REALLY love the cover, don't you?

Honorable mentions go to Greta Thunberg for your courageous activism. Your spirit—part of the mashup that became my Noah—lives on in her. Alana Levandoski, thank you for reminding me about banshees and, through your singing, giving me a taste of keening music. Thanks to Matthew Fox for showing the way from original sin to original blessing, Phillip Newell for strengthening my deep appreciation of Celtic spirituality, and Dorothy MacLean for being crazy enough to risk listening to plants. I also must mention my incredible team of doctors: Dr. Mohammad Al-Haddad, Dr. Jeffery Kons, and Dr. George Venious, along with the many unnamed caregivers who nursed me back to good health and a clear enough mind to find my way back to a half-finished storyline after my brush with mortality.

Finally, I'd like to introduce my readers to the *real* Noah—her last name is unknown to me. One morning in 2019, Beth and I were on holiday in Ireland, and we stumbled upon Kilkenny's hidden gem, *The Hole in the Wall*. We were greeted by Noah—a young, dreadlocked hippie barista who told us the history of the small public house and then served us mugs of deliciously strong Irish coffee. She quickly finished her chores and, in true Irish fashion, came and joined us in the small courtyard. In our conversation, she told us what it was like growing up in this small Irish city and then described her current life as a woodland forager. As the good-natured back-and-forth continued, at one point, she interrupted the conversation and went inside. When she returned, she was grinning at us, carrying a well-used ukulele. She asked if we'd like to hear a song—how do you refuse a question like that? And there we all were—Beth and I slowly sipping our coffee while this uninhibited, free-spirited sprite performed her "concert for two," singing the old Irish melodies like an ancient bard!

It was this simple, memorable, magical moment, combined with Noah's quirky hospitality, that sprouted like a seed years later and became my inspiration for *The Greenling*.

Noah, I've tried to track you down but haven't had much luck. I imagine you off in some remote forest, living off the land, with your ukelele in your knapsack. If someday you read this—thank you!

Works Consulted

Gratefulness, the Heart of Prayer by Brother David Steindl-Rast pages 207-208

Nature April 28, 2022 *"Zoonics Climate Change Increases Cross-Species Viral Transmission Risk"* (https://www.nature.com/articles/s41586-022-04788-w)

One Earth Magazine #6, 1978 interview with Dorothy MacLean

The Birth (Near Port William) from *Collected Poems 1957-1982*, by Wendell Berry

The Secret Life of Plants, Peter Tompkins and Christopher Bird

About the Author

DAVID BOORAM grew up creek stomping and geode hunting in the deep ravines of central Indiana, where he first experienced the magic of nature and learned about birds, frog-gigging, fishing, and organic gardening from his grandpa. He attended Indiana University, graduating with a BS in Religious Studies and Business Administration.

David founded Direction 4 Life Work, where he offered career counseling for 30 years to students and adults. In 2012, he co-founded Fall Creek Abbey, an urban retreat center, where he and his wife, Beth, have sought to renew the contemplative spirit through hospitality, presence, and conversation.

In addition, David companions individuals in his work as a spiritual director and trains others in the art of offering spiritual direction through the Fall Creek Abbey School of Spiritual Direction.

David describes himself as an ordinary mystic, lover of nature—especially the birds—a poet, contrarian, gardener, artist, and musician who pursues a life of gentle integrity, humor, creativity, and love.

He is the author of Wisdom for Old Souls, co-author of When Faith Becomes Sight and Prayers at Twilight, and creator of the popular Examen Qs and Couples Qs.